DEEP In The HEART

E. Randall Floyd

D1367269

IIII
HARBOR
HOUSE

AUGUSTA, GEORGIA

DEEP
In The
HEART

DEEP IN THE HEART
By E. Randall Floyd
A Harbor House Book/May 1998

Though largely a work of fiction, this book is based on true events. Most of the characters and settings actually existed. Where possible, the author has tried to present them in a historically accurate light. No living persons are represented in this book.

For information address:
Harbor House
3010 Stratford Drive
Augusta, Georgia 30909
Cover photograph of the 49th Regiment Georgia Volunteers flag courtesy of the Georgia Capitol Museum, Office of Secretary of State, Lewis A. Massey. Photograph of Confederate States belt buckle courtesy of George Juno and Russ Pritchard, Jr., American Ordnance Preservation Association, Ltd. Book Design by Lydia Inglett.

Library of Congress Catalog Card Number 97-95338
Publisher's Cataloging-in-Publication Data
Floyd, E. Randall, 1947-
Deep in the heart / E. Randall Floyd
First Edition
p. cm.
ISBN 1-891799-20-7
1. United States-History-Civil War, 1861-1865-Fiction.
I. Title
813.54-dc21   97-95338
        LCCN
Printed in the United States of America
10 9 8 7 6 5 4 3

To the memory of Dennie Floyd,
brother, friend and teacher,
who saw to it that I had a Boy Scout uniform.

ACKNOWLEDGEMENTS

AS ALWAYS, I WANT TO THANK a number of people for helping make this project possible. At the top of the list is my wife,
Anne, whose unwavering support for this and other projects
remains a modern American mystery; Wally and Ann Wildenradt,
two kind-hearted researchers with the patience of Job; Uncle Curt
(thanks for all those inspirational stories about the Civil War many,
many years ago); Ed Cashin and all my former collegues in the
History Department at Augusta State University who listened to
my many, many pitches about this book; Dan and Andrea O'Shea,
great friends and two of the most gifted artists I have ever known;
Lydia Inglett, a fair-haired goddess of the arts whose graphic genius
thankfully kept this project on track; Leslie Nelson, whose editorial
skills are unsurpassed; all the staffers and researchers at Virginia,
Louisiana and Mississippi battlefield sites who allowed me to peruse
their collections at will; Sandra and David Fenstermacher for loan-
ing me their valuable clips and maps of Vicksburg; Barbara Eaton,
for her kind assistance, and other staffers at Augusta-Richmond
County Public Library and the various branches for opening their
doors to me; all my students at Augusta State University who
helped make teaching Civil War history a real joy; the people of
Irwinton and Wilkinson County, Georgia; Dr. Sophia Bamford and
the people of Washington, Georgia, and Wilkes County, Georgia;
Sam and Margaret Smith of Swainsboro, Georgia; Mildred Fortson
of Lincolnton, Georgia; Mary Alice Jordan of Sandersville,
Georgia, and the Georgia Chapter of the United Daughters of the
Confederacy; Tom Sutherland and the Augusta (Georgia) Civil War
Roundtable; Mrs. Shelby Myrick of Savannah, Georgia, and the

National Society of the Colonial Dames in America in the State of Georgia for the use of their archival material; the Georgia State Museum and Archives; Annie Frances Davis of Birmingham, Alabama; Ken Thomas; Ernie Wyatt, Bill Bowers; Cliff Collins; the late, great General Joe Wheeler, whose ancestral homeplace is within walking distance of my own humble abode; all those other dead boys in gray (and blue) whose faces and names haunt the pages of this book. A belated thanks goes to three special teachers who offered me magic at a very young age: Mrs. Staten Lewis, who never once complained about those drawings on the back of my school papers; Mrs. Carolyn McCall, who introduced me to General Joseph Eggleston Johnston in the 7th grade; and Mrs. Fred Harrell, who now shares old classroom secrets with my mother, Ida Floyd, at Bethany Home in Vidalia, Georgia. Thanks also to Albert and Marjorie Shelander, whose insatiable curiosity about history in general and the Civil War in particular usually turns quiet little visits to the seashore into classroom exercises; B.B. and Betsy; Jane and Steve; Mary and Mitch; and to all those many others, not named here, who contributed in countless ways to the making of this book. I thank you from the bottom of my heart.

E. Randall Floyd
Augusta, Georgia, 1998

CHAPTER 1

THE BOY STOOD ON THE STEPS of the little country church, quietly surveying the horses and mules hitched out front. How easy it would be, he thought, to hop on one and ride away to freedom. He'd ride all day and night, not once stopping to rest, and before he knew it, he'd be in Baltimore or Philadelphia or maybe even all the way to Canada where he'd heard his kind was welcome.

He closed his eyes and pretended he was astride one of the horses right now, a great big stallion, flying across the Mason-Dixon. He could almost hear the thunder of the horse's hooves striking the clay, could almost feel the wind whisking through his hair as he galloped closer and closer to freedom...

The sudden, shrill clanging of organ music jarred him back to the present. His eyes popped open and he looked around. He was still standing on the church house steps. Not one of those old horses or mules had moved. Not one of them had carried him away to freedom. He sighed. It saddened him to think he was still in Georgia.

The boy's name was Moses Washington Collins, but everybody just called him Indigo on account of the dark, almost purple color of his skin. His pa had always told him his skin was that way because his ma had eaten too many muscadines when he was a seed sprouting up inside her belly. Indigo still laughed every time he remembered that story, even though, even today, he found it odd that he'd never developed much of a taste for the dark, juicy grapes that grew so plentifully in the fields and woods around his home.

He was barefooted, but otherwise dressed in his Sunday best—frayed coat, white shirt and trousers held together at his narrow waist by a rope. The straw hat on his head was tattered and bent, but he wore it proudly because it had once belonged to his grandfather, and now his grandfather—God rest his soul—was dead and turning to dust in an old field grave near Sparta.

Indigo had never been to a white church before, let alone a white wedding. But today was special. His job was to wait around until the service was over, then drive Mister Wiley and his new bride into town so they could catch the train to Savannah where they would spend their honeymoon. As a reward, Mister Wiley, who owned the little spread Indigo's ma and pa worked, promised to let the boy take care of Sable while he was away. Sable was Mister Wiley's prized Tennessee Walker, one of the finest mounts in the whole county. Indigo couldn't think of anything he'd rather do than take care of Sable—even if it meant waiting around all morning swatting bugs in the hot April sun for Mister Wiley and his bride to finish saying their vows.

Indigo was beginning to wonder how long it took white folks to say their vows when he heard a rider fast approaching. He looked down the road, a dry, dusty spit of clay that curved off to the west, and spotted a lone horseman racing toward the church. Indigo had never seen anybody ride so hard before. Great clouds of red-tinged dust billowed up behind the rider, and the sound of the horse's spiked hooves clacking and hammering on the clay reminded the boy of spring thunderclaps.

Seconds later the rider galloped into the churchyard and halted. He was a handsome, clean-shaven white man in his early twenties, and he wore a spanking new ash-gray uniform, the likes of which Indigo had never seen. His hair was long and golden, and it curled down around his shoulders almost like a girl's. Matching rows of brass buttons gleamed across his broad chest. His boots were jet black and shiny and rose almost to his knees. A long sword curved away from the saddle at his side.

Indigo shrank back when the uniformed rider dismounted and strode toward him, long spurs jangling.

"I'm looking for Sheriff Poindexter," the officer announced in a soft drawl.

Indigo had never seen a soldier this close before and didn't know how to respond. His eyes went from the officer's shiny boots and jangling spurs to the gleaming sword and holstered revolver clipped to his slender waist.

The officer reached inside his breast pocket and pulled out a slip of paper. "Would you please see that he gets this?" he said, handing the note to Indigo.

Indigo pretended to read the note, which was hand-scrawled on official-looking paper. Even though he couldn't make out all the words, Indigo recognized the state seal and the signature of Joseph Brown, the governor of Georgia.

"It's very important," the officer added quickly.

Indigo suddenly perked up. It wasn't every day that a fourteen-year-old black boy, the grandson of African slaves, was put in charge of delivering an important message to the high sheriff of Wilkinson County.

"Y-Yes, s-s-sir," he stammered, trying hard, but failing, to suppress the stutter that had plagued him since early childhood.

He was gone in a flash, bounding up the steps two at a time, the note clutched protectively in both hands.

———

RED LEVEL METHODIST CHURCH was small and plain and packed to capacity that morning. Sunlight streamed through the open windows, flooding the narrow sanctuary and casting a shimmering halo around the wreathed altar where a tall, white-haired preacher clad in black lorded over the young bride and groom.

"Martha Ann Walker," the Reverend Isaac Thurmond intoned in a high, quaking voice, "do you take this man, Wiley Nesmith, to be your lawfully wedded husband, to love and cherish, honor and obey, for as long as you both shall live, till death do you part?"

"I do," the bride said softly.

She was a pretty girl of eighteen, petite and perky, and she wore a simple white dress with ruffled sleeves and collar. No veil concealed her soft round face, the flawless texture of her rose-kissed cheeks and ruby-red lips. Her eyes were green, the color of the sea, and they twinkled in the warm glow of the altar candles as she gazed adoringly at the groom, a handsome, slender six-footer with dark, deep-set eyes and wavy brown hair cropped close at the collar.

"...By the power vested in me, I now pronounce you man and wife."

Indigo entered the church just in time to see Mister Wiley lean forward and kiss the bride. It was a slow, awkward kiss, and Indigo couldn't resist smiling.

Suddenly, Greta Underwood's heavy foot crashed joyously down on the organ pedals, rattling the church with music. Wincing, Indigo lingered at the back of the church and surveyed the crowd. He recognized just about everybody in the congregation. Mister Wiley's kinfolk were all there—his ma and six brothers and two sisters and their families. Plus, there was Mayor Futch and his two good-for-nothing boys, Theodore and Lawrence, both of whom looked bored and ready to bust their sizable guts.

Then he spotted Sheriff Poindexter sitting three rows from the front. He waited another moment, quietly screwing up his courage, then tiptoed over to the sheriff and gave him the note.

Hiram Poindexter was a big, craggy man with long, white hair and a thick mustache that curved downward at each end, almost touching just above his chin. A grave look came over him as he read the note. When he finished, he got up quietly and headed for the door, Indigo right behind him.

A middle-aged black couple sitting on the back row saw the sheriff get up and leave, followed by the boy. They looked at each other in stark amazement. Was something wrong? Was their boy in some kind of trouble?

"FOLKS, THIS IS MAJOR ANDERSON," Sheriff Poindexter said. "He's come all the way from Milledgeville to bring us some important news."

The sheriff stood at the bottom of the steps, hands on hips, a grim look fixed on his cracked, sun-worn face as he carefully appraised the crowd. Moments earlier the church doors had swung open and the well-wishers surged through, only to stop in their tracks when they saw the sheriff and the boyish officer at his side.

"Milledgeville?" someone muttered, and an awed murmur swept through the crowd.

The officer stepped forward, spurs jangling. He removed his hat and bowed courteously to the bride and groom. "Forgive me," he said graciously, "I deeply apologize for intruding upon this sacred ceremony. However, like the sheriff said, I do bring news of great importance."

Major Anderson paused long enough to size up the crowd. Then, in a voice cracking with emotion, he announced, "It is my honor and duty to inform you that Fort Sumter in the harbor at Charleston, South Carolina, has fallen. A state of war now exists between our country and the Republican government of the United States of America."

A stunned silence fell hard across the crowd.

Momentarily, a tall, silver-haired gentleman whose eyes seemed buried beneath bushy gray eyebrows, spoke up. "*Our* country, officer?"

"Yes, *our* country," the major replied proudly. "The Confederate States of America!"

With those words the crowd burst into cheers. Some of the men threw their hats into the air, hugged their wives and danced around with joy. A freckled young man, who didn't look old enough to shave—or to understand the magnitude of the moment—rushed forward and clasped the major's hand. "God bless you, sir, for delivering us this wonderful news. Long live the Confederacy!"

The young man's outburst was electrifying. Almost at once, the crowd erupted in another resounding chorus of cheers.

Before the cheering had died down, a heavy, thick-bearded man in his mid-fifties, hefted up his stomach and bellowed: "At last! This is the moment we've all been waiting for." The man could scarcely contain himself. He shook his fist skyward and loudly proclaimed, "We're free people now. Free! And I say it's high time we Southrens showed Mister Lincoln and those black Republicans in Washington they can't push us around anymore!"

The crowd roared in agreement. There was more hooting and hollering until the Reverend Thurmond, frail and thin in his dusty black frock, tottered forward. In a tremulous voice, he asked, "Pray tell, Major Anderson, what does all this Carolina business have to do with us here in Georgia?"

Every eye fell on the young major. One pair in particular belonged to a tall, striking redhead named Catherine Potter. Catherine's full, red lips moistened with excitement as she gazed adoringly at the dashing young officer with his blond curls and fetching uniform. Her fascination for the young officer did not go unnoticed by her husband, Joseph Potter, a tall, bespectacled man with a pointed chin and billowing sideburns, who placed a protective arm around his wife's tightly corseted waist.

Major Anderson cleared his throat and said, "Our new government needs every man it can muster to do his duty for the Confederacy. I've just come from the state capital where the governor is in the process of raising new volunteer regiments. He's calling for every able-bodied man between the ages of eighteen and forty to sign up immediately so that, if called upon, they can serve our glorious cause."

Catherine Potter pulled away from her husband and leaned toward the bride. "Isn't this so exciting?" she whispered in her sister's ear. Licking her lips, she added, "And that Major Anderson—isn't he just the most handsome man you ever did lay eyes on?"

Martha Ann Walker—*no, as of today, Mrs. Martha Ann Nesmith*—ignored her sister's brassy observation. All this talk about Abraham Lincoln and black Republicans had left her feeling cold and faint. And more than a little angry. How dare this Major Anderson come gallivanting out here in his fancy uniform and jangling spurs and interrupt the most important day of her life? How dare he?

The major raised his arms for silence. "Sheriff Poindexter has been instructed to oversee the raising of a local regiment. He'll call the first meeting in a few days for the purpose of electing officers and establishing a program of training. Every able man among you will be expected to respond."

"What's the hurry?" someone asked.

The major drew a sharp breath. "We expect the Federals will try to retake Fort Sumter soon. There's a rumor going around that Lincoln is raising a large army of volunteers for just such a purpose. We should all pray that South Carolina holds well until the rest of our sister states can mobilize and hurry to her aid."

"All honor to Carolina!" exclaimed another spirited voice. "Let us Georgians not fail in emulating the Carolinians' bravery and patriotism."

The old man with the bushy gray eyebrows grumped, "If you ask me, this is all a lot of tomfoolery."

"Why, what do you mean, Jacob?" someone in the crowd asked. "This is the moment of glory we've all been waiting for."

Old Jacob Logenheim glared at the man. "Glory be to horse-feathers," he snorted. "You're all crazier'n a bunch of dried-up doodlebugs." He rubbed his grizzled chin and huffed, "All this talk about bravery and glory. It's tomfoolery, I tell you, nothing but tom-foolery. Why, I fought the Injuns and the British back in 1812 and the Mexicans in '46, and let me tell you young hotheads a thing or two about war. There ain't nothing glorious about gittin' yourself shot up and maybe killed for a bunch of gol-dang politicians."

The young man with the freckles rolled his eyes and laughed. "Don't pay old Jacob no mind," he cracked to the major. "He's just sour that he won't be able to join up with the rest of us boys when the time comes."

Mayor Franklin Futch, flanked by his two boys, shoved his way through the crowd until he stood face to face with the young major. "Sir," he said imperiously, "I am the mayor of Irwinton, the county seat. Please inform the governor, who happens to be a close person-al friend of mine, that the people of my town are prepared to offer their full cooperation in whatever manner he and President Davis deem necessary."

"I shall inform him," the major replied.

Mayor Futch turned toward the crowd, puffed out his chest and said, "I have long believed that it would come to this. For too long the Northern class has trampled over our sovereign rights as states in its haste to dominate and spread its abominable control over our way of life. I now fear the worst, my fellow citizens. A dark cloud is forming over the land. It is coming fast and it is coming hard, like a storm in the night."

"And it's likely to blow us all away," Jacob Logenheim grumbled.

The rotund mayor gave the old man a reproachful look before resuming his regal pose. "But I say to all of you, should war now come and the shedding of blood be necessary in the defense of our homeland, my boys and I shall find our duty on the front lines where all brave men and true sons of the South must assemble!"

"Here! Here!" several men shouted at once.

"To arms! To arms!" someone else shouted. "Our Southern soil must be defended against all tyrants!"

The emotional outpouring thrilled Catherine Potter to the bone. Her whole body tingled with excitement as she listened to the cheering, the stirring oratory and bombastic boasts. She felt herself being pulled, swept along, as if caught up in a great tidal current surging toward some distant and unknown shore. Her heart pounded so hard it almost hurt as she continued to follow Major Anderson's every move, cling to his every word.

"Remember," the major thundered, "We are all in this together. And the Confederacy needs every one of us to do our duty."

"You can count on the boys of Wilkinson County," came another outburst.

His mission completed, the major remounted his horse. As he did so, he couldn't help noticing the flaming redhead with the sparkling blue eyes staring hard at him. He smiled courteously, blushing slightly, then raised his hand in a smart salute. "Till we meet again," he proclaimed, "long live the Confederacy!"

The pair of sparkling blue eyes followed him as he turned his horse around and sped away.

"Long live the Confederacy!" Catherine heard herself exclaiming.

"Long live the Confederacy!" the crowd roared back. "Long live the Confederacy!"

The roaring continued until long after the handsome young major with the golden curls and jangling spurs had disappeared down the road in a sparkling cloud of dust.

CHAPTER 2

"WHAT A PERFECTLY HORRID THING to have happen on your wedding day," Martha Ann Nesmith heard her sister say.

They were sitting next to each other at the head of a long table in the churchyard, munching on pineapple cake and sipping lemonade. The wedding was over, and now the reception was winding down. It would soon be time for Martha Ann and Wiley to leave for their honeymoon.

Most of the guests had waited around to see them off. Some wandered the cemetery in search of departed ancestors. Others, still fired up about the thrilling news out of Charleston, held court in the shade, debating war and politics while children climbed trees, fought chinaberry wars and scampered among the headstones.

Catherine Potter fanned herself and sighed, "But you have to admit, it's all rather exciting, Martha Ann, dear."

Martha Ann flinched at her sister's words. How could talk of war and politics ever be exciting, she wondered. She was still angry with that arrogant young major for having interrupted her wedding—and with everybody else who had thought his news about the fall of Fort Sumter was the grandest thing in the world.

Didn't they understand that this was the most important day of her life? Didn't any one of them care that she and her husband were about to leave on their honeymoon?

A shadow fell across the table. Martha Ann looked up and saw Zeke Taylor leering down at her. Zeke was a massive, slab-shouldered man with thick black eyebrows and a square-shaped face almost hidden behind a scraggly brown beard.

"There you are," Zeke said, slurring his words. His breath reeked of whisky and stale tobacco.

"Hello, Zeke," Martha Ann replied coolly.

The big man leaned over and smiled. "I came to collect my kiss," he said. "It ain't fittin' to go to a wedding and not kiss the bride."

Without waiting for an invitation, Zeke leaned down to kiss her. As he did so, Martha Ann drew back, and the big man lost his balance and crashed to the ground.

"Hey," he bellowed, picking himself up and thumping the dust off his coat.

"What'd you do that for? I can't kiss you if you don't keep still."

"Go away, Zeke," Catherine said sharply. "Can't you see she doesn't want you to touch her, let alone kiss her?"

Zeke narrowed his eyes and glared at Catherine. "Now ain't you a fine one to complain about kisses," he sneered. "I don't reckon there's a man in the whole county what ain't tasted those hot, wet lips of yours at one time or another."

"Zeke, please," Martha Ann pleaded. "You're drunk. Why don't you go and leave us alone?"

The big man wiped the slobber from his thick lips and laughed. "I'll go," he roared, "but not before I get my kiss."

"You'll go now," a voice behind him commanded.

Zeke spun around and saw Wiley Nesmith. Wiley's tie was loosened, and his shirt sleeves were rolled up past the elbows. His fists were balled tight, and the look in his eyes meant business.

"Easy, now, Wiley," Zeke said with mock fear. "There ain't no call to go getting upset. I just wanted to kiss the little bride, that's all."

"She doesn't want to kiss you."

Zeke grinned. "Well, that's what everybody keeps saying, but I ain't heard her say it yet with her own mouth." He took a menacing step toward Wiley. "What do you say we just let her make up her own mind about that?"

Wiley's glare hardened. "I told you to leave."

Zeke poked a thick, sausage-like finger against Wiley's chest. "Maybe you think you're man enough to make me."

Wiley's heart was pounding so hard it hurt his chest. He knew he was no match for Zeke Taylor, no match at all. The big man would fall on him like an oak tree and probably kill him. But there was no way Wiley was going to stand by and let the brute insult his wife on her wedding day.

Zeke drew back his fist, ready to pound Wiley into oblivion when a deep voice growled, "That's enough, Zeke."

Zeke recognized the voice and froze, his big fist hanging in the air. He turned slowly around and saw James Madison, the oldest of the Nesmith boys, lumbering toward him. Zeke lowered his fist and backed away from Wiley. James Madison Nesmith was the last man in the county he wanted to tangle with.

Zeke gave a nervous laugh. "Shoot, James Madison, I was just having a little fun, he said, forcing a crooked smile. "Ain't no need for everybody to get so riled up over nothing."

James Madison picked up Zeke's hat and flung it at him. "You best be leaving now, Zeke. And don't be coming around my family again unless you're sober."

"I was just having a little fun…"

"You heard him, Zeke." This time it was Sheriff Poindexter's deep, gravelly voice that got Zeke's attention. "If you don't get on your horse right now and leave I'm gonna run you in."

Zeke glowered at the sheriff, then back at Wiley. "I'll go," he snarled. "I reckon I know where I'm not wanted." He clomped unsteadily over to his horse and climbed up. Looking down at them, he snarled, 'But you Nesmiths are gonna be sorry. I'm gonna see to it that all of you get what's coming to you. Every last one of you!"

When Zeke was gone, James Madison turned to Wiley and said, "What are you trying to do, little brother? Get yourself killed on your wedding day?"

"I was doing just fine till you and the sheriff showed up," Wiley snapped. Then he smiled and shook their hands. "But thanks anyway."

"If I were you I'd steer clear of Zeke for a few days," the sheriff suggested.

"Don't worry," Wiley replied.

"If he gives you any trouble, just let me know. I've been itching for an excuse to put that old boy away for years."

Still trembling, Martha Ann rose and reminded Wiley that the train would leave for Savannah in less than two hours.

"Has anybody seen Indigo?" Wiley asked, glancing around.

"Here I am," a voice called down from the sycamore tree. Wiley looked up and saw Indigo and Garrett, Wiley's fourteen-year-old brother, waving down at them. The boys wasted no time tumbling down from the tree. Somehow they made it to the ground without spilling a drop of lemonade from the cups in their hands.

"Time to go," Wiley said to Indigo.

While they waited for Indigo to bring the wagon around, well-wishers crowded around the newlyweds for last-minute goodbyes. Wiley hugged his mother's neck, then shook each one of his brother's hands. Martha Ann did the same with her family.

It was Catherine who got in the last word. "My dear, you are simply going to love the Pulaski Hotel. The room I reserved for you has a balcony overlooking the river and a big canopy bed, and they put fresh flowers in your room every day."

She followed her sister to the wagon and watched her climb up. "You must promise that you will write me a nice, long letter and tell me everything about Savannah. Spare no details. Oh, I do hope you get there before it falls to the Yankees!"

CHAPTER 3

THE TRAIN RIDE TO SAVANNAH seemed to last forever. That was because they stopped at almost every station along the way, picking up volunteers anxious to get to Savannah so they could enlist. Most were fresh-faced farm boys with dirt under their fingernails. Some climbed aboard barefooted and carrying nothing more than a handful of pitiful rags strung across their backs. Others were well-groomed and fashionably attired and accompanied by black man-servants who hauled trunks bulging with tailored uniforms and polished swords and gleaming silver place servings.

But all of them—young and old, rich and poor—had fire in their eyes and a rage in their bellies, and they sang and cheered and made solemn vows to defend their sacred homeland to the death should it be invaded by Lincoln's legions from the North.

Martha Ann sat next to the window, watching the flat country-side roll slowly by. It would be dark soon. Long, purple shadows twisted and curled across the broad fields and vast cypress swamps that seemed to stretch on forever toward the horizon. Every now and then they'd pass a solitary farmhouse, tightly shuttered against the creeping gloom, and she'd think of all the long, lonely nights she had spent on her parent's plantation waiting for this day.

She closed her eyes and wistfully recalled the first time she met Wiley. It had been at a New Year's Eve dance fifteen months earlier. She and Catherine had gone to the dance together, but it had been Catherine—younger, prettier and not above flirting with any boy who looked at her—who had all the fun. It was bitterly cold that night, so cold that Martha Ann was about to go home when a handsome, dark-haired boy she'd never seen before walked over and offered her his coat if she'd dance with him.

She accepted his offer, and they had danced for hours, she and this tall, dark-haired boy, not once changing partners. And while they danced, Martha Ann Walker had fallen head over heels in love with Wiley Nesmith.

Six months later he asked her to marry him. He had just driven her home after church and was about to help her down from the buggy when he suddenly stopped and said, "Martha Ann, I know this is kind of sudden-like, but there's something I've been about to bust to ask you for weeks now."

He fidgeted with his hat for a moment, then reached up and took her by the hand. "What I mean is, we've known each for about six months now, and I've got to tell you, I ain't never met a girl half as pretty as you, nor one who I've enjoyed kissing so much."

Martha Ann only pretended to be horrified. "Why, Wiley Nesmith, I didn't know you made it a practice to go around kissing all the girls."

"Oh, no, no," Wiley stammered, "that's not what I meant, not what I meant at all…"

"Then just what did you mean?" Martha Ann teased, trying hard not to giggle.

Wiley sighed. "What I meant to say was…Well, I really like kissing *you*, only you. You've got nice lips."

"What about the other girls? Do they have nice lips, too?"

"No, no, they…they…" Wiley fidgeted some more, obviously in great pain. "What I mean is…" He drew another deep breath. "Well, actually, you're the only girl I've ever kissed. And I sure do like your kissing."

"Well, I like to kiss you, too."

"You do?" Wiley asked, suddenly blushing and brightening interchangably.

Martha Ann nodded. She had to bite her lip to keep from laughing.

More boldly, Wiley asked, "Then…what would you say if I asked you to marry me? To be my wife?"

"I'd say yes."

THE TRAIN FINALLY PULLED INTO SAVANNAH around ten o'clock that night. Even at that hour the station was swarming with volunteers and mobs of spirited citizens who stamped and cheered and waved newly stitched Confederate flags. A band played somewhere in the background.

The place was so busy it took Wiley half an hour to collect their bags, then another half-hour before a buggy became available to take them to their hotel.

A light rain was falling as the little surrey clip-clopped across the darkened cobblestone square. Wiley slipped an arm around his new wife's shoulders and pulled her close. "Happy?" he asked, his voice scratchy in the soft night air.

Martha Ann snuggled close against her husband. "Very," she purred. In fact, she could not possibly imagine a happier moment in her life. She had just married the man she loved, and now she was going to spend her honeymoon in the most romantic city in the South.

Wiley pressed his face against her hair and drank in the sweet, damp fragrance. "I love you, Mrs. Nesmith," he whispered.

Martha Ann lifted her face and saw the reflective glow of the street lamps shining in Wiley's dark eyes. "And I love you, Mr. Nesmith."

It was almost midnight by the time they got to the hotel. The driver, a young black boy with big, bulging eyes and spindly bow-legs, helped them down, then brought their bags around to the lobby.

"Thanks," Wiley said, tipping the boy a quarter.

The boy's eyes looked like they were going to pop out of their sockets. "Thank you, sir!" he beamed, unable to believe his good fortune. He tipped his hat and scampered out the door.

After Wiley checked them in, a black porter wearing a Pulaski Hotel name tag led them down a long, carpeted hallway, across a walled garden out back, then up three flights of stairs to their room on the third floor.

The room was clean and spacious and covered with a soft Oriental carpet. In the middle stood a huge, four-poster bed with an arching white canopy trimmed in lace frills. It was, quite simply, the biggest, grandest, most comfortable-looking bed Wiley had ever seen.

Humming a happy tune, the porter opened a set of French doors that looked out over the garden and Johnson Square beyond. The sweet smell of wisteria and honeysuckle floated in, along with the damp night air.

"This is the honeymoon suite," the porter beamed. He was a squat, powerfully-built man in his late twenties or early thirties, and he spoke with the fast, clipped accent so prevalent among book-smart blacks. "It's the best in town."

"I'm sure," Wiley said, eyes wandering around the elegant room.

The porter headed for the door. "If there's anything else you need, sir, just call on me. My name's Samson. I'll be your personal porter while you're here." He bowed graciously, then exited the room.

When they were alone, Wiley rushed over to his wife and took her in his arms. "Can you believe it? We're really here."

Martha Ann did find it hard to believe. Her thoughts drifted back to earlier in the day when that arrogant young major had galloped out to the church and interrupted their wedding. For one frantic, heart-stopping moment she had feared that Wiley and all the other boys were going to be called away to the army and the honeymoon would have to be postponed. In her mind's eye she saw herself standing alone on the church house steps, bouquet of roses in hand, Wiley waving goodbye, promising to return soon as he rushed off to war.

But her fears had been for naught. After the wedding and a brief reception in the churchyard, Indigo had driven them to the train station, and they'd left for Savannah right on time.

Now, alone in their cozy hotel room, all talk of war and Mister Lincoln's black Republicans seemed far, far away.

They walked out onto the balcony and gazed across the city. Even though it was past midnight, Savannah still hummed and throbbed with excitement. Late-night revelers tromped past their windows below, singing, laughing, waving colorful flags and banners, and huge, roaring bonfires illuminated the skyline and riverfront promenade two blocks away.

"Have you ever seen anything so beautiful in all your life?" Martha Ann said softly. "It's almost like we're standing at the edge of time waiting for the world to be born."

Then, almost as if it had been ordered specially for them, a brilliant burst of fireworks sent a shower of green and golden sparks arcing high over the river. Somewhere down along the waterfront a brass band began to play.

They stood on the balcony another five minutes, kissing like secret lovers in the dark, then went back inside the room, undressed and climbed into the big, soft bed.

"Oh, Wiley," Martha Ann moaned when he finally entered her, his musk-thick fragrance like a mist around her, glutting her body and soul with undreamed of desire.

When it was over, they fell asleep in each other's arms, their bodies shrouded in the soft, flickering glow of the bonfires and lingering aroma of wisteria and honeysuckle.

NEXT MORNING THEY WERE AWAKENED by a soft knocking at the door. Wiley got up, trod to the door and saw Samson—all smiles and fresh in a white linen jacket—standing outside with a newspaper and vase of flowers.

"This is for you, sir," Samson said, handing Wiley the newspaper. "And these," he added, handing him the flowers, "are for the new bride."

Wiley didn't quite know what to say. He'd never had anyone bring him a newspaper before. Of course, this was only the second time in his life he'd spent the night in a hotel. Were they always this friendly to out-of-town guests?

After Samson had gone, Wiley opened the newspaper to the front page. His mouth nearly fell open when he read the main headline. "Dear God," he muttered.

"What's wrong?" Martha Ann called from the bed.

Wiley's face had turned ashen gray. "Abraham Lincoln has issued a call for seventy-five thousand troops." He looked across the room at his wife. "They're going to try to force us back into the Union."

SAVANNAH WAS A CITY on the verge of a nervous breakdown. That spring, as war fever swept both sides of the Mason-Dixon, all people talked about was the coming Yankee invasion. Everybody knew it was only a matter of time before Union gunboats sailed into Charleston Harbor to try to retake Fort Sumter. Would the brave Carolinians be able to hold? If not, Savannah would be in grave peril.

Rumor had it that old Winfield S. Scott, the new general-in-chief of the Federal army, was already working on a secret plan to blockade the Southern coast. What a disgrace it would be to fall to that old traitor!

For weeks, city fathers had been preparing for the worst. Extra troops had been dispatched to Fort Pulaski, the old stone citadel guarding the main approach to the harbor out at Cockspur Island. Farther south, a new earthen works garrison called Fort McAllister had been constructed at the mouth of the Ogeechee River to protect Ossabaw Sound.

By late April, the cry, "Let the Yankees come if they dare!" reverberated throughout the old Colonial capital as anxious citizens and hastily formed militiamen busied themselves with preparations against attack.

In many ways, Georgia's oldest city already resembled a city under siege. Day and night the cobblestone squares echoed with the tramping of many boots and the lumbering clatter of wagons and artillery caissons. Snappy young officers strutted about, laughing, joking, delighting the young belles with their swagger and gallant vows to defend Savannah at all costs. Flashy new military companies with names like the *Georgia Hussars, Jasper Greens, Phoenix Riflemen, Oglethorpe Light Infantry, Rattlesnakes, Hyenas* and the *Chatham Artillery* paraded and drilled. One newly formed company, the *Savannah Cadets*, was composed of youngsters no older than twelve and thirteen.

Along Factor's Row, the bustling commercial district facing the river, bright new Confederate banners rippled and cracked in the warm breezes that fluttered in from the sea. It was here, near the original spot where the first settlers landed in 1733, that the invaders would more than likely try to gain entry to the city. To guard against that, most of the waterfront area had been transformed into a fortress. Warehouses that once bulged with cotton and tobacco had been converted into troop garrisons and supply depots. Handsome, multistoried mansions that once hosted glittering balls and chamber recitals now served as hospitals and recruiting stations.

Up and down Bay Street, huge cannons and rifle pits ringed by stacks of cotton bales and turpentine barrels pointed toward the quietly flowing river. Even the colorful promenade, once the domain of elegantly attired strollers and picnickers, now teemed with soldiers and bummers and prostitutes.

The rumble of war was still far away, but Savannah would be ready when it came to Georgia.

———

"LOOK AT THEM, parading around like this was some kind of little boy's game."

Martha Ann, dressed in a white cotton gown and slippers, stood on the third-floor balcony of the Pulaski Hotel, gazing down at Johnson Square below. It was only eight o'clock in the morning, but already the square and surrounding oak-shaded avenues and parks were abuzz with the sound of soldiers and civilians preparing for war.

Even this far away, Martha Ann could hear officers calling out cadences to boys and old men, many of whom, it appeared, didn't know their left foot from their right. Every now and then a mounted officer would come galloping onto the scene, swinging a saber and barking orders—more to impress the pretty young girls in their hoop skirts and bonnets, Martha Ann imagined, than anything else.

Wiley got up from the four-poster bed, slipped into his robe and strolled out onto the balcony. The fresh morning air felt good but sticky on his bare skin.

He put an arm around his wife's waist and drew her close. "Looks to me like they can't wait for the Yankees to get here," he said.

"I think they've all lost their minds," Martha Ann replied. "I think everybody in this whole town has completely lost their minds."

AT BREAKFAST THAT MORNING they ate hotcakes and sausages in a little walled garden behind the hotel. The hotcakes were filled with blueberries and cream cheese, and the sausages were cut into little squares and stuffed with peppers.

Wiley had never tasted anything so delicious in all his life.

They drank lemon-scented water and fresh-squeezed orange juice out of crystal glasses. When they finished, the waiter brought them a pot of steaming-hot coffee and sweet cream and sugar in little white porcelain bowls.

From where they sat they could see the broad river, its dark, murky currents sweeping rapidly toward the sea. A small steamboat chugged upstream, puffs of white smoke billowing from its tall chimney. A bright red Confederate flag fluttered from its tallest mast.

"More coffee, sir?"

Wiley looked up and saw the waiter, a slight, curly-haired lad barely in his teens. He wore black trousers, a bow tie, white shirt and a starched white jacket that seemed to swallow his small frame.

"Yes, thank you," Wiley said.

While pouring the coffee, the boy smiled and said, "First visit to Savannah?"

Wiley laughed and said, "Does it show that much?"

Martha Ann reached across and touched Wiley's arm. "We're here on our honeymoon. We were married yesterday."

The young waiter smiled and said, "Congratulations to both of you."

"What about you?" Wiley asked. "Are you from around here?"

"Born and bred. Course, I'll be leaving pretty soon."

"Oh?"

"I'm joining the Confederate army." The boy said it in a way that made it seem as natural as joining a church choir. "I'll be leaving for Charleston in two weeks."

Martha Ann cleared her throat. "Forgive me, but aren't you a little young?"

"I'll be sixteen my next birthday," the boy shot back. "Besides, I have an uncle up in Charleston who says he can get me in General

Beauregard's outfit. He's a state senator. Name's Justin Stiles. Ever hear of him?"

Wiley shook his head. "Nope. Can't say as I have."

"Uncle Justin says that *everybody* up in Carolina's joining up. Half the state's already in uniform and drilling for the invasion." The waiter paused, looked at Wiley. "What about you, Mister? Are you joining up, too?"

Wiley grimaced. "If I have to," he replied without emotion.

"It's the only fittin' thing to do," the boy asserted.

As he turned to go, he raised his right fist and shouted, "God bless the Confederacy!"

A young couple sitting at a table across the room jumped up and returned the salute. "God save the Confederacy!" they cried out.

Within seconds everybody in the restaurant was on his feet saluting the Confederacy and singing praises to Jefferson Davis.

———

THEY SPENT THE REST OF THE MORNING strolling the promenade down by the river. The air was warm and soft and smelled like the sea. They watched an old black fisherman haul in a basket of fish, then found an empty bench at the end of a small wooden pier and sat down to watch the birds and a small flotilla of sailboats drift past.

Later that afternoon it started to rain, and they ducked inside a cozy little restaurant facing the river and ate fried fish and oysters.

The restaurant was crowded and noisy. Soldiers sang and clapped, while big-busted girls sat on their laps or danced and played patriotic tunes on an old piano in the corner. The whole place was smoky and smelled like warm beer and fish, but most of the customers were so drunk with spirits and song they didn't notice.

When they finished eating, Wiley said, "Let's get out of here."

They went straight to the room, took off their wet clothes and climbed into the big, four-poster bed. They spent the rest of that that rain-soaked night in Savannah making love on satin sheets and pillows so soft and smooth Wiley thought of glassy lakes and summer clouds.

Around seven o'clock the next morning, Wiley got up and

walked over to the window. It was still dark and gray, and a light rain was falling. He looked down and was surprised to see a squad of young, gray-coated cadets singing as they marched across the square, their proud, handsome faces lit and glowing in the shimmering spring rain.

The song they were singing carried a soft, haunting melody. But it was the words, more than anything else, that captivated Wiley's senses as he stood at the window watching the young soldiers-to-be troop past until they vanished like phantoms in the early morning fog.

They were gone so fast Wiley wondered if they'd ever been there at all. Until those words came back to him:

> *I wish I was in the land of cotton,*
> *Old times there are not forgotten,*
> *Look away! Look away! Look away,*
> *Dixie Land.*
> *In Dixie Land where I was born in,*
> *Early on one frosty morning,*
> *Look away, look away, look away*
> *Dixie Land.*
> *Then I wish I was in Dixie,*
> *Hooray! Hooray!*
> *In Dixie land, I'll take my stand,*
> *To live and die in Dixie.*
> *Away, away, away down South in Dixie.*
> *Away, away, away, down South in Dixie...*

CHAPTER 4

WILEY WAS AMAZED at how much the town had changed. In less than a week, the time he and Martha Ann had been away on their honeymoon, Irwinton had been transformed from a sleepy little country town into a roaring military camp. The most noticeable changes were the bright red flags and banners that flew everywhere—over the sprawling new courthouse and town square, the tiny post office and school, the park, the livery stable, even the train depot.

It seemed strange that the Stars & Stripes were nowhere to be seen.

"Isn't it *grand*?" a prim, middle-aged woman sitting across from them gushed as the train pulled into the station. The woman leaned over and whispered to Martha Ann, "I'm from Macon. My husband's with Colonel Lawton in Savannah. Has your husband joined the grand Confederate army yet?"

"No," Martha Ann replied tartly—perhaps too tartly, based on the woman's shocked reaction.

"Well, my goodness," the woman huffed. "I would suggest that he get a move on it before all the good positions are filled. Then again, the war might be over before he gets to go to the front. Wouldn't that be simply awful?"

Martha Ann turned away from the woman in disgust. Outside the window she saw gangs of boys and men trooping about in civilian attire, muskets slung haughtily over their shoulders. Scruffy sergeants trailed after them, barking orders and calling out cadence.

As the train screeched to a hissing halt in front of the depot, she could see two barefoot boys armed with pitchforks standing guard over a rusty old cannon in front of the depot. Where had that old thing come from, she wondered? It looked like it belonged in a cabinet of curiosities. Or a junk pile.

"God help us all," she murmured. "Everybody here has gone crazy, too."

———

INDIGO WAS THERE WITH THE WAGON waiting for them when they stepped down off the train. As usual, he was barefooted and wearing his grandfather's straw hat.

"Hello, Indigo," Wiley called out. "Did you take good care of Sable?"

"Yes-s-sir," the boy said proudly. "Just like you t-told me to."

Wiley tossed the bags into the back of the wagon. "You didn't spoil him too much, I hope."

"Oh, no, sir, I wouldn't d-do that, M-Mister Wiley."

Wiley helped Martha Ann onto the wagon, then pulled himself up beside her. He turned to face Indigo and said, "You know, I've been thinking that maybe Sable needs more attention than I've been able to give him. A fine horse like that doesn't need to be cooped up in a stall all day long. He needs to get out, ride more. What do you think?"

Indigo gaped in disbelief. What was Mister Wiley trying to tell him? That he could keep Sable on a regular basis?

Then the bombshell: "What would you say if I let you keep Sable over at your house? I think that pasture on the far side of the cornfield would work out just fine. Of course, you'd have to water him every day and groom him and see to it that he eats properly. And, if you had time, I think it'd be a good idea to take him out for a ride at least once a day. What do you say?"

Indigo's reaction was swift and convincing. "Oh, yes, sir," the boy replied hastily. "I c-could do that. W-wouldn't be no problem. N-no problem, at all."

"Good. I'll speak to your pa about it soon's we get home."

The boy couldn't believe his good fortune. He grabbed the reins nervously and held them for a moment. "Anyp-place special you'd like to g-go?"

"Yeah," Wiley replied, settling down next to his wife. "*Home.* Get us there as fast as you can."

They had seen enough of the Grand Confederate Army for one week.

———

MONROE COLLINS WAS ON TOP OF THE BARN hammering shingles into place when he saw the wagon lumbering up the road. The sun was just beginning to set, and he had to squint before he recognized who it was.

"Lord, have mercy," he grinned, then put down his hammer and hurried down the ladder.

Monroe was a big man, with massive shoulders and an intimidating pair of arms that could snap a pine sapling in half or pull a mule out of a ditch. Underneath that power, however, beat the heart of a kind, gentle soul who rose before dawn every day to pray with his family and rarely spoke above a whisper.

He hurried across the lot and opened the gate, just as the wagon pulled into the lane.

"Welcome home, Mister Wiley, Miz Martha Ann," Monroe said excitedly. He helped them down from the wagon, then said to his son, "Boy, get those bags on inside the house. Hurry now! And don't forget to put the wagon away and make sure the horse is fed and brushed down. And when that's done, there's a heap of corn that needs to be shucked up at the house."

"Yes, Pa," Indigo replied dutifully. He was still so excited about Mister Wiley's offer to let him take care of Sable that even the thought of chores didn't bother him.

When Indigo was gone, Monroe scratched his head and said, "That boy, I don't know what I'm gonna do with him. All he ever does anymore is ride that horse. And when he ain't riding it, he's feeding it and grooming it. And when he ain't doing that, he's dreaming about doing it."

Wiley smiled. "Well, I suppose that's partly my fault, Monroe," he said, then explained the deal he had made with Indigo.

"How's Sarah?" Martha Ann interjected.

"Oh, she's just fine," Monroe replied. "Why, she's over there at the house right this minute cooking up a special homecoming meal for you: crackling cornbread and fresh collard greens. It's supposed to be a surprise."

Wiley licked his lips in mock hunger and said, "Then we promise not to let on."

<hr />

IT *WAS* GOOD TO BE BACK HOME, Wiley thought as they opened the front door and stepped across the threshold for the first time as man and wife. At least nothing here had changed.

Monroe put the bags down in the living room.

"Thanks for looking after the place," Wiley said.

"Wasn't nothing."

When Monroe saw that special look in Wiley's eyes—that-*we want-to-be-alone-now-look*—he dismissed himself politely by saying he'd go tell Sarah they were back.

At the door he turned around and said, "Oh, I almost forgot...James Madison came by earlier today. Said he and Miz Elizabeth would be dropping back by this evening. Said he wanted to talk to you about a meeting in town in the morning."

"A meeting?" Wiley asked.

Monroe shrugged. "Army talk," he said. "Must be about forming the regiment. That's all everybody's been talking about all week long."

<hr />

THE HOUSE THAT WILEY AND HIS NEW BRIDE lived in was small but comfortable. It had been built in the early 1800s by James Nesmith, Wiley's father, who had brought his family down from the Carolina high country after winning a hundred acres in a Georgia land lottery. In those days Wilkinson County was still wilderness, a raw, untamed region near the old Spanish border that was as lonely as it was remote, as dangerous as it was beautiful. But the land had been good and full of promise, and James Nesmith had prospered. The family had grown over the years, along with Nesmith's modest land holdings along Big Sandy Creek in the western part of the county.

Wiley was born on August 20, 1840, the youngest of six brothers and two sisters. There would be one more boy, Garrett, who came along five years later, the same year the old man succumbed to yellow fever.

In later years, the farm had been left to Wiley because the older boys had moved away to start their own families in different parts of the county. Both sisters were married and lived away, one in Alabama, the other near Athens. Garrett, the youngest, went to live with James Madison, the oldest, and his wife, Elizabeth, who also took care of their ailing mother, Jane Price Nesmith, now in her sixty-second year.

Wiley's life had taken a dramatic turn on New Year's Day, 1860. That's when he met Martha Ann Walker at the town dance. From the moment he set eyes on the pretty sixteen-year-old belle from across Turkey Creek near Danville, he knew she was the one for him.

Six months later Wiley proposed, and Martha Ann accepted. So did her father, Jeremiah Walker, but only after Wiley had assured him he would be a good provider for his daughter.

———

"A FATHER CAN'T BE TOO CAREFUL when it comes to such things," Jeremiah Walker had told Wiley one Sunday after church. "My daughter's welfare and future happiness mean everything to me."

They were sitting on the front porch of the Walker home enjoying a smoke. A cool breeze was blowing in from the cornfields surrounding the rambling, steep-gabled farmhouse that Walker and his four sons had built some ten years earlier.

Jeremiah Walker, a big, balding man with gray whiskers and a bulldog-like face, leaned over, looked Wiley straight in the eye and said, "A husband's got to be able to take care of his wife. Know what I mean, boy?"

"Yes, sir," Wiley replied somewhat nervously. He was trying hard not to choke on the thick cigar stuffed in his mouth that his future father-in-law had given him, along with instructions on how to use it.

When Wiley told him about the farm he had inherited, Walker's broad, tanned face lit up. "Good enough," he declared, slapping his leg for emphasis. "Now we can have ourselves a wedding."

The Walkers weren't wealthy, but they owned several slaves. Not long after the engagement announcement was official, Jeremiah Walker told Wiley he was giving him a slave family as a wedding present.

"Monroe's a good man," Walker explained. "Ain't never had a minute's worth of trouble with him or his wife, Sarah. You take care of them, son, along with the boy. Treat 'em right and fair, and they'll lay down their lives for you."

At first Wiley didn't know how to respond to what he knew was a very generous offer from his new father-in-law. In all his years, Wiley had seen only a few Negroes—mostly those who came to town with their masters on Saturdays to buy goods at the commissary or to gather at the old Meeting Place. Every now and then he'd spot a gang of them out at old Zaddock Simmons' place hoeing cotton or corn. But that was about it. There just weren't that many blacks—free or slave—in Wilkinson County.

And that was just fine with Wiley, who had always felt uneasy about what some whites called the "peculiar institution." In his way of thinking, it wasn't right for one man to work as another man's slave. Even though he suspected that Negroes were inferior to whites, Wiley was convinced they were human beings too, and that slavery itself was wrong, if not a complete sin. The whole country would be better off, he believed, if the Negroes were just shipped back to Africa where they'd come from. They'd be happier there, he reasoned, back among their own kind, provided they wanted to go.

Then, two months before the wedding, tragedy struck when a tree fell on Jeremiah Walker and killed him. It happened late on a Monday afternoon only hours after the old man had left Wiley's house in Wilkinson County. He had spent the afternoon helping Wiley frame in a new corncrib.

Politics had dominated their conversation most of the afternoon. Politics was something that Wiley didn't know or care much about. But as for Walker, a two-term justice of the peace and former state legislator, politics was the noblest calling on earth.

"The way I see it," the big man had said in a curious nasal drawl that sometimes made it sound like the words came out of his nose, "the people of the Southern states have no choice but to leave the

Union and go their separate way. We need our own country, boy, a country based on the things we believe in. I just don't see how we can continue to stay part of a government that's morally corrupt, one that treats us like second-class citizens."

Walker paused long enough to re-light his cigar. "Take the tariff, for example," he continued. "Ever since this republic was founded, a handful of rich Northern bankers and merchants have used the import tariff to make ungodly profits at the expense of the South." He leaned toward Wiley and said, "You know what I'm driving at, boy?"

"Yes, sir, I think so."

"The truth is," Walker continued, heaving one massive leg over the other, "it's been the South that's made this country great. The South and its agricultural commodities, mostly cotton. Without cotton the North would be nothing but a stony wilderness full of 'skeeters and Injuns. That's because it's Southern cotton that makes those Northern factories hum, boy. It's cotton that makes those moneylenders rich. Hell, it's cotton that makes the whole world go 'round." He paused, flicked ashes over the side of the porch. "Look at old England over there across the ocean. Without cotton—without *our* cotton—those people would be back in the Middle Ages."

Walker chewed on his cigar some more. "Like old James Hammond said, boy, cotton is king. No power in its right mind would dare go against the will of the cotton states. Now, here comes this Lincoln fellow and all those other damn fools who call themselves Republicans who have taken over the government. They don't understand economics, boy, haven't got a lick of business sense. All they yap about is the darkies, about how they're being mistreated and such."

Walker chuckled at that thought. "Well, what do they know about the darkies, I ask you? What would they do with 'em? They sure as hell don't want 'em up there contaminating their fine, pure cities. And you don't hear the folks out in the Western territories bellyaching for their company. I tell you, if those darkies were freed tomorrow, it wouldn't be long before those Yankee money-grubbers would be beggin' us Southrens to put 'em back in their chains."

Walker leaned back and scratched his bearded chin. "Hell, boy, is any of this making sense to you?"

"Oh, yes, sir," Wiley started. "I couldn't agree with you more."

The old man shifted in his rocker, as if he was about to say something uncomfortable, something he'd rather not bring up. A faraway look clouded his face as he narrowed his gray eyes and said, "I'm gonna let you in on a secret, boy. There's gonna be bloodshed. A powerful lot of blood is gonna flow before this sectional crisis passes."

It wasn't exactly the words, but the way Walker said them that chilled Wiley to the bone. *Blood. Bloodshed. A powerful lot of blood...*

What did it all mean?

Wiley nodded thoughtfully, pretending he understood everything Jeremiah Walker was saying. As a Southerner, Wiley was mindful of the grievous injustices being perpetrated against his region by the North—what some newspapers were calling "the crime of the North." And, although he didn't completely understand all the complexities of the sectional crisis, it seemed clear to him that the Federal government in Washington was doing everything it could to stir up the slaveholding states, to deliberately drive them out of the Union, just like Mister Walker was saying.

"Yessiree," Jeremiah Walker continued, rocking back on his heels and blowing smoke rings from the long, dark cigar, "I can see it now, plain as a woodpecker's nose. War's a-coming, boy. Make no mistake about it, war's a-coming."

Then he got back on his horse and rode home and died.

———

A FEW DAYS BEFORE THE WEDDING, Wiley and Indigo had taken the wagon down to Danville, loaded up Martha Ann's things and moved his bride-to-be into their new home. The boy's ma and pa had arrived several weeks earlier and were a big help getting Martha Ann settled in.

Wiley had given the slaves the little cottage at the far end of the field. It wasn't big, but it was clean and comfortable, had a good wooden floor, sturdy stone chimney and a deep cistern with plenty of fresh water. Sarah had gone to work on the place right away, cutting weeds, planting flowers and putting in a little vegetable garden out back. Indigo helped Monroe repair the roof and make a fence to keep the chickens in and the hogs and wild critters out. As a final touch, they built a picket fence from scraps of wood in the barn and painted it with whitewash.

Even before they arrived, Wiley had already made up his mind to free his slave family before the wedding—with or without his father-in-law's blessings. Jeremiah Walker's untimely death had removed any opposition to his plans. One week after his funeral, Wiley had gone into town and filed the necessary papers to emancipate the couple and their son. The action had cost Wiley some friendships, but none he couldn't live without.

"You mean…we're *free?*" Monroe asked Wiley the day the emancipation took effect. He and Sarah, both of whom had been born into slavery on a Sparta plantation, were having a hard time grasping the concept of freedom. "We can go anywhere we want to…just like white folks?"

Wiley nodded. "But, remember, you're always welcome to stay here. I can't pay you much, but you can live in the little house free of charge, and we can continue to farm the spread together."

It was an offer too good to pass up. Besides, where would a couple of beat-up old ex-slaves without any schooling go anyway?

"We'll stay," Monroe decided.

SARAH BROUGHT THE FOOD OVER AT SIX SHARP. She was a big, bosomy woman with bright, twinkly eyes and a silvery cloud of hair that flowed around her dark, round face like a wispy halo.

As a slave, Sarah had never gone to school, but that didn't stop her from teaching herself how to read and write—skills she had passed down to her only child, Indigo. But her education went far beyond book-learning. From her grandmother she had learned many of the old ways—conjuring, rooting, casting spells, removing spells and other closely guarded secrets, some of which even her own husband didn't know about. Sometimes Monroe teased her that she was the kind of woman who could raise the dead if she put her mind to it. So far she'd never had reason to.

Sarah set the table, served the plates, lit the candles and left just as Wiley and Martha Ann finished unpacking.

Their first meal together at home was a pleasant one. They ate fried pork chops and crackling bread, collard greens and mashed potatoes. For dessert, they ate almost half of the blackberry pie Sarah had baked fresh that afternoon.

After supper they went out on the front porch to watch the sun go down. They sat on the steps, listening to the gentle sounds of twilight. It was Wiley's favorite time of day, always had been. As a boy he used to enjoy sitting on the porch listening to his pa talk about the old days. There was usually a story or two about the Indian wars and how brave Colonel Clark and his band of buck-skinned rangers had driven the savages westward to lands beyond the wild Ocmulgee. On stormy nights he'd sometimes talk about the powerful hurricane that swept through the region long before the coming of the Spaniards, leveling the ancient forests and wiping out whole tribes.

Sometimes Wiley could almost hear the old man's voice whispering to him in the dark, just like he used to. It was strange. Wiley's pa had died when he was only a little boy, but he had never forgotten what he looked like or the sound of his voice.

"So this is what the world looked like when you were a little boy," Martha Ann said, her eyes wandering off toward the darkening fields and woods beyond. In the distance, giant bullbats wheeled and soared, while down in the canebrakes, crickets and bullfrogs and whippoorwills made their melancholy music.

"This is it," Wiley said softly.

Martha Ann drew in a deep breath of air and sighed. "This explains a lot."

Wiley was about to ask her what she meant when they heard, then saw, a wagon rumbling up the road toward the house.

"Looks like we've got company," Martha Ann said. "Our first visitors."

"Must be James Madison and Elizabeth," Wiley said, getting up and walking across the yard toward the gate.

He reached the gate just as the wagon rolled up.

"Whoa," James Madison said, tugging hard on the reins.

"Well, well, look what the night wind blew in," Wiley joked, reaching up and shaking his brother's hand. "Evening James

Madison, Elizabeth," he said. "What brings you two out this way this time of night?"

James Madison, a tall, bearded man with coarse black hair and thick eyebrows bunched together over his nose, swung his long legs slowly down from the wagon and stretched. "We heard you got back on the four o'clock run," he said in his customary mellow drawl. "Thought we'd drop by to welcome you newlyweds back to Georgia." He gave Wiley a playful poke. "So...how was the big city?"

"Come on inside and we'll put on a pot of coffee and tell you all about it."

James Madison shook his big head. "We'd love to, little brother, but we can't stay. As you can see, it's getting kinda late for us old-timers to be out on the road."

"Besides, we know you must have a million things to do," Elizabeth interjected. She was a tall, handsome woman in her late thirties, a year or two younger than her husband. She had gloriously dark eyes that seemed to burn with rare energy. Her hair—the color of Georgia clay—was piled up in a bun beneath a dark bonnet.

Elizabeth hugged Martha Ann and said, "We brought you a few things from town we thought you might need." She looked at her husband. "Make yourself useful, James Madison, and get them down."

James Madison did as he was told. He reached into the back of the wagon, grabbed a box of groceries and handed them to Wiley.

"Thought these things might come in handy," he said.

Martha Ann peered inside the box. There was an assortment of fresh vegetables and fruit, a sack of flour, a can of coffee, several jars of homemade dewberry jam, a roll of print fabric and a package of darning needles and thread. She was at a loss for words. "You shouldn't have," she stammered, genuinely touched. "This is so kind of you."

"Consider it a little welcome into the family," Elizabeth said.

While Martha Ann and Elizabeth chatted, James Madison pulled Wiley aside and asked, "What did you think of all the commotion in town?"

Wiley rolled his eyes. "Looks like they're expecting the whole Yankee army to come marching into town any minute," he said heavily.

James Madison gave a hearty laugh. "Yeah, I reckon it does," he said, rubbing his thick beard. He opened a can of tobacco, pulled out a plug and stuffed it between his cheeks. "What was it like in Savannah?"

"Same thing. Soldiers and cannons everywhere. The whole town looked like one big fort."

"Those folks have got serious problems. I wouldn't want to be in their shoes right now, not with them Yankee invaders breathing down their necks."

Wiley nodded. "What about Ma and the boys?"

James Madison sighed. "Ma's about the same. Up one day, down the next. The boys are itching like everybody else to sign up." He spat out a thick wad of tobacco, then looked straight at Wiley and said, "This thing ain't going away, you know."

Wiley frowned. "Nope, I reckon not."

"Best thing we can do is be ready."

"I suppose so."

James Madison wiped his hands on his pants and said, "Well, I reckon we best be shoving off. It's gonna be midnight before we get back to the house."

He nudged his wife, indicating it was time to go.

"Thanks for coming over," Martha Ann said to Elizabeth. "Maybe we can see each other again real soon."

"Get Wiley to bring you to church," Elizabeth said. "It's what everybody around here does."

James Madison helped his wife onto the wagon, then climbed up behind her. "Oh, almost forgot," he said. "There's gonna be a meeting in town in the morning to discuss forming the new regiment. Me and the boys are going."

Elizabeth punched her husband playfully. "Honestly, James Madison," she huffed. "Did you have to go and tell them that? Their first night back home from their honeymoon?"

"He needs to know, Elizabeth," James Madison shot back.

Wiley looked up and saw the serious look in his brother's eye. "What time?"

"Eleven. At the courthouse. Think you can make it?"

"I'll be there."

CHAPTER 5

IRWINTON WAS A NOT A BIG TOWN, but what it lacked in size it more than made up for in charm. At least that was what Wiley was thinking the next morning as the wagon carrying him and Martha Ann lumbered slowly into town.

Shaded avenues guarded the main thoroughfare, and behind the bushy boughs of elms, oaks and spruce pines loomed long rows of handsome, two-story houses separated by rolling, grassy lawns and manicured gardens.

The grandest house was a Greek Revival mansion that belonged to Mayor Franklin Futch. Futch had built the house in the early 1850s, shortly after moving from Augusta where he had made a fortune in the sawmill and railroad business. In Irwinton he had continued to prosper as a sawmill operator and planter. But his luck hit a dead end two years earlier when his wife, Cora, came down with the fever. Cora's death had left him alone in the great big house, with only the two boys, which a pair of black nannies was helping him raise.

As Wiley drove past the mayor's house—known as Acorn Hall— he couldn't help wondering if Futch's pledge to offer his two boys to the cause was real, or if their daddy's high-faluting words at the wedding had been nothing more than political aggrandizement.

Since ancient times, the land on which Irwinton now stood had been the center of a thriving Indian civilization. But various treaties since the Revolutionary era had led to the rapid removal of all tribes to new homelands westward beyond the Ocmulgee. A steady stream of settlers, squatters and land speculators, mostly from Virginia and the Carolinas, quickly spilled into the region, clearing forests, draining swamps and planting corn, tobacco and cotton. The township of Irwinton, named after a hard-drinking, gun-toting frontier governor named Jared Irwin, soon sprang up and quickly rose to prominence as the leading frontier community in the state. In the years immediately following the War of 1812, as the Indian threat was removed and more and more land-hungry settlers pushed into the backwoods, there was even talk of making the upstart frontier community the capital of the state. Such was not to be, however. That honor would pass back and forth between Louisville and Augusta, before finally winding up at Milledgeville thirty miles away on the Oconee.

Four dirt roads led into town, but the main square had been bricked over several years back at the height of the cotton boom. Wide, wooden sidewalks protected by shingled overhangs paralleled row after row of freshly painted storefronts. Bins of fresh produce and dry goods lined the sidewalks, as if storekeepers were anticipating brisk business today.

At the center of town stood the courthouse, a massive red brick building with towering white columns, a clock steeple and white-trimmed wings jutting off to either side. Built in the early 1850s to replace the old courthouse, which had been destroyed in a fire, the new structure was the focal point for community and political gatherings. It was there that most local business and civic affairs were tended to, where senators and governors and lesser politicians came to pound and plead their causes, where rank-and-file citizens came to judge and be judged.

Wiley pulled up in front of the courthouse and stopped. He was amazed at the number of people already in town. Horses, wagons and buggies seemed to jostle for every inch of space around the crowded square. He finally found an unoccupied hitching post, dismounted and tied up the mare.

"Here we are," he said, reaching up and helping Martha Ann down. "Watch your step."

Arm in arm, they started walking toward the courthouse. The daffodils and jonquils lining the walkway were already in bloom, even though it was only late April and an unseasonable chill lingered in the damp morning air.

Halfway across the lawn they heard their names called. They turned and saw five of Wiley's brothers—James Madison, William, Albert, Charles and John—striding briskly toward them.

"Morning, boys," Wiley called out, shaking hands with each. "Are we late?"

"Nope, it's just about to begin," James Madison announced. He tipped his hat to Martha Ann and said, "Morning, Martha Ann. Good to see you again."

"It's good to see you again, James Madison. Did Elizabeth come with you?"

"I'm afraid she was feeling a little under the weather this morning."

"I'm sorry. Is there anything I can do for her?"

James Madison shook his head. "Nope. I think she's just upset about…" He hesitated, groping for the right words. "You know, all this blasted war talk."

"They're all tired of it," added Albert, who, at thirty-five, was the second-oldest brother. He was a tall, lean man with narrow shoulders and a slight stoop in his back. He rarely smiled and wore the gaunt, weathered look so common among frontier dirt farmers. "Nancy threatens to leave me every time I bring up the subject."

Just then Garrett came running up. He was a tall, gangling lad of fourteen, with big, cow-brown eyes and shaggy blond hair that curled down around his ears. "They're starting!" he yelled. "Hurry, or we'll be late!"

Martha Ann grabbed Wiley's arm and said, "You'd better go."

"Will you be all right?"

"Of course. I'll just go over to Catherine's and look around."

She didn't tell him that her main reason for going to her sister's store was to buy cloth—just in case she had to make him a uniform.

They kissed and went their separate ways.

———

THE CROWD QUIETED DOWN when Mayor Futch, flanked by the Reverend Thurmond and Sheriff Poindexter, stepped out onto the courthouse steps and waved his arms.

"Thank you all for coming this morning," Futch shouted. He was puffing on a long, thick cigar and dressed in a fancy new three-piece suit and matching stovetop hat he'd bought special for this occasion. "We've got a lot to talk about, so I suggest we get right to it."

As he stared out over the crowd, the mayor couldn't help thinking how good it felt to be mayor, how grand it felt to be in charge at such a historical moment. He fairly bristled with pride as he contemplated the awesome responsibility before him.

He flashed the crowd another smile, then motioned the sheriff forward.

"The mayor's right," Sheriff Hiram Poindexter declared in his usual somber drawl. He removed his hat and wiped the sweat from his bulging forehead. "Now, most of you know why we're here. The governor has asked us to form an infantry regiment, just in case Lincoln decides to invade our country."

At the mention of Lincoln's name the crowd of mostly men and boys erupted in a chorus of boos and hisses.

The mayor stepped forward and waved his arms for silence. "Now, now, people, try to control yourselves. This is not the time or place to vent your wrath against that black Republican traitor. I pray to our merciful God that we'll all have an opportunity to do that later."

He paused to collect his thoughts, then continued, "Now, it appears to me that the first order of business is to ask for a show of hands of those among you who'd like to don the proud uniform of our country. Let me see those hands!"

Almost every hand in the audience shot up. "Me! Me! Me!" they shouted in unison.

"That's what I thought," the mayor replied, impressed by the show of hands and tangled mob of men and boys surging around the platform.

The Reverend Thurmond stood behind the speaker's podium, a worried look on his thin, leathery face. He'd seen plenty of mob action in his time, but nothing to compare with the rising tide of emotional energy he'd seen building in town all week. Mobs could be dangerous and counterproductive, even when organized for the noblest of causes. He honestly couldn't understand why so many of his fellow citizens were so hell-bent to run off to war and maybe get themselves killed for reasons few of them truly understood. In his heart he blamed the extremists on both sides—the abolitionists in the North and the so-called "fire-eaters" in the South—for stirring up the hellish passions that were tearing the country apart.

Without waiting any longer, he stepped in front of the mayor and faced the crowd. "My friends," he said, his thin voice cracking above the deafening roar, "I have something to say, and I beg you to please hear me out."

He waited for the clamor to subside. He drew a deep breath and said, "I urge every one of you to think about this day and all that is being asked of you. We are about to embark upon a dark and dangerous journey, a journey not one of us knows where it will end up."

He hesitated, took another breath. "If you do this thing," he continued, "if you sign up today to become soldiers, many, many of you may soon be marching off to confront the enemy on battlefields far to the north. I pray only that you now ask yourselves if that is what you want. If that is what you want for your families. Your community."

A startled look stole across Mayor Futch's round, reddened face, but he kept quiet while the preacher spoke.

"Before you answer," the elderly minister went on, mindless of the sweltering heat and tiny rivulets of sweat streaming down his forehead, "remember this: If you go, some of you—indeed, *many* of you—might not come back."

A husky voice in the crowd shouted, "We ain't scared of none of them clodhopping Yankees, preacher!"

The crowd seemed to explode in a medley of frenzied laughter and cheering.

One little man dressed in a natty brown suit pushed his way toward the courthouse steps. He was Hamilton Dewberry, publisher of the local newspaper. Dewberry was in his early seventies, but surprisingly agile for a man his age. He carried a pad and pencil in one hand, a thick book in the other.

Dewberry climbed the steps and then turned to face the crowd. "This man," he thundered, pointing toward Reverend Thurmond, "speaks the *truth*! You should all listen to him before it's too late."

"Oh, go on back to your little newspaper," one tall, well-dressed man hissed. "Nobody needs the opinion of an abolitionist!"

Dewberry fixed his gaze on the hissing man. "I am no more an abolitionist than you are, Clarence Oxendine," he shouted. "But I am not a secessionist. And I do know the law." He held up the thick book. "This is a copy of the Constitution of the United States of America. Nowhere in here do we find the right for a state to secede from the Union."

Mayor Futch stiffened. He hitched up his belly and snorted, "Now, Hamilton, don't you think that's a matter of interpretation? After all, the North has been violating our rights as sovereign states for years now. Need I remind you of the Dred Scott case?"

"You need remind me of no such thing," the publisher thundered back. "You know as well as I do that Judge Taney's ruling was no more binding than that of a Southern debating society. It was a stacked court from the beginning."

"What about old John Brown?" a young man in the crowd fired back. "Look what he tried to do up there in Virginny."

"John Brown was a madman," Dewberry replied, a disgusted tone in his voice. "He was no more a friend to the North than he was to the South."

Mayor Futch drew a sharp breath. "Why, Hamilton Dewberry, John Brown was a cold-blooded murderer. You seem to be forgetting what he did to those poor people out there in Kansas."

"I haven't forgotten," Dewberry said grimly. "But he was tried and convicted in a fair court of law and paid for his insane crimes by dangling from the end of a rope."

The publisher paused for a moment and looked out across the unfriendly crowd. "Think about it," he reasoned. "How can we, a mere nation of farmers, possibly hope to wage a successful war against a nation of merchants and engineers?"

"We'll do it," growled Bunk McGowan, one of Irwinton's leading planters and secessionists. Bunk was a giant slab of a man whose black eyes gleamed with unbridled passion. "We'll do it, by God in high heaven, and we'll win!"

Dewberry stood his ground. "But the Northern states are so much richer than we are, don't you understand that, Bunk? And they have almost all the industry. Why, I hear they're cranking out five thousand infantry rifles per day. And us? What do we have? Our best factories combined can produce no more than a hundred or so. We just don't have the skilled manpower, nor the capital, nor the resources to keep up with the North in a buildup of arms."

"So what?" someone yelled. "We'll fight 'em with what we've got—pocketknives and pitchforks if necessary!"

Dewberry stared hopelessly at the sea of faces pressing against the platform. The fools, he thought. The blind, bloody fools. To think they could win a war against one of the mightiest industrial and military powers on earth.

"There's something else you should consider," he finally said. "Who do you think will be doing the fighting, anyway? Will it be the rich slave owners in Sparta and Charleston and Savannah? Will it be the rich factory owners in Augusta and Richmond?" His eyes blazed with newfound fury. "*No!*" he shrieked. "It will be *you*, my friends—you and your sons and fathers and brothers who will be fighting and dying, not the rich and powerful planters and money-grubbers in Richmond and Charleston."

At that moment two well-dressed men, both in their late sixties, stepped out of the courthouse and stood next to the publisher. One was Dr. R.J. Cochran, a retired physician. The other was Judge N.A. Carswell. Both men were Democrats, but their anti-secessionist views were well-known around town.

"Now, it's my turn to say something," Dr. Cochran said in a soft, somber voice. "I have lived in this community most all my seventy-five years. I know every one of you by first name and even brought many of you into this world. But what I want to say is, I have served my country under the flag of the Union. And so long as God permits me to live, I will defend that flag with my sword, even if my own hometown assails it!"

"*Traitor!*" someone shouted.

Judge Carswell, frail and bespectacled and leaning on a cane, bristled at the charge, but held his calm. In a trembling voice, he said, "Good governments can never be built up or sustained by the impulse of passion. We must not be hasty. Let the fanatics of the North break the Constitution, if such is their felt purpose. Our people simply don't have the resources to wage a war against a country as strong and powerful as the United States. And we'd be alone in such a struggle, utterly alone, because no power on earth would dare come to our aid."

A young man pulled out a Revolutionary-era sword and waved it around. "Don't listen to these old fools, boys," he shouted defiantly. "We'll raise a great Southern army and drive the Yankee invaders all the way back to Canada. The day will come when our own glorious flag will float over the dome of the old Capitol in Washington!"

"He's right," exclaimed another man. "All it will take is one battle to resolve this problem once and for all."

When Dr. Cochran and Judge Carswell saw their argument was going nowhere, they turned slowly around and trudged back inside the courthouse.

Several people jeered.

"Go on, traitors, run, hide," Bunk McGowan shouted, "but you won't be able to escape the evil that Satan and his brazen cohort Abraham Lincoln have loosed upon this land!"

Dewberry glared at McGowan, then shook his head in sorrow. "God have mercy on you," he rasped. "God have mercy on all of you." He made a couple of notes in his pad, then, eyes brimming with tears, turned and walked away.

In the end, a decision was made to form a new regiment called the 49th Regiment of the Georgia Volunteer Infantry, nicknamed the "Wilkinson County Invincibles." It would consist of four or five companies and outfitted by a sponsor or group of sponsors. Samuel T. Player, a popular schoolteacher in his late thirties, was elected regimental captain. He would lead the men to Camp Davis near Savannah for training and permanent duty assignments.

By three o'clock that afternoon, several companies had been raised and volunteers sworn in. James Madison, Albert, Charles, John, William and Wiley were among the Wilkinson County boys who agreed to serve the Confederate cause. Of the Nesmith boys, that left only Garrett, the youngest, who would stay behind to look after the farms and Mother Nesmith.

But Garrett was thinking otherwise.

———

"IT'S NOT FAIR," THE BOY PROTESTED to his older brothers. "I want to go, too."

They were standing in front of the courthouse, the seven of

them still heady from the meeting that had lasted well into the afternoon. Other men drawn to the marathon assembly still milled about the square, talking, shouting, debating spiritedly, none of them seeming to want the meeting or this day to ever end.

It was as if the fires of rebellion, after smoldering for so long, had finally flared into an inferno and were now burning a swath through the soul of Dixie.

Only Garrett seemed unhappy about the day's events.

"Please, James Madison, can't I come, too? I promise you won't have to worry about me none."

"Somebody has to stay back and take care of Ma," James Madison told his little brother. He placed a friendly hand on his kid brother's shoulder. "That's your job."

"He's right," agreed John, who at thirty was the third oldest. "Don't worry. We'll tell you all about the war when we get back."

"But you heard what that Major Anderson said back at Wiley's wedding," Garrett persisted. "The Confederacy needs every man it can get."

William laughed. "That's the whole point, squirt," he teased. "They need men. Not boys."

Garrett's cheeks grew red with rage. "But I *am* a man," he retorted. "I can shoot a gun and ride a horse as good as any of you. Maybe better. I'm going to join the cavalry, you'll see."

"The cavalry," James Madison sneered. "That'll be the day."

Wiley was finally forced to intercede on his little brother's behalf. "Come on, boys, leave him alone. Can't you see that in his heart he's as brave as any one of us?"

Tears of rage and bitter disappointment flooded down Garrett's smooth cheeks. In another couple of years the boy would be shaving. But Wiley knew the others were right. Garrett was only a boy. He didn't think the Grand Confederate Army wanted boys going into battle.

Garrett stormed off when he realized nobody was going to listen to him. He crossed the street, jumped on his horse and rode away.

"I'll show them," he said to himself. "I'll show them all."

CHAPTER 6

MARTHA ANN HATED SHOPPING ALONE. As she strolled down the sidewalk, occasionally stopping to inspect bins of fruit and vegetables or to examine a store-made dress, she found herself missing Wiley immensely. It was an unconscious thing, an unbidden desire to feel his warm breath on her cheek, the strength of his strong arms around her waist. She knew it was silly. After all, he was only across the street at the courthouse. *Get a grip on yourself, girl! The meeting will be over before you know it, and both of you will be on the wagon heading home.*

She wandered on, trying to put Wiley out of her mind, at least for a few minutes, to focus on what she had come to town for, and that was to buy a few bolts of cloth in case she needed to make Wiley a uniform. It seemed strange to her that government agents were going around asking citizens to provide not only their own guns and horses but also their uniforms. You'd think that an army big enough to wage war would be able to outfit its own soldiers with uniforms.

She stopped when she came to Potter's Dry Goods and Clothing Boutique and went inside. The store was small and dark and reeked of musty boots and cracked leather. Stacks of coats and pants lay piled up everywhere, as did boots, dusters, hats and a variety of other clothing items. On a wall near the potbellied stove at the back hung a dozen or more saddles, blankets, harnesses and stirrups, while a bewildering variety of hats, caps and bonnets lined the wall just inside the door. Up front there was a glass display counter crowded with jars and bottles of varying sizes and shapes, each filled with pens and buttons and other items Martha Ann couldn't identify.

Martha Ann worked her way down a cluttered aisle until she

came to the cloth section. As she fingered the material, a tall, thin man wearing a silk vest and a green banker's visor crept out from the back of the store.

"Martha Ann," Joseph Potter called out cheerfully. "What a pleasant surprise."

"Hello, Joseph," Martha Ann said to her brother-in-law. She loosened her bonnet and smiled. "I thought I might find Catherine. Is she here?"

Joseph shook his head and sighed. "You know your sister. She couldn't stand being cooped up in here with all that excitement going on across the way."

Martha Ann glanced wistfully out the window toward the court-house. "Yes, I suppose it is exciting in a grim sort of way," she said without emotion. Then, more excitedly: "I've never seen so many people in town before."

"We've never had a war like this before," Joseph replied. He took off his wire-rimmed spectacles and wiped them with a handkerchief. "I heard you and Wiley were back. How did you enjoy Savannah?"

"It was wonderful, thank you," she replied. Then: "But a little crazy, if you know what I mean."

Joseph smiled knowingly. "I know exactly what you mean." After a pause, he asked, "What brings you to town this morning?"

She nodded toward the courthouse.

"Ah, you mean the meeting," Joseph said, nodding. A trace of bitterness was in his voice.

"Wiley plans to sign up, you know."

Joseph examined his glasses, saw that they were clean, then clamped them back onto his long, bird-like nose. "So I hear. James Madison and the boys were in here earlier spreading the news. Sounds like the whole county's hell-bent to form a regiment."

"What about you, Joseph? Are you going to sign up, too?"

Joseph shrugged. "Oh, I don't think so, what with this store and all. If I went away, I honestly don't know who'd look after the place." He hesitated, then said, "Besides, I'm not entirely convinced this war is necessary."

Martha Ann felt herself flinch. "I don't think I quite understand what you mean," she said.

Joseph adjusted his glasses, then leaned over the counter and stared straight into Martha Ann's sea-green eyes. "The way I see it, a civil war like this is only going to benefit two kinds of people—the rich cotton planters down here and the wealthy bankers up North. They're the ones who stand to gain the most if this so-called Confederacy succeeds. People like us?" He shook his head and laughed. "Why, we're nothing more than cannon fodder for the ruling classes."

"But what about states' rights?" Martha Ann was floundering—and she knew it—as she tried to make sense out of what her brother-in-law was saying. "I thought this whole fuss was about our rights as Southerners to live our lives the way we wanted to."

Joseph grimaced. "That's what those bunch of fools in Montgomery and Richmond would like you to think," he said. Softening, he added, "No, my dear Martha Ann, I'm afraid it's a little more sinister than that. What they want, what this crisis is truly all about, is power—the power of a handful of politicians and bankers and industrialists to control the destiny of this nation and all its people for decades to come."

Martha Ann still wasn't sure she understood. She bit her lower lip and said, "Well, I just hope none of our boys have to go off to fight in a war that isn't necessary. President Davis says it will all be over by summer anyway."

"More lies," Joseph sneered. "Haven't you heard the latest? Abe Lincoln has ordered a naval blockade of the Confederacy. He's even raised seventy-five thousand men for the Federal army. That means it's only a matter of time before Virginia and North Carolina and maybe every one of the border states march out of the Union, just like we did. And then we're going to have ourselves a real shooting war." He shook his head and sighed. "No, Martha Ann, I'm afraid there is no possible way it will be over by the end of summer. Or next summer or many more summers to come."

The prospect of a longer, broader war suddenly made Martha Ann feel faint. She leaned against the counter, clutching her throat. Was it her imagination, or was the room suddenly starting to spin?

She would have collapsed on the spot had Joseph not caught her in time.

"Are you all right?" he asked.

"I...I think so," Martha Ann stammered. "It's just all so...so confusing, and I'm so afraid for Wiley."

Joseph helped her into a chair. "Would you like a glass of water?"

"No, thanks. Just need to sit here a moment. Catch my breath. I'll be fine."

When he saw that she was better, Joseph apologized for speaking out in such a manner. "Just forget what I said," he urged his sister-in-law. "Maybe he won't have to go off after all. Maybe none of them will."

Martha Ann pushed herself to her feet. "I do hope you're right," she said, steadying herself.

At the front door she turned and said, "Please tell Catherine I'm sorry I missed her."

"I will." Almost as an afterthought, Joseph said, "I'm sure she will see you in church Sunday."

Martha Ann closed the door behind her and stepped outside. The air was warmer now, and fresh, just what she needed to bring her back around. What had come over her, she wondered?

She was halfway down the block when she realized she had forgotten to buy any cloth.

———

CATHERINE WALKER POTTER was the kind of woman men liked to look at but knew they better not touch. There was something a little too wild, a little too raw about the tall, lusty redhead with creamy, peach-smooth skin and flashing, powder-blue eyes, something dangerous that drove all but the most reckless of men away almost as quickly as it attracted them.

That was unfortunate for Catherine, who reckoned, with some justification, that she was the most beautiful woman in all of Wilkinson County, perhaps all of Georgia, and certainly the most desirable. She enjoyed the attention men lavished on her, relished it. Craved it.

Too bad she was married.

Catherine's behavior had not gone unnoticed by the good people of Wilkinson County. In fact, it was a constant source of embarrassment to Martha Ann, Catherine's younger sister by two years.

Martha Ann knew how men looked at her sister, how the womenfolk gossiped behind her back and tried their best to keep their men out of reach whenever she came near. None of that seemed to bother Catherine. She continued to carry on, shamelessly at times, regardless of the snickers and catcalls from men and women she'd never met.

Catherine had moved to Irwinton four years earlier when she married Joseph Potter, an up-and-coming young merchant with a college degree and a promising future in politics. At first things seemed to go well for the young couple. There were parties and invitations galore, some from as far away as Savannah and Augusta and the capital at Milledgeville, where Joseph harbored hopes of serving in the legislature some day. On one visit to Milledgeville shortly after their honeymoon, Catherine even got to meet Robert Toombs, the hot-tempered young fire-eater from Wilkes County who all but swept the bewitching belle from Irwinton off her feet.

Back home in Irwinton, Joseph and Catherine Potter were the toast of the town. No longer did anyone debate whether young Joseph Potter should or would throw his hat into the political ring; it was only a matter of when and what state or national office he would seek.

Then something happened. Those who knew Joseph said he changed almost as soon as the honeymoon was over. Whether it was because of Catherine or some other reason, the once sociable dry-goods merchant with promising political aspirations started declining invitations to parties and other social events. He rarely ventured out of the store anymore, except to go home or the bank. He even stopped going to church. He became sullen and withdrawn, and his politics took a notable radical turn when he came out against Robert Toombs, Governor Brown and secession.

Some of his friends blamed it on Robert Toombs, Howell Cobb and other fire-eaters who had all but taken over control of the state government. Joseph's Unionist views had long been a matter of public record, and as the crisis worsened, his anti-secessionist stand stiffened. He never tired of warning friends and foes alike that no good would come out of secession. Most likely the country would be destroyed, and then France or England or perhaps even Mexico would waste little time trying to assert supremacy over the grand old republic.

But those closest to the brooding young merchant blamed

Catherine for his sudden and inexplicable fall from political grace. They saw the woman as vain and out of control, a temptress and amoral hussy whose reckless ways were destroying her once-proud husband.

But there was nothing anyone could do because the man loved his wife with a passion that knew no bounds.

That morning when Martha Ann saw her sister hanging on the arm of Fred Sherwood, the young son of the town banker, her first instinct was to walk away, pretend she hadn't seen her. The sight actually sickened her. If Catherine no longer had any respect for herself, why couldn't she at least think of poor, sweet Joseph?

"Why, Martha Ann, what a pleasant surprise."

Martha Ann almost cringed when she heard her sister's voice. She knew she was trapped.

She turned slowly around and saw Catherine and Freddy Sherwood heading her way. Predictably, Catherine was draped all over the young banker's arm. Shameless, Martha Ann thought. Absolutely shameless.

"Hello, Catherine," she said dryly.

"Oh, Martha Ann," Catherine gushed, "I've been meaning to get out to see you. I do hope you had a wonderful time in Savannah. How was the Pulaski Hotel? I'm just dying to sit down with you and hear everything."

As usual, Catherine looked gorgeous. She was dressed in a tightly corseted green silk dress trimmed in white lace and a matching jacket and feathered hat that more than flattered her generous curves. Instead of rolled up under her hat, as was the local fashion, Catherine's mound of red hair spilled around her shoulders in long, springy curls.

Catherine pulled away from her escort long enough to hug her sister and say, "What brings you to town today? No, wait...let me guess. Wiley's joining up." Without waiting for a reply, she clasped her hands and said, "Isn't it all so thrilling? I mean, all these handsome soldier boys everywhere."

She leaned against Sherwood and squeezed his arm. "Dear, you do know Freddy Sherwood, don't you?"

The young banker tipped his hat politely and said, "Morning, Martha Ann. By the way, a belated congratulations to you and Wiley. I wish you both a long and happy marriage."

"Thank you, Mr. Sherwood," Martha Ann replied coolly.

"If there's anything you ever need..." Sherwood grinned, as if caught up in a private joke..."I mean...at the bank...just let me or my father know. We've got connections, you know."

Catherine laughed. "Connections. Isn't he a dear?" She leaned over and whispered in her sister's ear. "And rich. Handsome, young and rich. Need I say more?"

Martha Ann closed her eyes. At that moment she wished desperately that she could disappear, vanish on the spot.

Fred Sherwood pulled out a fancy gold pocketwatch and looked at it. "My goodness, where does the time go? Would you ladies kindly excuse me? I must be getting back to the bank. Nice to see you again, Martha Ann." He winked at Catherine and said, "As for *you*, I'll see you later."

As soon as the boy was gone, Martha Ann turned on her sister. "Catherine...Why do you do that? *Why?*"

Catherine pretended to be taken aback. "Do what?"

"You know perfectly well what I mean."

"I declare, Martha Ann, I haven't the foggiest idea what you're talking about."

"What would poor Joseph say if he saw you flirting with that...that *boy?*"

"Joseph?" Catherine laughed. "The only thing Joseph Potter cares about is that silly little store of his."

"That's not true. He loves you, Catherine."

"Loves me?" Catherine rolled her eyes skyward. "Let me tell you something, dear sister. If my husband loves me so much, why doesn't he join up like all the other boys? Make me proud of him for a change instead of hiding in that dark, stinking old store all the time."

"He has his reasons," was all Martha Ann could think of to say.

"Well, the main reason is, I think he's a coward," Catherine said flatly.

"Catherine...Joseph is not a coward. How dare you say such a thing!"

"You don't know," Catherine said, a defiant tone still in her voice. "I've been begging him for weeks to enlist. I even told him I'd make him the nicest, fanciest uniform in all the Confederacy."

"Uniforms!" Martha Ann hissed. "Is that all you care about, Catherine? *Uniforms?*"

"Well, you have to admit that…"

Before she could finish, two young men brandishing Confederate flags came marching down the sidewalk and almost collided with them.

"Sorry, ladies," one of the young men, a tall, lanky fellow with curly black hair and flashing, steel-blue eyes, said. "We're hurrying over to the courthouse to sign up before all the positions are filled."

The second boy, equally handsome, said, "They're electing regimental officers, and we thought we might throw our names in the hat."

Catherine threw her hands up and squealed. "Officers! Isn't that wonderful?" She looked at Martha Ann, then back at the boys. "Would you fine gentlemen care to escort a lady across the way with you?"

The boys looked at each other and grinned. They couldn't believe their good fortune.

"Would we!" the first boy exclaimed. "Why, it would be an honor, ma'am."

Catherine locked her arm inside the taller boy's, and, with a twinkle in her eye, said to her sister, "Aren't you coming? They might even elect Wiley. You never know."

Martha Ann shook her head slowly. "I don't think so. I've still got errands to run."

"Well, toodle-do," Catherine laughed, dashing away on the arms of the pair of young, flag-waving volunteers.

Yes, Martha Ann told herself sadly, the whole world is going crazy.

———

ON HIS WAY HOME that afternoon Garrett rounded a sharp curve and almost crashed into Indigo and the big red horse he was riding. Garrett recognized the horse right way. It was Sable, Wiley's Tennessee Walker.

"Where are you headed in such an all-fired hurry?" he snapped. "You almost got us both killed."

"Me?" Indigo shot back. "It was you who alm-most ran into m-me."

Indigo was right, and Garrett knew it. He was still steaming over the business back at the courthouse and hadn't been paying attention to the road. Good thing it wasn't a wagon or his guts might be spilled all over the place.

"I'm sorry," Garrett apologized. "Are you okay?"

"So far's I can t-tell."

"Sure glad Sable didn't get hurt."

"Me, t-too," Indigo replied. He reached down and stroked the horse gently. As he did, he noticed the agitated look in Garrett's eyes. "Something ailing you, Garrett?"

"Nothing I can't deal with," Garrett replied tersely. He caught himself, then looked across at his friend. "Well, I might as well tell you. You'll know soon enough anyway."

"Know what?"

Garrett leaned forward. In a haughty tone, he confided, "You do know there's a war going on, don't you, Indigo? And that the Yankees might be invading Georgia any day now?"

Indigo's eyes grew wide. "Yankees? You mean President Lincoln's Yankees?"

Garrett nodded. "Thousands of them blue-bellies might be marching on Savannah this very minute." He paused, then gave Indigo a look that suggested he was about to reveal the deepest, darkest secret in the world. "Can you keep a secret?"

Puzzled, Indigo nodded.

"You promise?"

Indigo nodded again.

"You promise not to tell anyone, not a single soul?"

Indigo was about ready to bust a gut. "I p-promise," he blurted. "I won't t-tell a soul."

Garrett looked around to make sure there was nobody else on the lonely road. Only when he saw they were completely alone did he lower his voice and say, "I'm going to join the cavalry."

Indigo's eyes lit up. "The c-cavalry!" he exclaimed. The thought rolled around inside his head a moment before he said, "How are you g-gonna do that?"

Garrett ignored the question. "I'm gonna ride over to Milledgeville and try to sign up with a real live horse unit. I hear

General Walker from Augusta is over there trying to raise a cavalry division and is looking for every rider he can find."

Garrett let that thought sink in for a moment, then announced: "When I sign up, I'm gonna get me a uniform and a sword, a real shiny one, and pair of those high black knee-boots, just like Major Anderson wore back at Wiley's wedding."

This was shocking news, and Indigo was having a hard time absorbing it all. It seemed so unimaginable that Garrett, who was his best friend and same age, was going to join the cavalry and get a horse and sword. "A s-sword, too?" he asked incredulously. "Are you really? Are you really g-gonna join the c-cavalry and get yourself a real sword?"

Garrett smiled proudly. "You just wait."

Indigo drew a deep breath, then asked, "Can I c-come, too?"

Garrett flinched. "Well," he started, suddenly feeling oddly uncomfortable, "I don't know about that." He looked across at Indigo. "I don't think they allow—you know—your kind in the Confederate army."

CHAPTER 7

THE NEWS FROM THE FRONT that summer was good. Outnumbered Confederate forces under the command of P.G.T. Beauregard, the dashing Creole hero of Fort Sumter, had defeated a powerful Union army at Manassas Junction in Northern Virginia.

That victory, together with several smaller but notable Rebel successes out West and in the Shenandoah Valley, had left many Confederates convinced that the war would, indeed, be over before summer's end.

"Have no fear," newspapers across the South proclaimed, "our gallant boys in gray will be home in time for harvest!"

On the night of June 30, a blazing comet had suddenly appeared in the sky over Richmond. Southerners everywhere saw the fiery phenomenon as one more sign that their cause was just and divinely inspired. General Beauregard promptly declared that God was on the side of the South.

"A reckless and unprincipled tyrant has invaded our soil," the general told a group of newspaper correspondents three weeks before the bloody clash at Bull Run. "Abraham Lincoln, regardless of all moral, legal and constitutional restraints, has thrown his abolition hosts among us, murdering and imprisoning our citizens, confiscating and destroying our property, and committing other acts of violence and outrage too shocking and revolting to humanity to be enumerated."

Autumn came and went. There were more battles and more Southern victories, but still no sign of the war winding down. Far to the north, "Stonewall" Jackson, the brooding, demon-haunted hero of Manassas, was rampaging through the snowy wilds of the

Shenandoah Valley. In late December weary soldiers on both sides broke off hostilities and went into winter camp.

———

WILEY WAS AWAKENED by the mournful patter of rain against the roof. He rolled over slowly, anticipating the soft warmth of his wife.

She wasn't there.

He sat up and looked around. Where could she be?

The room was dark. Cold. He got up, tiptoed over to the mantel and looked at the clock: 3:45. He slipped on his trousers and went into the living room.

He found her in front of the fireplace, wrapped in a blanket and rocking gently back and forth in the old oak rocker that had belonged to his mother. In the reddish glow of the firelight, he could see that Martha Ann had been crying.

He walked over and stood next to her. Without saying a word, he leaned down and kissed the top of her head.

"I was worried," he said softly. "When I woke up and you weren't there, I…" He faltered, trying to choose his words carefully. "I kind of got scared that something might have happened."

He stood there a moment longer, listening to the hissing embers in the fireplace and the soft rumble of rain outside. When he bent down and kissed her on the cheek, he tasted her tears, warm and salty, against his lips.

"Hey, what are these for?" he asked, genuinely surprised. He knelt beside her and wiped away the tears with his fingertips.

"I can't help it," she sobbed. "It's this terrible war. I don't understand what any of it means or why it has to be."

She brushed back a loose strand of hair and wiped her nose with a lace hankie. "And when I think that you might have to go somewhere far away, leave me alone…"

She buried her face against Wiley's chest and wept.

Wiley had never seen Martha Ann cry before. He wanted badly to comfort her, to say the right words that would ease her pain. But Wiley had never been good with words. Besides, what could he say?

He glanced toward the mantel and saw his daddy's old musket hanging there, gleaming in the darkness. The fact that he might soon carry the old gun into battle sent a cold shiver racing down his spine.

"Even if I have to go," he finally said, drawing her close, "it won't be for long. Those Yanks don't want to fight us any more than we do them. But, if we have to go, we'll make them wish they'd never tangled with us Wilkinson County boys."

Martha Ann drew Wiley's hand to her cheek and held it there. "You will be careful, won't you?" she asked softly.

"Of course."

"And you'll write home every day?"

"Every day."

"Promise?"

"Promise."

THE REVEREND ISAAC THURMOND had every reason in the world to feel good that morning. For the first time in the twenty years that he had been pastor of Red Level Methodist Church, there was standing room only inside the little country chapel.

He sat in a high-back chair behind the pulpit, listening to the singing and quietly collecting his thoughts for the Sunday sermon. On his lap lay a tattered black Bible that matched his suit.

The pastor gleamed with beatific pride as he surveyed the packed congregation. The regulars were there, along with what looked like the whole Nesmith clan—the matriarch Jane, looking radiant but frail this morning, and her boys and their families: James Madison and Elizabeth, John and Beth, Charles and Maggie, Albert and Nancy, Wiley and Martha Ann. William, the only bachelor in the group, sat next to his mother. Most of the older folks sat in their regular pews, while the younger ones had to make do in the aisles and on the steps out front.

Everyone who could, stood, song books opened to the appropriate page, praising God and singing their hearts out.

The old church fairly shook with song.

Thurmond secretly praised the Lord for bringing all these people to church, even if it had to take a war to do it.

The moment the choir stopped singing, the elderly preacher rose and headed toward the pulpit. He raised his arms and everybody sat down. A hush descended over the congregation as Reverend Thurmond, somber as a thundercloud, opened the Good Book and began to read.

"O Lord, we call upon Thee to be with us in this time of great peril. We ask you to rescue us from the evil ways of men, to preserve us from wrongdoers who devise evil things in their hearts…"

"Amen," an old man shouted from the deacon's corner.

"Hallelujah, amen," echoed another deacon.

The preacher's voice trembled as it gradually rose, probing the far corners of the little chapel and filling the congregation with a mixture of fear and awe. "We call upon Thee, O Lord, to show us the right path, to guard, guide and lead us as we embark on this dark and dangerous journey," he intoned. "Be with us, O merciful Father, as our enemies surround us, as in the days of old, threatening our homes and fields and families, yea, the very faith that sustains us…"

Once more, the old men huddled along the front row in the deacon's corner erupted in a chorus of "Amens."

IN THE GRAVEYARD behind the church, Indigo and Garrett wandered among the moss-covered headstones, kicking toadstools and chasing dragonflies.

They came to an old stone marker and stopped.

"Garrett," Indigo said, leaning over the marker. "D-do you really th-think those Yankees are gonna try to invade us?"

Garrett sat down on the marker and sighed. "I suppose so."

Indigo got up and swatted at a dragonfly. "Then, does that m-mean me and my ma and p-pa will be f-free?"

"You're already free, Indigo," Garrett replied. "My brother freed you when Mr. Walker gave you to him. Heck, you're as free as I am. Free as that dragonfly."

While Indigo pondered that thought, he took off his straw hat and smoothed out some of the kinks. "I know," he said, "b-but what about the others? All my c-cousins and aunts and uncles and the r-rest of the s-slaves? Will they be f-free too if the Yankees come?"

"I don't know. I suppose so."

Indigo stood up and stomped a giant orange toadstool with his bare foot. "Well," he said, eyeballing the dragonfly that kept fluttering within reach. A split-second later he reached out and snatched the hovering insect. "If I am already f-free, then I can do anything I want to, right?"

Garrett looked up and said, "I guess so. Indigo, why are you asking me all these dumb questions?"

Indigo smiled. "Bec-cause I'm g-gonna join the cavalry, too, just like you. I'm g-gonna get me a horse and a s-sword and a pair of those f-fancy black b-boots."

"Indigo, you know you can't do that. The Confederates don't allow people like you…You know, your kind, in the army."

Indigo frowned. His mind was already made up. "Then I guess I'll just have to g-go join the Yankee c-cavalry," he replied, opening his palm and letting the dragonfly flitter away.

———

THE SERVICE DIDN'T END until nearly one o'clock, almost an hour longer than usual. When Garrett heard the church door swing open, he hurried around to the front and waited in the shade of the giant sycamore.

His heart skipped a beat when he saw Amy Skinner talking to a group of girls. He wanted to go over and say hello but didn't dare. Not with all his brothers standing around. He'd never hear the end of it if they caught him talking to a girl.

Deep down, Garrett liked Amy Skinner, liked her a lot. They went to the same school but lived on opposite sides of the county, so he rarely saw her, except at school and church. Several times he wanted to go up and talk to her at school, but each time he lost the nerve.

That's why his heart nearly stopped beating when he saw Amy, a pretty brunette with dark, almond-shaped eyes and unblemished skin, waving at him. In fact, it seemed that all the girls in the group were looking at him. Smiling at him.

He almost fainted when he saw Amy and three of the girls walking his way.

"Hello, Garrett Nesmith," one of the girls called out.

Another girl—all red hair and freckles—giggled and asked,

"Why weren't you in church?"

"I was with Indigo," Garrett shot back. "Besides, it was hot in there, and there wasn't any room."

Now it was Amy Skinner's turn. "And just what were you two talking about that was so important it kept you out of the Lord's house?"

Garrett shrugged. "You're just girls. You wouldn't understand."

A dark fury seized Amy. "What makes you so sure of that, Garrett Nesmith?"

Garrett couldn't think of any possible way to explain what he meant. "It's just…It's just that, well, we were talking about joining up. The…the cavalry," he fumbled.

The darkness in Amy's eyes vanished. The fury gave way to sheer adoration. "The cavalry!" she squealed, clasping her delicate hands. "Why, Garrett Nesmith, that's about the grandest, bravest thing in the world!"

"Will you bring me back a souvenir?" the red-haired girl ventured eagerly.

Amy brushed past her friends and kissed Garrett on the cheek. "That's for you," she said. "For your bravery."

Garrett almost came unhinged. It was the first time he'd ever been kissed by a girl. His hand went automatically to his cheek, still warm from Amy's kiss. He held it there, shaking, his face the color of crimson.

Unfortunately for Garrett, James Madison happened to turn and look at the exact moment Amy planted the kiss. When Garrett saw the big grin on his brother's face, he knew he was in for it.

"Oh, no," he groaned, looking around desperately for a place to hide.

James Madison lumbered over and collared his little brother before he could escape. "Don't you think you're a little too young to be kissing the girls, Romeo?"

"I didn't kiss nobody," the boy blurted defensively. "She kissed me."

Too late, he realized the damage had already been done. Whatever he said now, whatever he did, would only make matters worse. Every eye in the churchyard was on him now, staring straight at him, through him. He could hear them all laughing.

Garrett would never be able to face Amy Skinner again.

The rest of the brothers strutted over. William, always the wiseacre, snickered and said, "We don't want to keep Ma waiting, squirt." He nudged him with his elbow and winked. "You can kiss all the girls later."

Still swooning from the kiss, Garrett slipped and fell to the ground when he tried to mount his horse. That brought another round of sidesplitting guffaws from his brothers.

"And I thought you wanted to join the cavalry," James Madison croaked. He lifted the boy up with one hand and planted him in the saddle. "Well, I'd suggest you learn how to ride a horse first."

CHAPTER 8

I T WAS ALMOST TWO-THIRTY by the time the Nesmith clan sat down to eat. Sarah had prepared a feast: butter beans and summer squash, cornbread and rice and roast pork. Plus, there was a platter of hot buttermilk biscuits, blackberry jam, cane syrup and two fresh-baked apple pies for dessert. Two pitchers of sassafras tea and another of fresh-squeezed lemonade had been placed at the center of the table next to a colorful bouquet of fragrant spring flowers.

"James Madison," Mother Nesmith said from her position at the head of the table. "would you mind leading us in prayer?"

As he did every Sunday since his mother had moved in with him and Elizabeth, James Madison rose, bowed his head and prayed: "O Lord, we thank you for the food we are about to receive, for the many wonderful blessings you have bestowed upon us. We ask You to be with us as we go about this day and the coming days, especially as the clouds of war grow darker all around us. Bless us, O merciful Father, and keep us. And, most of all, we pray for our father, James Nesmith, a simple soul and obedient servant of Thine, who is with Thee now in Paradise. Amen."

"Amen," everybody said.

Immediately Garrett rubbed his hands and said, "Would somebody pass the biscuits?"

Jane Nesmith gave her son a reproachful look. "Young man," she said severely, "you just wait your turn. Have you forgotten? We have a guest today."

Martha Ann, still the newcomer to the family, smiled and said, "It's all right, Mother Nesmith. I understand how hungry men can get sometimes."

"Don't we all," Elizabeth agreed with a laugh.

The platters of food were passed around, and soon everybody's plate was piled high with generous helpings. Garrett was the first to dig in. Predictably, he was also the first to finish and ask for seconds.

A few minutes into the meal, William looked across at Garrett and said, "Hey, squirt, how about passing me some more of that squash?"

"My name's Garrett," the boy growled. "Stop calling me squirt."

The other boys thought that was funny. William, still chuckling, leaned across the table toward Garrett, and said, "Just what's a squirt like you figuring on doing in the cavalry, anyway?"

John nudged his little brother and said, "Yeah, if I was thinking about joining the cavalry, I'd learn how to stay on a horse first," he teased.

"You're just jealous!" Garrett fired back.

"Jealous?" Charles asked, winking at Wiley. "What are we jealous of, squirt?"

Trembling with rage, Garrett glared across at his brothers. "'Cause I can ride a horse and shoot a gun better than any one of you." He was fuming now. "And 'cause I'm gonna be in the cavalry. And the rest of you are gonna be nothing but foot soldiers. Just plain old ordinary foot soldiers."

Charles wiped his mouth with a white linen napkin. "The cavalry," he sneered, then burst out laughing.

"That's right—the cavalry! I might even ride with Colonel Forrest!"

"Forrest?" John replied in astonishment. He gave a hearty laugh, then said, "That'll be the day."

James Madison waited until the laughter died down, then pointed his fork at Garrett and said, "How many times do I have to tell you, boy…You ain't going nowhere. So you might as well get all that high-faluting talk about Colonel Forrest and the cavalry out of that pea-brain skull of yours."

Garrett was on the verge of tears as he said, "You can't make me, James Madison. None of you can!"

It was Mother Nesmith who finally settled the issue. "Boys, that will be quite enough of this bickering. James Madison, you and your brothers ought to be ashamed of yourselves, picking on your little brother like that. And on the Sabbath, too."

"Ma's right," Wiley agreed. "I think we ought to just lay off him a while."

William tilted his head toward Wiley. "I didn't hear anybody ask for your opinion," he snapped.

Mother Nesmith tapped her plate with a fork. "I said that's enough!" She paused long enough to collect herself, then continued, "It's bad enough that there's a war going on. Must you carry on like this? I'm just glad your father isn't around to hear all this infernal squabbling, God rest his soul."

The boys quieted down at the mention of their father's name and resumed eating.

After dinner, everybody adjourned to the front porch. A warm breeze was blowing in from the cornfield, bringing with it the sweet smells of freshly turned earth. The women sat in rockers making idle conversation while the men lounged on the steps and side of the porch, smoking cigars and pipes. Out front, Albert's and John's girls played hopscotch in the lane, while James Madison's two boys fought a furious chinaberry war.

It was Wiley who turned to Mother Nesmith and asked, "Are you sure you're going to be all right, Ma? There's no telling how long we'll have to be away."

The old woman grunted—whether in amusement or contempt, Wiley couldn't tell. "And why shouldn't I be all right?" she quipped. She winked at Martha Ann and said, "We girls will manage just fine. Besides, Garrett will be here to make sure the chores are done properly."

"Mother Nesmith's right," Elizabeth broke in. "We can manage just fine without you boys for a few days. It's you we'll be needing to worry about."

"Isn't that the Gospel," Nancy chuckled. Nancy was a quiet, serious woman, not yet in her thirties, but already the rigors of farm life and childbearing were starting to show in her round, rosy face.

Sarah, wearing a black dress and white apron, came out on the porch and said, "Will there be anything else, Mrs. Nesmith?"

"Thank you, Sarah, but I think that will be all," Mother Nesmith replied.

"Well, I'll be going now."

Martha Ann said, "Do you need a ride home, Sarah? Wiley and I will be leaving in a few minutes. You can ride with us."

Sarah shook her head and smiled. "Indigo is waiting out back with the wagon. You know that boy. If there's a horse around to take out, he's the first to mount up and ride." She laughed. "But, thank you just the same for asking, Miz Martha Ann."

As she turned to go, Sarah leaned over Garrett's shoulder and pretended to whisper, "So it's you who's been putting ideas in my little Indigo's head about the horse cavalry."

Sarah's accusation caught Garrett completely off-guard. "Well, I...uh, we...we've talked about it," he stammered.

"That's what I thought," the black woman laughed. She hugged Garrett, put on her coat and hat and left.

ON THE WAY HOME THAT AFTERNOON, Martha Ann sat as close as she could to her husband. Neither spoke as the wagon creaked and bounced down the narrow dirt road, kicking up small clouds of reddish-brown dust behind them.

The sun was going down. It would be dark soon. Bats roared and wheeled overhead, while farther back in the swamps and cane-brakes, the plaintive wail of whippoorwills echoed through the stillness.

Everywhere the shadows of twilight curled and lengthened, sometimes forming weird patterns on the road and along the edge of the woods.

As they rode along, listening to the melodic creaking of the wagon wheels and the steady clip-clop of the mule's hooves on the clay, Wiley's mind was far away. He had never been on a battlefield, had never even seen a man die. But he imagined it must be awful, just about the most awful thing in the world. Images of men charging into battle kept flashing through his brain—sometimes so real he could almost hear them screaming and shouting as the cannons roared and the lead balls flew and soldiers fell and died, their bodies ripped and mangled and sprawled in heaps on blood-soaked fields.

The question that kept gnawing at him was: Would he be able to hold up in the heat of battle? Or would he turn tail and run and thereby bring shame and scorn on his family?

Only time would tell.

It was Martha Ann who broke his train of thought. "I'm afraid," she said softly, so softly he almost didn't hear her.

He reached over and put his arm around her. "I know, Punkin," he said, using his favorite pet name for his wife. "Me, too."

Martha Ann leaned her head against Wiley's shoulder. "Sometimes I have this awful feeling, a terrible, dark dread. Every time I think about you going away..." She looked away, unable to continue. "Oh, Wiley," she finally sobbed, "do you really have to go?"

Wiley drew in a deep breath and held it. "You know I do," he finally said, letting the air out. "But everything's going to be all right, you'll see."

Still leaning against his shoulder, Martha Ann closed her eyes. The twilight air, once so pure and sweet, now chilled her to the bone. She shivered. "Wiley?" she started. "Please promise me you'll be careful, that you won't do anything foolish or try to be a hero."

A faint chuckle escaped Wiley's lips. "Now what makes you think I'd try to be a hero, Punkin? Heck, I'll only be a private. Privates aren't supposed to take chances and be heroes. They just do their job and count the days till they can come back home."

"And you will come back, won't you?" Martha Ann asked pleadingly.

The question seemed to hang in the air for a moment while Wiley thought of an appropriate response. "Of course, I'll be back," he assured her. "I'll be back in time to harvest the crops. I promise."

The wagon rolled on a few more yards, then Martha Ann asked, "Do you really think the war will be over that soon? It's been going on almost a year now."

"All depends."

"On what?"

"Lots of things. If Maryland and Kansas and some of the other Border States come in on our side, we'll stand a pretty good chance of getting this thing over with in a hurry. If England or one of those other foreign countries sides with us, then old Abe Lincoln will have no choice but to let us go our separate ways."

"But what if they don't?" Martha Ann asked fearfully. "What if nobody comes to help us? What if we're left all alone to fight the Yankees?"

Wiley sighed. "Then God help us all," he said heavily.

———

THE NEXT MORNING, Martha Ann stood alone in the shadows of her kitchen, slowly stirring a pot of peas with a long wooden handle. Through the open backdoor she could see Wiley down at the woodpile splitting logs, his bare chest sweaty and rippling with muscles. Wiley was a handsome man, a good man, and Martha Ann looked forward to a long, happy life with him. When he proposed to her, he had promised to love and take care of her—a vow he had made good until his decision to volunteer for the cause.

Now, with war clouds drifting closer and the blood of young men already spilled in massive quantities on both sides, the future no longer looked as bright and promising as it once had.

She tasted the peas. A bit on the salty side, but that's how her Wiley liked his vegetables. She gave them another vigorous stir, then moved the pot off the burner, away from the heat. Then she untied her apron, draped it across the chair and walked outside.

Wiley stopped chopping when he saw her coming. He leaned against the axe handle, wiping beads of sweat from his furrowed brow with a handkerchief.

"Supper's almost ready," Martha Ann said. "I hope you're hungry."

"I could eat a bear," Wiley replied heartily. He picked up the axe and handed it to Martha Ann. "But, first," he said, "there's something I've been meaning to teach you." When he saw the blank look on his wife's face, he grinned and said, "A woman on her own has got to know how to chop wood."

"Oh, Wiley, you know I can't do that."

"Sure you can. There's nothing to it."

"I can't. Honest."

Wiley sighed. "How do you know until you try?"

"I just know," Martha Ann replied, pushing away the axe.

Wiley grabbed the axe in both hands and held it tight. "Watch close," he said, moving toward a thick pine log. "You hold it like this. See? Then you swing it down sharply at an angle. Like this."

To demonstrate, Wiley raised the gleaming blade high over his head, then brought it crashing down, splitting the log cleanly into two sections. "See?" he said, smiling. "Like I said, there's nothing to it. It's all in the shoulder and the eyes."

Martha Ann shuddered and stepped forward. "I don't know about this…"

Wiley gently wrapped her hands around the stout oak handle. "Come on," he said. "You can do it."

Martha Ann fought back a powerful urge to be angry. Chopping wood was man's work, that's all there was to it. At least that's what she had been raised to believe. She had never chopped a stick of wood in her entire life. Why was Wiley making her do this now?

"Well," Wiley asked, "what are you waiting for?"

"This is the silliest thing I've ever heard of," Martha Ann huffed.

But she could see that Wiley was in one of his "instructive" moods. She knew that, as much as it might hurt her pride and dignity, the only way out of this was to go along with him. "All right, mister tough guy," she hissed, grasping the handle firmly. "Stand back."

Wiley did as she said.

Martha Ann took a couple of deep breaths, then raised the axe high over her head. With a defiant grunt, she swung it downward at a sharp angle—completely missing the log and burying the blade deep in the soft dirt.

Wiley hooted with laughter.

"See?" Martha Ann shrieked. "I told you I couldn't do it."

Still chuckling, Wiley put his arms around his wife's tiny waist. "It's not a snake, Punkin," he said. "You don't have to kill it. Try again."

"Oh, Wiley…"

"Just do it," Wiley said patiently. "Nice and slow, just like I showed you."

Reluctantly, feet planted firmly apart and a defiant sparkle in her eyes, Martha Ann drew the axe high over her right shoulder again. She held it there a full three seconds, glaring first at her husband, then down at the stupid log. She swung the axe downward with a mighty, clanging thrust that severed the log in two.

"Whoo-weee!" Wiley shouted, clapping his hands. "Would you look at that? See? What did I tell you, huh?"

Martha Ann had to admit she was pretty astonished herself. She stared unbelievingly at the two halves of the log at her feet. Except for the fact that she was out of breath and both her hands tingled from the impact of the axe, she was unshaken by her feat.

"I did it," she said to herself. Then, more loudly: "I actually did it, didn't I?"

She threw the axe down and fell into her husband's sweaty arms. Like children, they careened and pranced around the pile of logs, laughing, shouting, swinging each other around in never-ending circles. The giddiness of the moment made them forget about the war. Suddenly, the war seemed far, far away, a bleak affair for other people in other places to worry about.

Today, now, here, on this sunlit meadow in a remote corner of Georgia, life seemed wonderfully normal, untouched and unshaken by the cataclysmic events already reshaping the country far to the north.

And that was just fine with Wiley and Martha Ann, who continued to dance and roll around on the grass, already becoming dewy with the onset of twilight.

"Let's go to the house," Wiley finally said.

"Do we have to?" Martha Ann purred. "It's such a gorgeous afternoon. Can't we stay out here until the stars come out? I want to stay out here forever."

"What about supper?"

"Forget supper."

Wiley rolled over and pressed his lips against his wife's. "We can see the stars from our bedroom window," he said, gently nibbling her ear.

Martha Ann rose slowly. She stared into her husband's dark eyes and said, "I love you, Wiley Nesmith. I love you with all my heart."

"And I love you, Martha Ann Nesmith," Wiley said.

They kissed again, long and deep, and while they kissed the first star rose high in the eastern sky.

CHAPTER 9

MARTHA ANN GLANCED AT THE CLOCK on the mantel. It was a few minutes past six, almost time for Wiley. She hurried into the kitchen, saw to it that supper was ready. Then, for the umpteenth time, she went into the dining room to make sure the table was set just right. It had to be perfect that night. Perfect.

As she passed the mirror in the hallway, she paused long enough to adjust her hair and to smooth out the wrinkles in her dress. Then, almost without thinking, she let both hands slide slowly down to her abdomen. She closed her eyes and began to gently rub the barely noticeable bulge there. The sensation was electrifying. Several seconds later she opened her eyes and flashed a secret smile at her image in the mirror.

She lit the candles on the table in the dining room, went out on the front porch and waited for her man to come home.

Some time later she heard Wiley's heavy footsteps clomping up the back steps. She hurried back inside, rushing around to make sure nothing was out of place.

"Anybody home?" she heard him call out, teasingly, as he did every afternoon when he came in from the fields. Then: "Something sure smells good," he said, thumping the dirt and mud from his boots at the back steps.

Wiley stopped cold in his tracks when he saw Martha Ann standing in the doorway, a fixed smile on her face. The sight of her almost took his breath away.

"My lord," he crooned. He took off his hat and hung it up on the rack behind the door, not once taking his eyes off his wife.

He was surprised to see her wearing her finest dress, the one he had bought her in Macon a few months back. He was surprised because the only time he'd ever seen her wear it was on Sundays when they went to church.

"What's the special occasion?" he asked.

Martha Ann smiled coyly. "Oh, nothing special," she replied. "I just thought it was time we had a nice, proper supper together." More softly, she said, "I just wanted to look nice for you."

"Well, you're nice all right." Wiley stopped, sniffed himself. "But look at me—standing here smelling like a fresh-butchered hog."

Martha Ann moved past him toward the kitchen. "Well, you just go get yourself cleaned up. Supper's almost ready. Peas and dumplings tonight."

Wiley stopped. Peas and dumplings! That was his favorite dish. A broad smile broke across his tanned, dirty face. Now he knew this had to be some special occasion.

Martha Ann couldn't help smiling as she watched her husband scurry out to the back porch to wash up. While he was outside, she finished setting the table.

When Wiley returned a few minutes later, fresh-shaven and wearing a clean, white shirt, his eyes nearly popped out when he saw the table. He recognized his mother's silver flatware, the fancy blue plates and matching bowls that had belonged to his own grandmother.

They sat down at opposite ends of the table and ate.

"TEN DAYS. That doesn't leave us much time, does it?" Martha Ann sat across from Wiley, sipping a cup of hot dandelion tea while he polished off his second portion of peas and dumplings. She liked to watch Wiley eat. He liked her cooking, and that was good, and he always ate heartily, but never stuffed himself the way most men did. Almost without thinking, she reached down and touched her abdomen. So warm and alive. She yearned to tell him the news.

"We're luckier than some," Wiley replied. He broke off a chunk of cornbread, swirled it around his plate before putting it in his mouth and swallowing it. "Over in Savannah I hear another group's marching off day after tomorrow. That's five regiments this month alone."

Martha Ann sighed. Was there no end to the need for more soldiers? Every day it seemed that more boys were called away, mostly
to Virginia where General McClellan was expected to launch an
invasion against Richmond any day. Half the men in Wilkinson
County were already either gone to meet that challenge or were
about to leave. William had been the first of the Nesmith boys to be
called away. His regiment was now with Johnston in Virginia protecting the Peninsula from Federal advances from the Chesapeake.
Charles' regiment, the 57th, had been in Mississippi since Christmas
guarding Vicksburg.

"I think it's unfair," Martha Ann said sadly. She paused long
enough to take another sip of tea, then added, "You'd think they'd
give you more time to plan these things. After all, Virginia is a long
way off."

"It's not that far," Wiley replied. He pushed back his plate and
said, "Besides, that's where Johnston needs the most men."

"I was hoping it wouldn't be so far away."

Wiley gave her a reassuring smile and said, "It won't be for long."

Her face contorted. "How do you know that?" she asked.

Wiley sighed. "That's what President Davis says."

A wave of hopeless apprehension swept over Martha Ann at the
mention of the Confederate president's name. "Well, what does he
know?" she blurted. She was trying, God knows she was trying, to
control the rage welling up inside. "This war might go on for
months. Years. And all he does is sit up there in his fancy high office
in Richmond and beg the people to remain patient, to sacrifice
more, to send more men…"

Martha Ann's outburst came out of nowhere and caught Wiley
by surprise. He leaned back in his chair and sighed. He longed to
share his true feelings with her—his secret fear that the war might
be much longer and bloodier than anybody anticipated—but he
didn't want to say anything that would cause her any more grief, not
now, not when he was so close to leaving.

Besides, what possible good would it do now? It would only
make things worse. And how could he tell her the truth when he
didn't even know what it was himself?

"Look," he said softly, "I doubt the North can keep up this invasion much longer. Pretty soon those old boys in blue will get tired of being away from home and will make Lincoln call the whole thing off. You'll see."

Martha Ann felt the tears coming on long before her eyes started misting up. She had wanted to be strong. How she had wanted to be strong! At least for this one night, this one special night. In fact, the war was the last thing she had wanted to talk about tonight. But it seemed like every sentence, every word always drifted back to the war one way or another.

When Wiley saw tears forming in the corners of her eyes, he got up and walked around the table. He took Martha Ann's face in his hands, gently kissed her forehead and said, "I promise you, Punkin"—he always called her Punkin when he felt affectionate— "it's going to be all right. Everything is going to be all right."

He brushed back a loose strand of hair and kissed her again. "I'll come home every chance I get. They call it furlough in the army."

He studied his wife's eyes. They were green and shimmering now with tears. He wanted to kiss her again and keep kissing until the pain and the fear went away, along with the anger and uncertainty.

As he looked at her, it suddenly occurred to him that something else might be troubling her.

Martha Ann chose that precise moment to clear her throat and say, "I'm sorry." She blew her nose. "I hate weepy women." Hesitated. "It's just that…Well, I think you should know that…" She struggled to find the right word. "That…"

Wiley could see she was holding something back. He looked at her, eyebrows arched, smooth forehead creased, waiting.

Martha Ann said, "You…You're going to be so far away, and…and…" She couldn't continue.

Wiley leaned closer, searching her eyes. What was she trying to tell him? "Yes, and?"

Martha Ann drew a deep breath. Her whole body felt like it was lifting off the floor. Why was she having such a hard time with this? "Well," she began falteringly, "Virginia is an awful long way from here, and…and…well, I just thought you should know that…" She hesitated again, blew her nose. "I just thought you should know…" She couldn't complete the sentence, no matter how hard she tried.

Wiley studied her a moment longer, then thundered, "*Know what?*" His curiosity finally got the best of him, and he asked, "Is there something else you want to tell me, Punkin?"

Martha Ann smiled. It always made her feel good when Wiley called her Punkin. "No," she said quickly, too quickly. Then: "Yes!" Then: "No. I mean, yes, there is something else. I...I've been wanting to tell you, but just didn't know how."

At last he was getting somewhere. Still puzzled, though, Wiley asked: "Tell me what?"

Martha Ann looked down. In a soft, wavering voice, she said, "You're going to be a father."

"WHAT DID YOU SAY?" WILEY ASKED, blinking in utter amazement.

Martha Ann looked up, straight into her husband's eyes. "I said...You're going to be a father. We're going to have a baby. A baby boy."

Wiley rose slowly to his feet. "Did you say...*a baby?*"

Martha Ann nodded happily, tears streaming down her face.

"A baby," he murmured. Then: "Are you...*sure?*"

"Yes, my love," she replied, still crying and smiling at the same time.

She took his hand and placed it against her abdomen. "Here, feel. He's going to be a strong one. Just like his father."

Suddenly, Wiley felt as if he were floating, suspended in blackest space, a million questions exploding in his head. He was delirious with joy. "A boy," he said to himself. "Imagine that. A real boy. My own son."

He went to his knees and took both of Martha Ann's hands in his own. "That's wonderful, Punkin. Wonderful." He kissed both her hands, her arms, then was on his feet kissing her neck, her face, wrapping his arms around her tightly, as if to protect her and the little seed inside her from all danger. Then: "When?"

"September."

Wiley stood up. "September?" He frowned. "Why, that's only six months," he said, his mind still reeling.

A gray look came into his eyes, and he turned away. "God knows where I'll be in six months." The grayness was quickly replaced by a brilliant burst of light. "But I'll come home. You can count on that, my little Punkin, I'll be here when the time comes. Oh, you can count on that." He drew a heavy sigh. "Imagine that! Me, a father."

"You *will* come home?" Martha Ann asked fearfully. "Won't you? I mean, I do so want you to be here with me when the time comes."

Wiley kissed his wife gently on the lips. "Of course, I will. There aren't enough Yankees in the whole Union army to keep me away."

"Promise?"

Wiley hugged her tightly. "I promise."

"Oh, Wiley, I love you so much."

"And I love you."

They embraced again.

Suddenly, Wiley drew back. "Oh, my God—the farm," he blurted. "I'll have to tell Monroe and Sarah so they can help you out more around here."

Martha Ann smiled. "I already have. They agreed to keep a close eye on the place and to help me when it comes time for the baby."

Martha Ann wasn't sure Wiley had heard her. He was now on his feet, circling the room, deep in thought. "There's so much to do," he muttered, more to himself than to her. "I'll pay them, of course. And…And I'll send you money home every month, enough for food and supplies and some extra for Monroe and Sarah."

Martha Ann couldn't help giggling at the childish change that had come over her husband. "Everything will be fine, Wiley. Really it will."

"The back fence needs some fixing. And…and the hogs and cows. Well, Monroe knows how to do all that, I reckon. But you're going to need some more help around the house. I guess Sarah is good at that. And Ma'll be happy to come over and help out with the baby."

Martha Ann threw back her head and laughed. "Wiley, would you just calm down? Please? We'll be fine, both of us. Don't worry." In a more serious tone, she said, "You're going to have many more important things on your mind now, my darling. And you mustn't fret over us back here. You'll be in the army. You must make a good soldier and make both of us proud to be your family."

CHAPTER 10

A LIGHT RAIN WAS FALLING the day the citizens of Wilkinson County turned out to see their boys off to war. All morning long they had been gathering at the little depot on the edge of town, anxiously awaiting the arrival of the train that would take the spirited young warriors to Savannah, and from there North Carolina and, finally, the battlefields of Virginia.

Any minute now the whistle would blow, and the fresh-scrubbed farm boys, dressed in their spanking-new uniforms, would clamber aboard to set forth on their "long and dangerous journey," as the Reverend Isaac Thurmond had once phrased it.

It was a grand and glorious occasion, in no way diminished by the gray skies and torrential rainfall that had ripped through town during the night, transforming streets and walkways into quagmires. Between showers that morning there were parades and marching bands and fireworks displays that lit up the leaden skies.

Then, precisely at noon, Governor Joe Brown, a slight, balding man with slumped shoulders and narrow, fierce eyes that flashed behind thick spectacles, ascended a specially built platform and offered a long and stirring tribute to the gallant men of the Georgia 49th.

"Fellow Southerners, your soil has been invaded by an abolitionist horde," the governor proclaimed in an imperious, high-pitched voice that rocked the crowd to a frenzy. "I now call upon you to rally...to go forth and drive the invaders back into the sea!"

"We will rally!" a young man in uniform shouted. His exultation was contagious.

"God save the Confederacy!" another soldier shouted, and there was more wild cheering. Hats flew into the air by the hundreds as men and women hugged and kissed and little children sang and scampered between legs.

The governor smiled as he calmly surveyed the jubilant crowd. He spread his arms wide for silence. Then, hitching up his trousers, he thundered: "All we ask is to be left alone! All we've ever asked is to be left to our own ways, our own destiny." He paused, took a deep breath and continued. "We take no special pride in sending the flower of our manhood forth to battlefields far from home, to have you assail the flag that for so long guided all of our hearts and common destinies. But now a great tragedy has befallen our great land, and we must fight. *We shall fight!* And I say to you proudly that we shall bring sure and certain terror to the hearts of those who would oppress our noble cause…"

At carefully arranged interludes, fireworks would go off, igniting the crowd's passions to an even higher pitch. Brass bands would kick in with rousing medleys. Bells would chime and women would swoon and children would wave flags and men would howl and roar and pump their fists toward merciful heaven.

WHEN THE TRAIN WHISTLE SOUNDED at two o'clock that afternoon, an eerie silence descended upon the crowd. For the first time, the reality of war came crashing down. In a few moments the soldiers would be gone, on their way to battlefields far from home. A few would go on to fame and glory; some would never return.

The date was March 22, 1862. The war was still young, not quite a year old. Names like Manassas, Wilson's Creek, Forts Donelson and Henry and Pea Ridge were already household words. But those struggles, bloody as they were, would soon pale in comparison to the monumental bloodbaths that lay ahead.

For the time being, the boys in gray, huddled along the tracks waiting for the train that dreary day, could bask in their own quiet innocence at the glory being lavished upon them by the cheering crowd.

EARLIER THAT MORNING Garrett Nesmith and Indigo Collins had climbed on top of the baggage shed to get a better view of the rail-side festivities. Now, as they listened to the governor's impassioned speech and the jubilation of the crowd, they were not disappointed.

As Garrett watched his brothers, enthralled by their uniforms and the adulation being heaped upon them, a single thought continued to possess him: Somehow, some way, he was going to join the cavalry. It might not be today. It might not be next week, or even the next month. But he was determined to enlist, to serve his country in the ranks of the cavalry. Of that, he was certain. He would not be denied.

From below a girl's voice suddenly called out: "Why, Garrett Nesmith, is that you up there?"

Garrett looked down and almost fell out off the roof when he saw Amy Skinner standing below. She was dressed in a pretty pink dress and blue coat and matching bonnet. Her cheeks were rosy and damp from the light mist swirling across the train yard.

Oh, no, Garrett thought. Not her! The last thing he wanted was for Amy to see him crouched up there on the roof of the baggage shed like an ordinary schoolboy. How undignified—and him about to become a cavalry trooper!

He hoped his embarrassment didn't show. "Oh, hello," he said sheepishly.

Amy scrunched up her face and asked: "What are you two doing up there?"

It was an innocent question, but Garrett had a sinking sensation that she was making fun of him.

"Uh, waiting for the train," he stammered.

"Up there?"

"Uh-huh. The view is better up here."

Then Amy did the strangest thing. She hitched up her skirt and clambered up onto the shed.

"You're right," she said, settling between Garrett and Indigo and gazing across the train yard. "The view is much better up here. Look!" she added, pointing toward Garrett's brothers boarding the train. "Aren't those your brothers?"

"Yeah," Garrett mumbled, his voice deflated, flat.

The girl's dark eyes twinkled with excitement. "Just look at them all," she said admiringly. "They're so handsome. Every one of them is so handsome."

Amy's words only deepened Garrett's anguish. It was bad enough that she had caught him sitting on top of the shed. Now she was clearly making fun of him because he was not wearing a uniform.

"I'm waiting so I can join the cavalry," he suddenly heard himself say.

Amy's eyes seemed to catch fire. They were so big and bright Garrett could see his own reflection in them. "Oh, Garrett," she gushed, squeezing his arm. "I'm so proud of you. I can't wait to see you in your uniform."

Indigo perked up and said, "I'm g-gonna join up, t-too."

"Why, Indigo," Amy replied, turning toward him. "I'm doubly happy for you, too. She swung back around to Garrett and asked, "When are you boys planning to leave?"

Garrett thought hard for a moment. "Soon" is all he could think of to say.

"Y-Yeah, r-real soon," Indigo stammered back.

———

ACROSS TOWN, Catherine Potter stood staring out the window of Potter's Dry Goods and Clothing Boutique. For some time she had watched the crowds come and go, the parades, the marching bands, even the governor's procession as it wound past the town square on its way to the train depot.

Any other time and she would have been out there in the middle of things, frolicking in the fun, flirting, cheering the boys on. She had even met the governor once and would have probably invited him over to tea. With or without her husband's approval.

But not today.

Today Catherine Potter remained inside the store, the stinking store, seething, angry, ashamed—repulsed by her husband's cowardly reluctance to sign up for the service.

"You're a disgrace," she had chastised him earlier that morning. "What kind of man would choose to stay back and let others go off and do his fighting for him?"

"A very wise one," Joseph had replied, calmly thumbing through a receipts ledger that lay open on the counter.

But when Joseph saw the dark look that filled Catherine's face, he closed the book and looked straight at her. Even in the dim light he couldn't help but be struck by her great beauty. "Catherine," he said gently, trying to choose his words carefully, "this war is all wrong. Can't you see that? When will you and the rest of these people come to your senses and realize it is also immoral and unconstitutional, an evil thing?"

"You and your fancy words," Catherine spat back. She thumped the counter with her tiny fist. "There's nothing real about you, Joseph Potter. You're just a fake, a nobody, a...a hopeless, boring clod who would rather stay here and rot in this horrible little store than go out and do something exciting."

Most men would have withered under so fierce an assault. But not Joseph, who merely turned away. He was used to such outbursts from his wife, and he knew how pointless it was to argue with her, especially when she was like this. That was something he had learned a long time ago. Just let her rant, he reminded himself, let her sulk and screech and rage like the flaming banshee she could be at times. It would pass. It always did. Then she'd fly into his arms, all weepy and shaking, and they'd kiss and make love, and her fury would finally go away.

At least until the next time.

"You're just a coward," Catherine hissed.

Joseph flinched, but refused to buckle. The words hurt, of course. They cut deep into his heart, his manhood. But he knew not to let his wife's words get to him, to dismantle what little dignity remained in his soul. She could be mean at times, heartless, cruel. But deep down, there was the soft, loving woman he had married five years ago. Others might not understand Catherine, but Joseph did. That's why he could still love her after all this time, all this pain. Whatever demons dwelled within Catherine Potter's heart would never possess the power to drive Joseph away from her.

———

JANE NESMITH sat on a small wooden bench beneath the dripping overhang, frail and fading, bundled in black. She was alone, except for Sarah, who sat next to her holding her hand. The black woman's warm presence comforted her, but did little to ease the ache she felt in her heart for her sons—Wiley, James Madison, Albert, and John—who were about to march off to war, something she had prayed she would never live to see happen again. She had already seen two of her sons off—William and Charles—and the pain this morning was no less subdued.

She recalled a similar day long ago when her brother, Herschel, had been called away to fight the British invaders down in Florida. She was much younger then, only a child, really, but she remembered how Herschel, so handsome and dashing and utterly innocent in his crisp blue uniform, had promised to bring her back a souvenir from the Florida campaign. He never came back, and the only souvenir she got was a letter, now yellowed and crumpled in the bottom of her trunk, from his commanding officer saying that he had fallen in action.

Jane Nesmith had naively believed she would never know such heartache again. Now, as she watched her sons, handsome and dashing and full of fresh innocence in their bonny gray uniforms, she knew she was wrong.

They had said their farewells earlier in the day, mother and sons, along with comforting final words with the Reverend Thurmond. Now, as the band played on and the flag-waving festivities continued, it was the wives' turn to spend a final few moments with their men.

MARTHA ANN leaned against Wiley, quietly fighting back tears. She had wanted to be strong, not to crumble and wilt, but now that the time had come for Wiley to leave, all resolve had abandoned her. When she raised her eyes and looked at him again, so handsome in the gray tunic and light blue trousers she had made for him just last week, his father's old but polished musket perched at his side, a wave of despair swept over her.

"Oh, Wiley," she said, willing herself not to cry, "you will come back to me, won't you?"

Wiley felt his wife's pain. It penetrated his own body like a knife, plunging deep into his heart. He had to strain to keep his voice from trembling. "Of course, I'll be back, Punkin. I promised you, didn't I?"

"Promise me again," Martha Ann said with palpable urgency.

Wiley cradled her face in his hands. "I promise," he whispered, gazing deep into her eyes. "I'll be back before you know it."

"And you will be careful," Martha Ann interjected.

Wiley nodded.

"Are you sure you have everything?" she asked nervously, checking his canteen and bayonet, the blanket roll draped over his shoulder and the leather cartridge box at his side. "Sewing kit? Mess kit? Skillet?" Then: "Writing paper! What about writing paper? And a pen?"

Wiley smiled. "I've got everything," he said reassuringly. He drew her close again, sniffed the fragrance in her hair. "Now stop fretting like an old mother hen."

"Don't worry, we'll take good care of him," John laughed. He and Albert had wandered over from a few ranks away. For no particular reason, Martha Ann secretly liked John better than Wiley's other brothers. Next to James Madison, he was the hardest working and certainly the most handsome—tall and blond, with soft blue eyes and a warm smile. She and Beth, John's wife, had never really been close, but she liked her a lot, too.

Albert, stooped and frail and aged beyond his years, leaned on his musket and cracked, "That's right. We won't let him out of our sight."

"That'll be the day," Wiley retorted. "I'll probably have my hands full looking after you boys." He glanced around. "Anybody seen James Madison?"

"Last I saw of him he was with the captain," John said. "I think they're trying to make a sergeant out of him or something."

Just then a brilliant burst of sunlight penetrated the dark overhanging clouds. For a moment the whole train yard was transformed into a sparkling wonderland of light. In that brief moment of shimmering radiance, all trace of fear and despair seemed to vanish like phantoms in the night, replaced by jubilation and the wondrous hope that always comes with the dawn.

But the effect was only fleeting. A split second later the sun was gone, along with the shimmering radiance, and the whole town was blanketed once more in low-hanging clouds of gray.

"See you on the train," Albert said to Wiley. He dipped his hat to Martha Ann, then, following John, disappeared in the mass of gray-clad troops surging toward the tracks.

As soon as they had gone Wiley turned to Martha Ann and said,

"Guess it's time." He patted her abdomen and smiled. "Promise me you'll be extra careful," he choked. "Remember, you've got two to take care of now."

He wrapped his arms around her then, clasping her tightly as if to protect her from every danger in the world.

Martha Ann thought her heart was going to break. Never before had she felt so sad, so lonely, yet so full of pride at the same time. She despised this war for taking Wiley away from her. She despised it for what it was doing to her life. At the same time, she couldn't help but feel monumental pride in her husband, her town, her new country.

"Here it comes!" someone shouted, and every tear-filled eye turned to watch the flag-draped troop train rumble to a clanking halt in front of the depot. Great clouds of hissing steam belched from the locomotive. Several officers wearing tall black boots and swords strapped to their sides jumped off the train and motioned for the men to start boarding.

"Men of the 49th—all aboard!" one of the officers ordered.

Captain Samuel Player, looking trim and handsome in his tailored uniform, climbed onto the platform and relayed the boarding instructions. His sword gleamed in the bright sunlight, and the twin rows of brass buttons on his chest glittered like cut glass.

Wiley took both of Martha Ann's hands in his own, kissed each one, then found her mouth. It was a long, sweet kiss that both wished could have lasted forever. Pulling back, Wiley said, "I have to go now. Remember, that I love you, Punkin. I'll always love you. Forever and forever…"

"And I love you," Martha Ann whispered back. She threw her arms around his neck and held him again, not wanting to let go. If she closed her eyes and held on long enough, she might wake up and find it was all just a dream, a horrible dream. So she continued to hold on until she felt Wiley's fingers gently prying her arms away.

"Please," he said tenderly. "I've got to go."

He kissed her one last time before turning loose and slowly backing away. Then he was gone, swept away by the surging tide of gray.

Martha Ann stared after him, searching the crowd for some sign of her husband. Then, overwhelmed by a desperate urge to find him, to hold him, to kiss him one last time, she lunged into the shoving masses, looking this way and that, peering over shoulders and jumping up and down.

Only later did she see him, leaning out a window and waving frantically. "Goodbye!" he and every other soldier on the train were shouting at the top of their lungs.

Martha Ann fought her way forward, not once taking her eyes off him. "I love you!" she shouted over and over, not sure if he could hear her.

Then the train roared to life again and began to move—slowly, chugging, churning, an iron monster come to life, heaving, shuddering, crunching down the pair of gleaming iron rails.

From every crowded window, soldiers waved and called out to loved ones, pledging their love, promising to return, while masses of weeping women and cheering boys rushed along, waving handkerchiefs and yelling.

Martha Ann followed the train, too. She followed it until the caboose finally rounded a wooded bend and was gone.

CHAPTER 11

THE TRAIN PULLED INTO SAVANNAH STATION shortly before dark. The mayor of the city, tall and dignified in black tails and a stovetop hat, was on hand to greet them, along with a group of pompous-looking aldermen, several high-ranking officers and a throng of flag-waving citizens.

Wiley was amazed when he looked out the window of the train and saw the mob of people lining the tracks. Young boys and gray-haired old men, giggling girls and well-frocked women of all ages, many of them waving flags and handkerchiefs, pressed against the tracks as far as the eye could see, cheering, shrieking.

Wiley was reminded of the night he and Martha Ann had arrived at the station for their honeymoon. He smiled wistfully as he recalled the carriage ride to the hotel, the torchlight parades, the young waiter hell-bent to enlist. Most of all he remembered that wonderful little room overlooking Johnson Square. He could almost smell the sweet fragrance of wisteria and honeysuckle wafting through the room. Had it really been almost a year?

John, who sat next to Wiley on the ride over from Irwinton, leaned past him and said, "Would you look at all that? You'd think we just won the war."

"I think that's what they expect us to do," Wiley replied.

Captain Player strode into the car, relaxed, fresh and regal in his crisp, gray uniform. He fixed his gloved hands on his narrow hips and looked around. "Remember who you are, gentlemen," he said to the men of the 49th. "The eyes of Wilkinson County are upon you this day. Indeed, the eyes of the entire Confederacy are upon you!"

"Yes, sir," the men roared in unison.

At the rear of the car, a thin, sallow-cheeked boy stood up clutching an old musket. "Cap'n," the boy asked tentatively.

Wiley turned around when he thought he recognized the voice. It was Petie Clanton, old Bart Clanton's boy. What was he doing there, Wiley wondered? If he recalled correctly, Petie couldn't be a day over fourteen, the same age as Garrett. Too young to be in the army, that was for sure.

In a high-pitched voice that cracked with adolescent innocence, Petie asked, "Is this where we fight the Yankees?"

The boy's question triggered an outburst of laughter. Even Captain Player smiled at the boy's naiveté. "No, son," the captain replied in a fatherly tone. "This is where we *train* to fight the Yankees."

A puzzled look stole across the boy's thin, pockmarked face. "Train?" he said disappointedly. "You mean, I won't get to shoot no Yankees yet?"

"Not yet, I'm afraid," the captain answered. "God willing, there'll be plenty of time for that yet."

———

AS THE MEN OF THE 49TH clomped down from the train, a civilian band struck up, filling the cavernous station with stirring strains of martial music. The music and clamor of the crowd were electrifying. When the band broke out in a stirring rendition of "Dixie," the crowd almost went berserk.

"God bless you boys!" a woman shouted, tossing a bouquet of flowers into the ranks.

Wiley turned in time to see brother John snatch the flowers in midair. "These Savannah gals sure are the friendly type," he clucked.

It was a thrilling moment, one Wiley would never forget for the rest of his days. As he stood there, watching the tumultuous crowds and listening to the music, it seemed incomprehensible that, less than four hundred miles to the north, boys in blue and gray were already spilling blood on Virginia soil. Or, at that very moment, an enormous Yankee invasion fleet was being assembled along the shores of the Chesapeake Bay to march on the Confederate capital at Richmond.

Mayor Richard Arnold raised his hands, and the cheering gradually died down. Smiling broadly, he said, "They tell me you're called the Wilkinson County Invincibles."

"*Yes, sir!*" almost every man in the regiment yelled at the top of his lungs.

"Well, here in Savannah we've got a new name for you," the mayor said. "*Heroes.*" He paused, carefully measured the impact his words were having on the audience, then continued. "We welcome you to our fair city in this, our moment of peril. We thank you for coming, and we commend you for your unselfish devotion, your uncompromising patriotism and sacrifice and willingness to defend our just and noble cause. May the god of battle be with you as you prepare to go forth to defend our sacred homeland..."

More wild cheering, followed by a round of speeches from stout-chested bigwigs and brass. Then, one by one, the various companies started filing out of the station on their way to the riverfront where they were treated to artillery salutes, rousing musical medleys and a dazzling display of fireworks.

As the bands played and the crowds cheered and the flaming rockets arced higher and higher over the dark waves, Wiley couldn't help thinking how strange it all seemed, dream-like. Never in his life had he imagined being a part of such a grand spectacle. Any second he expected to wake up and find himself in bed back at the farm, Martha Ann's warm breath on his neck.

The celebrating continued well into the night. There was dancing and feasting and more music and speeches and fireworks. Negro musicians, some dressed in elegant white jackets, others barefooted and clad in plantation rags, sang and danced and played banjos and fiddles. It was a sight that brought howls of laughter from spectators, many of whom formed circles around the shuffling, gyrating performers, egging them on with clapping hands and stamping feet and Confederate dollar bills tossed at their flying feet.

Finally, sometime around midnight, the party broke up. The civilian revelers went home to bed. The soldiers, groggy from all the excitement and weary from the long day's events, crawled inside their blankets and slept that first night under the stars along the cool banks of the Savannah River.

NEXT MORNING they were awakened by the shrill blast of a bugle.

"Time to rise and shine, little brother," Wiley heard someone say. He opened his eyes and saw James Madison's big, bearded face looming over him.

Wiley sat up and stretched. "Didn't we just turn in?" he asked, yawning and rubbing the sleep from his eyes. "What time is it, anyway?"

"Four o'clock."

"Four o'clock?" Wiley groaned. "Why do you suppose they woke us up so early?"

James Madison rocked back on his heels and laughed. "Boy, you're in the army now. Better get used to the wee hours."

Wiley crawled to his feet. The air blowing in from the bay was cool and damp and smelled like the sea. Beyond the dark river, the sun was just beginning to rise. Thin fingers of pink light poked skyward above the dark tree line across the river. All around him, the boys in gray were beginning to stir.

The Wilkinson County Invincibles had arrived.

CHAPTER 12

AT SEVEN SHARP A BUGLE SOUNDED, and the men began to move out. Their destination was Camp Davis, one of several small military training facilities ringing the outskirts of Savannah. There the men of the 49th would spend the next several weeks learning the basics of army life—marching and drilling, fighting and shooting.

Fighting and shooting. That was the part most of the men had been waiting for. They could do without the marching and drilling. What good was all that when fighting and shooting Yankees were all that really mattered?

But for the past several weeks, ever since the regiment started officially organizing, it seemed as if all they did was march and drill, march and drill.

By their second day in Savannah, some of the excitement of army life was already beginning to wear thin. The long, hot train ride from Irwinton, with men pressed so close together they found it hard to breathe, had given them an early taste of what lay ahead. The fine welcome at the station had helped restore spirits, as did the mirthful night of celebrating. But now, as they trudged through the gloomy pine barrens on their way to Camp Davis, some were beginning to have second thoughts about army life.

———

THEY REACHED CAMP DAVIS around noon. A dark, husky major by the name of Hawkins met them at the perimeter, introduced himself as the camp commander, then led them to an assembly area at the center of the compound.

After the men had formed, the major folded his arms and said, "I hope you boys enjoyed yourselves in town last night." He paused, a wicked grin twisting slowly across his broad, leathery face as he surveyed the double ranks of raw recruits massed before him. "Because I'm here to tell you that life has changed for you in a big way."

The grin widened into a sinister smirk. "For the next few weeks, you boys will belong to me. You can forget about your mammies and your pappies and your sweetie-pies back home. I'm gonna be on your backs day and night, like a bear claw on honey. By the time I'm finished with you boys, you're gonna be wishing you were back home with the womenfolk picking cotton."

The major strutted forward, hands hooked to his black leather belt, silently appraising the men. "Not all of you will make it," he growled, twirling a thick mustache that turned up toward his cheeks. "But those of you who do will soon be on the front lines ducking Yankee bullets…"

OVER THE NEXT FEW DAYS, Camp Davis became a living hell for the men of the 49th. Up before dawn, marching all day with full packs and muskets, drilling with bayonets until after sundown. The only breaks came at mealtime. After "night training," they'd crash into their blankets for a few hours of shut-eye. At four o'clock sharp the bugle would rattle them out of their blankets, and they'd be up and at it again.

The day always began with an extended beat of snare drums known as the "long roll." Breakfast and roll call would follow, then high-strutting officers would lead them on a five-mile march into surrounding swamps, where they'd practice dry firing on the run, parrying with bayonets and hand-to-hand combat.

Staying in step was a problem for some of the boys who didn't know their left foot from their right. Occasionally, sergeants would tie wisps of hay to their left foot and wisps of straw to their right.

Setting the men to march, drill sergeants would call out, "Hay-foot, straw-foot, hay-foot, straw-foot"—until they finally got the hang of it.

A familiar chant would sweep through the ranks of the recruits as they marched about camp:

> *March! March! March, old soldier, march!*
> *Hayfoot, strawfoot,*
> *Belly-full of bean soup,*
> *March, old soldier, march!*

It wasn't until the third week in camp that the men of the 49th were taken to the firing range. A rotating team of sergeants took them through the drills of loading, aiming and firing, even though most of the men, having grown up in the country, were already quite familiar with firearm basics and were excellent shots.

"I know what a lot of you boys are thinking," one sergeant said. "You're thinking this is a waste of time because you already know how to shoot."

The sergeant pointed to Petie Clanton and ordered him to step forward. Looking sheepish and out of place, the boy did as he was told.

"Here," the sergeant said, tossing the boy a cartridge box. "What's your name, boy?"

"Clanton...sir," the boy said nervously. "Private Petie Clanton."

"Do you like to hunt, Private Clanton?"

"Yes, sir. I do it all the time back home."

The sergeant grinned. "Well, good, Private Clanton. I want you to pretend you're back home hunting a big old gobbler." The sergeant leaned close, so close his nose almost touched Petie's. "Think you can do that, Private?"

"Yes, sir," Petie wheezed. He was so scared that sweat was pouring down his face.

The sergeant spun around and pointed toward the woods. He lowered his voice and said, "There he is. You see him. It's a big, fine specimen, full of feathers and a red beard that drags the ground. He's over there, see, less than a hundred yards away." He glared at Petie. "What you gonna do, Private Clanton?"

"Huh?"

"What are you gonna do, you nitwit? You ain't gonna let that big old gobbler get away, are you?"

The boy shook his head. "No, sir," he replied sharply.

"Then shoot him, damnit. Show us how you'd shoot him." The sergeant turned around again and jabbed his finger toward a white-painted barrel about a hundred yards across the field. On top of the barrel rested a fifty-pound bag of flour painted Yankee blue. "There's your bird. Shoot him before he gets away. Now!"

Private Clanton swallowed hard. He glanced around, saw the fellows looking at him, waiting for him to make a move. The sweat was now pouring down his face. Gulping so loud you could hear it all the way down the line, the boy reached inside the cartridge belt and pulled out one of the cylindrical-shaped paper cartridges. He slowly twisted off the end, dropped it into the muzzle of his musket, rammed in a piece of wadding and drew a bead on the target.

Squinting, he pulled the trigger.

The musket boomed. One hundred yards away, the blue target exploded in a shower of white powder.

A loud cheer rose up from the ranks.

"Way to go, Petie!" John Nesmith shouted.

"You did it!" another soldier exclaimed.

Relief washed over Wiley like a great tidal wave. So did pride. Pride in the fact that one of the hometown boys—one of the Wilkinson County Invincibles—had shown what kind of stuff he was made of. Even if he was only a boy.

Private Clanton lowered his musket, a proud grin worming its way across his thin, pockmarked face. He turned slowly toward the sergeant.

"You're *dead*, Private Clanton," the sergeant snarled. "*Dead! Dead! Dead!*"

The boy's jaw dropped. He didn't understand. Nor did anybody else.

Wiley wondered what the sergeant was talking about. The boy had plucked his target dead center.

James Madison, standing next to Wiley, leaned over and whispered, "What's the matter with that fool sergeant? Ain't he got eyes? The boy hit it fair and square. We all saw it, plain as day."

They didn't have to wait long for an explanation.

"Took you too long to load your firearm, you dimwit," the

sergeant snapped. "In the time it took you to load and pack, the enemy would've killed you three times over. You've gotta fire faster, boy, faster! Do you hear me?"

All color had drained out of Petie Clanton's face. He stood pale as a ghost, quivering with confusion. "Y-Yessir," he replied, not sure at all what the gruff sergeant meant.

"Gimme that," the sergeant ordered, snatching Clanton's musket with one hand, the cartridge box with the other. "Gentlemen," he said, "Billy ain't about to wait around for you to load up your squirrel guns. If you want to live, you gotta learn to load quick. Quickness is the name of the game here."

He backed up a couple of steps, turned around and said, "Observe, gentlemen. Here's how you do it in combat—if you want to live."

With lightning speed, he spread his legs, seized a cartridge from the box, twisted the end off with his teeth, dropped it into the muzzle, rammed in wadding, aimed and fired—all in less than thirty seconds. Then he spun around and fired, striking another barrel dead center.

He lowered the smoking musket and slowly eyeballed the men. "There are only two kinds of soldiers," he rasped. "Those who can get off two rounds a minute and shoot straight—and those who can't. Those who can't soon become dead soldiers. Dead soldiers, gentlemen, ain't no good to the Confederacy. Never forget that."

———

OVER THE NEXT FEW DAYS there were many more lessons about life and death on the front lines. The most memorable advice came one day when a lumbering, flat-faced sergeant named Kramer went before them and offered a long list of "do's" and "don't's."

"Ven you go into battle," the husky sergeant explained in a thick, German accent, "remember zee following rules: Do not shoot until you see zee enemy clearly. Look for his eyes, gentlemen, but remember to fire low, preferably at zee chest area so you von't overshoot. Don't vorry if you only vound Billy; an injured man has to be taken from zee field by healzy vones, putting zem out of action, too."

The sergeant had bushy red eyebrows that rose up and down as

he spoke. "Und anozer zing," he shouted. "Alvays pick out your target. Vatch how he moves. Is he fast? Slow? Does he run
sidevays?"—here, the sergeant imitated a soldier scampering side-
ways. "Oder," he added, lumbering straight toward them, "does he
run straight on at you like zis?"

The men were soon roaring with laughter at the sergeant's antics
and colorful accent. Most of them couldn't remember the last time
they had laughed.

"You do zat before you fire," Sergeant Kramer went on, "und you
von't miss a zing. Und, vhen pozzible, pick off zee enemy's
offiziers—particularly zee mounted vones. Shoot all zee artillery
horses you see vizin range. Under all conditions hold your ranks.
Ven ordered to charge, do so at vonce und move rapidly. Do not stop
to smell zee roses. You are much less likely to be killed vhile going
steadily forvard zan if you hezitate oder retreat. But, in zee case you
have to fall back, do so gradually und in order. Remember zat more
men are killed during disorganized retreat zan at any ozer time."

As for charging artillery batteries, Sergeant Kramer offered this
advice: "Do not be terrorized by cannonfire. Artillery ist never as
deadly as it seems. A rapid forvard movement reduces zee battery's
effectiveness und hastens zee end of its power to destroy.

"Anozer zing: Do not pause oder turn aside to plunder zee dead
oder to pick up spoils. Battles have been lost by indulgence in zis
temptation. Do not heed zee calls for assistance of vounded comrades oder stop to take zem to zee rear. Details have been made to
care for casualties; und zee best vay of protecting your vounded
friends is to drive zee enemy von zee field."

Finally, he hitched up his considerable belly and said,
"Straggling under any guise vill be severely punished. Covards vill
be shot. Do your duty in a manner zat vill make your regiment und
country proud of you…"

———

A FEW DAYS BEFORE CAMP broke, the men of the 49th received
two special visitors—General P.G.T. Beauregard, the hero of Fort
Sumter and Manassas, and the honorable Robert Toombs, former
United States senator and Confederate secretary of treasury.

The Creole general, handsome, wavy-haired and clad in a double-breasted jacket and knee-high riding boots, stood on a platform reviewing the troops. Somehow he looked shorter—and much thinner—in real life than in the tawdry drawings circulating camp.

"In a few days you will be joining our gallant comrades far to the north who, like you, have responded to our nation's call." The general's voice was low and weary, almost melancholy. One could almost discern a black cloud hovering somewhere at the edge of his consciousness. "The eyes and hopes of eight million proud Southerners go with you," he intoned in that same brooding tone. "You are expected to show yourselves worthy of your race and lineage, worthy of the women of the South, women whose noble devotion in this war has never been exceeded at any time in history."

When Toombs, a portly brigadier with large, baggy eyes and a receding hairline, took to the podium, he urged the new soldiers to follow their leaders faithfully and to "take the initiative… Carry the war into the enemy's country with all due haste. History and God are on our side. We must now invade. We must carry the war into Africa. Our banners will wave in the streets of Washington in a few days…"

———

THAT NIGHT, their last at Camp Davis, Wiley sat down beneath a star-studded sky, pulled out his pen and writing paper and wrote a letter to his wife:

Camp Davis
April 5, 1862

My dear loving wife,
At last training camp is over, and I'm proud to say that all of us Nesmith boys made it through without too much trouble. I think I can safely tell you that it would take a lot more than another war to make me go through it again!
We break camp first thing in the morning and go our separate ways. I have orders to go to Virginia to join Gen'l. Johnston near Richmond, where I hear there's been a lot of fighting lately. I have been assigned to

"A" Company, the Georgia 49th Regiment under Colonel Andrew J. Lane. I'm happy to say that Capt. Player will be going along with us. He's a good man—a little high-strung at times, but a good man, and I think he's going to make a fine officer.

James Madison is supposed to be heading somewhere in that direction, too, but his final orders have not arrived yet. The other boys still don't know where they're going to wind up. I hope their orders arrive before I leave in the morning. It would be nice to know where all my brothers are going.

The stars are out in great number tonight, so I guess that's a good sign. As I sit here, gazing straight up into the high blackness, I can't help but think of you and all the nights we used to sit out and count these very stars. How far away you seem; but, like the stars, I can look up and see your bright eyes looking down on me from the heavens.

My darling, I send all my love to you and pray that we will meet again soon. Until then, I remain your loving husband,

Wiley

PS I will drop you a few lines on the way to Virginia. Oh, almost forgot to tell you that old Bart Clanton's boy, Petie, has joined up and will be going with us to Virginia. He proved himself well in training. You ought to see him shoot! But he's just a boy, no older than Garrett. Lord, what is this world coming to?

CHAPTER 13

THE OLD-TIMER SQUATTED on a makeshift bunk outside the station, a tattered gray overcoat slung casually across his narrow shoulders. His right arm was cased in a sling, and a thick, dirty bandage streaked with blood covered most of his head and left eye.

"Take a good look, boys," he rasped, showing off his wounds to the green recruits from Georgia. "This is what's waitin' fer ye up in Virginny."

The old trooper was one of a hundred or so veterans crowding the Goldsboro station when Wiley's train pulled in. Most of them sat quietly in the shadows, nursing wounds and grudges, while a few limped about on canes and crutches.

The sight of so many wounded men thrilled the young Georgians who leaned eagerly out the windows for a better look. They shook hands, passed out tobacco and listened to stories about life and death in the Virginia trenches.

"Little Mac's up there waiting on you boys, and he's growing right impatient," one grizzled private cracked. He advised them to write their names on a piece of paper and pin them to their breasts. "That way, when you fall, they'll know where you're from and how to contact your next of kin."

Such stories had thrilled the young recruits, but also generated a certain amount of anxiety, especially later when they crossed the Virginia line. As the train drew closer to Petersburg, they grew strangely quiet. There were fewer jokes and less swearing and considerably more sweating and praying. Guns were checked and re-checked. Cartridge boxes and cap pouches were examined over and over to make sure the right amounts of paper, powder and ball were in each. Bayonets and bowie knives were polished and honed to perfection.

They were relieved when they pulled into Petersburg Station and found no Yankees waiting for them. Instead, there were pretty girls and flowers and lots of home-cooked food prepared by local citizens. It seemed as if the whole town had turned out to greet them, to thank them for coming to help turn back McClellan's invaders.

Before leaving Petersburg, the 49th was assigned to a brigade commanded by Joseph Reid Anderson, a dapper, fifty-year-old West Point graduate with twinkly eyes and wavy brown hair curling back from a V-shaped hairline. Anderson's force consisted of units not only from Georgia, but also from South Carolina, North Carolina and Louisiana. As they moved northward toward Richmond, Anderson's brigade fell under the command of A.P. Hill's "Light Division," part of the Department of Northern Virginia under General Joseph Eggleston Johnston.

———

THE VIRGINIA COUNTRYSIDE was even more beautiful than Wiley had imagined. He stared in wonderment as the long gray columns snaked past grass-covered meadows, with spectacular views of smoke-ringed mountains in the distance, unable to shake the feeling that he was entering another world, a world far removed from the flat pinelands and moss-draped swamps of Georgia. A riot of flowers seemed to blossom everywhere at once—along the roads, in the woods, the meadows, the wide, sprawling fields. And what fields they were! Wiley had never laid eyes on more handsome fields! Broad and rolling, rich with black soil, freshly turned, and crops almost ready for harvesting. The houses they passed were big and sturdy and far older than the fancy plantations back home.

As he trudged along, Wiley's mind drifted back to his own little farm down in Wilkinson County. He wondered how Martha Ann was holding up, what with all the chores and planning for the baby. In her last letter she had reassured him that everything was fine; Monroe and Sarah were a big help, she said, as were Garrett and Mother Nesmith. Elizabeth and Nancy had been out several times to see her and always saw to it that she had a ride to church.

You must think now of yourself, she had advised him. *Be sure to eat right and get plenty of sleep…Our son is going to need a strong, healthy father…*

Our son…

The words stuck in his brain like a recurring pleasant dream.

"I THOUGHT THERE WAS A WAR going on up here," remarked Burrell Delk, a bushy-haired young private who had come on board at Greensboro. "Look around you, boys. Where are the Yanks?"

Delk reminded Wiley of a headstrong puppy—anxious, eager and bouncy. Too bouncy for his own good, Wiley thought. In the days ahead, that kind of recklessness could get him in a lot of trouble.

"Don't worry, boy," retorted Tom Johnson. At age twenty-eight, Johnson was already one of the oldest men in the company. That's why some of the boys referred to him affectionately as Gramps. "We'll see 'em soon enough."

TWO DAYS LATER they came to a tiny crossroads town on the outskirts of Richmond called Seven Pines. It was here, they were told, that McClellan's invaders would try to pass through on their way to the Confederate capital city.

"Whatever happens, we must not allow them to succeed here," General Anderson had told the men on the afternoon of their arrival at Seven Pines. As he spoke, the steady boom of artillery and crackle of musketfire could be heard in the near distance. "Do you hear that?" the general asked, pointing his sword toward the east. "The Yankees are on the other side of those woods. They're coming strong, and they're coming fast. Our job is to hold the line, boys, drive them back into the James."

The general lifted his hat, speared it with his sword and raised it high. "The fate of the Confederacy is in our hands!" he proclaimed.

The response was electrifying. The men cheered and yelled, threw caps and bags into the air. Up and down the lines, multicolored regimental flags fluttered and cracked in the acrid wind.

They spent the rest of that first afternoon digging trenches and constructing breastworks. Every time they'd finish one set of earthworks, a tall, white-bearded officer would appear out of nowhere on a dappled gray horse and order them to get busy on another one. Then, when that one was finished, he'd have them build another. And another.

"Dig, dig, dig," groaned Delk. He was standing waist-deep in a trench, his white cotton shirt smeared with dirt and mud. "Who is that there feller, anyway?"

Gramps chuckled. He pushed back his mud-flecked field cap and said, "Why, son, don't you know by now? That there feller's Robert E. Lee, the king of spades."

Delks looked confused. "King of *what?*"

"Spades," Gramps replied. "Every time he comes around, it's dig, dig, dig."

Private Delks spat a wad of tobacco against the trench wall. "Then I wish he wouldn't come around so much."

THAT NIGHT, a torrential rainstorm swept down from the hills, drenching the Virginia countryside. Swamps were flooded, and streams crested their banks. By dawn the fields and woods surrounding Seven Pines had been transformed into a murky, muddy domain. Tents and field equipment washed away. Small livestock penned in low-lying areas drowned. In some places men stood knee-deep in muck. Wagons bogged down up their axles and had to be abandoned. Artillery limbers got stuck, and extra teams had to be brought in to help pull them out of the mud.

In spite of the miserable weather, the main thing on the minds of the soggy men in gray as they turned in on the night of May 29 were the Yankees.

ON THE MORNING of his third day at Seven Pines, Wiley was awakened by the thumping roar of cannonfire, followed by the shrill blast of a regimental bugle. He was on his feet in a hurry, gearing up and scrambling to get into his boots.

Burrell Delk, who shared Wiley's tent, was on his feet in a flash. "Hey, sounds like this might be our lucky day," he announced.

"You gotta be dreaming," said Gramps, who rose slowly on the far side of the tent. "Those Yanks ain't about to start a fight in this kind of weather. They're too educated for that."

"I say, bring 'em on," Delk shot back. "The sooner we get to 'em, the sooner we get this whole thing over with and go back home."

Suddenly, there was a loud, piercing whine, and every man froze. Gramps yelled "incoming!" a split second before a tremendous explosion rocked the tent and sent the men crashing to the floor.

Moments later Second Lieutenant Joshua Walker, a lean, lanky Louisianian, stuck his head inside the tent and yelled, *"The enemy is at hand! Rally, boys, rally!"*

There was a crazed look on the young officer's powder-smeared face as he hovered in the smoke-filled doorway, dripping wet, his sword drawn and gleaming, his long, jet-black hair and mustache a tangled mess. A moment later he was gone, clomping back out into the pouring rain.

Wiley grabbed his musket, checked the weatherproofing of his cartridge pouch and followed the other men outside, where another officer was barking frantically at them to form up. In the downpour, nobody seemed to know what to do. There was confusion galore as mounted officers thundered about in the muck, waving swords and shouting orders. Wild-eyed soldiers scurried in all directions, seemingly lost and bewildered in all the commotion.

Somehow the men managed to find their respective companies. Shoving and pushing, they finally linked up in formation, and with that, some measure of order was restored.

The first order of business was roll call—not an easy task, considering the droning roar of rain and the incessant crackle of musketfire and boom of artillery in the near distance. Off to their right a couple of hundred yards away, several long lines of Confederate infantrymen were already moving into defensive positions between two tall farmhouses. Horse-drawn artillery batteries sloshed and clattered in all directions, while mounted officers frolicked about, brandishing swords and revolvers. High above it all fluttered the Stars & Bars, impressive even in the rain and drifting fog, as was the sea of multicolored regimental flags that rippled and cracked in the damp morning air.

It was a stirring sight, and Wiley was mesmerized by the flurry of so many men scampering about, the increasing babel of noise, the drifting clouds of gunsmoke that seemed to be everywhere at once, choking, clogging, burning eyes and nostrils.

"Looks like Delk's gonna get his wish after all," Gramps whispered to Wiley.

And then it happened—right in the middle of roll call, a split second after Delk had sounded off. Another shell, whistling, arcing high overhead, landed in the front ranks, right where Delk was standing. The impact blew the bushy-haired boy to bits. Wiley and half a dozen other boys were knocked to the ground. Incredibly, no one else was hurt.

Wiley got up slowly, coughing and gagging, the sound of the explosion still ringing in his ears. Then he looked down and saw Delk—or what was left of him, which wasn't much.

Groaning, other soldiers staggered to their feet. When they saw the remains of their comrade, several fell to their knees and heaved their insides out onto the rain-soaked ground.

It had happened so fast. Still dazed, Wiley stood staring at the scattered parts of human anatomy that had once been Delk. It didn't seem real. Only seconds ago the boy had been laughing and joking, anxious to get it on with the Yanks so that it would be over with and he could go back home. Now he was dead, not enough of him left to bury in a breadbox.

"Get back in your ranks!"

Wiley lifted his eyes and saw a mounted officer galloping in his direction, shouting and waving a sword at the befuddled men. The officer drew to within a few yards, then whirled around toward a top-heavy sergeant and snarled, "Sergeant…get a detail over here to take that dead boy away!"

The sergeant gave a smart salute and said, "Yes, sir!" He paused, then: "What about the others, sir?"

The officer's eyes found Wiley first, raking him over with their burning intensity, before scanning the other boys of Company A.

"They're fine," he snapped. "See that they get back in their proper ranks. The enemy will be approaching any minute!"

"Okay, you heard the major," the sergeant bawled. His name was Levi Veal. He was a big, sad-eyed fellow with a red, bristly beard cropped short on his round, leathered face. Wiley had met him back at Savannah, but couldn't remember where he came from. "Get back in formation and prepare to face the enemy!" Sergeant Veal roared.

The men of the 49th re-grouped quickly, then waited. And while they waited for the next command, it suddenly occurred to them that this was it, the real thing, not just some boring backwoods exercise. All those long weeks of practicing and drilling and marching now belonged in the past.

Like never before, each man suddenly became aware of his own mortality. Any minute now—any second, really—any one of them could die.

Just like Burrell Delk.

CHAPTER 14

DRUMBEATS, MUFFLED AND LOW, echoed somewhere far down the line. It was a sad, lonely sound, full of foreboding and deep, dark despair. In all his life, Wiley had never heard a more dreary, soul-numbing sound. He thought of old cemeteries and ancient bones rotting low in the earth. He thought of widows and mothers draped in black, teary-eyed children waiting at the door for fathers who would never come home.

Soon that infernal, steady cadence would follow the men into battle. For many, it would be the last sound on earth they heard.

Suddenly, a group of mounted officers materialized like phantoms out of the fog. Their faces were grim and smeared, their uniforms tattered and streaked with powder and mud. They halted in front of the 49th, directly opposite Wiley. One of the officers, a frail, stooped general wearing a red plaid shirt under a rain-blackened field jacket, trotted forward and dismounted. He had hollow eyes and pale cheeks that were sunken so far back he looked almost cadaverous.

"Gentlemen," the hollow-eyed general rasped. "We have just received word that General McClellan's Yankees are advancing just beyond that rise." He took off a yellow glove and pointed toward a thickly wooded area beyond the field. "Our orders are to form a line of assault and drive them back before they can gain that field."

Gramps leaned over and whispered in Wiley's ear. "Know who that is, boy? That's General Ambrose Hill, hisself. I hear tell his girlfriend ran off and married Little Mac. So, I figure he might have a score to settle with that two-timing Yankee rascal."

General Hill stared straight at the somber line of troops assembled before him, as if trying to read each man's mind. He was about to make another announcement when a shell, screeching down from the heavens, fell on top of an artillery caisson behind him and blasted it to splinters.

The explosion had been less than thirty yards away but didn't seem to faze the melancholy general.

He brushed himself off and resumed speaking as if nothing had happened, nothing at all. "When you go into battle, boys, I want you to remember your names!" he croaked, thumping his chest with his fist. "*Remember your names!*"

Without another word, he climbed back onto his horse and rode away.

———

"YOU READY, BOY?" Gramps asked Wiley.

Wiley swallowed hard. "As much as I'll ever be," he replied.

"Kinda spooky, ain't it?"

Wiley drew in a shuddering breath. "Kinda."

They were massed along the front line, a solid wall of gray snaking across a field on the outskirts of Seven Pines. Any second now the drums would roll again and the signal given to move forward.

In the meantime, every man watched and waited. Whether out of sheer nervousness and dread or old-fashioned discipline, they checked their weapons and equipment over and over, making sure that each piece was in place.

"Whatever happens, don't turn tail and run," Gramps reminded Wiley.

"Don't worry."

"You just stand your ground, and move forward when you're told to move forward. You'll be all right if you just keep your head down, and don't go trying to play the hero."

"Don't worry," Wiley repeated.

When the order finally came to form up, Wiley spotted a familiar face two ranks behind him. It was Petie Clanton, the fuzz-faced kid from back home. It was the first time he had seen him since Camp Davis.

He wanted to go over and say hello, but there wasn't time. The ranks were forming up, preparing to move out. Wiley offered up a secret prayer that, if nothing else, the boy had at least learned how to keep his head down.

———

WILEY HEARD THE CRACKLE OF MUSKETFIRE and clanging of canteens and swords and the thunder of many boots long before the Yankees finally emerged from the woods on the far side of the field. When he saw them, a solid wall of blue less than five hundred yards away, his first instinct was to drop his musket and run. How could any one army hope to stop such a charge? It wasn't possible. They would all die.

Then he thought of Martha Ann, how she would feel if she were to hear he had turned coward. He thought of his son not yet born. He thought of his mother and all the others back home—Reverend Thurmond, Mayor Futch, Sheriff Poindexter. What would they think if one of their own suddenly turned tail and ran?

He couldn't let them down. They were depending on him, him and the 49th. President Davis was depending on them. The Confederate States of America was depending on them. They had to hold. Had to drive the Yankees back and save Richmond. What was it General Hill had said?

Remember your names, boys…Remember your names!

Wiley suddenly understood what the general had meant.

Captain Player, riding high on a frisky bay, rode before Company A, urging his men forward. "Let's go, boys, let's go!" he screamed, waving his handsome, jewel-tipped sword. "For your homes…For your families…For the honor of Georgia…Forward!"

Player's words seemed to energize the entire line. Almost as one they surged forward, sweeping across the open field, an undulating wave of gray, yelling, screaming, firing at will. Wiley felt his fears gradually giving way as he rushed ahead, shoulder to shoulder with his comrades, their weapons drawn and cocked, boots thundering and sloshing across the grassy plain.

It was the most thrilling moment in Wiley's life. All around him men were screaming and yelling as they charged forward, some falling and dying, others plunging onward through the rain, gleaming weapons held high, banners fluttering high overhead. He felt himself surrounded by the deafening roar of cannonfire and the steady popping of muskets. Shells whistled and fell, whistled and fell, exploding like giant firecrackers amid the swarming Confederates. One by one and in massed groups the men fell, grabbing their chests, pitching face-forward into the mud. Every now and then Wiley came across a wounded comrade, but the momentum carried him past their pleading lips, beyond their outstretched hands and shell-blasted bodies. He couldn't stop, couldn't slow down, even to offer a drink of water from his canteen...

The living poured on ahead, bullets kicking up clumps of earth and grass all around them, shrieking, whining through the air, making thudding noises when some poor soldier's chest or head got in the way. Ten yards to his left, Wiley saw Sergeant Veal catch a bullet and go down, clutching his huge belly. The big man was dead even before he hit the ground, his guts spilling out onto the rain-soaked ground.

On the opposite side of the field came the Yankees, an equally determined foe, muskets leveled and clouded with gunsmoke, swords and bayonets flashing.

All of a sudden Wiley glimpsed Old Glory rising high over the dim, blue battle line, and a lump rose in his throat. The sight of the grand old flag left him more than a bit confused and dazed. The longer he stared at it, the more disoriented he became. It suddenly occurred to him that the flag he was charging was the same flag his daddy had fought for back in 1812, the same one his uncle had died for down in Florida.

Then he saw the flag dip, flutter to the ground, as the Yankee carrier fell. Wiley started, then felt a curious sense of relief when, an instant later, another solider snatched up the flag and continued the advance.

A moment later Captain Player was back at the head of A Company, leading the charge. "*Forward, boys, forward!*" he yelled over and over, his steely-gray eyes clouded with fury. "*For the glory of the Confederacy! For the glory of our homeland!*"

Wiley thought he had never seen a braver or more stirring sight. The young captain continued to gallop back and forth, oblivious to the hail of bullets raining down all around him, urging the men on.

"Rally, Georgians, rally!" he continued to rail. "Remember who you are...*You're the Wilkinson County Invincibles!*"

"Yahoo!" screamed Gramps, who actually seemed to be enjoying the savage charge.

A moment later the scruffy private cut loose with a shrill, blood-curdling yell that seemed to well up from some deep abyss in his soul. The yell echoed up and down the Rebel line, an unnatural, shrieking fury, until it finally caught on. Soon every man in the ranks was imitating that same ear-piercing scream as they swept up the sloping hillside toward the enemy.

"That's it! That's it!" Captain Player shouted, delighted at the frenzied state of mind the mesmerizing yell produced in his men. "Keep it up...We'll have them on the run in no time..."

Wiley felt something tug at his leg. He looked down and saw a skinny, bone-white hand clamped around his ankle. He tried to shake free, but stopped when he recognized the boyish face staring up at him.

"Help me...please," Petie Clanton begged.

When Wiley saw the gaping hole in Petie's stomach, his guts twisted and splayed grotesquely in the mud, he almost screamed out. *Oh, God, no, not little Petie...*

"Can you help me, Mister Wiley?" Petie asked, his eyes blank and bloody and brimming with tears. "Please?"

Wiley glanced around for help. When he saw no medic, he bent down beside the boy and started loosening his collar.

"Water," the boy pleaded. "Please...water."

Wiley unscrewed his canteen, tilted the boy's head back and poured. The cool liquid poured past the boy's cracked and bloodied lips, streaming down toward the fires that blazed in his belly.

"T-Thanks," Petie said weakly. He licked his lips thirstily. Then: "Am I gonna die, Mister Wiley?"

Wiley blinked back a sudden rush of tears. *Of course, you're not gonna die,* Wiley heard himself screaming inside his head. *You're only fourteen years old, boy, the same age as my kid brother. There's no way I'm gonna let you die...*

Stroking the boy's forehead, he said, "No, Petie, you're gonna be just fine."

Petie smiled, tried to rise. "It hurts, Mister Wiley, it hurts real bad..."

A wave of nausea washed over Wiley when he looked down at the horrible belly wound and realized there was nothing he could do. He cradled the boy's head and rocked him slowly. "I know it hurts, Petie," he said comfortingly. "I know. Just try to hang on until we can get you some help."

He looked up and scanned the field for a medic. "Will somebody help me, please?" he yelled. "I need help over here!"

The boy coughed. It was a deep, ragged cough that brought up blood and bits of tissue. Then Petie's hands were on Wiley again as he strained to pull himself up. "Will you tell my pa, Mister Wiley? Will you tell him that you saw me...that you were with me?"

Wiley bit his lip to keep from crying. "I'll tell him," he nodded.

The boy leaned back in Wiley's arms and smiled. It was the sweetest smile Wiley had ever seen.

A shell whistled high overhead and exploded somewhere nearby. Wiley didn't flinch. He couldn't take his eyes off the brave little boy from his hometown who had answered the call to serve his country. Wiley closed his eyes, willing the boy to get better, but knowing in his heart there was no hope.

Another cough. More blood and ragged bits of tissue belched up from the boy's mangled guts.

"I'll tell him how brave you were," Wiley said, tears streaming down his own cheeks. "I'll tell him how you charged straight at those Yankees and ran them like rip."

"Thanks," Petie said, eyes glazing.

The smile was still on the boy's lips when he died.

———

THE BATTLE CONTINUED TO RAGE until late in the afternoon. Then an amazing thing happened: The Yankee lines slowly started falling back.

It happened shortly after the two lines had drawn to within fifty yards of each other. For almost an hour each army had stood its ground, firing point-blank into the opposing ranks. The firing had been so hot and heavy that the barrels of some muskets actually melted in the hands of soldiers on both sides.

About dusk, Yankee units started slowly withdrawing. Soon they were marching in full retreat from the field of battle. Amid a flurry of drumbeats and bugle calls, they quietly gathered up their dead and wounded and fallen banners and started trudging back into the dark woods from which they had emerged that morning.

The Confederates were stunned. For several moments nobody could believe what was happening. Some front line officers thought it might be a ploy, a trick of some kind, so they ordered their men to maintain their positions.

"Steady, boys," Captain Player shouted warily. "Hold your positions…"

When it became clear that it was not a trick, that the Yankees were actually on the run, the air was split by the deafening roar of jubilant rebels. They threw hats into the air and cheered so loud and long their throats felt like they were on fire. Bleeding, mud-caked soldiers embraced one another and danced around, some falling and rolling around in the mud like happy hogs.

The battle was over. The Confederate army, outnumbered and outgunned more than two to one, had stood firm in the face of the fiercest, bloodiest Yankee assault to date. The South had another much-needed victory.

More than that, Richmond had been spared.

Only later did Wiley and the men of the 49th learn of another fateful consequence of the great battle of Seven Pines: General Johnston had been wounded and taken from the field of battle. Robert E. Lee, the "king of spades," was now in command of what would soon become known as the Army of Northern Virginia.

CHAPTER 15

GARRETT NESMITH HEARD THE SOUND of approaching hoofbeats long before the rider galloped into view. He closed the barn door, dropped the slat and headed across the lot toward the house.

He reached the front gate just as Zeke Taylor, the mail carrier, rode up.

Zeke waited for the dust to clear, then groused, "Where is she, boy?" Zeke was a big, bearded man with broad, slab-like shoulders and long, muscular legs that dangled around the horse like a pair of logs. Above his right eye was a jagged scar—the result of an old knife fight. Besides being the mail carrier, Zeke was also captain of the local Security Council. The Security Council's job was to keep tabs on the colored community, slave and free. If any blacks got out of line, the Security Council was authorized by the state legislature to deal with them as it saw fit. Punishment was usually swift and severe. "Run get her. I ain't got all day here, you know."

Garrett reached up to take the letter. "Then give it to me," he snapped. "I'll see that she gets it."

Zeke yanked the letter back out of reach. "Not so fast there, boy. I said it's for her. Personal." He glowered menacingly at the boy. "Now, you go fetch her—now."

Garrett glared back at the big man. He didn't like Zeke Taylor. Nobody did. Zeke Taylor was a bully and a brute, and he drank too much. And Garrett knew he didn't ride all the way out here just to bring Martha Ann a letter.

He was just about to tell Zeke to get off his brother's property when Martha Ann stepped out onto the porch. "Who is it, Garrett?" she called out, shielding her eyes in the bright afternoon sunlight.

When she saw Zeke, her heart sank. Oh, well, she thought, might as well get this over with. She wiped her hands on her apron and walked slowly across the yard toward them.

When she reached the gate, Zeke grinned. "Why, howdy, Miz Martha Ann; ain't you a right regular sight for sore eyes?"

"Hello, Zeke," Martha Ann said as politely as she could allow herself. "What brings you out this way?"

Zeke shifted his gaze down to Garrett. "Boy," he said sternly, "ain't you got something else to do?"

"No," Garrett shot back contemptuously.

Zeke's face contorted with anger. "Well, why don't you go find something?" he snarled, fingering the scar over his eye. "Can't you see I need to talk to Miz Martha Ann in private?"

Garrett tensed. He wanted nothing more than to drag the big man down out of the saddle and put a good licking on him. But that would be a stupid thing to try to do. Zeke would kill him, and Garrett knew it. So, instead of challenging him, Garrett looked across at Martha Ann, as if waiting for her to tell him what to do.

"It's okay, Garrett," Martha Ann said, nodding curtly. "I'll be all right."

Garrett gave Zeke one final, defiant glare, then huffed back toward the barn.

When Garrett was gone, Martha Ann looked at Zeke and asked, "What do you want, Zeke?"

Zeke dismounted and took a step toward her. "Here," he said, waving the letter in his hand, "I've got something for you."

When she reached for the letter, Zeke grabbed her wrist. "Not so fast," he teased, yanking her toward him.

"Zeke! Let go, you're hurting me!"

Zeke relaxed his grip, then turned her loose. "Sorry," he said, raising both hands in mock apology. "I don't know what came over me, Martha Ann."

Rubbing her wrist, Martha Ann said, "Just give me the letter and go. I'll pretend this never happened."

Zeke ran his eyes up and down her body. "You know, I was thinking. It must git awful lonely out here at times, what with Wiley gone so long and all."

Martha Ann drew in a faltering breath. "Zeke...I think you'd better go now..."

"I mean, a beautiful young woman like you, way out here all by herself. It just ain't right. Know what I mean?" He lowered his eyes until they fastened on the bulge in Martha Ann's abdomen. He licked his lips. "Little old seed like that sprouting up inside must create a powerful craving..."

From the barnyard, Martha Ann heard footsteps approaching. She and Zeke turned at the same time and saw Garrett and Indigo striding across the lot toward them. Garrett was carrying an axe. Indigo clutched a pitchfork.

"I think you better go now," Martha Ann warned.

Zeke pushed back his hat and grinned at the two boys. "Well, well, well. What is this?" His gaze fixed on Indigo. "Some kind of nigger rebellion? I might have to speak to the Council about this."

Indigo felt every muscle in his body tighten. He raised the pitchfork slightly, and when he did, Zeke backed slowly toward his horse. "Easy, there boy, easy," he chuckled. "I didn't mean no harm. Just funnin' around, that's all."

He climbed back on his horse and looked down at them. "See? I'm leaving. No harm done."

From the saddle he threw the letter down at Martha Ann's feet. His lips twisted into a cruel grin. "Better take your time reading it, little mamma. I suspect it'll be the last one you see from your husband for a long, long time."

Zeke kicked the horse and galloped away.

"Are you all right, Martha Ann?" Garrett asked.

"Yes, fine, thank you," she said, relieved, but still shaken. "Thank you both."

Indigo said, "That Mister Zeke, he's one m-mean customer. That's what my pa says."

"Your pa's right," Martha Ann replied, still rubbing her aching wrist.

"I'M GLAD YOU CAME and g-got me, Garrett, c-cause there's s-something important I've b-been meaning to tell you."

Garrett and Indigo were sitting on a bale of hay inside the crib, shucking corn and tossing the dried ears down into the horse's trough. They had been there more than an hour, reliving the incident with Zeke, each bragging to the other about what he would have done had the big man not backed down.

"What is it?" Garrett asked, reaching for another ear of corn.

Indigo put down the two ears of corn he was holding and turned to face his friend. "Rem-member what I said to you about the c-cavalry?" he asked. "About j-joining up?"

"I remember," Garrett replied.

"Well...just between you and m-me, I'm g-gonna do it."

"Do what?" Garrett asked dumbly.

"Join up, t-that's what. I'm gonna j-join the Yankee c-cavalry."

Garrett faced Indigo in surprise. "The Yankee cavalry?" he asked incredulously.

Indigo nodded. "Gonna get me a p-pair of them fine f-fancy boots and spurs and a long s-sword with my name c-carved right there on the handle. Best of all, I'm g-gonna get my own horse. A big, strong c-chestnut g-gelding with a b-black blaze."

Garrett stared hard at Indigo, trying to figure him out. "How? How do you think you're gonna do all that, Indigo?"

"There's a way," Indigo started to explain. "It's c-called the Underground Railroad. It's g-gonna take me to f-freedom first, up North somewhere. And when I g-get there, I'm gonna join up with a c-cavalry unit. Maybe even one of Sheridan's. You ever h-hear of General Sheridan, Garrett?"

"Of course I've heard of General Sheridan," Garrett answered. He ran his fingers through his blond hair, then said, "Indigo, how many times do I have to tell you...you're already free."

Indigo shook his head. "Ain't the s-same thing," he replied. "If I go up North and join the c-cavalry, then I'll be really f-free. Can't no man ever call me n-nigger again."

Garrett reached for another ear of corn, shucked it clean and tossed it down into the trough. "I don't know," he said, shaking his head. "It sounds kind of dangerous to me. What exactly is this Underground Railroad anyway? I mean, where does it run? I ain't never heard of such a thing, myself."

Indigo laughed. "It ain't a real railroad," he explained. "It's just a b-bunch of places—s-secret places—where slaves can go and get help if they w-want to be f-free. There's one not f-far from here, in fact. Over near Augusta. That's where I'm p-planning to go."

"How do you know all this?"

Indigo put his hand on Garrett's shoulder and said, "I'll t-tell you, Garrett, cause I trust you. But you have to p-promise never to tell a soul. Never."

"I promise."

"If you b-break that p-promise, it could hurt a lot of innocent p-people. Maybe even get some k-killed."

"I said I promise, didn't I?"

Indigo drew in a deep breath and held it for a moment, as if he were about to reveal the meaning of life and death. In a hushed, wary tone, he said, "In town, there's a p-place where a lot of my p-people—you know, black folks—go to talk about things."

Garrett knew about the place. So did everybody else. The Meeting Place was an old warehouse at the edge of town where blacks liked to gather to socialize, mostly on Saturday nights. What did The Meeting Place have to do with Indigo's Underground Railroad?

"The Meeting Place," Garrett shrugged. "Big deal. I know all about it already. Everybody does."

"Yeah, The Meeting Place. Well, a c-couple of months back, a sp-pecial visitor came and told us about the Underground Railroad. S-She said she'd help anybody who wanted to go up North. And s-she'd do it for f-free."

"She? You mean a woman's doing all this?"

Indigo nodded. "Her name is Harriet T-Tubman. Used to be a slave herself. Then one day s-she escaped from her owner up in Maryland and helped f-form the Underground Railroad. She's b-been helping others escape ever s-since."

Garrett didn't say anything for several seconds. Then: "So, when are you planning on leaving?"

"Soon. Miz T-Tubman's supposed to c-come back and tell us

what to do. Right now, I r-reckon she's off s-setting it up for us s-so we can go when she gets back."

"What about your folks, Indigo? Do they know about this? What do *they* think?"

A sad look came into Indigo's eyes. "That's the hardest p-part. They want me to go, so I can be f-free. But, at the s-same time, they're k-kind of afraid." His eyes suddenly focused brightly. "But when I f-finish with the c-cavalry, I plan to go to school somewhere up North, g-get a job and s-send for them."

Garrett thought that over for a moment, then said, "I'm happy for you, Indigo—that is, if you really want to go. It sounds like a real good plan." He hesitated. "You know I'm planning on joining the cavalry, too?"

Indigo nodded enthusiastically. "Yeah. Imagine that," he said. "B-Both of us in the c-cavalry. Maybe we can meet up with one another s-sometime. Wouldn't that be s-something?"

"I doubt it," Garrett said softly.

Indigo looked confused. "Why not?"

"Think about it," Garrett said. "You'll be wearing blue. I'll be wearing gray."

———

MARTHA ANN WAS STILL SHAKING when she sat down to read Wiley's letter. As she tore open the envelope, she couldn't help wondering what she would have done had Garrett and Indigo not been there to chase Zeke off.

The letter, written in pencil, was only one page long. It was dated June 2, 1862:

Seven Pines, Virginia
In Line of Battle

My darling wife,
I wanted to write sooner to let you know I arrived safe and sound in Virginia after a stopover in North Carolina. The train ride was no thrill, but it was better than marching up here on foot, I reckon.
We are at a little place outside Richmond called Seven Pines. The

countryside is pretty, but it has rained every day since we've been here.

Yesterday we had our first big fight. The Yankees came charging at us out of the woods like a bunch of screaming banshees. I'm proud to say we held our own, and soon had them on the run. A lot of boys fell on both sides. We lost our share, but nobody you'd know except for Old Bart Clanton's boy, Petie. I was with him when he died. I plan on writing a letter to his pa as soon as I can find the time.

It isn't easy watching a man die. It's something that stays with you a long time, never turns you loose, even when you're trying to sleep. I keep seeing Petie's face in my dreams, the pain in his eyes, the tears rolling down his cheeks. He might have been only a boy, but one thing I can truly say is he died like a man.

I thank God that he saw fit to take care of me in battle yesterday. I ask you to say a prayer for me—for all of us—that we may stand firm and do our duty and not break and run when next we meet up with the enemy.

I also hope and pray that you are doing fine and that Garrett is coming over and helping you around the house like he's supposed to.

I keep thinking about the little one, too, and what it'll be like to have my own son. I've thought of several names, but we'll go over them when I come home. I don't know when that will be because they need all of us here on the front lines to protect Richmond from the Yankees.

I will write again as soon as we chase McClellan and the rest of the blue-bellies back to Washington.

Your loving husband,

Wiley

CHAPTER 16

H AMILTON D EWBERRY LEANED BACK in his swivel rocker and fanned himself with an old magazine. The August heat was stifling. A slight breeze wafted in through the open window behind his desk, but it was hot and sticky and only made things worse.

Any other night he'd lock up the office and go outside on the porch or maybe take a walk to cool off.

But not tonight.

Tonight was production night, the night he and Rufus, his young black assistant, put the paper out. It was a ritual they repeated every Wednesday night. They'd lock themselves inside the office of the *Independent* where they'd stay until the newspaper was printed and bound and ready to hit the streets. That usually meant all night. Then, with the first crack of dawn, the two of them would hurry out the door with fresh bundles of newspapers under their arms to begin the distribution process.

When that was done, they'd slump back to the office to start the cycle all over again.

That was the trouble with the newspaper business, Dewberry thought wistfully as he stared out his window into the dark night. It never ended. There was always some story to cover and write up, plates to be made for the artwork, ads to be solicited and bills to be paid. It was a never-ending process that made a young man old in a hurry. Why anyone would want to go into the newspaper business in the first place was beyond Dewberry.

Now what kind of question was that, he asked himself as he gazed across his cluttered office. He smiled as he scanned the dozens of framed mementos, engravings and awards that covered his desk and walls—relics of a long and illustrious journalism career that spanned more than six decades. Newspapering was the only life Hamilton Dewberry had ever really known. As the son of a successful newspaper publisher from Charleston, Dewberry had learned the ropes at a very early age. He had written, edited, sold advertising space and distributed copies of the newspaper on Charleston street corners. He was as much at home in the back shop where the newspaper was set in type and printed as he was in the front office where the big stories were written and the great decisions made.

On his sixteenth birthday, his father had made him vice-president of the company.

"Son," his father had told him on the day of his big promotion. "It is just as I feared—you have more ink in that body of yours than Dewberry blood."

After graduating from college—Yale, class of 1810—Dewberry worked for several large newspapers "up North," earning a good living and a national reputation as a crusading reporter and editor. In the late 1820s he traveled throughout Europe, covering the bloody post-Napoleanic revolutions as a correspondent for his father's paper as well as several national publications.

When his father died of a stroke in 1838, Dewberry, then in his late thirties and still a bachelor, went back home to Charleston to take over the family business. It was an exciting time to be in the newspaper business, what with westward expansion, the Indian problem and "Manifest Destiny" all the rage. Within months the enterprising young publisher had tripled his newspaper's circulation by capitalizing on the great news events of the day—the relocation of the Indians out West, the Seminole wars down in Florida, the Texas annexation dispute, the coming war with Mexico and, of course, the growing sectional crisis.

A decade after taking over the helm, Dewberry sold the paper for a handsome profit and went on the road again as a correspondent. He followed the troops to Mexico, where he was wounded twice and captured by Santa Anna's forces on one occasion. The worst part of his ordeal came after his rescue by American soldiers. General Winfield S. Scott, the American commander of the

Mexican Campaign, charged Dewberry with violating the news blackout and threw him in jail. While incarcerated, he came down with scurvy and would have died in that rotting black hell had the war lasted another month.

At a newspaper convention in Savannah in 1852, the much-traveled journalist met Delbert Anderson, the aging owner of the *Irwinton Independent*, the small but official news organ of Wilkinson County. One night over drinks, Anderson talked Dewberry into buying the *Independent*. The paper was losing money, Anderson said, and needed Dewberry's golden touch to bring it back around.

A month later, Dewberry—now in his mid-fifties and still a bachelor—found himself the proud new owner of one of the smallest but most progressive weeklies in Georgia. He set to work right away building up the paper's circulation and advertising base using some of the same methods he had used at his father's paper. Especially popular was a new front-page opinion section called Opposing Viewpoints. Here some of the greatest minds of the day debated politics, art and popular culture. A frequent contributor was William Lloyd Garrison, the fiery abolitionist from Massachusetts, who happened to be an old friend and fellow journalist and newspaper editor. Another was Edward A. Pollard, the noted Virginia journalist and historian who favored the extension of the slavery system into Central and South America. Hotheads and radicals from all quarters took advantage of the *Independent* to spew their flaming rhetoric. In the process, the newspaper's circulation soared.

So did profits.

In time, Dewberry had been able to hire an assistant, a twenty-five-year-old free black named Rufus Tyler. Tyler was a natural. He caught on to the newspaper business in a flash, starting in the back shop running the press, then quickly working his way up to writing and editing copy.

But this was still the Deep South, so Dewberry wisely refrained from allowing his apprentice to sign his name to articles.

"Are you sure you want to run this?" Rufus Tyler asked.

Dewberry looked up and saw his apprentice standing in the doorway. His shirt sleeves were rolled up past the elbows, and he wore a green visor over his clean-shaven head. In his hands, still dripping wet with black ink, was the front-page galley proof.

Dewberry, still fanning, waved him inside his office.

"Let's have a look," he said, putting down his fan and lighting up a fat cigar. He scanned the page proof, muttering to himself as he carefully appraised every word, every line of the article.

When he got to the end, he said, "I don't see anything wrong. Print it."

"But, Mr. Dewberry," Rufus persisted, "Don't you think this is a little—shall we say—inflammatory, even by George Bickley's standards?"

George Bickley was the highly imaginative Virginia writer and founder of the Knights of the Golden Circle. The Circle's goal was to promote a "golden circle" of slave states from the American South through Mexico and Central America to the rim of South America.

Dewberry personally detested Bickley and his crack-brained scheme, but occasionally bought articles from him because a number of his subscribers enjoyed reading his work. The price of doing business, he kept reminding himself every time he set Bickley's name in type.

"This stuff sells newspapers," Dewberry explained.

Rufus rolled his eyes and sighed. "You're the boss," he said, but it was clear his heart wasn't in it.

Dewberry followed his apprentice into the shop where the rest of the page was being set up. When the last story and headline was in place, Dewberry looked at the clock and said, "Why don't you run on home, Rufus? I can take it from here."

"Are you sure? I can stay a little longer if you like."

Dewberry yawned. It was already past two o'clock. They'd been at work since late that afternoon getting the paper ready for the press.

"No," he said. "You run along home to that little wife." He patted Rufus on the back and winked. "I'm sure she's still up waiting on you."

The black man's face twisted in an embarrassed grin. "Yes, sir, Mr. Dewberry." He reached for his coat. "You're the boss."

When he reached the front door, he turned and said, "See you at six."

"That's six sharp," Dewberry corrected him. "We've got a lot of papers to distribute in the morning." After a brief hesitation, he smiled and said, "Thank God for that."

After Rufus had gone, Dewberry walked over to his desk, pulled the shades and sat down. He opened the bottom drawer, pulled out a bottle of whiskey and poured some into a coffee cup. He downed the whiskey in a single gulp, filled the cup again and downed that one, too. Sighing, he wiped his mouth and put the bottle back. Then he reached for a pad and started to write what would be the lead editorial in the next edition. The headline was "A Prayer For Sanity in an Age of Madness."

A few minutes into the piece he was interrupted by the sound of shattering glass. He looked up, listening. It sounded as if it had come from the back room.

Still clutching his pen, he got up slowly and walked into the back room. He looked around, searching for the source of the noise. When he felt a draft, he noticed that the back door was standing wide open.

Now, how did that happen? he wondered. Maybe Rufus had come back for something. "Rufus?" he called out. "Is that you?"

On the far side of the room, a pair of shadows moved. Dewberry reached for the lantern, but before he could light it up, two men entered through the back door and stared at him.

"Who are you?" Dewberry asked, squinting to make out the forms in the darkness. "What are you doing here?"

Behind him, several pairs of strong arms seized him by the shoulders and threw him to the floor. He screamed as he fell, lashing out with his fists, but to no avail. Suddenly, another man was on top of him, hog-tying his hands and feet.

When it was done, the pair of masked intruders standing in the doorway stepped into the room and shut the door behind them. In the dark, one said, "This is what we do to Yankee-loving abolitionists."

Dewberry's anger quickly gave way to fear as he watched the masked men clomp closer toward him. "Help!" he croaked, but he knew no one would hear him at this time of night. "Help!"

The last thing the elderly publisher saw, before a heavy fist crashed hard against his nose, shattering the bone, was a jagged scar just above the right eye of the masked man who slugged him.

Rufus Tyler lived near the railroad tracks on the other side of town. He was halfway home, when he remembered he'd left his hat back at the office. It was his best hat, the one Mabel, his wife, had given him last Christmas. If he went home without that hat, there'd be big trouble.

He turned around and headed back down the shadowed street toward the newspaper office.

"Hurry," said a low, muffled voice. "We ain't got all night."

"Relax, would you?" Zeke Taylor groused. "We've got to do this right, so that the other traitors in this town will get the message once and for all."

They worked quickly, going from room to room dousing the furniture and walls with kerosene.

When the kerosene can was empty, Zeke grinned and said, "Let's do it."

"What about him?" one of the other men asked, nodding toward the unconscious publisher.

"Leave him be."

The intruders opened the back door and hurried outside. The last man to leave was Zeke. Before closing the door behind him, he struck a match, lit a wad of paper and tossed it into the room.

Within seconds the whole back room was engulfed in a solid sheet of flames.

"Oh, my God," Rufus said when he saw the flames shooting out the back of the newspaper office.

He started in the direction of the fire station, but thought of Mr. Dewberry and ran toward the newspaper office instead. The single thought that kept going through his head as he sprinted down the dark street was that his employer must have fallen somehow, hit his head and, in the process, knocked over a lantern. How else could the fire have started?

The second he reached the front door, he realized he didn't have a key. Without hesitating he kicked the door open and raced inside.

Thick puffs of bluish-black smoke rolled out of the back shop where Rufus had last seen Mr. Dewberry. He could hear flames crackling back there, see their flickering glow through the shadowed doorway.

Fighting the smoke and heat, Rufus darted into the back room and saw the unconscious form of his boss lying on the floor.

"Mr. Dewberry!" he shouted.

He bent down, grabbed the publisher by the arms and dragged him back into the front office. A split second later an overhead beam crashed to the floor, pulverizing a desk and scattering bright red sparks and clouds of smoke everywhere.

By now the fire had spread into the front area as well. Soon the whole building would be a roaring inferno. Rufus had to get the injured publisher outside in a hurry. He hoped it wasn't too late already.

He hoisted the old man onto his shoulders, fireman style, and dragged him toward the gaping doorway. He paused long enough to snatch up a couple of type-set galleys, then pushed open the door and staggered outside.

They barely had time to reach the sidewalk when the roof crashed in with a resounding bang. Sparks and cinders shot up into the night sky. For one awful moment, Rufus thought they were going to spread to other buildings and catch fire.

Suddenly, the old fire bell on the courthouse square was clanging away. Then Rufus heard a stampede of feet heading his way.

"What's going on?" someone shouted.

"My, God," screamed a woman in her nightgown and cap. "It's the newspaper—the whole thing's burning up!"

Not everything, Rufus thought, still clutching the scorched but undamaged page galleys.

CHAPTER 17

SOLDIER LIVES TO KILL. From the moment he puts on a uniform and swears allegiance to his country or cause, there remains but one universal truth, one fundamental purpose for his being, and that is to kill and kill again.

Or, as Sergeant Kramer used to say back at Camp Davis, "A soldier's job ist to attack und destroy zee enemy before he, himzelf, ist destroyed."

The German drill sergeant's words were very much on Wiley's mind that hot, rainy morning in mid-June as he and his battle-scarred comrades trudged through the gathering gloom.

He could almost hear Kramer's thick, heavy accent, the colorful way he called cadence and bellowed advice to the green recruits from Georgia.

"Men live und die on zee battlefield according to zheir own villingness und ability to follow vun simple rule: kill oder be killed. A good soldier vill go anyvhere, do anyzing, follow any order to accomplish his mission, vhich is to kill. He ist prepared to svallow all pride, bear any burden, endure any hardship—even, should it become necessary, to lay down his own life so zat his mission might succeed. Anyzing less vould be unzinkable."

But Seven Pines had taught Wiley another valuable lesson: When the moment of truth finally comes and a soldier stands face to face with his own mortality, sometimes even the bravest, most stout-hearted warrior among them will forget pride and causes and cry out for his mother.

Wiley wondered how many of his comrades would stand and fight this day—and how many would cry out for their mothers as they ran screaming toward the rear.

Until Seven Pines, Wiley had never seen a man die. Burrell Delk, the skinny little loud-mouth from Carolina, had been the first. There had been others, many others, including little Petie Clanton and Sergeant Veal, before the Yankees cut and ran. Even Gramps had taken a ball in the leg and had to be evacuated to Richmond. The last thing Wiley heard before moving out after the fight was that Gramps' leg had to be amputated.

Horrid images of the battle still lingered in Wiley's mind: broken wagons; the screams of wounded and dying men; mutilated bodies ripped and shredded and lying face-up in the mud and rain; blank-faced officers rushing about, ordering stragglers and scattered units to re-group and press the attack; mangled survivors begging to be shot so they could be put out of their painful misery.

Of all the horrors he had witnessed at Seven Pines, the one that stood out was of Burrell Delk standing in line, laughing, cracking jokes about the Yankees, perfectly oblivious to the fact that death was only a few short seconds away. Wiley flinched as he recalled the piercing whine of the incoming artillery shell, how it whistled and shrieked and roared seconds before landing and blowing the boy's smiling face and youthful body into oblivion.

If he lived to be a hundred, Wiley would never forget the endless rattle of musketry that greeted the boys from Georgia their first day at Seven Pines. Nor would he soon forget the booming cannon, the frantic chorus of high-pitched yells by the infantrymen, the clouds of white smoke wafting over the long lines of advancing men in blue. Only a madman could ever wipe that grim spectacle from his mind and get on with his life.

When they had seen the Yanks retreating from the battlefield, some of the boys had mistakenly thought the war was over. Some cheered and hooted and danced around in each other's arms, delirious with the joy of victory and the sweet awareness they would soon go home. Ironically, others were disappointed that it had ended so suddenly. For them, disappointment turned to jubilation, however, when word came down the lines that they were re-forming for another strike at McClellan's right flank, which was rumored to be positioned just north of Chickahominy Creek a few miles northeast of Richmond.

For the most part, the men were in good spirits as they clomped forward through the mud and drifting fog. Many were eager to get at the Yankees again. This time, God willing, the boys in gray would teach the invaders a lesson they wouldn't soon forget—even if it meant marching all the way to Washington to catch up with their ornery hides.

THE REBS CROSSED the rain-swollen Chickahominy without opposition. By early afternoon they had reached the outskirts of Mechanicsville, a gloomy crossroads community of tumble-down shacks and log stores fifteen miles north of Richmond. After a short break, they were on the march again, this time heading straight toward their target—the Union right flank—which was strung out along a swampy region east of Mechanicsville known as Beaver Dam Creek.

Weariness had caught up with many of the troops. They had been marching since sunup, pausing here and there only long enough to grab a quick bite or to re-shoe a mount before pushing on. Now they were tired. Bone-tired. So tired that many of them dragged their guns behind them, indifferent to the mud and clay clogging up the firing mechanisms.

Few spoke as they staggered along, as if under a spell, three long lines of graybacks, drawn forward as if by some mystical force.

The woods grew increasingly thick and wet and wild the closer they got to the swamp. An uncommonly cool breeze blew in from the dark trees, chilling Wiley to the core. He could feel the tension, thick as an Augusta cotton patch, as they angled cautiously toward the woods. Strained, shadowy eyes peered warily from beneath the black, gleaming bills of field caps. Canteens rattled and banged. Horses and mules pawed and snorted and champed at their bridles. Long, curving sabers clattered at the sides of mounted officers. Wagon wheels creaked and groaned and squished through the ever-present mud.

Behind them came the sound of drumbeats, hollow and low, an eerie, muffled thudding, that seemed strangely out of place amid these otherwise tranquil, mist-choked hills.

Somewhere back in the ranks a young soldier was crying.

WILEY WAS IN A WORLD OF PAIN. His feet, blistered and cramped, ached so badly he felt he was going to pass out any second. But the biggest problem was his back. The stress in his shoulders was excruciating. He shifted the weight of his haversack, trying to find relief that way. But all it did was redistribute the pain. With his left hand he stroked the smooth walnut stock of his father's old musket. The familiarity of the piece gave him an odd sense of comfort, a fleeting connection with the innocent world he had left far behind.

"They say the Yankees are on the other side of that swamp," someone behind him muttered.

Wiley craned his head around and recognized the man. He couldn't remember his full name, but around camp he was known as Talmadge.

Talmadge was a remarkably big fellow from Alabama, well over six feet tall, with bushy black eyebrows and a luxuriously tangled beard the color of swamp water. His neck was thick and powerful, and the way it bulged out over his frayed collar reminded Wiley of a prize Brahman bull getting set to charge.

"I thought I smelled buzzard meat," cracked another private, one they called Buster. Buster, from somewhere near Atlanta, was a tiny spit of a man with a knobby head that bobbed up and down above his thick, brown blanket roll.

A third soldier, a snaggle-toothed private from Augusta named Smalley, spoke up: "I hear they got some of them fancy new repeating rifles."

"They're gonna need a lot more than that when I get my hands on 'em this time," Talmadge snorted.

The big man let go a wad of chewing tobacco thick enough to choke a fair-sized mule.

"Ain't that the truth," Buster chuckled. Only it was more like a wheeze than a chuckle. "I can't wait to get another one of them blue-bellies square in my sights."

Talmadge caught Wiley staring back at him and snarled, "What about you, boy? You ready to bag yourself another Yank?"

Wiley shrugged and said, "Not particularly." Even before he turned away, Wiley knew he had said the wrong thing.

"Now what in tarnation's that supposed to mean, huh, boy?" Talmadge growled back. "Ain't you itchin' to get at them Yanks like the rest of us?"

Wiley shrugged. "Maybe tomorrow. Right now all I want is a good night's sleep."

It was Buster who spoke up next. He cranked his head around and stared at Wiley. "Hey," he asked in a curious, almost threatening tone, "you ain't one of them queer fellers that high-tails it soon's the shooting commences, are you?"

Wiley let the question hang for a moment, then said, "I don't think so."

He was beginning to seriously wonder where their conversation was headed when he felt Talmadge's big hand drop like an iron weight on his shoulder.

"I don't like your attitude," the big man said, spinning Wiley around. "I think I'll just have to teach you a little lesson about proper army attitude."

Word spread quickly through the ranks that a fight was about to break out. In the time it took Wiley and Talmadge to shed their gear and roll up their sleeves, dozens of soldiers had gathered around them, eager to see a tussle. Now they were completely surrounded by their fellow warriors, who were recklessly urging them on, punching each other, laughing and cracking jokes as they waited for the fireworks to begin.

Wiley knew he didn't stand much of a chance against a man the size of Talmadge. The best he could hope for was that he would last long enough until some officer came along to break it up. Whatever happened, he couldn't back down. He'd be the laughing stock of the company if he did that, the company goat, probably for the rest of the war.

"Come on, Tal, show him what we do to shirkers," Buster screeched.

"Yeah," shouted Smalley. "We don't want no cowards marching with us, do we boys?"

The other soldiers roared their agreement.

Wiley thought: *This is madness—fighting among ourselves with the woods full of Yankees less than a mile away.*

Bracing himself, he fixed his eyes on Talmadge and said: "Okay, big man, what I want to know is, where were you when the rest of us were charging up the hill back at Seven Pines? I was there, right on the front lines. Shot myself half a dozen blue-bellies, too. Funny thing is, I don't remember seeing you there. I guess you must have had business at the rear."

A dark fury seemed to seize Talmadge. His eyes narrowed. His nostrils flared, and the veins in his thick neck stood out like blue ropes. The bull was about to charge.

Wiley saw the big fist coming and ducked. It went sailing harmlessly past his head.

The second time Wiley wasn't so lucky. The big man faked a left jab, then sank his right fist dead-center in Wiley's gut. Wiley staggered backward, gasping for air. Before he could catch his breath, another solid blow caught him square in the chin. The impact was so great Wiley felt the bones in his knees buckle as he cartwheeled to the ground.

The pain was instantaneous and immense. He lay there in the mud for several seconds, groaning and holding his stomach, then Talmadge's mountainous form was straddling him, both fists cocked and clenched like twin hammers.

"Had enough, Georgia boy?" he challenged. "Or do you want some more?"

Wiley hurt too much to answer. His chin—his entire jawbone—felt as if it had just been kicked by a mule.

He lifted his head and slowly rubbed his throbbing chin. A thin trail of blood trickled down from the corner of his mouth. Where had that come from? he wondered, dabbing at the blood with his finger.

He rose to his knees and coughed. "Is that all you can do?" he wheezed.

Growling, Talmadge reached down, grabbed Wiley by the collar and yanked him to his feet. "No," he sneered, pressing his face close to Wiley's. "There's more."

He slammed his fist hard into Wiley's chest. The impact sent him reeling backward again, crashing to the ground like a sack of potatoes. This time Wiley couldn't move. He lay still for several seconds, trying to collect his senses.

Then, somehow, he managed to drag himself to his feet again.

Two quick punches sent him sprawling again. He landed face-down in the mud. Each time he tried to get up, the big man would plant a log-like foot on his back and thrust him back into the mud.

"Stay down," one onlooker urged Wiley

Buster shifted toward Talmadge. "Yeah, Tal," he said nervously, "don't you think he's had enough?"

Talmadge turned on the scrawny private. "Had enough? Hell, I ain't even started with him yet."

Buster backed away quickly, his face white with fear. "Sure, Tal, sure," he stammered. "But you ain't...You ain't gonna *kill* him, are you?"

When Wiley opened his eyes and saw the big man's back turned, he pushed to his feet. With a sudden, willful burst of strength, he lunged forward, pile-driving Talmadge to the ground. Drawing upon every ounce of reserve strength in his body, Wiley pounded his foe with both fists—left, right...left, right...left, right, left, right—until, utterly exhausted, he fell over on top of him.

For what seemed like an eternity, both men lay still, unable to move, heaving in great gulps of air, their uniforms soaked and spotted with mud. Slowly, Wiley picked himself up off the fallen giant and dropped to one knee beside him. Any second now, he expected Goliath to rise from the dead and pulverize him.

Instead, Talmadge sat up and looked at Wiley in astonishment—then burst out laughing. The big man laughed so hard he lost his balance and rolled backward into the mud.

"That's the best lickin' I've had in a long time," he bellowed, crawling to his feet and wiping the mud out of his eyes, his beard. When he saw the perplexed look in Wiley's eye, he laughed again. "Reckon I had it coming, too."

He stuck out his hand. "Put it there, Georgia boy. For a little feller, you've got a pretty mean left hook."

Wiley blinked. It took him several moments to realize he was out of danger. "Yours ain't so bad, either," he sighed, rubbing his cut and swollen chin.

Just then Smalley straightened up and said, "Look alive, boys, we've got company. *Officers!*"

The soldiers scurried back into their ranks just as a cadre of mounted officers galloped into view. One of the officers, bearded and resplendent in a brilliant red cape and upturned hat, surged past on a handsome white charger.

"Wonder who that little dandy is," Talmadge muttered to no one in particular.

Buster's beady eyes lit up. "Why, don't you know, Tal? That's General Stuart, hisself."

"Who?"

"I've seen pictures of him," Buster said. "That's Jeb Stuart, General Lee's cavalry commander."

The soldiers watched spellbound as the famous general and his cadre thundered past, gradually fading like phantoms in the misty gloom of the swamp. Then, like phantoms themselves, the Wilkinson County Invincibles gathered up their gear and began to move out, silently, toward the darkening woods where a much more formidable and unforgiving enemy waited.

CHAPTER 18

Sarah Collins was in the front garden hoeing collard greens when Garrett came riding up on Sable, Mister Wiley's big Walker. As she watched him gallop into the yard, she was struck by how tall he looked in the saddle, how handsome. He'll be grown soon, she thought, just like Indigo. It was scary how fast those two boys were shooting up.

"Any news from Mister Wiley?" she called out, leaning on the hoe handle.

Garrett dismounted and hitched the horse by the barn. He reached into his pocket, pulled out a packet of letters and waved them around. "Three!" he shouted excitedly. "She's got three letters!"

Sarah clasped her hands with joy. "Glory be!" she exclaimed. "Miz Martha Ann is gonna be tickled pink."

Garrett raced up the steps, almost colliding with Martha Ann in the doorway. She was wearing a dark blue dress and white starched apron with a pink cameo pinned at the neck. Her soft brown hair was piled high on the back of her head in a braided bun.

"Why, Garrett, what brings you out here this time of day?" she asked.

Garrett slowed down long enough to catch his breath, then hurriedly showed her the letters. "They're from Wiley," he beamed, handing her the packet.

Ever since the incident with Zeke Taylor, Garrett had made it his business to ride into town at least twice a week to pick up Martha Ann's mail. The less they saw of Zeke Taylor, the better off everybody was.

For a moment all Martha Ann could do was stare at the three

brown envelopes bound together by a single blue ribbon. It was as if she was afraid to touch them for fear they might disappear. It had been weeks since she had heard a word from him. And now—three in one day!

"Well?" Garrett asked impatiently. "Ain't you gonna open them?"

Martha Ann laughed nervously. "Of course, I am, silly," she replied. "It's just that—well, I'm a little nervous, that's all."

Garrett smiled as if he understood. "Want me to do it for you?"

"Not on your life," Martha Ann fired back teasingly. She ruffled his hair playfully and said, "This is one thing I think I can manage all by myself."

They went into the living room and sat down on the sofa. But Garrett couldn't stay still. He bounded to his feet and started pacing the floor, eager for her to rip open the letters so he could hear the latest news fresh from the front.

Trembling, Martha Ann opened the first letter. It was a brief note from Richmond. There were only a couple of lines, because Wiley said he was in a big hurry to mail it before they moved out. But he did remember to tell her how much he loved her and that he was thinking only about her and the little one on the way.

Don't overdo it, he pleaded. *Let Sarah and Monroe and Garrett do your chores for you. You must save your strength for the days that lie ahead.*

As always, the letter was signed: *Your loving husband, Wiley.*

Garrett couldn't stand the suspense any longer. He leaned toward her expectantly and asked, "Any news about the fighting?"

"I'm afraid not," Martha Ann replied, shaking her head. "But he did say to give you his best."

Garrett was clearly disappointed. Then his eyes fastened on the second envelope as Martha Ann's fingernails slid beneath the sealed flap.

"I bet this one's real exciting," Garrett predicted. "I just know he's been in some big battle by now and seen lots of generals and stuff."

Once again, it was only a note—shorter, in fact, than the first one.

Martha Ann scanned the note. In a subdued voice she said,

"They're marching north again. They're with General Jackson."

Garrett gulped. "General "*Stonewall*" Jackson?" he asked incredulously.

Martha Ann nodded. "I suppose so." She folded the letter and put it away.

"That's it?" Garrett asked dejectedly.

"I'm afraid so." She looked up at him and smiled. "Unless you want to hear the real mushy stuff."

Garrett made a face and shrugged. "No way." He stalked over to the window and stared out. "Geez, you'd at least think he'd say something about General Lee. After all, he is marching with the Army of Northern Virginia."

Martha Ann looked at the third envelope. It was fatter than the first two, so surely there would be something more consequential.

She took her time opening this one and was rewarded when two pages fell out. Tucked between the pages was a bank transfer for twenty Confederate dollars along with a note telling her he would send her more next payday.

She put down the transfer and looked at the first page. She read slowly, savoring each word, each sentence, scrawled in Wiley's usual style of handwriting. As she read, she could almost smell her husband's musky scent, could almost see him sitting on a stump somewhere on a far-off Virginia hillside, his strong hand crafting each letter in each word.

She got up slowly and, leaving Garrett behind, walked out on the porch. She sat down on the steps and gazed across the fields and shadowy woods beyond. It would be dark soon. A thin mist was already creeping across the land.

As she looked out over the fields, watching the sun dip lower and feeling the onset of another dewy twilight, she felt her eyes growing moist and salty with tears. She drew in a shuddering breath, trying to hold back the flood of emotions that threatened to wash over her any second.

She missed Wiley so much. What she would give to see him walking up the lane at that very moment, the way he used to when he came in from the fields, his old shirt dark and sticky with sweat, his heavy boots covered with mud.

A wave of hopeless apprehension swept over her. What if he never came home? What if something terrible were to happen to him, just like poor Petie Clanton? No, no, a shrill voice deep inside her soul countered, you mustn't think like that, you mustn't!

———

OUT IN THE GARDEN, Sarah leaned against the hoe, her own heart breaking for Martha Ann. She started to come over, but thought better of it. This was one grieving period the poor girl had to get through on her own. It was the only way.

———

MARTHA ANN HEARD GARRETT clomping through the house. She pulled up her apron and dabbed at her eyes. It did no good to dry them, of course. The tears would simply keep coming and coming, not stopping until long after sleep had claimed her deep in the night. No, it was impossible to stop the tears. She might as well try to stop the dew from falling on the grass.

When Garrett saw how upset she was, he screwed up his face and asked, "Is there anything I can do?"

Martha Ann shook her head slowly. "No, no, I'm fine," she said, choking back the tears. "It's getting late. You best be running on home now."

Garrett fidgeted in the doorway. "Don't you worry," he said, trying to sound stronger and wiser than his fourteen years. "I'll be back over bright and early in the morning to check on you."

He hesitated for another moment, then turned to go. "Goodnight," he said softly.

"Goodnight, Garrett. Thank you for coming over."

Martha Ann watched the boy cross the yard to the barn, mount up and ride off into the purple gloom of twilight. She watched until she couldn't see him anymore, then went inside the house, lay down on her bed and cried herself to sleep.

Sometime during the night she was awakened by a violent rainstorm that banged and shook the house. She was afraid at first, then she remembered the letters from Wiley and an odd sense of security flowed into her. It was comforting to know that something Wiley had so recently touched was in the house, so nearby. Without thinking, she reached under her pillow and pulled out the three letters that had arrived earlier in the day.

Oh, Wiley, she moaned, caressing the crumpled, tear-stained letters with her fingertips, *where are you tonight, my love? Where are you?*

EARLY NEXT MORNING Martha Ann was awakened by the sound of someone banging on the front door.

She sat up and looked at the clock on the table by the bed. My goodness, it was past eight o'clock! She'd never slept so late in all her born days.

She jumped out of bed and hurried over to the mirror. She flinched at the strange woman looking back at her. Where did those dark rings come from, she wondered. How did her hair get so tangled—and so gray, she wanted to know.

She smoothed out her dress quickly and did the best she could with her hair, then hurried through the living room toward the door.

"Just hope it's not the preacher," she said out loud to herself as she threw the latch and swung open the door.

In the doorway, hat in hand, stood Monroe.

"Morning, Miz Martha Ann," Monroe said politely. "Me and Sarah was hoping nothing was wrong."

Martha Ann managed a smile. "Goodness no, Monroe. I just overslept, that's all." She breathed in deeply the fresh morning air.

It suddenly occurred to her that something was troubling the black man. "What about you, Monroe? Is something wrong? Is Sarah all right?"

"Sarah's just fine," Monroe said quickly.

"Then what...?" She stopped. "Is it Indigo?"

Monroe heaved a mighty sigh, slowly nodded. "Yes, ma'am, it's about my boy." He drew in another deep breath. "Miz Martha Ann, could I have a word with you?"

"Of course," Martha Ann replied, stepping back and waving Monroe into the living room.

Monroe stood just inside the door, looking around. The pain in his eyes was so intense Martha Ann could almost feel it herself.

"Now...what's this about Indigo?" she asked.

Monroe hesitated, as if he didn't quite know where to begin. "The boy...he's been talking awful foolish lately," he finally said.

"Foolish? What do you mean?" Martha Ann asked.

Monroe fingered the brim of his hat nervously. "He...He ain't making much sense these days, and his mammy and I are really beginning to worry about him."

"Oh, you know how teenage boys are," Martha Ann said, waving her hand as if to dismiss the thought. "I'm sure it's nothing serious. I wouldn't worry about it if I were you."

Monroe's gaze shifted to the floor a moment. When he looked up again he said, "No, Miz Martha Ann, I'm afraid it's more than that. A lot more." He fidgeted, as if trying to muster up the courage to say more. "It's this infernal war, Miz Martha Ann. It's got to where that's all he ever talks about anymore. Day and night."

Martha Ann breathed a sigh of relief. "Is that all? Monroe, you know that's all anybody talks about these days. I don't figure that Indigo's any different. At any rate, I don't see that as being any reason to get upset."

"Well, that's not the worst of it," Monroe said somberly. He hesitated, groping for the right words. "You see, the boy's talking about joining up."

Martha Ann hesitated. "Joining up?"

"Yes, ma'am. And I ain't talking about with the Rebel boys, either."

Martha Ann gasped, suddenly horrified. "Do you mean to say," she started, "that he wants to join the Yankees?"

Monroe nodded.

"But why? Why on God's green earth would he want to do a thing like that?"

"He says if the Rebels won't have him, then he'll go with the Yankees. Long's they let him ride in the cavalry."

"Oh, no, not him, too," Martha Ann lamented. "That's all Garrett ever talks about these days."

"He's my baby, Miz Martha Ann, the only boy I got. I sure don't want to see him go off nowhere. Especially with the Yankees."

"Have you talked to him, told him how you feel?"

"Lord, Miz Martha Ann, that's all we been doing for weeks now.

Talking. I've even threatened to whip him within an inch of his life. But his mind done seems to be made up, with or without mine and his mammy's blessings. I thought if you said something to him—I mean, I know how much he respects you, and all—maybe he'd change his mind."

Martha Ann said, "I'll see what I can do. Meanwhile, I suggest you give it some more time, Monroe. Maybe he'll change his mind on his own accord."

Monroe shook his head sadly. "I sure hope so," he said. "It's about to kill his poor mammy."

CHAPTER 19

THE STORM CAME OUT OF NOWHERE, a howling, thrashing monster, banging and bellowing its way across the western end of Wilkinson County like a runaway locomotive. It struck the Nesmith farm at midnight, toppling trees, overturning wagons and sending the barn and shed roofs sailing off into the black, rain-driven night.

The little house trembled but held. Inside, Sarah Collins frantically worked to help Martha Ann bring forth the tiny miracle within her womb.

"It's gonna be all right, child," the black woman said reassuringly, wiping Martha Ann's forehead with a cold cloth. "You just got to breathe harder, push a little harder."

Martha Ann tried to do as she was told. She heaved and pushed, heaved and pushed, straining and screaming at the top of her lungs, while the wild winds shrieked and wailed and moaned around the trembling eaves and shuttered windows.

In the living room Monroe and Indigo paced the floor, listening to Martha Ann's tortured screams and the raging tempest outside. In the dim glow of the firelight, their ebony faces glowed like wet coal.

"Think she's g-gonna make it, Pa?" Indigo asked.

"Sure, she's gonna make it, boy," Monroe replied. "She's in the Lord's hands tonight."

Monroe leaned against the mantel, stared into the flickering flames. Every few seconds a gust of wind would howl down the chimney, scattering embers across the floor. Each time that happened, Indigo was on his feet in a hurry, stamping out the sparks before they could do any damage.

Monroe's eyes fixed on the oval portrait above the mantel. It was a full-length portrait of Wiley in his uniform, taken at Camp Davis just before his unit shipped out to North Carolina. It showed him in regulation battle dress, complete with haversack, bowie knife and musket.

"Monroe!" Sarah's voice booming from the bedroom.

Monroe turned and flew across the room. He pushed open the door and peered inside the bedroom. Sarah was bent over Martha Ann, both arms pressed against the woman's heaving, swollen abdomen. A pair of candles on either side of the bed cast eerie shadows on the bare walls and ceiling. Bedclothes lay scattered about, as did piles of discarded rags.

When Sarah saw Monroe standing in the doorway, she yelled: "Hot water! I need more hot water!" She handed him a ceramic pitcher. As he turned to go, she added, "And bring me some more clean rags. They're in the kitchen. *Hurry!*"

Monroe rumbled back to the fireplace and refilled the pitcher. He found a stack of clean, dry rags in the kitchen and took them in to Sarah.

"How is she?" he whispered to his wife.

Sarah shook her head, unwilling to talk about it. "Just go on back out there and keep the water hot and boiling," she instructed. "This might take a while."

Monroe cast another glance at Martha Ann's massive, perspiring form, then quietly walked out of the room.

When Indigo saw the worried look in his pa's eyes, he asked, "Is something wrong, Pa? Is she gonna be all right?"

Monroe looked at the portrait over the mantel. Fixing his gaze on Wiley's eyes in the portrait, he sighed and said, "Won't know for a while. Something seems wrong with the baby."

———

WHEN MONROE HEARD THE SOUND of a baby crying, he thought he was still dreaming. He had been drifting in and out of sleep for what seemed like hours. At one point he dreamed he was back at the old Sparta plantation, rocking Indigo to sleep in front of the fireplace. Sarah was kneeling next to them in the rocker, singing a sweet lullaby.

The words echoed sweetly in some forgotten corner of his mind:

> *Go to sleep, little baby,*
> *Dream while the angels serenade thee.*
> *When you wake, the sun will shine,*
> *And I'll be there by you…*
> *I'll be there by you…*

Then they were in some old field, and Indigo was learning how to pick his first cotton. The long rows seemed to stretch on forever, and their backs were breaking beneath bulging bags filled to overflowing.

Indigo started to cry when the overseer galloped over, a demonic glint in his pale blue eyes.

"*Hush that little young'un up and git back to work!*" the overseer commanded from the saddle. He was a stern-faced fellow with a long, crooked nose and a tall black hat. A long black whip lay coiled at his side.

"*I'm trying, Mr. Jacobs, I'm trying,*" was all the young father could say.

But Indigo wouldn't stop crying. He clung to Monroe's legs, unwilling to turn loose no matter how much the overseer threatened him or his mamma and papa begged him.

Mr. Jacobs reached down and uncoiled the long whip. With a snarl, he flung it back over his head, then cut loose. The whip rang out as it cracked over the boy's back. Once…Twice…Three times the whip lashed out.

All Monroe and Sarah could do was look on and watch, powerless to protect their baby from the cruel, singing whip that bit into Indigo's bleeding back.

Suddenly, the overseer was gone, and the fields were gone, and Indigo was astride a great big horse, galloping across a sunlit meadow near the old Walker place. Monroe could see him from some far corner of the field, laughing the innocent laugh of childhood as the wind blew through his hair and the horse's flowing mane.

"Pa," Indigo said. "*There's something I want to talk to you about.*"

Now they were standing in the barn behind the Nesmith house, grooming the pair of horses and mule. When Monroe saw the pained look on his son's face, he knew there was something important on his mind.

"*What is it, boy?*"

"*I've been thinking,*" Indigo said tentatively, and in Monroe's dream the boy's voice was deep and strong and didn't stutter once. "*The only way I'll ever amount to anything is to go away somewhere far off, maybe up North.*"

Monroe was intrigued. "*Up North? What kind of fool talk is that, boy?*" he heard himself asking as he whirled around to confront his son. "*There's a war going on, in case you haven't heard.*"

Indigo shook his head. "*It ain't our war, Pa. You know that.*"

Monroe stared at his son. "*Not our war? Then just whose war do you think it is, boy? I mean, if it ain't ours.*"

Indigo sighed. "*It's their war, Pa,*" he said. "*The white folks. It don't have nothing to do with us.*"

Monroe let out a little laugh. So that was it! It was clear that the boy had been hanging around The Meeting Place too much listening to those crazy, wild-eyed abolitionists who sneaked down from up North to spread their poison.

"*Boy, let me tell you something,*" he said, more firmly than he had intended. "*This war, this war those white folks are off fighting, it has everything to do with us. Everything.*" He leaned forward and looked the boy square in the eye. "*And when it's over, when Mister Lincoln finally whips the Rebels, as he will, then people like you and me are gonna be free. Really free. There won't be no more slaves in all the land. Black folks will be free to come and go as they please, just like the whites.*"

He straightened. More gently, he said, "*And then, when it's all over, if you still want to go up North to better yourself, then I'll help you every way I can.*"

"*But I can't wait, Pa,*" Indigo persisted. "*I want to go now.*" He paused. "*Listen, Pa, there's a way. I done looked into it. There's a group of people who want to help boys like me. It's called the Underground Railroad.*"

"*The Underground what?*"

"*Railroad. The Underground Railroad. Only it's not really a railroad, it's just…*"

"*So that's what all those secret meetings in town have been about, huh,*" Monroe concluded. "*I should have known it was something no good. What are you trying to do, boy? Get yourself strung up by the Security Council or something?*"

Indigo shook his head. "*No, Pa, it ain't nothing like that. It's safe. This old woman, see, this Miss Tubman, she's really special. I wish you could meet her sometime, Pa. She helped lots of slaves escape up North. She was even a slave herself once.*"

Monroe groaned. "*Now I've heard everything,*" he snorted. "*Slaves helping slaves to escape. Next thing I hear you'll be wanting to raise up a rebellion like old Nat Turner. Look where it got him.*"

"*Pa, I ain't talking about no rebellion. I just want to go up North. Make something of myself. Make you proud of me.*"

"*I'm already proud of you, boy. You never have to worry about a thing like that for the rest of your life.*"

"*I know, Pa, I know. But it just ain't the same thing.*"

Monroe drew back. "*What's so special about being up North, anyway? Just what you aiming to do once you get there?*"

Here Indigo paused. "*Join the cavalry,*" he said firmly.

"*The what?*"

"*The cavalry,*" Indigo said. "*I want to join the Union cavalry.*"

THE SOUND OF CRYING AGAIN. A baby, somewhere far off in the night...

"*Pa! Pa!*" Indigo shouted, shaking his father awake.

Monroe sat up abruptly and looked around. "What is it?" he asked groggily. When he saw the clock he realized he'd been asleep for more than an hour.

"It's the baby, Pa!" Indigo said excitedly. "It...It's done come."

Monroe was out of the chair in a flash, bounding across the floor toward the back bedroom. Sarah met him at the door, a relieved smile on her face.

"She...She's all right?" Monroe asked hopefully.

"They're both fine," Sarah replied wearily. Then: "It's a girl. Born three minutes ago."

"A baby girl," Monroe muttered, almost in disbelief. He swallowed hard. He'd never seen a baby girl before, never even thought about one. He let out a little yelp, grabbed his wife and hugged her. Tears of joy trickled down his face, not so much for him and Martha Ann, but for the man in the Confederate uniform whose portrait hung above the mantel.

Monroe would have given anything if Wiley could have been there at that moment to share in the sweet sound of his own baby girl cooing in the next room.

Monroe pulled back. "But I thought you said there was a problem."

Sarah shook her head. "The Good Lord took care of it," she said. "The baby came out just fine when her time came."

"Hallelujah," Monroe said softly. "Let us rejoice!"

They were still rejoicing when the sun rose, warm and bright, burning away the rain clouds and exorcising the dark demons of the night.

CHAPTER 20

MIDNIGHT. APRIL 16, 1863. A light rain was falling over the Confederate city of Vicksburg. Three young soldiers, sleepy and miserable in the sticky heat, slouched beneath billowing regulation ponchos as they paced back and forth in front of a handsome, hilltop mansion overlooking the river. Even though the hour was late, lights still burned in every window of the flag-draped house. Spirited laughter mingled with mirthful music could be heard reverberating within.

The soldiers watched as a steady procession of carriages came and went, clip-clopping up and down the winding, cobblestone drive. Well-frocked civilians and bearded officers wearing gleaming black boots and gilded gray uniforms hurried in and out of the rain, polished sabers clanging at their sides.

The occasion was the city's Grand Gala, the main social event of the year. Everybody who was anybody was there that evening—senators, congressmen, planters, mayors, bankers, artists, poets, publishers and military men of notable rank. Most conspicuous of all was a tall, slender, immaculately tailored general with sad eyes and a flowing gray beard named John C. Pemberton. Pemberton commanded the Confederate forces stationed around Vicksburg. It was his army's job to protect the vital river bastion from Yankee invasion. Rebel cities and forts to the north and south had already fallen to Union onslaughts, but as long as Vicksburg held—as long as Vicksburg controlled the "Father of Waters,"—the Trans-Mississippi West still belonged to the Confederacy.

But a Yankee invasion was the last thing on the minds of Pemberton and most of those attending the Grand Gala. Amid the waltzing and flowing champagne, the Northern-born general charmed his gentrified hosts not only with his generous smile and dashing flair, but also with his grand reassurance that their proud city of five thousand citizens was perfectly safe. No Federal force, he nobly promised, not even Sam Grant's blue-clad army of thugs, was big enough or strong enough to challenge the riverside citadel.

Few had reason to suspect that, at that very hour, Union gunboats under the command of Rear Admiral David Porter were steaming upriver toward the Confederacy's "Gibraltar of America." Within days, Sam Grant's land forces, already on the move to the north near Jackson, would descend upon Vicksburg like a pack of hell-sent demons.

———

THE TRIO OF GUARDS snapped to attention as another gilded military carriage drove up. They saw the pair of officers bundled inside—both clearly inebriated—and waved them past with a sharp salute.

As soon as the drunken officers were safely out of ear range, one of the guards, a wiry, undersized private with a bird-like nose and dull, beady eyes, nodded toward the retreating carriage and cracked, "There go our leaders, boys. Ain't they a grand sight? Sure ain't no mystery why we're losing the war."

"Ain't that the truth," drawled a second soldier. His name was Thomas Crawford. He was a big, brooding Irish corporal whose craggy face and lantern jaw were haloed in sandy whiskers.

Crawford glanced up at the big house where the festivities were taking place and sneered, "How much longer you lads figure they're gonna keep this up, anyway?"

"I reckon till the war's over," chuckled the third sentry, Private Charles Nesmith of Wilkinson County, Georgia.

Like most of his comrades with the 57th Georgia Infantry, Charles had aged remarkably in the sixteen months he had been away at the front. Action at Baker's Creek, Big Black River and half a dozen other major fights from Tennessee to Mississippi had left him with the lean, haggard look so common among foot soldiers who had reached their manhood in the trenches.

Corporal Crawford spat a thick wad of tobacco juice onto the cobblestones and watched the rain wash it away. "Least they could do is offer us a pot of hot coffee," he groused.

"Some of those fancy cakes they're filling their bellies with wouldn't hurt none either," chuckled Lucas Altman, the thin-faced private with the bird-like nose.

Charles and his two comrades had been standing guard duty for nearly eight hours straight. They were tired and bellyaching hungry, ready for dry clothes, a hot meal and a soft bed. They had seen enough of drunken officers and Vicksburg's high society for one night.

Yet, they knew things could be worse. They could be out in the rifle pits, waist-deep in mud and mites and mosquitoes. Or—even worse—they could be upriver on the front lines where all the fighting was going on.

Miserable as they were, at least they were safe here in the city, guarding the generals and pampered socialites of Vicksburg.

SHORTLY PAST MIDNIGHT Charles noticed a strange, flashing light arcing high across the dark sky far to the south. He blinked hard when he saw another—then another. All at once he heard what sounded like the muffled booms of incoming artillery and mortar rounds. In a flash he realized they were under attack. But *how? Where?*

There was no way the Federals could be approaching by land. Not with better than thirty thousand well-armed defenders ringing the city. It couldn't be from across the river, either, because there the ground was inundated with swamps and canebrakes and quivering pools of quicksand. Any military movement in that terrain would be tactical suicide.

Only when Charles saw—and heard—the Confederate batteries south of the city opening up did he realize the attack was coming from the river itself.

Minutes after the initial bombardment, the streets below began filling up with dazed and bleeding people, civilians mostly, screaming, running in all directions. One after the other, and sometimes in clusters, houses, schools, churches and barns were blasted into smoking rubble. Warehouses and wharves hugging the banks of the river exploded and tumbled into the water.

The clang of fire bells split the night air as crackling flames shot skyward. Ambulances clattered madly about town. Half-dressed people, oblivious to the bursting shells overhead, fell to their knees in the pouring rain and called out to God to protect them. The overall scene was one of madness and chaos as more buildings caught fire and exploded, chimneys toppled and soldiers scurried to form ranks.

An officer clutching a bottle of champagne emerged from the mansion behind Charles and exclaimed, "My God...it's Grant!"

He was quickly joined by several other officers and ladies. They stood on the veranda, seeing—but not believing—the shocking events unfolding all around them.

"No, it can't be," one white-whiskered colonel declared. "It must be Porter. It has to be Porter. I'd know that devil's work anywhere!"

"Damn his soul to hell!" another officer bellowed.

The officers staggered down the steps and made for their carriages. Others pouring out of the house followed suit, some of them stumbling and sliding on the rain-slickened driveway. A few managed to swing onto their mounts, only to collide with fellow riders. Women screamed. Carriages bounced and careened out of control and overturned. Long-bearded politicians took one look at the mess and hurried back inside.

A number of onlookers, Charles included, simply stared out over the burning city, transfixed by the spectacle, unable or unwilling to accept the reality of what was happening. Vicksburg was under attack. One might have sooner expected the moon to fall into the sea.

Lucas Altman jumped out of the way of a swaying carriage. "What do we do?" he asked Corporal Crawford, who was in charge of the guard detail.

Crawford scratched his sandy whiskers and waited, much like a bearded prophet, for the right answer to come down from on high. He finally shrugged and said, "Damned, if I know, boy."

CHAPTER 21

MARTHA ANN USED TO LIKE going to town. But that was before the war. The war had changed things, too many things. Like a lot of people, Martha Ann wondered if life would ever be the same again in her little hometown, even if, by some magical means, the war should end tomorrow and all the boys came marching home.

That morning, as she and the baby rode into town with Monroe, Sarah and Indigo, Martha Ann couldn't help noticing how Irwinton had physically deteriorated over the past year and a half. Once a bright, cheerful place with neatly manicured gardens and fresh-painted houses and storefronts, in some ways it now resembled a ghost town. A riot of weeds sprouted up everywhere—sidewalks, yards, even the middle of the thoroughfare. Abandoned buildings and shops along Main Street stood cracked and peeling, their windows and doors boarded up.

The saddest sight was the courthouse, once the pride of Wilkinson County. Beneath its bright canopy of Confederate flags and banners, the massive landmark loomed gray and forlorn, a fading mistress down on her luck. A number of small shops around the courthouse had been converted into granaries where foodstuffs collected under the "tithing tax" were stored.

But the changes were more than physical. Like some insidious disease, the war seemed to have infected the common psyches of the people, sapping their vitality as well as their resources. Where happy, industrious shopkeepers and vendors once thronged, nowadays the downtown area seemed more populated by roustabouts and drifters, some of them no doubt army deserters and other renegades on the wrong side of the law.

That morning, however, Irwinton was busier than usual, busier than it had been in months. People Martha Ann hadn't seen since before the war smiled and waved, some stopping to inquire about the baby and Wiley. No doubt all the excitement was due to the big meeting at the courthouse later that morning to discuss taxes and the "impressment laws" recently enacted by the Richmond government.

Monroe found an empty post directly in front of the feed and seed store and pulled in. He hopped down from the wagon and held the baby while Martha Ann and Sarah climbed down.

"I shouldn't be more than a couple of hours," Martha Ann said, straightening her bonnet and smoothing her skirt. "Monroe, why don't you take Indigo over to Abernathy's and get yourselves some cold apple cider? Tell him to put it on my account."

To Sarah she said, "Are you sure you and Joanna are going to be all right?"

"Oh, Lordy, yes," the black woman smiled. Her smile broadened when Martha Ann handed her the baby. "We're gonna just take us a nice long stroll around the square, then sit and play under the shade tree. Now, you just run along to that meeting, and don't worry none about me and the baby."

Monroe said, "If it's all right with you, Miz Martha Ann, me and the boy are gonna go over to The Meeting House for a spell."

"You can do whatever you want, Monroe," Martha Ann said. "Just try not to be late. We've got a lot of chores to do before we head back home."

She pulled back Joanna's blanket and gave the sleeping infant a soft kiss. "Bye-bye, sweetheart," she whispered. "Mommy's going to miss you." Then: "If she starts coughing again, I think I'll take her straight over to Dr. Scully's."

Sarah patted Martha Ann's arm. "I think a little fresh air is all this child needs."

"I hope you're right, Sarah."

Monroe waited until Sarah and Martha Ann were out of hearing range, then turned to his son and said, "Are you sure you want to go through with this, boy?"

An urgent look came into Indigo's eyes. "I got to, Pa," he said passionately. "I've d-done made up my m-mind."

Monroe sighed deeply. "Well, come on, then, let's get it over with."

IT WAS GOOD TO SEE so many people in town for a change, Martha Ann thought, as she crossed the street toward her sister's shop. Maybe they should call a meeting every Saturday, if that's what it took to get things back to normal.

Greta Underwood, the church organist, was coming out of the store as Martha Ann walked up.

"Hello, Martha Ann," Mrs. Underwood said stiffly. "I missed you at church last Sunday."

"The baby was sick."

"Oh…I'm sorry. I hope it isn't anything serious."

"Just a little cough. She's much better now."

"Well, you let me know if there's anything I can do."

"I will."

"Then I'll see you at church in the morning," Greta Underwood said, waving goodbye as she turned and bustled away down the sidewalk.

Martha Ann went inside the store and looked around. There were several customers milling about, none she knew.

"Well, look what the wind blew in," Catherine said, gliding over to Martha Ann and hugging her neck. "It's good to see you again."

Martha Ann hugged her sister back. "You too, Catherine." She looked around. "How's Joseph?"

Catherine drew back. "Please," she said, frowning, "let's not ruin this beautiful morning by getting off on that subject." She brightened. "Where's that precious little niece of mine?"

"Sarah's keeping her so I can attend the meeting."

Catherine looked disappointed. "Well, you simply must let me see her before you leave town," she said. She reached behind a counter, rummaged around for a moment until she found what she was looking for. "Here," she said, handing her a shiny new porcelain baby rattler. "I've been saving this special for her."

Martha Ann blinked in rare astonishment at the beautiful—and, she knew, expensive—gift. "Oh, Catherine," she said appreciatively, "you shouldn't have. It—It's so beautiful."

Martha Ann suddenly felt guilty—guilty for all the terrible things she'd said and thought about her sister in the past. She was still her sister, her only sister, regardless of how she lived her life. The shame she hid in her heart for Catherine had made her almost forget just how kind her sister could be at times.

"Thank you, Catharine," she said softly, putting the toy in her bag.

Catherine reached across the counter and placed her hand on Martha Ann's. "Any news from Wiley?"

Martha Ann hesitated a moment. "He's still in Virginia, that's about all I know."

"Any chance he'll get to come home soon?"

Martha Ann sighed. "We keep hoping. It seems like every time he puts in a request for a furlough, something happens and the regiment has to move out."

"I'm so sorry," Catherine said. "I know how hard it must be on you."

Martha Ann brushed back a tear. "We're managing," she said bravely.

"You must be very proud of him."

The gentleness of Catherine's words touched her deeply. "I am," she said, choking back tears.

—— —— ——

AFTER LEAVING CATHERINE'S STORE, Martha Ann realized she still had half an hour to kill, so she decided to browse some of the few remaining shops in business.

She crossed the street and went into Mary Graham's Dress Shop. She hadn't intended to buy anything, but the moment she laid eyes on the pretty blue dress in the showroom window, she knew she was in trouble.

"That's the one for you, dearie," Mary Graham said approvingly from the corner of the store.

Mary Graham was a sweet, dainty widow in her early sixties. She had twinkling blue eyes and strong white teeth that sparkled when she smiled, which was often. She wore her hair piled high in a bun and was a bit on the plump side, but behind that matronly countenance beat the heart of a savvy businesswoman. Over the years she had worked hard to build up one of the most successful dress shops in middle Georgia. And she wasn't about to let a little war mess up business.

"It's beautiful," Martha Ann gushed, unable to take her eyes off the dress.

Mary Graham pulled the dress off the rack and handed it to Martha Ann. "You just go back there and try it on, dearie. Then let's have a look."

Martha Ann hesitated. She knew she had no business even looking at such a fancy, store-bought dress. And when she saw the price tag, she shook her head. "I'm afraid it's way too expensive, Mrs. Graham," she said. "But thank you, anyway."

The elderly store owner's eyes twinkled. "Oh, pooh," she persisted, "You just go back there and slip into it anyway." She yanked off the tag. "And don't you worry about the price."

Martha Ann agonized for a long moment. "Well, it can't hurt anything to just try it on," she reasoned, then hurried into the dressing room before she could change her mind.

It didn't take long to take off her clothes and slip into the new dress. A few moments later she was standing in front of a full-length mirror, marveling at the dress and how good it felt on her.

"It's stunning," Mrs. Graham said, clasping her hands in delight. "And look at that, would you? A perfect fit. Child, you look absolutely gorgeous."

Martha Ann agreed. She hadn't looked or felt as good as this in months.

"It *is* beautiful," she sighed, fingering the delicate fabric. She was suddenly gripped by a dark panic. How could she even think of buying such a dress when soldiers were going hungry on the front lines? "But I can't. Not with Wiley away and all. It just wouldn't be right."

Mrs. Graham nodded her head patiently, as if she understood everything. Then she looked around to make sure nobody else in the store was listening. "Listen, dearie," she said almost in a whisper. "If it's the money you're worried about, you can always pay it back on the never-never. Little bit here, little bit there. Nobody will ever know but just us two."

Martha Ann felt like she was being tortured. The dress was positively beautiful. It made her feel good just looking at it. But she couldn't. She just couldn't. "I'm sorry," she said, "but I can't. It—It wouldn't be right."

Mrs. Graham saw the anguished look in Martha Ann's face and smiled. "Tell you what, dearie," she said, pulling her aside. "You just forget about the price. I want you to take the dress. It's yours. Compliments of the house."

Martha Ann stared at her image in the mirror. She was stunned, flabbergasted by Mrs. Graham's more than generous offer. "Oh, Mrs. Graham, I couldn't do that," she suddenly heard herself say. "It wouldn't be fair."

"Nonsense. Now you just march right back in there, and take if off so I can wrap it up nice and neat for you." She winked. "It's the least an old woman like myself can do to show my appreciation for all the sacrifices you and your husband are having to make right now for all of us."

"But…"

"No, not another word," Mrs. Graham said, raising her hands as if to block any more discussion of the matter. "I insist."

She herded Martha Ann back into the fitting room. "Now you go on and change, and I'm going to pick out a nice matching hat to go with it. And when I see you at church Sunday morning, I expect to see you wearing it."

CHAPTER 22

WHEN MONROE AND INDIGO REACHED The Meeting House, two burly black guards stepped in front of them. "Hey, where do you niggers think you're going?" one of them growled.

Monroe didn't recognize either man. It was clear by the way they talked and dressed that they weren't local.

"My boy and me are here for the meeting," Monroe explained.

"It's all full up," the big guard said gruffly. He folded his arms as if daring Monroe to try to get past him.

"But we came a long way just to be here," Monroe pleaded. "Besides, this meeting is very important to my boy here."

The guard pressed menacingly toward Monroe. "Didn't you hear me, *nigger?*" His lips curled into a twisted snarl. "I said there ain't no room. Now, take your boy here and *git!*"

Indigo stared to say something, but Monroe cut him off.

"Look," Monroe said sternly, sizing up the pair of brutes with his eyes. "I don't know who you fellows are or where you came from, but me and my boy come here nearly every Saturday morning. This is our place, see, our special place." He glared at the big guard and added, "Now, if you don't mind stepping aside…"

Before he could finish, the second guard came over and shoved Monroe backward to the ground.

"Hey!" Indigo cried out. "You can't do that to my pa!"

Both guards threw back their heads and roared with laughter.

Monroe picked himself up and slowly dusted himself off. "You shouldn't have done that," he said, motioning for Indigo to get behind him.

The first guard never saw Monroe's fist coming. It slammed into his nose and sent the big black man hurtling backward into a stack of barrels. Before the second guard could react, Monroe grabbed his forearm and wrenched it up, forcing the man to his knees.

"*Owwww*," the big guard wailed. "Let me go, you damn fool, let me *go!*"

"Not until you apologize to my boy here," Monroe said, tightening his grip.

"You must be crazy, nigger," the guard shot back.

Monroe yanked the arm even higher. The guard screamed out in pain again.

"I said apologize…or, I swear, I'll break it."

The guard was on the verge of tears. "Okay, okay," he blurted. "I'm sorry. Now…will you just let go?"

Monroe let go of the man's arm and pushed him to the ground. "Next time you outside niggers come down here, try to be a little more polite." Turning to Indigo, he said, "Come on, son, let's go."

They went inside the warehouse and sat down on a couple of crates near the back. Up front, a frail, elderly black woman was speaking in a low but powerful voice.

"…There is a road to freedom," the old woman was saying, as she leaned over a makeshift podium. Her hair was white as snow, and she wore a black dress that seemed to swallow her small frame. In the dim light of the warehouse, Monroe thought she looked like a shriveled-up scarecrow. "…All you have to do is just get on that road and keep following it till it ends…"

As he listened to her words, Monroe gradually became aware of feelings long submerged. Almost without thinking he reached out and put his arm around his son.

———

ACROSS TOWN AT THE COURTHOUSE, the meeting had begun with an impassioned speech by Bart Clanton, who had been appointed head of the Citizens Committee Against War Taxes. Clanton was a stooped, rail-thin farmer from the east end of the county whose only son had fallen at Seven Pines in the summer of '62.

"They took my boy," Clanton cried out, "but that wasn't enough."

He raised both fists and shook them angrily. "Now they want to take my cattle and hogs. Well, I, for one, say enough is enough!"

"I'll second that," someone from the audience shouted. "The Yankees can't do us no more harm than our own government has done."

"That's right!" a woman shrieked from the rear of the room. "If we let them keep the current policy, we won't have to worry about the Yankees invading. We'll all starve to death before they get here!"

Mayor Franklin Futch, who had been sitting in a chair up front taking it all in, rose and motioned for silence. He pulled out a white silk handkerchief and dabbed at the sweat pouring down his bald, egg-shaped head.

"Ladies and gentlemen," he began, "please...please, this is no time for harsh words about our own government, which is doing everything in its power to get us through this crisis."

He waited for the moaning to die down, then continued: "We're all in this together, remember? We have to stick together, be strong—one united front. Mercy, this is not the time to be threatening revolution."

A husky, ruddy-cheeked man dressed in ragged farm clothes rose slowly and said, "But, Mayor, maybe what we need is another revolution to straighten out the mess this government has put us in."

Caleb Dirkens, a frail, white-bearded farmer who was sitting next to Martha Ann, stood up and shouted, "We've had just about enough of Mr. Davis and his government up there in Richmond. The same thing is true of Joe Brown and his pressmen." The old man spat, wiped his mouth and continued: "Why, they came out to my house just two days ago and took away my wagon. My last wagon! Any day now I figure they'll be coming for my mule. How am I supposed to do my plowing then?"

AT THE BACK OF THE ROOM, almost hidden in a frayed black overcoat and scarf that covered his badly scarred flesh, Hamilton Dewberry sat passively listening to the proceedings. Rufus, his black apprentice, sat next to him, taking notes and occasionally leaning over to identify the speaker or to explain what was being said.

The "mysterious" fire that had gutted the office of the *Irwinton Independent* had left its publisher blind and badly disfigured but had failed to destroy his spirit. If anything, Hamilton Dewberry had emerged from the tragedy more determined than ever to report and comment on the news, regardless of whose toes—or egos—he had to step on in the process.

"Be sure to interview Caleb Dirkins before he leaves," Dewberry said to Rufus. "That man has more passion in his back pocket than all the crowned heads in Richmond."

"Yes, sir," Rufus replied, making a note to do just that.

MARTHA ANN GLANCED across the room and saw Elizabeth, James Madison's wife, leap to her feet and raise her hand. In a calm, deliberate voice, Elizabeth said, "I would like to address this assembly, please."

The room grew strangely quiet as every head turned toward Elizabeth.

"Why, of course, Elizabeth," the mayor said, smiling. "Please go right ahead."

Elizabeth cleared her throat. "Most of you know my husband, James Madison, who is off with General Lee somewhere in Virginia. Now, in all the time he's been away at the front, I haven't received more than a few dollars. He keeps saying that the Army of Northern Virginia has no money to pay the soldiers with. And they're already down to half-rations of meat and bread, eating wild berries and persimmons and bark off trees just to keep from starving."

Here and there rose low, muffled utterances of agreement.

Drawing new energy from the crowd, Elizabeth continued, "I hear they're having bread riots up in Richmond and that they're spreading to other cities all across the South." She paused, and her eyes seemed to ignite as she surveyed the crowd. "Now, I ask you— all of you—do we want to have that kind of situation here in Irwinton? Do we?"

Another murmur rumbled through the audience. Elizabeth straightened and said, "If we are to avoid that kind of situation here, then I beg you, Mister Mayor—I beg you—do something to stop them from impressing our livestock and farm produce! Make them keep their hands off our property!"

Several women sprang to their feet and applauded. "Listen to her!" one woman shrieked. "If you won't do anything to help us, then I say we'll have to take matters into our own hands to protect what's ours!"

"Ladies! Ladies!" Mayor Futch retorted, pounding the podium for order. "I assure you the governor is doing all he possibly can right now. Need I remind you that he has already cut taxes for the families of soldiers off fighting on the front lines? And he tells me he's doing the best he can to see to it that confiscated food is distributed properly to widows and parents of our fighting men."

"That's not enough!" another woman shouted.

Elizabeth, who was still standing, said, "The women and children are suffering horribly, Mister Mayor. They're starving to death, every day in the streets. Right here in Irwinton. We need food! And we need it now!"

Several women jumped to their feet again and shouted in unison: "Food! Food! We need food!"

Soon every woman in the room was on the floor demanding food. "Food! We need food!" they chanted, pumping defiant fists into the air. "We need food! We need food! We need food!"

Frantic now, Mayor Futch waved his handkerchief and pounded the podium in a futile attempt to restore order. "Ladies!" he called out, "ladies, please..."

But his voice was drowned out in the rising chorus of female protesters.

The meeting dissolved when the chanting protestors, led by Elizabeth, stormed from the courthouse. Before exiting, Elizabeth spun around and shouted: "We'll get food, Mister Mayor. You'll see. There won't be any more children starving in the streets of Irwinton. Go tell that to the governor!"

On the way out, she leaned toward Hamilton Dewberry and said, "And you may quote me on that, Mr. Dewberry."

CHAPTER 23

THE YOUNG LIEUTENANT WALKED into the tent and snapped to attention. Directly in front of him, swathed in a halo of cigar smoke, stood a small, dapper man with short, sandy hair and a wispy beard that curled down to his chest. The man was General Joseph Hooker, Lincoln's new commanding general of the Army of the Potomac. In the early morning light the general looked frail, almost ethereal, as he and several field officers leaned over a low plank table covered with maps and charts.

When the general looked up and saw the lieutenant standing in the doorway, his eyes lit up. "Ah, come in, Lieutenant," he said, waving him forward. "I trust you have something for me."

"Yes, sir," the lieutenant replied nervously. He took a couple of hesitant steps forward and stopped. It wasn't everyday a lowly lieutenant was invited inside the commanding general's tent.

"Well?" the general said, waiting. "Let's have it, man, let's have it."

"Oh—yes, sir," the lieutenant stammered. He reached into a satchel, fumbled around for a moment, then pulled out a stack of documents. "These came just this morning," he said, handing the documents to the general.

Hooker was obviously pleased with what he saw. He smiled as he thumbed through the stack of maps and photos taken only hours earlier by members of the balloon reconnaissance team. Excellent, he thought. Just what he had been waiting for.

"You and your men are to be commended, Lieutenant," the general said, folding up the documents and stuffing them inside his long blue coat. Turning toward the other officers, he said,

"Gentlemen, it is just as I expected. General Lee is on the move, and I think I know exactly where he is headed."

He got up, buttoned his coat and fastened on his sword. "We have work to do, gentlemen. Shall we get started?"

FOR MONTHS, "Fighting Joe" Hooker had been monitoring Lee's movements in and around a densely tangled forest twelve miles west of Fredericksburg known as The Wilderness. Recent reports reaching him from the field indicated that Lee was in trouble and probably on the run. At long last, the confident Union commander felt he had his cagey Confederate adversary right where he wanted him.

As soon as the spring rains let up and the Virginia roads cleared, he planned to go after Lee and destroy him. He had a score to settle, and he wanted to settle it personally. A lot of his men felt the same way. Most couldn't wait to get another crack at the Confederates after what they had done to them at Fredericksburg. Back in December, twelve thousand of their comrades had been slaughtered during a senseless assault against heavily fortified Rebel positions. It was an assault that cost the former Union commander—Ambrose Burnside—his job. Now that job belonged to Hooker, and by God in high heaven, "Fighting Joe" Hooker was going to make those Rebels pay. It was his intention to hound Lee and his ragged band of Rebels into extinction.

"May God have mercy on General Lee for I will have none," he had proclaimed after his appointment to top command.

Everything was falling into place that week in late April as the spirited Union commander moved the bulk of his army across the Rappahannock River. He had guns, he had food, he had men— more than twice as many as the Army of Northern Virginia, 130,000 to 60,000. The only hitch in the plan—the only thing that worried Hooker as he hurried to finalize plans for the big offensive—was Jackson. Thomas J. Jackson—or "Stonewall," as those simpleton Rebels called their hero—was the unknown factor. Lee alone he could handle, but Lee and Jackson together—well, that was a beast of a different stripe.

Still, Hooker aimed to keep his pledge to Lincoln to lay waste to

Lee, take Richmond and bring the war in the East to a rapid conclusion. "The Confederate army is now the legitimate property of
the Army of the Potomac," he boasted. "The enemy must either
ingloriously fly or come out from behind his defenses and give us
battle upon our own ground, where certain destruction awaits him."

His plan was to circle behind Lee's unprotected rear, catch him
by surprise and, in a word, crush him. All this was supposed to happen near Chancellorsville, an insignificant little country crossroads
community a few miles down the Fredericksburg Turnpike.
Chancellorsville was not really a town, just a solitary farmhouse in
the midst of a cultivated clearing. It was there that Hooker would
set up headquarters and oversee his army's great victory. It was there
he would plot the demise of Robert E. Lee and seal the fate of the
Confederacy. A victorious campaign against the Confederates at
Chancellorsville would not only figure into Lincoln's political for-
tunes, but undoubtedly lead to another star for Hooker.

On the morning of May 1, after several delays, Hooker's
columns finally began their long awaited advance.

———

THE ONLY THING Hooker hadn't counted on was The Wilderness.

The Wilderness was a vast, no-man's land of thick, tangled woods
and impenetrable swamps that surrounded the Confederate army
like a giant protective shield. Even in broad daylight it was a dark and
gloomy place, an uncharted region of shifting shadows and soaring
pines and giant scrub oaks, underskirted by a dense, wiry underbrush
that limited visibility to only a few paces in any direction.

For the Federals, it was impossible to imagine a more unlikely
place for battle between two grand armies than The Wilderness.

But the forbidding terrain suited Robert E. Lee perfectly.
Outnumbered and out-gunned, the wily Virginian saw the brooding forest as a defensive commander's dream come true. Not only
did his men know The Wilderness well, here Hooker's superior
artillery and ground troops would be of no tactical advantage.

All Lee had to do was wait for the feisty Northern commander to
make his first move.

He wouldn't have to wait long.

THE SUN HAD BEEN UP less than half an hour when the order came down to move out. As if in a trance, the weary men in gray rose from their humble breakfast fires, swung their muskets over their shoulders and set off down a narrow dirt trail called the Orange Plank Road. The road knifed straight through the heart of The Wilderness toward Chancellorsville, where they had been told the enemy was waiting in full force.

In the distance, cannons thumped and boomed, and the crackle and rattle of musketfire rose and fell, rose and fell, forming small clouds of gunsmoke that drifted higher and higher above the distant tree line.

Skirmishers, Wiley reflected, staring off in the direction of the ruckus. The real action probably wouldn't come until they reached Hooker's main line at Chancellorsville.

The day was still young, but already the smell of gunpowder lingered hot and heavy on the soft morning air as the men plodded along, four abreast, laughing, joking, making small talk, anything to keep their minds off the danger ahead. Most of them marched light. Knowing they were going into battle, they carried only what they needed—blanket, canteen, bayonet, knife, musket, cartridge box, and haversack stuffed with rations and tobacco. Many carried small Bibles stuffed in their front pockets or tucked away in their haversacks.

Wiley recalled the words of one old-timer the night before the big charge at Malvern Hill. They had been sitting around a campfire when a grizzled old veteran had wandered over and sat down by the fire.

"Boys," he'd croaked, rolling a smoke. "When you're out there on the field tomorrow, pack light. Don't pick up anything 'ceptin' food and tobaccy."

The soldier had been in his early forties, but in the flickering firelight Wiley had thought he looked incredibly ancient—weathered, broken, like a castoff old hound. "Git hold of all the food you can," he had advised. "Steal it, if you have to. Let your aim be to secure food and food and still more food, and keep your eyes open for tobaccy. Fill your canteen at every stream we cross. Something else: Never wash your feet till the day's march is over. If you do, they will surely blister…"

Wiley had never forgotten the man's words. That morning, as

they pressed toward the enemy, the old-timer's advice was still very much on his mind.

———

THROUGHOUT THE RANKS, it was common knowledge that the Federals were massing near Chancellorsville for another push toward Richmond. Orders were to engage the enemy there, using The Wilderness as a protective screen, and drive them back to the Rappahannock. The fact that Hooker's men outnumbered Lee's better than two to one did little to offset the mood of the spirited gray coats as they tromped steadily forward amid a sea of colorful regimental banners and gleaming muskets.

It was a magnificent sight—a six-mile-long column of creaking wagons and marching men, clattering canteens and swords and jangling spurs, horses and mules snorting and pawing the ground, bugles blaring, and the slow, steady pounding of drums. Boots and bare feet skudded and scraped across the clay, made soft and moist by heavy rains the previous night.

At the head of Wiley's column rode Samuel Player—now a major—handsome in his dusty gray field coat and plumed hat. A regular sport, Wiley mused, proud of the way the young major from back home had conducted himself so far. Leading scared boys into battle was no easy job; yet, Major Player seemed to have a natural gift for rallying the weak-hearted, urging them on with his spirited words and fearless bravado. Twice the major had had horses shot out from under him, only to get back up, grab another mount and continue the charge as if nothing had happened. Wiley knew of at least one occasion when the major had taken a ball in the leg. Rather than leave the field, he had had the wound patched up right there on the spot, then limped back to the fight.

They had gone no more than a couple of miles when the dark woods on the left seemed to explode in a solid sheet of flame. There were popping sounds and more popping sounds as the Confederates scattered, some screaming and falling, rolling in the dirt, clutching their bellies as blood and guts and bits of blasted bone flew across the road. Others lay still, their eyes upturned and glassy, fingers gnarled in death.

More Confederates fell, long lines of them, chests and heads exploding as volley after volley of hot lead rained down on them from the trees. Thick puffs of gunsmoke swirled and spiraled among the pines as the unseen enemy fired and reloaded, fired and reloaded, an endless roar of muskets and pistols raking the Rebel lines.

The ambush had caught the Confederates by surprise. Regimental commanders whirled on their steeds, shrieking at the men to hold their positions, to stay within their ranks. One commander, a long-haired colonel with sky-blue eyes and sporting a coffee-colored beard and yellow gloves, took a ball in the chest and toppled from his horse. He rolled next to Wiley, sat up and said, "Close up, boys, keep pressing! Keep moving!" then sank back and died.

Wiley froze, mesmerized by the sight of the dead officer at his feet. He couldn't move, couldn't tear his eyes away from the handsome beard, the once-sparkling blue eyes now frozen in death. Bullets spat and pinged all around him, kicking up small clouds of dust, but still he couldn't move. One bullet actually grazed his hat, knocking it off his head.

Suddenly, Talmadge was beside him, pushing him to his feet. "Come on, boy, git a move on it," he barked. "You're gonna git yourself killed if you stay here." He looked down at the dead colonel. "Besides, ain't nothin' you can do for him now."

Talmadge was right. The officer was dead. There was nothing Wiley could do for him now. As he looked around, he saw that a lot of soldiers were dead, and there was nothing he could do for them either.

When he picked up his hat and saw the jagged hole in the brim, he realized how close he had come to joining the dead himself.

He got to his feet and fired blindly into the trees. He reloaded and fired again, not bothering to aim, just pointing the muzzle in the general direction of the gunsmoke and pulling the trigger.

Major Player came riding up just then, sword arcing above his head. "Aim low, boys!" he shouted. "You're bound to hit something."

Then the major was gone in a cloud of dust, heading down the line to rally other units of the 49th.

The fighting ended almost as quickly as it had begun. The

Federals pulled back into the woods, fading like phantoms. The aroused Confederates continued to pour rounds into the shadowy trees until long after the last of the blue coats had vanished in the brush. Led by Major Player, several massed units of Rebels gave chase, charging into the woods, shooting and screaming like avenging angels. They beat the bushes with their rifles, poked and probed with bayonets.

A few moments later they staggered back out onto the road, dragging wounded prisoners and pushing others before them at bayonet point.

Talmadge, his tattered uniform grimed by the smoke of gunfire and campfire, looked at Wiley and said, "You okay?"

Wiley nodded. "I think so," he said, leaning against his musket. "Where do you think they came from?"

Talmadge made a grunting sound, then spat a wad of chewing tobacco onto the road. "Shoot, boy, these woods are crawling with blue-bellies. See those?" he asked, pointing toward a pair of observation balloons floating high overhead. "They got eyes in the sky. They know every step we're taking."

That didn't seem fair to Wiley. If the Yanks had observation balloons, the Rebs should have them, too. It didn't seem right that one side could have them and the other not.

Just then another officer came galloping up on a rust-colored horse. "Re-group! Keep moving!" he screamed over and over. "Re-group! Keep moving!" until he was swallowed up by the ringing clouds of blue gunsmoke.

Soon the men were on their feet and moving forward again. Only now the bugles were still, and the drums lay strangely quiet against the young chests that carried them.

Late that afternoon, an eerie calm settled over the black woods surrounding Chancellorsville. The hollow roar of artillery could still be heard here and there, mixed with the faint crackle of musketry. But they seemed too far away to be bothered with as the Confederates settled down to assess their losses. Hospital wagons crowded the narrow road, stopping to pick up the wounded and the dead. The wounded were ferried to field hospitals hastily set up behind the lines, where surgeons, their arms and white cotton frocks smeared with blood, sawed off limbs and sewed up holes in soldiers left by Minié balls and shrapnel. Burial details rounded up the dead and quickly disposed of them in temporary mass graves. Black orderlies drove crude wooden markers bearing the names of the dead into the soft earth.

The Southern boys had done their job. Under Lee and Jackson, they had successfully halted the Union drive, even turned it back.

"ANYBODY SEEN BUSTER?" Smalley asked.

The private had just wandered over and sat down on a log facing Wiley and Talmadge. His face was black with smoke and dirt. The pain in his eyes revealed his concern for his missing friend.

"I've been looking all over the place," Smalley muttered. He was on the verge of tears. "Nobody seems to know where he is."

Wiley looked up. "Have you checked the hospital tent?"

"Yep. Tried 'em all. He ain't there."

Talmadge clicked his teeth. "Maybe he up and skedaddled."

Smalley thought about that for a moment. "Naw—Buster wouldn't do a thing like that." He got up and started walking toward the woods. "I'm gonna go look in the woods. He might be hurt or something."

"You be careful out there," Wiley said.

Before fading into the trees, Smalley turned around and yelled, "If you see him, be sure and tell him I'm looking for him. I don't know what I'd do if anything happened to that boy."

"WE SURE RUN those old boys like rip," Talmadge crowed. He was perched on a log next to Wiley, rubbing down his musket with a rag. "Too bad it got dark. Another few minutes and we could have picked their tail feathers clean."

Wiley agreed. "There's always tomorrow," he joked.

"You got that right," Talmadge replied. "Them old boys better get 'em a lot of shut-eye tonight 'cause they're gonna need all their strength when I jump back on their blue hides in the morning."

It was amazing how much the big man liked to fight. He'd

charge into battle like a screaming demon, totally unaffected by bullets whizzing past his head or cannonballs bursting all around him. There was an air of invulnerability about him, an almost mystical, god-like quality that made Talmadge one of the most feared warriors in Lee's army. That was one of the reasons why Wiley always made it a point to stick close to the big soldier.

Another was the fact that they had become fast friends, almost like brothers. It had started right before Seven Pines when Wiley had stood up to the big man. Instead of backing down, as most sensible men would have done in that situation, Wiley had fought back, even getting in a few good licks before they called it a draw and shook hands.

Now they were constant companions—bunking together, marching together, sleeping together, fighting together.

Talmadge was a quiet, almost secretive man, not given much to talking about himself. But Wiley had learned that he came from a small farm near Selma, Alabama. That was about all he or anyone else knew about the big man, except that he was one of the best soldiers in the Confederate army.

Wiley had just sat down to pen a letter home to Martha Ann when a rider came galloping into camp. He was dressed in civilian clothes and carried a bulging satchel strapped across his chest.

Another newspaperman, Wiley speculated. Sometimes it seemed as if there were more newspapermen running around in this war than soldiers. For the life of him, he didn't know why they needed so many. All they did was write lies that kept the folks back home upset.

Several sentries raced forward, muskets at the ready. "Halt!" they shouted at the civilian rider.

The rider halted, his face frothing with rage. "Hold your fire, you damn fools!" he shouted. "Ain't there been enough friendly killing for one night?"

"What's your business here, mister?" one of the guards asked.

"Let me pass, you idiot," the civilian sneered. "Can't you see I'm on an urgent mission here?"

"You ain't going nowhere, hoss, till you tell me who you are and state the nature of your business in this here camp."

Talmadge got up and walked slowly over to the rider. "Hold on a minute, boys," he said to the guards. Looking the civilian up and down, he said, "You mentioned something about friendly killing, mister. What kind of friendly killing would you be talking about?"

The civilian yanked off his hat and scratched his head. In the dim light he looked to be in his mid-twenties, with a fine shock of jet-black hair and a full beard. "What I'm talking about is, General Jackson has been shot. Shot by some of our own boys."

Every soldier within earshot sprang forward. They surrounded the rider, beseeching him to tell them more.

"All I know is, he was coming back in from a ride a little while ago, and was shot by some North Carolina guards who thought he was a Yankee spy."

"A spy?" one of the guards breathed.

"Oh, no—not Jackson," the other guard moaned.

"Is he gonna be all right?" Talmadge asked.

The rider shrugged. "Don't rightly know, friend. They say he took three balls. Two officers with him were killed outright. Plus a courier."

"Good God, this is terrible," a young private wailed. "Old Jack dead. It can't be true."

"Who's in command of his corps?" Wiley asked.

"Hill was," the rider responded. "Then he got hurt. Now Stuart's running things."

"Jeb Stuart?" Talmadge asked.

"The very one," the rider said. He put back on his hat, grabbed the reins and said, "Well, I've got to get to Lee's tent to tell him the bad news. Then I've got a story to write, boys. This one will make all the papers."

He stopped long enough to salute the men and say, "Give 'em hell tomorrow, boys!" then nudged his horse and galloped away into the dark Virginia night.

"TOMORROW" BEGAN with a blistering artillery bombardment, one of the fiercest of the war. For hours the ground around Chancellorsville shook and trembled as Confederate guns, crowded onto a low rise known as Hazel Church, pounded nearby Union positions.

Shortly after dawn, waves of barefooted, bloodstained Rebels screaming "Remember Jackson!" surged across the smoking fields, mindless of the solid yellow line of fire being laid down by the frantic Union troops before them. As the Rebels pressed their wild advance, the Federals finally broke and started to pull back. The fiery-eyed boys from Georgia, North Carolina, South Carolina and Texas gave no ground. They soon swarmed over abandoned Union rifle pits and breastworks, blasting and stabbing everything that moved.

The battle at Chancellorsville was over. It had raged for four days, finally resulting in Hooker's dramatic withdrawal across the Rappahannock. The campaign that Hooker had confidently predicted would bring about a much-needed Northern victory had ended in disaster.

There would be no political glory for Lincoln this day, no new star for "Fighting Joe" Hooker.

Sad for the South was the loss of "Stonewall" Jackson. Jackson died eight days after being shot in the forest at Chancellorsville— ironically, not from the wound itself but from pneumonia and complications that set in following surgery to amputate his arm.

"Jackson has lost his left arm," a tearful Lee announced to his men, "but I have lost my right arm."

CHAPTER 24

WILEY AWOKE to the sound of birdsong. It had been so long since he'd heard a bird singing he had to think for a moment before he realized what it was.

It was only five o'clock in the morning, but already the camp was astir with activity. Reinforcements clad in clean gray uniforms—not one of them of shaving age—had arrived late yesterday. Lean, lanky officers and gruff, snorting sergeants bullied them about, offering them a taste of what life on the front lines was really all about.

They were put through the usual drills—marching, turning, saluting, parrying, standing at parade rest, standing at attention, presenting arms—then ordered to start chopping wood and digging latrines.

Watching the greenhorn recruits being put through the drills was enough to make a crusty old veteran weep. But not Wiley. Wiley was smiling that morning. Smiling because there would be no marching or drilling or fighting for him this day. No, sir, not this day. He even caught himself doing something he hadn't done in a long, long time: whistling. What was this war coming to, he wondered happily, as he quickly dressed and packed and hurried out of the tent toward the command post.

When he saw the long line of soldiers queuing up outside the major's tent, his heart sank. Oh, well, he thought. I've waited almost two years for this furlough. Reckon a few more minutes won't hurt.

He took his place behind a young, freckle-faced private with cow-brown eyes and a shock of dirty blond hair.

The young private turned around and asked, "Going far?"

"Georgia," Wiley replied cheerfully.

"Georgia, huh?" the boyish private grunted. He made a whistling sound through his teeth. "That's a right far piece, ain't it?"

"I reckon I can make it."

The youthful private rubbed his chin and said, "I'm heading down your way, too. South Carolina." He stuck out a bony hand. "Name's Cooper. Nash Cooper. You can call me Coop."

"Howdy, Coop," Wiley said, shaking his hand. "I'm Wiley Nesmith."

The line surged a few inches forward. "You married?" Coop asked.

"Yep."

"Any chul'in?"

"Any what?"

"Chul'in…You know…chul'in'?"

It took Wiley a couple more seconds before he understood. "Oh…children," he laughed. "Yeah, sure. Baby girl. Name's Joanna."

"Joanna. That's a right purty name for a little gal."

"Thanks."

"In fact, I knew a gal once back home named Joanna. Purtiest little thing you ever laid yore cold eyes on. Almost hitched up with that one, I did." A sad look came over Coop's boyish face. "But an old rattler up and bit her on the foot and she died. Two nights a'fore we were supposed to see the parson."

"I'm sorry," Wiley said, struck that a boy so young looking could have come so close to getting married.

Coop suddenly brightened. "What's she like? Yore little Joanna? I bet she's somethin' to crow about."

Coop's question caught Wiley off-guard. It suddenly occurred to him that he didn't know—didn't have a clue as to what his own daughter looked like.

"Don't rightly know," Wiley replied. "I left before she was born. But her ma says she has the biggest blue eyes and curliest red hair in all of Wilkinson County. That's where I come from."

Coop flashed another boyish smile. "Gonna be a real heart-breaker, that one, I bet."

"You best believe it."

"How come you never went back to see her?"

Wiley drew a deep sigh. "I've been busy," is all he could think of to say.

"You mean… you ain't never had no furlough?"

Wiley nodded. "Came close a couple of times," he explained. Then: "Every time I got things worked out the army messed it up."

"I hear you," Coop said knowingly. "All this marching and campaigning. It's enough to make a coon dog climb a bay tree. How much longer you figure this war's gonna be lasting, anyway?"

"Your guess is good as mine."

Coop scratched his nose and said, "You'd think old Abe Lincoln and Jeff Davis woulda done kissed and made up by now, on account it ain't getting' nobody nowhar."

———

IT TOOK THEM A FULL HOUR to reach the commander on duty. Actually, there were two officers—a captain and a fresh-faced lieutenant—who greeted them from behind a plank desk that had been set up under a shade tree.

When it was Wiley's turn, he approached the table and gave a smart salute.

"Name?" the captain called out to him in a weary, almost watery voice. He was a squat, freckled fellow whose thick lips, flat nose and big, bulging eyes gave him an odd, frog-like look.

"Private Wiley Nesmith, sir. Reporting for furlough."

"Nesmith, huh," the captain grunted. He rifled through a stack of papers until he found what he was looking for—a piece of paper with Wiley's name on it. "Here we are."

A lump the size of Texas rose in Wiley's throat. He couldn't believe he was actually standing here in line, about to go home. He was so excited his knees were knocking.

"Private Nesmith," the captain said, "you've been approved for a week-long furlough." He looked Wiley square in the eye and asked, "Just where are you planning to spend all that time, son?"

"Home, sir."

The captain's right eyebrow arched upward in surprise. "Home? Why, it says here you're from Georgia. Don't you think that's a mighty long way off for such a short leave of absence?"

"I reckon I can make it, sir."

The lieutenant, an officious little fellow who had been standing with his arms folded while carefully scrutinizing Wiley, leaned down and whispered something in the captain's ear. The conference ended abruptly, with the frog-faced captain facing Wiley again.

"Son," he said, "you wouldn't want to reconsider your travel plans? Like I said, Georgia is a far…"

"Begging the captain's pardon," Wiley broke in, "but I aim to go to Georgia. I haven't been home the whole time I've been in the army. That's better than a year now." Softening, he added, "You see, sir, we have this little baby, a girl, and I've never even seen her. But her ma says she's sprouting up faster'n a weed. Anyway, Martha Ann—that's my wife, sir—she lives on the farm alone, and, well, sir, I just figured it was time I got to go home, to see my family, sir."

The captain drew a deep breath and held it. "I see," he said, slowly exhaling. "That's fine with the army, I suppose. Just so long as you're back here in a week. Seven days. If you aren't back on time, the army might think you were staying away on purpose. Do you understand what I'm saying, Private?"

"Yes, sir, I understand, sir."

The young lieutenant leaned forward. In a high, nasal tone he asked, "You wouldn't be thinking about—skedaddling—would you, Private?"

Wiley almost choked. Swallowing hard, he asked: "Skedaddling? You mean, deserting, sir? Oh, no, sir, not at all, sir."

The lieutenant whispered something in the captain's ear, then straightened up and looked at Wiley. "Why should we believe you, Private? Soldiers desert all the time. They go home, kiss the wife, play with the babies. Then, when the time comes to leave, they have second thoughts."

"Hold on a minute, Lieutenant," the captain interjected, cutting off the arrogant young officer with a wave of the hand. He pulled another page from Wiley's file. His eyes grew wide as they scanned the page. "Says here you were at Seven Pines. Beaver Dam Creek. Malvern Hill. Fredericksburg." He read on: "My God, you were at Chancellorsville, too." He looked up at Wiley and said. "Son, you've sure seen your fair share of action, haven't you?"

"Yes, sir, I reckon I have," Wiley replied.

The captain's eyes went back to the page. "Wounded twice— flesh wounds, nothing major." He looked up. "Looks like you're quite a soldier, son."

"I do what I have to, sir."

"Very well." He signed a form and handed the papers to Wiley. "Here are your orders. You're ready to go home."

Ready to go home.

The words sent a shiver down Wiley's spine. "Thank you, sir, thank you," he said, reaching quickly for the orders.

Just then the lieutenant placed his hand on top of the orders and held it there. Glaring at Wiley, he grinned and said: "Remember, Private, seven days. The army shoots deserters."

"That'll do, Lieutenant," the captain snapped, handing Wiley his orders. The lieutenant drew back, suddenly red-faced.

Wiley stuck the papers in his pocket, saluted and did a smart about-face. Before he had taken two steps, the captain called out, "Oh, and, soldier?"

Wiley turned slowly, suddenly fearful the captain had changed his mind, that his furlough was going to be denied after all.

"Sir?" he asked, slowly turning around.

The frog-faced captain gave a big-hearted grin and said, "Give my best to your family down in Georgia."

Wiley thanked the captain again, spun around and hurried away, not stopping or looking back until he was well clear of the command tent.

———

BACK AT HIS TENT, he finished packing right away. He crammed everything he had into his haversack, then grabbed his bedroll and musket. The last thing he did was sling on the knapsack containing a stack of unmailed letters to Martha Ann. No use mailing them, he told himself, not when he could deliver them in person.

He stepped outside the tent and almost collided with Talmadge.

"Going somewhere?" the big man teased, looking Wiley over. When he saw the gleam in Wiley's eye he yelled, "Hot damn, boy! You did it! That furlough finally came through. Congratulations."

"Nothing to it," Wiley cracked.

Talmadge was grinning so hard it looked like his mouth was going to slide off his face. He thumped Wiley on the back and asked, "When you heading out?"

"There's a troop train pulling out of Richmond for Savannah first thing in the morning. If I hurry, I can catch a ride on the hospital wagon that leaves at noon."

Still grinning, Talmadge said, "I'll be a hog-tied polecat. You really are going home, ain't you? You're gonna finally git to see that little whippersnapper." Then, suddenly mellow, he added: "And you couldn't have picked a better time, either, hoss."

"Wiley looked at him. "What do you mean?"

Talmadge scratched his beard. "I reckon you ain't heard."

"Heard what? What are you talking about, Tal?"

The big man sighed. "There's a rumor going around camp that Lee's fixin' to head us up North. Somewhere in Pennsylvania, wherever the hell that is."

"Pennsylvania? None of our boys have been that far north yet." Then: "All I can say is, it's about time."

Talmadge shifted uneasily. It was hard to tell if he was happy or sad about the news. Normally, he'd be itching to get at the Yanks, no matter where they were.

"One thing's for sure," Talmadge said. "We figure on eatin' high on the hog when we git up there. I hear they got enough food to feed Lee's whole army for a year and then some."

Wiley paused. "When's all this supposed to happen?"

Talmadge shrugged. "Nobody knows yet. Couple of days, maybe. Soon's things settle down here. But I doubt old Lee's gonna wait much longer. I figure he wants to strike while he's got 'em on the run."

Talmadge reached out and grabbed Wiley's hand. "But, hey, don't you worry none about that, boy. You just git on down there to Georgia, and kiss that little darlin' girl of yours for me."

Then he reached inside a small bag tied around his waist and pulled out a tiny silver crucifix. "Been totin' this thing around long enough," he said. "I'd be pleased if you'd give it to the little one."

A sad, faraway look came into Talmadge's eyes as he handed the little crucifix to Wiley. Wiley held it for a moment, feeling its weight in the palm of his hand, then turned it over and read the inscription: "*Margaret Rose Talmadge. Selma, Alabama, September 13, 1948.*"

"It belonged to my little girl," Talmadge said softly. "We called her Mary."

Looking up, Wiley saw tears forming in his friend's eyes. It was the first time he had ever seen Talmadge this close to crying. "Tal...I didn't know you had a little girl."

"Well, that was a long time ago."

"Where is she now?"

Looking away, Talmadge said, "Fever got her back in '54. Along with her ma."

Wiley felt as if his heart had been ripped out. For the longest time he just stood there, unable to say anything, staring at the tiny silver crucifix in his palm and reading the little girl's name over and over.

"I'm sorry, Tal," he said softly. "I didn't know..."

Talmadge wiped his face with the back of his big hand and said, "Ah, that was a long time ago."

Wiley stuck the crucifix into his haversack next to Martha Ann's letters. "Thanks, Tal," he said, mindful of the pain still visible in the big man's eyes. "My little girl—Joanna—I know she's going to love it."

He reached for his musket. "Well, guess I better be shoving off if I'm gonna make that train."

"Yeah. You better git going."

Looking back, Wiley said, "You take care, you hear? Keep that big, ugly head of yours down, or you'll scare the Yankees to death!"

Then he was gone—gone to see his family!

CHAPTER 25

THERE WERE SIX OF THEM IN ALL—Wiley, Coop, two privates from North Carolina, a bow-legged sergeant from Atlanta and a young, wavy-haired lieutenant from Savannah who didn't look old enough to shave.

Wiley couldn't help thinking: The Confederacy must be in pretty bad shape to be bringing in boys like this to lead grown men into battle.

But he had to admit the young officer cut a striking figure in his shiny black knee-boots, red scarf and clean, well-tailored uniform.

"Probably fancies himself a real dandy," Coop smirked as they watched the showy officer strut ahead of the small squad of homeward-bound soldiers.

Home.

Wiley still couldn't get over the fact that he was finally going home.

They had set out from camp earlier in the day, hoping to make Richmond in time to catch the night train heading south. They had missed the hospital wagon by half an hour, so the six of them set out on foot, still hopeful of making the night train if they hurried.

Because they had to leave in such a hurry, Wiley hadn't had time to drop a line to Martha Ann letting her know he was coming. Not that it really mattered. Knowing how slow the Confederate Postal Service was, he'd probably beat the letter home anyway.

The squad hadn't gone more than a couple of miles when one of the North Carolinians, a stoop-shouldered runt of a man with cracked, leathery skin and carrot-colored hair, called out to the lieutenant: "How much farther you figure it is to Richmond?"

"Ten miles," the lieutenant replied crisply, never once breaking stride.

The soldier from North Carolina made a groaning noise. He sat down and started tugging off his boots.

The lieutenant whirled around and demanded to know what the soldier thought he was doing.

"These old boots are killing my feet, sir. You reckon we could stop and rest a spell?"

The glare in the young officer's eye was enough to freeze raindrops. "Soldier, if you can't keep up with us, we'll have no choice but to leave you here," he said sternly. The lieutenant straightened, adding, "I might warn you, however. These woods are crawling with Yankee skirmishers."

At the mention of Yankees, the disgruntled private jumped to his feet and hurried to catch up with the others.

Wiley was impressed by the way the young lieutenant had handled himself. Such composure usually came with more experienced officers. But the lieutenant simply looked too young to have been in the military long enough to have achieved that measure of authority. Maybe he was one of those West Point graduates, Wiley reckoned. That would account for a lot.

———

SOME TIME LATER the road widened, and they came to a small abandoned crossroads community. Several houses and barns had been burned to the ground, obviously torched, while those still standing looked empty and grown over with weeds and vines. Except for a shutter banging somewhere in the wind, an eerie silence prevailed over the empty town.

As they marched past the ruins, Wiley couldn't help wondering what had become of the people who once lived in those tumble-down homes surrounded by dilapidated barns and sheds. It saddened him to think of the children who might have once romped and played in the weed-choked yards. Where were they now?

On the far side of the town, they came to a fork in the road and turned right toward Richmond. The road narrowed as it dipped behind a hill, weaving past more shell-blasted fields and gutted houses and barns. As accustomed as he had become to death, Wiley was still moved by the number of graveyards they passed, most of them new and randomly set up, marked by simple, hastily con-structed wooden crosses.

Eventually, they came to a dark forest that pressed in close against the road. Instinctively, the sergeant slowed down and looked around, eyes furrowed beneath bushy red eyebrows. Catching up with the lieutenant, he said, "Sir...I've got a funny feeling about these woods..."

The lieutenant halted, looked at the sergeant. "What kind of feeling, Sergeant?"

The big sergeant scratched his scraggily beard. "I don't rightly know, sir," he replied, still looking around. "It's just that...well, it's too quiet, sir, if you know what I mean."

The lieutenant glanced quickly around, as if listening for some-thing the others couldn't hear. "I see what you mean," he agreed.

The sergeant pressed the point. "I gotta be honest with you, sir, I ain't never seen it so quiet." He scanned the bushes again. "Listen...Why, you can't even hear a cricket."

The lieutenant's hand went automatically for his Colt Revolver. "Sergeant, I suggest you have the men look alive," he said.

"Yes, sir," the sergeant said. He turned toward the men and in a low voice said, "Keep your eyes peeled, boys. Billy's out there some-where."

Yankees? That's impossible, Wiley thought. Not this close to Richmond. Marauders, maybe. Or deserters. But not Yankee troops. Please, God, not Yankee troops this close to Richmond...

Farther along, the woods thinned and the men relaxed. They even stopped to pick blackberries and blueberries growing along-side the road. Wild grapes, though not quite ripe, also grew in thick clusters.

The men ate their fill of the delicious berries and grapes, then stuffed their pockets with more.

A couple of miles down the road they rounded a sharp curve and saw the hospital wagon—the same hospital wagon they had been scheduled to take earlier. It was parked in the middle of the road, apparently abandoned, its loose canvas tarpaulin making a snapping sound in the breeze. The horses were dead, their carcasses already attracting a flock of buzzards.

They drew their guns and advanced cautiously.

The lieutenant waved his swords at the buzzards, and they took off. He walked toward the back of the wagon, pulled back the flaps and peeked in. "God in heaven," he murmured, then made a gagging sound as he backed away.

The sergeant rushed over to the wagon and poked his head through the flaps. When he saw the bayoneted and mutilated bodies of the dozen or so patients inside, he let out a little gurgling sound, then wheeled around and heaved his guts out onto the ground.

"Yankee bastards," he snarled, steadying himself as he wiped the vomit from his mouth. "They'll pay for this."

From all indications, the hospital wagon had been ambushed by marauders. No legitimate, self-respecting soldier could have committed such grisly atrocities. All twelve patients, some of them double amputees, had been bayoneted and shot. The team doctor and driver had been gutted. The nude, mutilated body of a female nurse was found strung up from a nearby tree. From all indications, she had been raped and tortured before someone ran a sword through her neck.

They ripped off parts of the canvas tarpaulin, wrapped up the bodies and buried them in a shallow mass grave. The lieutenant said a few words, then they turned soundlessly away and resumed their journey toward Richmond.

———

THEY WERE LESS THAN A MILE from the outskirts of Richmond when Coop turned to Wiley and asked, "Ever been to Richmond?"

"You could say that," Wiley replied. "I was with Johnston's command last summer."

"I hear it shore is a purty town."

"I wouldn't know. I was too busy fighting Yankees to notice."

"I hear you," Coop cackled, then slowed down to munch on some more berries.

A few minutes later, one of the North Carolinians caught up with Wiley and asked, "Where you headed, buddy?"

"Georgia," Wiley answered.

The North Carolinian made a clicking sound with his tongue, then scratched his head and said, "Say, that wouldn't happen to be anywhere near Macon, would it?"

"Sure is," Wiley replied. "We're so close we're regular neighbors."

"You don't say," the North Carolinian continued. "I've got a brother from down your way. Ever hear tell of a little dinky place called Griswoldville?"

"Sure," Wiley said. "It's only a crow's call from Irwinton, my hometown. Nice little place."

The stoop-shouldered private seemed genuinely thrilled that Wiley was familiar with the town where his brother now lived. "He went down there before the war, married a little gal and got himself a job in a gun factory. By the way, my name's Coleman. Wilbur Coleman. Wilmington's my home."

"Wiley Nesmith."

Coleman stuck out his hand. "Well, put it there, Wiley Nesmith. Looks like we're gonna be at least headin' in the same direction for a while." He paused. "You married, Wiley Nesmith?"

Wiley nodded. "What about you?'

Coleman shook his head and guffawed. "Naw. Ain't been a gal born yet that could chain me down. I got too much livin' to do before I go and git myself all hitched up to some little hussy."

Wiley laughed. "Well, each to his own, I guess."

They trudged on in silence for a while, happy to be on their way to Richmond, and from there, home, wherever home was.

A few minutes later Coleman nudged Wiley. "Say, Wiley Nesmith, when we get to Richmond, what say you and me have us a little fun? I hear there's this little place down on River Street where the gals like their men rough and ready." He nudged Wiley again and winked. "If you know what I mean."

"I'm a married man, remember?" Wiley countered. "Besides, I got a train to catch."

"This one place—The Silver Spur, I think it is—they say it has the coldest beer and best-tasting sippin' whiskey in all Virginny. And I tell you, Wiley Nesmith, right now I could sure go for a plug of that." He gave Wiley a knowing wink. "And maybe one of those purty little gals down on River Street. Know what I mean?"

Wiley said, "Maybe some other time, Wilbur. My train leaves at eight."

"Shoot, boy, you got plenty of time. We can round us up a couple of them little hussies soon's we git there and have us *some* kinda fun. Make you forgit all about Chancellorsville and what those blue-bellies did to that hospital team back there."

Wiley didn't much care for all this talk about loose women. But whiskey? Now, that was a different matter. A good glass of bourbon would sure hit the spot. He could almost smell it, taste it sliding down his parched and thirsty throat.

But no—that wouldn't do, wouldn't do at all, because of what whiskey might lead to. "Guess I'll have to pass," he lamented.

Coleman leaned closer—so close Wiley could smell the months of sweat—and said, "Come on, buddy, I can show you to some places that'll make you whistle a brand-new tune."

"I bet you could," Wiley mumbled, wondering how he was going to be able to get the pesky private off his back. "But I can't take a chance on missing my train."

Coleman finally said, "In that case, you reckon you could spot me a couple of dollars? I'll wire it back to you in Georgia soon's I git to Wilmington and git it from my brother."

Wiley honestly thought about lending Coleman the money—just to get him off his back, if nothing else. But the fact was, he was a little short of cash himself. In his back pocket was an envelope containing forty dollars—a little more than four months' pay. Money he'd been saving up for more than a year to go home on. Money for Martha Ann and Joanna. He couldn't afford to part with a penny of it.

He shook his head. "Sorry, Wilbur, but I can't."

Coleman started to say something else, but before he could finish the sentence there was a loud, popping sound, then another... and another.

Coleman's eyes suddenly grew wide, and a moaning sound issued from his mouth. He dropped his musket and toppled backward to the ground, dead, a dark red hole spiraling through the middle of his forehead.

A split second later the woods on both sides of the road erupted in gunfire.

"Ambush!" the lieutenant shrieked, reaching for his sword and pistol. "Take cover!"

Wiley dropped to the ground, his eyes fixed on Coleman, whose body was already turning cold and stiff next to him in the dust. A mixture of rage, anguish and fear swept through him as he contemplated how close Coleman had been to going home. He rolled his eyes skyward, tears streaming down his face. Why? he asked. Why take him now?

Wiley knew he didn't have time to wait around for an answer. If he didn't find cover fast, a bullet might find him, too.

He got to his knees and scanned the perimeter. Which way should he go? Where should he run? All around him, the woods seemed ablaze with gunfire. Thin, white puffs of smoke lifted through the trees, and every now and then he could catch a glimpse of a wispy shadow darting among the trees.

He looked over and saw the second North Carolinian sprawled in the dirt. He couldn't tell where the Tarheel had been hit, but it didn't really matter because he could tell the man was dead.

Coop had dropped to the ground and lay on his belly. His gun was jammed, and Wiley saw that he was desperately trying to adjust the mechanism when a ball caught him in the shoulder and spun him over on his back.

"I'm hit!" Coop yelled, grasping his chest.

Then a flurry of bullets raked his body, and Coop lay still in the road.

Only the lieutenant stood firm, waving his sword defiantly and firing his revolver randomly into the woods. He kept yelling for the men to rally, but there was no one left to rally. That was because the big sergeant from Atlanta was dead, too, crumpled like a stuffed rag doll on the far side of the road where he had fallen in a desperate break for the woods.

In spite of the confusion and hot lead spewing all around him, Wiley couldn't take his eyes off the young lieutenant, who continued to stand his ground, teeth clenched, legs spread, blasting away at the unseen enemy until the chamber on his revolver clicked empty.

Then, out of ammunition, he drew his sword and let go a blood-curdling scream, the same piercing Rebel yell that had driven the men of the 49th surging across the blood-soaked hill at Malvern Hill.

Wiley watched until a musket ball ripped into the lieutenant's chest, spinning him to the ground. Supported by his sword, the young officer managed to pull himself to his knees, his fancy tunic now stained with blood and dirt. He staggered, oblivious to the hail of bullets whining past, jaw jutted forward, teeth still clenched, waving his sword until another ball caught him in the neck.

He fell silently to the ground again, still clinging to his sword, the red scarf around his neck fluttering like a wind-blown feather as he went down.

CHAPTER 26

THEY MOVED AMONG THE DEAD, searching, probing with their bayonets. "Finish 'em off with your bayonets, boys," a ruddy-faced corporal ordered. "These Rebs ain't worth wasting precious powder on."

The marauders did as their corporal commanded. They moved quickly, silently, methodically running each of the dead Rebels through. One of them, a short, round-shouldered private with a pockmarked face and drooping mustache, squealed like a pig when he found one of the bushwhacked Rebs still twitching.

It was Coop. Coop lay on his back more dead than alive, his chest caked with dried blood. He was in a world of pain. White-hot fingers of fire scratched and clawed across his chest and neck. His head felt like it was about to burst. Strangely, below his waist he felt nothing.

But his eyes worked, and when he saw the mustachioed Yankee soldier looming over him, something in him withered, died.

"Lookie, here, Corporal," the Yankee crowed. "We done found us a live one here."

"Run him through," the corporal growled, without even turning around.

The Yank positioned his bayonet square against Coop's heart, then hesitated. He blinked. "Why, this one's just a baby, Corporal. A little Johnny Reb."

When Coop saw the bayonet poised above his chest and understood what was about the happen, he gritted his teeth and begged, "Don't kill me...Please don't hurt me no more."

The Yankee stared down at the young Rebel, trying to make up his mind what he should do. He hadn't counted on finding one alive, let alone one this young. To make it worse, here was this little Rebel with eyes as big as blue saucers begging for his life.

Hell, the soldier wondered, what was this army coming to when it had to go around slaughtering boys so young?

He swallowed hard, sighed, then glanced around to make sure none of his buddies had noticed his reluctance. Some might misinterpret his hesitation as weakness. But the truth was, the longer he watched the wounded Reb writhing and groaning beneath the bayonet, eyes wide and pleading for his life, the less sure he was of what he should do.

"Please," Coop continued to beg, wheezing and coughing up clots of blood. He wrapped both of his bleeding hands around the sharp bayonet. "If you kill me…I won't get to go home and see my ma and pa. They…They're expecting me."

"Come on, Reb, cut that out," the Yankee grumbled. "Don't be no crybaby, you hear?"

Coop closed his eyes and coughed again. Up came more blood, spurting from his chest and the corners of his mouth. When his vision cleared, he saw the big corporal looming over him, a long sword dripping wet with blood at his side.

"What's the problem here, Snodgrass?" the corporal blared. "You having trouble finishing off this little Johnny?"

The soldier called Snodgrass said, "Look at him, Corporal. He ain't but nothin' but a kid."

"Hell, Snodgrass, half the Confederate army ain't nothing but kids. Kids with guns that kill our own boys. Now do it!"

Snodgrass sighed. He looked down, trying to avoid Coop's pleading eyes. "This ain't nothin' personal, Reb," he said, then rammed the long bayonet deep into Cooper's chest.

Their grim mission accomplished, the Federals gathered in the middle of the road to compare their souvenirs—watches, framed photos, money and other valuables. They were too busy laughing and stuffing their pockets to notice movement in the bushes off to their right. Had they been more observant, they might have seen the musket, might have heard its hammer cock, might have even taken into consideration the fact that someone might have survived the ambush.

Wiley squeezed the trigger, and the musket shuddered in his arms. Thirty yards away, the Yankee corporal grabbed his chest and dropped to his knees. Before he died, he swung his head slowly around and saw a glint of metal protruding from the bushes.

"Goddamn Reb done killed me," he muttered, then fell flat on his face, dead.

The rest of the Yankees bolted into the woods. Some left in such a hurry they dropped their guns and souvenirs.

Then blackness closed around Wiley.

WILEY AWOKE to the overpowering stench of human sweat, dried blood and urine.

He was lying on a bed in some kind of room. The room was dark and dirty, full of blurred shadows and the moans of dying men.

Voices kept floating through his head, vaguely familiar voices that spoke to him from the dark. They seemed to come from far away, blurry mutterings that rose and fell, laughing, whispering, crying.

He looked up and found himself staring into the eyes of a white-bearded stranger. The stranger was sitting on the bed beside him, holding his hand.

In a kindly voice that creaked with weariness, the stranger said, "Welcome back, soldier."

Wiley didn't know what the stranger was talking about. Welcome back from where, he wondered?

He tried to rise, but a stabbing pain that began in his right shoulder and radiated down through his chest prevented him from moving.

"Where am I?" he finally asked. He hardly recognized his own voice.

The stranger smiled and said, "You're in a hospital, son. Chimborazo. You're safe." He leaned closer and examined Wiley's eyes. "How do you feel?"

Wiley rubbed his head. "My head. What happened?"

The stranger gave a weary shrug. "I was hoping you could tell me. A patrol found you a few miles outside town. From what we've been able to tell, it looks like you were on the tail end of some kind of ambush." The white-haired stranger paused while he checked bandages around Wiley's shoulder. "By the way, I'm Dr. Ballentine."

Wiley winced as the painful memory of the ambush came rushing back. They had been on their way to Richmond, the six of them, when the woods had exploded in gunfire. Cooper. Coleman. The young lieutenant with the high boots and the red scarf...

He closed his eyes, trying to remember, yet struggling at the same time to block out the painful memory of it all.

"There were others," Wiley began.

Dr. Ballentine shook his head slowly. "All dead. You and a young lieutenant were the only ones to make it out of there alive. He was shot up pretty bad, but managed to tell us what happened. How you saved his life by killing a Yankee marauder. Said you're a hero."

"I...I can't remember," Wiley croaked.

"They came at you out of the woods," the doctor explained, trying to jog Wiley's memory. "You fellows didn't have a chance, according to what the lieutenant said. You took a ball the size of a walnut in your shoulder."

"I did?"

"Lucky for you that you fell in those bushes. They didn't even know you were there until you shot that Yankee corporal."

It was all coming back now. The ambush. The white puffs of smoke. Men running around. Screams. The Yankee soldier with the drooping mustache who bayoneted Coop. The ball that came out of nowhere and slammed into his shoulder, knocking him into the bushes...

The doctor stood up, arms folded. "Apparently that was the same gang that ambushed one of our ambulances and murdered everybody on board. We found their bodies. Somebody had at least taken the time to give them a Christian burial."

More memories washed over Wiley: the hospital wagon. The mutilated corpses. The nurse hanging upside down from the tree, her nude body slit open and drained dry of every drop of blood...

"I...I remember," Wiley whispered, trying to blink away the grisly vision. "They were...the same ones who bushwhacked us..."

The doctor nodded slowly. "That must have been a terrible experience for you," he said soothingly. "What with that bullet in your shoulder. You should know that we were able to successfully remove it."

"That young lieutenant," Wiley started, "the one with the red scarf...Is he...I mean, is he all right?"

The doctor shook his head slowly. "I'm afraid not," he said, rubbing his eyes. "He died during surgery. We did everything we could. He just...didn't make it."

The doctor walked over to a window and looked out. Hundreds of white canvas tents seemed to cover every square inch of the hospital grounds. Countless numbers of wounded and sick soldiers sprawled everywhere—on wagons, on cots, on the ground. White-clad doctors and nurses scurried about, tending to the dead and dying. Mule-driven ambulances clopped and creaked along, halting long enough for orderlies to unload new patients or to pick up the dead and haul them away.

Here and there, gathered in great piles outside surgical tents, tottered huge mounds of human limbs—legs, arms, feet, hands, fingers—grotesque monuments to standard medical practice in the field of battle.

And nowhere could one escape the wild shrieking of men going into surgery or the sorrowful moans of those coming out. No sound this side of hell could have been worse than those tormented screams as hacksaws whirred and ripped through bone and quivering tissue.

Dr. Ballentine turned away from the window and walked back over to Wiley. "We tried our best, son. But he'd lost too much blood, you see. But before he died, he told us all about the attack. Said you were a real hero."

The doctor's mind seemed to wander a bit, then came back. "So, we've put you up for a medal."

A medal...

A medal for what? Killing a Yankee? Doing his duty? How many other Yankees had he killed in the line of duty these past few months? Twenty? Fifty? A hundred? Should he be awarded a medal for each one, for each life he had taken? If so, he'd need a good-sized wagon to carry them all around in.

Wiley could have cared less about a medal. The very thought repulsed him. He had other things on his mind besides medals.

Like the brave young lieutenant who had stood his ground during the attack, never once wavering. And all the others who had died on that dusty little road outside Richmond.

Tears came to his eyes when he thought about the senselessness of it all.

Then he thought about home. *Home!* Martha Ann...Joanna...

"Doc...I...I was going home. When can I leave?"

The doctor leaned down and placed a gentle hand on Wiley's shoulders. "I'm sorry, son, you should know that all furloughs in your division have been cancelled."

"Cancelled?" Wiley almost shrieked.

"A few days ago Lee's Army of Northern Virginia, which I understand your regiment is a part of, ran into some pretty bad trouble up North. Your division got caught right smack in the middle and suffered heavy losses."

Wiley groaned. He suddenly remembered something Talmadge had told him before he left. Something about Lee planning to take the boys up North.

But where?

"Can you tell me where it happened, Doc?"

The doctor rubbed his chin thoughtfully. "Somewhere on the Pennsylvania line," he said. "I think they said it was near a little place called Gettysburg."

"Gettysburg," Wiley murmured. The word rolled off his tongue slowly. Gettysburg...What kind of place was that?

"From what I've heard, it was nothing short of murder. Picked our boys to pieces. They say that General Pickett lost half his division, including a lot of boys from your home state of Georgia."

The doctor got up again and picked up a chart at the foot of Wiley's cot. "So, you see," he said, flipping through the chart, "I'm under orders to send you back to your regiment as soon as you're well enough to travel. And the way things look, that shouldn't be more than a couple of days."

Wiley was crushed. His unit had been battered by the enemy. Now he wasn't going home.

What else could happen?

"But, I was going home," he whimpered, eyes brimming with

tears. "It isn't fair, Doc. It just isn't fair."

The doctor looked at him and in a fatherly tone said, "Don't worry, son. You'll get to go home soon." Then: "This war can't go on much longer."

Doctor Ballentine was wrong on both counts.

CHAPTER 27

WHOMP! WHOMP! WHOMP! Charles Nesmith awoke to the familiar sound of incoming artillery. He had never been asleep, really, only drifting in and out of that nameless black state of unconsciousness known to all hardened veterans of the front lines.

He was in a trench, a mud-filled trench on the outskirts of Vicksburg. The trench was part of a maze of earthworks and barricades guarding the northeastern approach to town called the Great Redoubt. Less than five hundred yards beyond the trenches, hunkered down in their own rifle pits and hastily constructed breastworks, were the men in blue who were trying to kill him.

Charles lifted his eyes and looked around. The first thing he saw was Corporal Crawford, crouched low against a soggy embankment. He was busy loading his musket, an old Tower of London model called a "mule" because of the way it kicked. The corporal's muddy uniform was so ragged and worn Charles half expected it to peel off his back any moment. For the first time, Charles noticed his friend wasn't wearing shoes.

When Crawford saw him staring at his blackened and swollen feet, he winked and said, "Injun-style, lad. That's what me pappy used to call it."

Charles felt sick. He didn't know if it was the sight of Crawford's feet or the scurvy that was sweeping across camp.

"Better ready yourself, lad," Crawford rasped. "They're a-fixin' to make another run at us pretty soon. I can feel it in me bones."

Charles couldn't help but admire the grizzled old warrior's spunk. Wounded twice. Three fingers missing—thanks to an overzealous surgeon back at Perryville. Not a decent meal in more than three months. And probably dying of scurvy.

Yet, here he was, teeth clenched, eyes blazing, belly on fire, ready to fight on. To the death, if necessary.

What manner of men has this war created? Charles wondered. Men willing to go for days without food. Men willing to go into battle without ammunition or weapons that worked properly. Men who never complain, men who live from moment to moment, one battle to the next. Men who go for months or years without seeing or hearing from their loved ones back home.

Death and suffering had become the Confederate soldier's constant companions. They were with him in camp, on patrol, in battle, even in his dreams.

The thought occurred to Charles: What could be so bad about death? Death had its own peculiar way of dealing with hungry men.

Wearily, Charles pushed himself to his feet and checked his own musket, an Enfield. He saw that it was loaded and ready to fire, then leaned back against the wall and stared up at the sky. Huge, billowing clouds rolled and tumbled across the vast expanse of blue. It was a comforting sight, really, to see something so innocent and pure and so very far away from the war-scarred earth.

Charles honestly didn't know how much more of this war he could take. He didn't know how much more any of them could take.

It was early morning, July 3, 1863. The siege at Vicksburg was now in its third month. Between constant bombardment by land and sea and repeated infantry assaults, the Confederate army was simply worn out. Ammunition was down to the last few rounds in most units. Some had already exhausted their powder and shot and were pulling back to await supplies many knew would never come.

Worst of all was the hunger. Hunger was a raging lion. A grinning demon. It gnawed and tore at the insides of starving civilians and soldiers alike. It drove men mad, sent them scurrying into dank caves and snake-infested swamps in search of rats, squirrels, snakes—anything to put in their hollow bellies. The bones of cats and dogs had long become a common sight around campsites. Mule meat—a delicacy now—sold in butcher shops for ten dollars a pound. People with money were only too happy to pay the price.

As Charles watched his comrades swarm into position, he couldn't help thinking back to that night in April when he and Crawford and Altman were standing guard duty at the Grand Gala. Compared to now, that had been an innocent time, a different age. He could almost hear the tinkling music, the laughter; could almost smell the fragrance of honeysuckle and magnolia blossoms wafting on the soft night air. In his mind's eye he could still see the pretty girls in their hooped skirts and the handsome officers in their fancy dress uniforms as they came and went in their fine carriages. Back then, how could anyone have known what sad fate lay in store for their proud city?

Before the siege set in, Vicksburg had been the pride of Dixie, a showplace of beautiful homes, elegant shops, sprawling river-front parks and a prosperous, happy population far removed from the turmoil of war. Now, with Grant's campaign in the West in full flower, the once-handsome city with its gleaming monuments and white-columned mansions and shaded magnolia lanes was teetering on the brink of total collapse.

Where was Johnston? Where was his thirty-thousand-man army? Why didn't they come?

For months, the people of Vicksburg had been anxiously waiting for the exhalted Confederate general to come dashing to their rescue. And when he did, they would show Grant a thing or two. Together with Pemberton's forces, they would save the city and drive the Yankees clear back to Tennessee. Isn't that what President Davis had promised them? Isn't that what the newspapers kept saying?

But the hours had passed, and the days had passed, and still there was no sign of Joe Johnston and his gallant army of gray coats. The bombardments continued, night and day, and Grant's Federals pressed steadily closer to the city. A string of recent defeats at Champion's Hill, Big Black and Milliken's Bend had left the beleaguered Confederates reeling in confusion and frustration.

And with the fall of Port Gibson twelve miles upriver, the city of Vicksburg was now cut off from the outside world. They were, in a word, trapped.

Still, the defiant Rebels prayed for a miraculous intervention by Johnston. The newspapers continued to confidently predict that "the undaunted Johnston is at hand…We may look at any hour for his approach."

But more hours came and went and still no sign of their savior. Once-soaring spirits sagged. As citizens and soldiers, down to quarter rations now, scurried among the ruins for dogs and cats, their once-grand expectations of a glorious victory were now giving way to pessimism and despair. Alone and in groups, some ragged Confederate defenders put down their rifles, climbed out of the pits and walked away.

A few days earlier, Charles and a group of soldiers had sent a letter to Pemberton. "If you can't feed us," the letter begged, "you had better surrender, horrible as the idea is, than suffer this noble army to disgrace themselves by desertion…This army is now ripe for mutiny, unless it be fed."

The arrival of General Richard Taylor's three brigades back in June had given their spirits a much-needed lift. But it wasn't enough. They needed at least a division to stand a fighting chance against Grant's seventy thousand blue coats.

Charles himself had begun to ponder the unthinkable. Perhaps Johnston would not arrive in time after all. Perhaps the rumors were true that the general didn't think the city could be saved. Perhaps Vicksburg would fall, just like New Orleans and Jackson and every other major Confederate stronghold in the western theater.

And if that happened, how much longer would it be before Atlanta and Richmond and Charleston suffered the same fate?

———

CHARLES NEVER SAW the Union sniper who fired the bullet. He never saw the flash of the muzzle, nor the puff of smoke, nor the conical Minié ball whirling through the air toward him.

But he heard the impact of the ball striking hard against his chest. It was a dull, metallic thud that caused his eyeballs to bulge outward in shock, his bones to vibrate. Then he felt the bullet go in deep, felt the burning pain as it ripped through his lungs before exiting below his left shoulder blade.

At first he didn't know what had happened. He thought maybe Crawford had accidentally backed into him or poked him with his rifle barrel. Only when he looked down and saw the blood oozing warm and sticky from the hole in his chest did he realize he'd been shot.

The last thing Charles remembered, before tumbling into a deep, black hole, was that strange look on Crawford's grizzled face, and the words, "You've been hit, lad."

CHAPTER 28

THE STENCH OF BURNING OIL and rotting carcasses lay heavy over the fallen city of Vicksburg. Everywhere one looked, thick, choking plumes of black smoke rose high above the horizon, adding to the misery and suffering of civilians who had been unable to flee before Grant's triumphant legions surged into the last Rebel bastion along the Mississippi.

Some survivors had fled into the snake-infested swamps to escape the invaders. Others took shelter among the craggy caves and manmade hollows along the bluffs, still hopeful that Joe Johnston might come to their rescue.

But Joe Johnston never came.

———

THE TRAIN ROLLED IN WITH THE FOG, belching smoke and spewing noxious fumes into the air. No sooner had it shuddered to a halt than Yankee guards were rushing about, prodding the Confederate prisoners aboard at bayonet point.

"Move it along there, Reb," one thick-lipped sergeant snarled, poking and jabbing a wounded boy of about eighteen. "Keep it going, keep it going."

"Hey, Billy," the boy's bedraggled companion drawled, "take it easy, why don't you? Can't you see the boy's hurt?"

The sergeant pushed back his cap and grinned. "Well, now that's about to break my heart," he sneered. "But you better tell him that he ain't hurt nearly as much as he's gonna be if he don't git a move on it!"

It took a little more than an hour for all the prisoners to be shackled and herded inside the long line of boxcars. When the last door finally clanged shut, the whistle sounded, and the train lurched forward.

"Where ya'll takin' us, Yank?" an emaciated-looking private yelled through a slated door to a guard stationed outside on the platform.

The guard, a thin, freckled private clad in a dusty blue field jacket, leaned across his rifle and smirked, "I reckon you'll know soon's you get there, Reb." He laughed. "Now, you boys just settle back and enjoy the ride."

"You ain't takin' us across the Mason-Dixon, are you?" another Reb rasped.

The Reb's question, lost in the fog and the clanging roar of the locomotive as it pulled away from the station, went unanswered.

———

INSIDE THE CARS, grim-faced Confederates watched silently through slatted rails as the train rumbled past the smoldering ruins of the city to begin its long, slow journey northward. Every now and then they would catch a glimpse of a solitary figure darting among the shadows, no doubt groping for something to eat.

Sometime later, in a darkened corner of a car near the rear of the train, Charles Nesmith awoke to a world of pain. He tried to sit up, but the burning sensation in his chest wouldn't let him.

"Easy, lad, easy," Charles heard a familiar voice say. He looked up and saw Corporal Crawford's big, bearded face looming over him.

"Where are we?" Charles asked weakly.

"On a train," Crawford answered, "somewhere in Mississippi."

Charles coughed, and when he did it felt like arrows of fire were shooting through his chest.

"Here," Crawford said, unscrewing his canteen lid and tilting it toward Charles' parched and swollen lips. "Drink some of this. It'll help."

The cool liquid flowing down his throat did seem to quell the fire raging in his midsection. When he finished, Charles wiped his lips and said, "I'm gonna die, ain't I?"

Crawford hesitated a moment, then let out a nervous burst of laughter. "Hell, no, lad. You're gonna be fine, just fine." He pulled out his handkerchief and pressed it against his buddy's blood-soaked chest. "Now you just lay still and rest some more."

Gently, Crawford repositioned the blanket roll beneath Charles' head, then adjusted the bandages. That seemed to give the boy some relief, but what he needed was a doctor. The big Irishman had seen a lot of wounds in his time, but none as bad as this.

"Don't lie to me," Charles gasped. He grabbed Crawford's shoulder and said, "I want to know the truth. Am I dying?"

Crawford avoided his young friend's eyes. He'd already done everything he could for the lad, ever since he took the ball square in the chest back in Vicksburg. He'd plugged up the hole the best he could, patched up the wound and kept him warm and full of water until the Yankees found them in the trench. What else could he do?

"No," he finally told the private. "You ain't dying. What you're doing is going home."

Charles seemed to relax for a moment. His hand slid slowly away from Crawford's shoulder. A faraway look came into his eyes as he said, "I ain't afraid of dying. Dying don't mean nothing to me."

Another coughing spasm wracked the boy's frail body. A full minute passed before the convulsions subsided, but in that time the wound in Charles' chest opened again.

When Crawford noticed more blood oozing up through the bandage, he ripped off his handkerchief and pressed it tightly against the gaping hole.

"Hold on, lad, hold on."

A delirious smile stole across Charles' face. Gagging and wheezing, he looked into Crawford's eyes and said, "We sure showed 'em, didn't we? We showed 'em good."

Crawford pressed down on the bandage harder, willing the blood to stop. "Sure did, son," he said, forcing a laugh. "A few more lads like me and you and we'd a had those old Yanks high-steppin' it clear back to Tennessee."

Charles smiled weakly, then—mercifully—surrendered to a greater darkness.

ON THE OPPOSITE SIDE OF THE CAR, almost hidden in the grainy shadows, a young, shackled soldier sat staring at Charles.

The soldier had smoldering blue eyes and long blond hair that flowed around his pale, bearded face much like a halo, giving him a beatific, almost Christ-like appearance.

But the fury that blazed in the young soldier's eyes was anything but Christ-like. Some might have said it bore the mark of the beast.

"Lunatics," the young soldier muttered. His voice was clear and direct, but aimed at no one in particular.

Crawford craned his head around, searching the darkness until he found the young soldier who had spoken out. "What did you say?"

"They're all lunatics," the soldier mumbled, a blank stare on his handsome, dirty face.

Something in the soldier's voice—pain, despair, a dark, primal rage—chilled Crawford to the bone. Without understanding why, he found himself curiously drawn to the strange young soldier with the smoldering blue eyes.

"I don't rightly follow you, Private," he said to the soldier.

The soldier didn't once take his gaze off Charles. "Look at him," the soldier sneered. "Dying like a dog. And for what?" He gave his chains a fierce shake. "I'll tell you why, since you're all either too blind or too stupid to figure it out for yourselves."

The boy must be stark raving mad, Crawford concluded. Either that or he's spoiling for a fight.

"Look around you, friends," the soldier shouted to the other soldiers on the train. "Who do you see? Ragged little boys and dirty old men with rotting teeth. Scum of the earth, the blight of Cain. That's what you see." His eyes blazed anew as he continued: "Do you see any officers on this train? Do you see any gentlemen?" He waited a moment, then—another rattle of chains, and: "This is not our war, friends. It's *their* war, I tell you—the officers and the planters and the gentlemen who would have you give up everything you own and sacrifice your own lives for their greedy, ungodly aims."

The room went grimly silent while the other prisoners listened, mesmerized by the strange young man's impassioned outburst.

"What would you know about gentlemen and officers?" an old trooper yelled from another corner. "You're just peckerwood trash like the rest of us."

The soldier didn't bother to dignify the trooper's question with a response. Instead, he lowered his shaggy head onto his manacled arms, closed his eyes and wept.

Crawford, still confused, glared across at the testy young soldier, trying hard to figure him out. "In case you've forgotten, Private, we're at war with the Yanks. Just whose side might you be on, anyway?"

The bearded private lifted his manacled hands and pointed toward Charles. "His," he said softly, tears streaming down his cheeks. "I'm on *his* side."

———

CHARLES AWOKE when another bolt of pain shot through his chest. He reached for Crawford's arm again. "Crawford?" he called out in alarm. "Where are we?"

"Still on the train."

"Are we going home?"

Crawford took Charles' hand in his own and squeezed it. "That's right, lad. We're going home. Now go on back to sleep. We'll be there before you know it."

"But I want to be awake when we get there."

"Don't worry, I'll see to it that you're awake."

That seemed to please Charles. He lowered his head again and closed his eyes. "Don't forget...Don't forget to wake me," he said, drifting off to sleep again.

Crawford's eyes brimmed with tears. "I won't," he promised.

———

CHARLES WAS OUT for more than an hour. While he slept, the train made several stops, picking up more prisoners each time. Two new Rebs were shoved inside their already over-crowded car. One was an old man on crutches, the other a hollow-chested boy missing an arm. The pair of prisoners found a spot in the far corner and settled down among their rags and bleeding bandages.

Only later did Crawford learn they were father and son and had fought side by side at Port Hudson against Nathaniel Banks before surrendering to William Tecumseh Sherman at Jackson.

They had just crossed the Tennessee line when Crawford heard Charles stirring beside him.

"Crawford?" Charles called out. "I...I can't see anything. Where are you?"

Crawford scooted next to him and placed a reassuring arm around his shoulders. "I'm here, lad, right beside you."

Charles clutched his heaving chest. "It hurts...God, it hurts so much..."

Crawford unscrewed his canteen and splashed a few drops of water onto his handkerchief . "There," he said, swabbing the boy's face, "just try to take it easy. Won't be long now. We're going home, lad. We're going home."

Charles rolled his eyes toward Crawford and said, "You got to write them, Crawford. Tell them...Tell them what happened."

Crawford bit his lip to keep the tears from showing. "I will, son, don't worry. I will."

"You've got to promise."

"I promise."

"Tell them...Tell them..."

Charles let out a little gasp, then stiffened. His eyes grew wide, as if they were focusing on some distant object, then glassed over. There was one final, convulsive shudder before his body went limp in Crawford's arms.

Crawford lowered his head against the boy's chest and wept like a baby.

Across the room, a soft, familiar voice whispered in the dark: "Lunacy...It's all lunacy."

CHAPTER 29

T HE THING MARTHA ANN LIKED MOST about living in the country were the sunsets, especially during the long, hot summer months when the sky turned golden red and the sweet smells of the forest drifted in through the windows on cool breezes.

Before he went away, she and Wiley used to sit for hours on the back porch, listening to the melancholy murmur of crickets and whippoorwills and watching the flaming sun simmer and fade, gradually giving way to the soft glow of moonbeams and starlight.

Of course, they were younger then, and the times were more innocent. Neither had reason to suspect those far-off golden twilights would ever end. Little did they know that bugles would one day blow and flags would unfurl and the tramping of many boots would thunder across the land like a mighty drum, calling out the gray-bearded men and curly-haired boys with glory in their eyes.

It all seemed so foolish now, this war—sad, an awful dream, a nightmare that never ended. But still the drums kept pounding, and the bugles kept blowing, and the soldiers kept kissing the womenfolk goodbye and marching off to glory—only to discover, in the end, there was no glory, only darkness and death and despair as the nation crumbled and fell apart and bled on the high altars of passion.

That evening, as she stood alone on the porch watching the sun slowly melt behind the trees, Martha Ann Nesmith wondered how many more boys must die on those nameless battlefields far away before leaders on both sides came to their senses and put an end to the carnage. She didn't know much about the politics of this terrible war, nor did she care to. The only thing that mattered was that it was wrong, shamefully wrong, and that what she wanted most in all the world at that moment was for her husband to come home, to hold her in his arms, kiss her and love her once again.

In the pale glow of the rising moon, Martha Ann suddenly felt lonelier than she had ever felt in her life.

It had been more than a year since Wiley had gone away, more than a year since he had touched her, held her close and kissed her goodnight.

A warm glow spread through her as she closed her eyes and visualized what it would be like to feel his warm body pressed close against hers once again.

She sighed, glanced across the dark field toward Monroe and Sarah's little cottage. A single yellow light shone in the window, and a thin trail of blue smoke wafted up from the stone chimney. Probably just sitting down for supper, she mused. It comforted her greatly to know the black couple was there, just across the field, hardly more than a stone's throw away. She wondered what she would have done without them these past months. In all probability, she would have had to sell the place and move to town and throw herself at the mercy of family members, or—Heaven forbid—some relief agency.

But Monroe and Sarah, God bless them, had stayed on to help, even though they were technically free and could have gone anywhere they wanted. They were such good people—more like her guardian angels than tenant farmers. It pained her to no end that she was unable to pay them more.

The sound of the baby's crying broke the mood. Martha Ann allowed herself to drink in one last gulp of the sweet night air before hurrying inside the house.

"POOR LITTLE BABY," SHE COOED, lifting the child gently from her crib.

She swung the baby around playfully, singing to her, making crazy faces. When the baby continued to fret, Martha Ann nuzzled her face and said, "I think I know just what you want."

She went to the rocker, lifted up her blouse and began the pleasant ritual of nursing. While the baby fed, Martha Ann hummed an old tune, one her on mother used to sing to her a long time ago, one she had heard Sarah humming on numerous occasions:

> *Go to sleep, little baby.*
> *Dream while the angels serenade thee.*
> *When you wake, the sun will shine,*
> *And I'll be there by you.*
> *I'll be there by you.*

While she rocked and hummed, Martha Ann's thoughts drifted back to the day she had told Wiley he was going to be a father. He'd been excited, of course, convinced as he was that it was going to be a boy. Until the baby came, Wiley's letters had been full of anxious talk about all the things he was going to do with "my boy" when he got back home. Fishing. Hunting. Showing him how to carve and whittle, raise hogs, catch dragonflies and snakes. He'd raise his son in a God-fearing household, and when the time came, he'd see to it that his boy got the two things that mattered most to a boy—a spirited horse and a trusty gun.

Then Joanna came, and Martha Ann just knew Wiley would be crushed to learn it was a girl instead of a boy.

She couldn't have been more wrong.

If anything, Wiley seemed even more excited about the prospect of coming home to a little girl, his very own "little darling," as he referred to the baby in his letters, which usually arrived at the rate of two or three a week.

She had just finished putting Joanna to bed again when she heard the sound of heavy footsteps dragging up the front porch steps. Thinking it was either Monroe or Indigo, she rose from the rocker and started toward the door.

Halfway across the room she stopped. What would Monroe or Indigo be doing coming over this time of night?

She hesitated a moment longer, weighing the possibilities. Of course, it was Monroe, she reasoned, probably coming over to remind her about the trip to town next Saturday. Who else could it be?

Steadying herself, she threw back the latch and opened the door. When she saw Zeke Taylor standing in the doorway, the smell of whiskey strong on his breath, her first instinct was to slam the door shut and run grab a kitchen knife. But she hesitated, and that was all the time Zeke needed to step across the threshold and into her parlor.

"What do you want?" she gasped.

Zeke tipped his hat and smiled. "Evening, Martha Ann," he said. "I was just passing by and thought I'd...*hic*...stop in and pay my... *hic*... respects."

Zeke was drunk, that much was clear. Not only was he weaving, his words were slurred, and his breath reeked of onions and stale tobacco.

The look in the big man's bloodshot eyes made Martha Ann's blood run cold.

"Well?" he drawled. "Ain't you gonna...*hic*...be polite and ask me to take a seat?"

Martha Ann drew her shawl tightly around her shoulders and backed away. "Zeke Taylor, have you lost your senses? You get away from here right now, this instant, do you hear me?"

The strength in her voice surprised even herself.

But Zeke just smiled. He had that same crazed, devilish glint in his one good eye. "Now, that ain't no way to talk to a neighbor," he said, pretending that his feelings were hurt. He continued to sway back and forth.

"You're drunk," Martha Ann said distastefully.

The big man tottered closer. "I've had a little nip," he said, then hiccuped again. "And I'm likely gonna have another'n." He winked. "Thought you might like to join me."

"Get out!" Martha Ann shrieked. "Get out of my house this instant!"

"Whatsamatter? I ain't good enough for you, huh? That it? I bet it's because I ain't no...*hic*...soldier boy."

"Zeke...please!"

Zeke reached inside his back pocket and withdrew a small flask of whiskey. He unscrewed the lid, took a swig, then offered it to Martha Ann. "Good stuff. Sure you don't wanna little nip?"

Martha Ann knew she had to act—act fast—or suffer horrible consequences. But what? What could she possibly do? What could any woman do to protect herself against a brute like Zeke Taylor?

A tidal wave of dark thoughts swept through her mind. If anything happened to her, who would take care of the baby? She couldn't let that happen. She had to protect the baby, get her out of the house. But how? Where would they go?

She turned to run, but Zeke reached out with one brawny hand and caught her shawl. The shawl slipped free and fell to the floor. He lunged for her again, this time catching her arm before she could break free.

"Come here you little hussy," he slobbered, yanking her toward him.

"Owwww," she screeched, "you're hurting me!"

"I said come here," Zeke commanded. "I know what you want."

Again, Martha Ann screamed.

This time Zeke slapped her.

"Now, you just pipe down, woman, I ain't gonna hurt you none if you'll just shut up. Jus' gonna have us a little fun here, that's all."

"No, Zeke, please…"

Zeke slapped her again. "I told you to shut up," he blubbered.

He pulled her against him and gave her a slobbery kiss. She spat on him, clawed at his eyes with her free hand.

Zeke had drawn back and was about to hit her with his fist when a deep voice behind them growled, "You best take your hands off her, Mr. Zeke."

Zeke wobbled slowly around. When he saw Monroe's massive form standing tall in the doorway, his thick lips twisted into a savage grin.

"Well, well," he slurred. "If that don't…*hic*…beat all I've ever seen. A nigger standing up to a white man." He leered around toward Martha Ann and said, "Martha Ann, Wiley'd bust a gut if he knew that nigger was on your property."

To Monroe, Zeke pointed his finger and snarled, "Do you know who I am, boy?"

"I know who you are," Monroe replied.

"Then you know you better git yore black hide out right now while the gittin's good!"

"Not till you turn Miz Martha Ann loose," Monroe said.

Zeke flinched. No nigger had ever sassed him—and lived to talk about it.

"I'm a good mind to kill you, boy, right now," Zeke growled.

Just then Indigo stepped onto the porch and stood next to his father. He was brandishing an axe. The sharp blade gleamed liked a snaggled smile in the pale moonlight.

Zeke's mouth fell open. "What the..?" he began.

"Just let her go," Monroe said.

Zeke looked at the axe again, then back at Monroe. Smiling, he turned Martha Ann loose and took a step backward. "You're making another big mistake, boy," he snarled, "a mighty big mistake."

Monroe said, "I reckon I'll just have to live with it, Mister Zeke." His eyes narrowed. "Now you git on out of here," he said, thumbing toward the door, "before I turn my boy loose on you with the axe."

Zeke did as he was told. He backed slowly around Monroe and the boy. When he got to the bottom of the steps, he looked back and shook a defiant fist. "You're one dead nigger!" he yelled. "You hear me, Monroe? I'm gonna git you for this, you and your stupid, stuttering boy. You'll see!"

Zeke staggered and almost fell before he reached his horse. Somehow he managed to reel himself into the saddle.

Weaving, he shook his fist again and shouted, "You jus' remember that, boy. You're gonna be awful sorry you messed with Zeke Taylor! We've got ways of dealing with bucks like you! You'll see!"

When he was gone, Monroe walked across the room to Martha Ann and said, "Are you all right, Miz Martha Ann?"

Martha Ann reached for her shawl and wrapped it around her shoulders. "Yes, thank you, Monroe." She was still trembling. "I...I don't know what got into Zeke."

"Demons, Miz Martha Ann."

Martha Ann gave Monroe a quizzical look. "Demons?"

"Yes, ma'am. Demons done gone and got hold of Mister Zeke. They been messin' with his head for a long time now." He gave her a reassuring smile. "But you're gonna be all right now, Miz Martha Ann. Mister Zeke won't be bothering you no more tonight."

CHAPTER 30

IT WAS RAINING THE DAY Private Charles Nesmith came home from the war. That didn't stop the people of Wilkinson County from turning out by the hundreds to welcome home one of their fallen heroes. All morning long they had been converging on the small train station at the edge of town—silent, grim-faced men and woman and sad-eyed children wearing black armbands and clutching tiny flags. The scene was remarkably similar to that of two years earlier when so many of these same citizens had been on hand to see the Wilkinson County Invincibles board the train and ride off to war. What a grand occasion that had been! Children dancing and playing in the rain. Fireworks and picnics and parades lasting into the wee hours. Stirring patriotic speeches by starry-eyed politicians, including the governor of the state.

Back then, no price had been too steep to pay for freedom, no sacrifice too great for their glorious cause.

But today there would be no rousing speeches by deep-throated politicians. No parades and fireworks. No pumpkin-slinging contests. There would be no singing and torchlight dancing in the streets. No laughing children.

Today the town was draped in funeral black. Businesses were closed. Confederate flags up and down Main Street had been lowered to half-staff. Even the horses and buggies were decked out in black plumes and crepe. From one end of town to the other, the silence was as profound as a public hanging.

Most of the notables were there—Sheriff Poindexter, Mayor Futch, the Reverend Thurmond—just as they had been two years ago. Only now they were older, less inclined to miracles.

MARTHA ANN MARVELED at how well Mother Nesmith was holding up. Her grief was strong, yet the proud old woman carried her suffering well.

They sat on a bench beneath a baggage overhang next to the tracks. Mother Nesmith had wanted to be as close to the train as possible so she could be the first to touch her boy's casket when they unloaded it off the train. Martha Ann sat on one side, holding her hand. Maggie, Charles' widow, sat on the other, gripping an umbrella that protected the three of them. Behind them stood Garrett, gaunt and stiff, an angry look on his face.

Mother Nesmith was dressed in her finest black dress. Her narrow shoulders, slumping so low as to be nonexistent, were covered by a matching shawl. Her eyes, puffed and swollen from several days of tears, still misted as she stared down the long tracks waiting for the whistle to blow.

Then, all at once she heard it—the whistle—a long, piercing shriek that split the damp morning air.

Mother Nesmith flinched.

"Here it comes!" someone called out.

A baby started crying. Several women began to wail as the train shuddered closer.

Soon others were weeping—women and children and stout-chested men who didn't even try to conceal their grief.

Mother Nesmith perked up. "Is he here?" she asked, her voice low and scratchy. Then: "Is my boy home yet?"

Martha Ann reached out and squeezed the old woman's hand. "Almost, Mother Nesmith," she replied. "Almost."

Another long minute passed before the train rounded the wooded bend and chugged into view. The big locomotive rumbled straight toward them now, hissing, belching fumes and columns of smoke as it slowed, its single light stabbing through the gloom like a giant, watery eyeball.

After what seemed like an eternity, it finally clanked up to the platform and stopped. There was a screech of brakes and grinding steel wheels. A gush of steam hissed out from below, but nobody moved back or even seemed to care.

Before the steam and smoke had cleared, a young Confederate captain dressed in a fancy, double-breasted uniform stepped down from the train and faced the crowd.

"Which one of you is here to collect the body of Private Charles Nesmith?" he asked officiously. His right hand clutched the hilt of a gleaming, gilded sword that dangled at his side.

Martha Ann helped Mother Nesmith to her feet. Then Maggie rose. The three of them moved toward the young officer.

The captain removed his hat when he saw Mother Nesmith walking toward him. "Are you the mother?" he asked.

Mother Nesmith nodded. "I am."

"And I am the wife," Maggie said solemnly.

The officer bowed, then said, "I am Captain Roderick Matheson." He looked first at Maggie, then at Mother Nesmith. "I am truly sorry for your loss. You can both be proud of him, the gallant manner in which he gave his life in defense of his country."

The perfunctory tone of the officer's voice convinced Martha Ann that he had given this speech many times before.

Mother Nesmith made a whimpering sound, then sagged. Garrett rushed forward and helped Martha Ann steady her.

The captain cleared his throat, waiting for her to regain composure. Finally, he said, "Private Charles Nesmith was a genuine hero. He went bravely to his death so that we may be free from the tyranny of the North, so that the principles of our proud country can endure." He paused again to wipe the rain from his face, then turned toward Mother Nesmith. "He fell in Vicksburg, Mississippi..."

"I know that," Mother Nesmith broke in.

"He fell from wounds received in the chest."

Mother Nesmith blinked back tears. "I know that, too."

"A soldier who was with him wrote and told us all about what happened," Maggie explained softly. "About how he died on a prisoner-of-war train."

"The Yankee doctors let him die," Garrett hissed.

The captain gave the boy a dismissive glance. "President Jefferson Davis sends his sincerest condolences to both of you ladies. So does his commanding general, Joseph Eggleston Johnston."

"Where was Johnston when they needed him?" Garrett fired

back bitterly. "I hear he let Vicksburg fall because he was too scared of General Grant."

The officer's handsome face lost some of its composure. "I wouldn't know about that, son," he said, straightening. "Besides, this is not the proper time to discuss official military policies."

"He let my brother die," Garrett continued, half-blinded by rage. "He let all of them die."

The captain didn't bother to challenge the boy's outburst. His job had taught him to respect the power of grief.

He stepped aside while porters unloaded the shiny metal coffin. Another soldier came off the train and handed the captain a ragged canvas haversack and a folded Confederate flag. The officer gave them both to Maggie.

"On behalf of the President of the Confederate States of America," he said perfunctorily, "I want to thank you for your husband's service and unselfish duty to his country. He is a true hero and should always be remembered as such."

The captain withdrew the gilded sword at his side. In one swift movement, he touched the coffin, the flag, finally bringing the gleaming blade around in an upward "Order Arms" position. With that ritual out of the way, he re-sheathed the sword, snapped to attention and saluted the coffin.

"Good soldier, I bid you farewell," he said. "You now belong to the ages."

He did a smart about-face and climbed aboard the train.

Seconds later the whistle shrieked once more, and the big locomotive roared to life, belching more clouds of smoke and hissing steam until it finally began to roll away.

Then it was gone, fading in the rain and the drifting fog like a gleaming apparition, leaving the people of Irwinton alone to grieve over their fallen son.

Mother Nesmith stared at the gleaming coffin. She waited for the right moment, then stepped slowly toward it. She placed a gloved hand on top and held it there, silent in her own thoughts.

"My baby," she moaned.

Then she threw her arms across the coffin and wept.

The Reverend Thurmond, looking old and gray in the rain,

came up behind Mother Nesmith and placed an arm around her shoulder. "It's time to take him home now," he said.

Mother Nesmith straightened. "I know," she told the white-haired preacher. "And this time, when I get him home, nobody can ever take him away from me again."

CHAPTER 31

WILEY'S WOUND TURNED OUT to be worse than Dr. Ballentine had thought. He spent nearly four more weeks convalescing at Chimborazo, the giant Confederate hospital. He wrote home almost every day, promising Martha Ann he'd come home as soon as he was able to arrange another furlough.

"I've let you down again, my darling," he wrote. "But I promise I'll be home soon. Like Dr. Ballentine said, this war can't last much longer..."

Upon his release from Chimborazo, Wiley had to sign a form promising to head straight back to his unit. He was warned that any soldier caught disobeying that order would be tracked down and shot.

But there was one stop Wiley had to make before leaving town.

He hitched a ride into Richmond aboard a commissary wagon. For two dollars, the driver, a short, squat black man with reddish, twinkling eyes and the shiniest buckteeth Wiley had ever seen, agreed to drive him across town to Hollywood Cemetery.

"What you want to go over there for, mistuh?" the driver asked. "Ain't nothin' in that place but a bunch of ol' haints and boogers."

"I have my reasons."

The driver shook his head and said, "Well, suh, you ain't gonna catch me messin' 'round with no haints and boogers, no-suh-ree."

It was a hot August morning, and a soft, scented breeze stirred among the boughs of pines and poplars lining the narrow river road leading into town. They drove past handsome homes and well-tended gardens. Flag-draped boats of all shapes and sizes— steamers, ironclads, sailboats and a variety of military cutters— puffed slowly up and down the James River, some of them belching smoke and steam, others meandering quietly along. Artillery batteries and pockets of sharpshooters lined the banks guarding the nautical approach from the east. The shore batteries had been put up following an ill-fated Union river assault almost two years earlier. That drive, led by the Federal ironclad *Monitor*, had been turned back at Fort Darling, a few miles downstream. Defenders of the Confederate capital quickly realized how vulnerable the city was to a river approach and hastily constructed the elaborate network of forts and batteries.

They pulled into the city limits of Richmond and turned onto a cobblestone roadway that cut straight through a congested industrial district. It was here that Wiley came face to face with the heart and soul of the Confederacy: cotton. Cotton seemed to be everywhere, mounds of it piled high on wagons and boats and rusty flatcars. Towering bales filled streets, yards and long, rickety wharves where hissing steamboats rocked and waited. Even the air seemed possessed by the stuff. Wispy white fibers danced and floated like wind-blown snowflakes.

They passed several brick warehouses crowded with Federal prisoners.

"Yankees," the driver sneered. "They're to blame for this whole damn war."

Wiley learned that the black driver's name was Jeremiah Wannamaker—named, he said, after a cousin up North. Jeremiah was a jovial, watermelon-shaped man who shook like jelly when he laughed, which was often. He made clucking sounds with his teeth as they drove along, occasionally slowing down to point out an interesting sight.

"Now, lookee yonder," he said, pointing to a magnificent, white-columned building. "That's Mistuh Jefferson Davis' home. See that high porch? That's where his boy fell off and killed hisself. Sad thing, that. Near-bout broke that old man."

Jeremiah made a big point of making sure Wiley understood he was a free black. "Yessuh," he said proudly, "I been free goin' on five years now, ever since my cousin, Abraham Wannamaker of New York City, paid off my old master. Five hundred dollars. That what it took to cast them ol' shackles off and set my soul free. Now, I is free

as a butterfly, free as a bird, free as the dew on an Alabama cotton
bloom..."

———

THEY FOLLOWED A WINDING DIRT ROAD until they came to
the top of a steep hill with a panoramic view of Richmond on one
side and the James River rapids on the other. Jeremiah stopped
when they came to a wrought-iron gate. A small ornate sign read:
"Hollywood Cemetery."

"Well, here it is," Jeremiah said. He pulled a rag out of his back
pocket and dabbed at his sweaty brow. "Want me to wait for you?
Be an extra dolluh if you do."

Wiley reached in the back, pulled out his gear and climbed down.
"No, that's all right," he said. "I'll be all right. Thanks for the ride."

Jeremiah leaned down from the wagon and rolled his eyes
toward the cemetery. "Just you remembuh what I told you, mistuh.
You see anything funny in there, you better skedaddle. Them ol'
haints ain't nothin' to be messin' around with."

Then he popped the reins, and the wagon lumbered away, leaving Wiley alone with the quiet dead.

———

HE WANDERED AMONG THE LONG ROWS of tombstones until
he came to the one he was looking for. It stood over a small grave,
one of several reddish clumps of earth sheltered by the outstretched
arms of a massive magnolia tree.

In the center of the group of graves was a small wooden marker
that read: Confederate War Dead. Above the marker fluttered a
small Confederate battle flag.

Wiley lowered his eyes to the small hand-carved headstone
before him and read: *William N. Nesmith, Private, Confederate States
of America. Died July 18, 1862.*

"Rest in peace, brother," Wiley said softly.

William had died at Chimborazo Hospital shortly after arriving
in Richmond the previous summer. They said it was smallpox, but
Wiley knew it could have been anything. Weary doctors on the
front lines accustomed to dealing with hundreds of mangled bodies

and desperately sick and injured men each day often listed as cause of death the first diagnosis that popped into their heads.

Whatever the cause, his brother was dead—another victim of this senseless war.

Wiley turned his face skyward. Tears welled up in his eyes as he contemplated the dark, fast-moving clouds gathering overhead. *How many others, Lord? How many more do you want? How many more of my brothers must be sacrificed in the name of this unholy war?*

He dropped to his knees and wept openly, unashamedly.

As he knelt beside William's grave, hat in hand, tears streaming down his cheeks, he recalled a Bible passage from childhood: *My spirit is broken, my days are extinguished, the grave is ready for me…*

Job's desperate lament seemed to sum up the deep anguish wracking Wiley's tormented soul at that moment.

Wiley leaned over the grave and wiped away a patch of moss that had collected in the corner of William's headstone. Placing his hand on the grave again, he whispered, "I'll tell Ma I saw you. She'll like that."

The wind had started to pick up. In the distance a crackle of thunder and jagged lightning announced that rain was not far away.

Wiley remained beside the grave for several more minutes, unable or unwilling to tear himself away. Finally, he forced himself to his feet. He touched the gravestone one last time, then picked up his gear and trudged slowly back down the winding path toward the bottom of the hill.

Jeremiah Douglas was waiting for him at the gate.

"Need a ride, mistuh?" the big black man called out.

Wiley smiled, relieved to see Jeremiah and his gleaming, buck-toothed grin. "Depends on how much it's gonna cost me," he joked.

"Hop on up," Jeremiah chuckled. "This one's on the house. The way I see it, I got to go back down the same way I came up. Won't cost no more, no less."

They left, just as the first raindrops started falling.

———

JEREMIAH LEFT WILEY OFF at a busy intersection downtown. A light rain was still falling, but not enough to slow anybody down.

"The post office is just over there," Jeremiah said, pointing to a massive brick building across the street. "You go in there and tell 'em Jeremiah said to fix you up with a mail coach headin' back to your reg'mint. They'll take care of you."

"Thanks, Jeremiah," Wiley said, "I'll do that." He reached up and shook the black man's huge hand.

"Anytime, mistuh, anytime. Now you just take care of yourself. Don't go gittin' yourself shot up by some damn no-count Yankee."

"I won't," Wiley promised.

"Remembuh, there's a lot of graveyards like that one up there on the hill full of dead Rebs who tried to be heroes. Ain't nothin' this side of the Pearly Gates worth dying for—except a good woman and a good bottle of gin. Now, you remembuh that, mistuh, and you'll come through this thing just fine."

"I'll remember."

Jeremiah clicked his tongue, and the wagon rumbled away, leaving Wiley standing in the rain.

CHAPTER 32

WILEY SPENT THE REST OF THE AFTERNOON wandering the streets of Richmond. He was struck by all the wondrous things to see and do—the tall buildings and spacious parks, the ornate factories that hummed and clanked with activity, the bustling waterfront, the broad, shady boulevards, the monuments and museums. There were fine shops and fancy restaurants at every turn, each one filled with happy, well-dressed citizens.

Wiley figured a visitor could spend a whole week walking the streets of Richmond and never run out of things to see and do.

In spite of all of its great charm and beauty, however, the proud capital of the Confederacy was beginning to show signs of decay brought on by the ravages of war. In some windows and on street corners hung posters and signs complaining about everything from conscription and high taxes to the mounting war dead and President Davis' ability to lead the war effort. Mobs of women and children roamed the streets, demanding food and an end to the war. Most of the better-dressed citizens hurried to get past the shambling rabble, only to encounter other marauding groups around the next corner.

A grimy pall of dirt and soot seemed to have settled over the entire city, no doubt belched up by the gunpowder and armament factories working around the clock in a frenzied effort to keep up with military acquisitions. Bridges, roads and public buildings suffered from lack of maintenance because the demands of the military had simply left too few men behind to do the job.

In many ways Richmond was already a city under siege. Shabby refugees from Yankee-occupied lands to the north crowded the streets and sidewalks. Children and destitute war widows begged and panhandled on street corners. Runaway slaves slouched in the shadows of side streets and alleyways. Politicians and self-styled prophets hawked speeches and slogans at every turn, while wounded, raggedly clad soldiers limped about, searching for handouts and whiskey.

It was a city whose soul had been deeply scarred by the war. And major recent defeats at Gettysburg, Vicksburg and elsewhere over the summer months had left many of its citizens wondering how much longer it would be before the Federals launched another major offensive against their city.

This time, they feared, the combined might of Robert E. Lee and Joseph E. Johnston might not be enough to turn the invaders back.

"How much longer can the Confederacy endure?" screamed a headline from the Richmond newspaper.

Wiley paused outside a store window to admire a line of fancy women's dresses. He imagined what one of them would look like on Martha Ann. For one brief moment he thought about going inside and buying her one, a pretty blue one with satin bows and billowing sleeves and a low-cut neckline trimmed in lace. But when he saw the price tag—five hundred dollars—he shook his head and walked away.

———

"WANNA BUY AN APPLE, MISTER?"

Wiley turned around and saw a little boy holding up a shiny red apple. The boy was about ten years old. He was frail and thin and had great big eyes and a shock of red hair packed down beneath a dirty, over-sized military forage cap. He was barefooted, and the pants and shirt he was wearing were nothing more than rags held together by multicolored patches.

Wiley's heart sank when he saw the boy, the sad, blank look on his filthy young face. "Sure, son," he said, reaching into his wallet. "How much?"

"Is five cents too much?" the boy asked hopefully.

Wiley took the apple and looked it over. "Say, this looks like a mighty fine apple. I'd say five cents is too low. What if I gave you ten cents? No—make that twenty-five cents."

The boy's eyes lit up. "Twenty-five cents?" He couldn't believe his ears. "Are you sure, mister?"

"Sure, I'm sure. Why, this is the finest-looking apple I've ever seen." Wiley rolled the apple around in his fingers. "I'd say twenty-five cents is about right."

Wiley gave him the money, rubbed the apple and took a bite. "Ummm, just as I suspected," he said, taking another crunch. "Delicious!"

"Gee, thanks, mister," the boy said happily.

He rolled the shiny coins around in his palm, then stuck them in his pocket. "Wait till I tell my ma."

The boy started to scoot away, then stopped. Turning around, he scrunched up his nose and asked, "Are you a soldier, mister?"

Wiley nodded, suddenly conscious of his uniform.

Another sad look filtered across the little boy's dirty face. "So was my pa," he said softly. "He was killed fighting the Yankees at Manassas." Squinting his eyes, he asked: "Are the Yankees gonna kill you, too, mister?"

Wiley patted the boy's head. "I hope not, son," he replied. "I hope not."

———

WILEY CAUGHT UP WITH HIS UNIT, now part of Thomas' brigade, A.P. Hill's division, near Culpeper. He had followed Jeremiah Wannamaker's advice and hitched a ride on a mail coach as far as Orange, then walked the rest of the way.

He arrived in camp just before dark, tired and hungry, his feet covered with blisters and his shoulder still sore from the wound. But as he wandered the compound searching for his regimental quarters, he realized how much better off he was than many of his comrades who had gone off to fight in that Gettysburg campaign.

The wounded lay everywhere—on wagons, in tents, beneath trees, on the open ground. There were so many it was hard to walk anywhere without stepping on some poor soul. Some sat or lay perfectly still, oblivious to the flies and stench of rotting death all around them. Others writhed and twitched in agony, moaning and crying out to God for relief.

Long rows of freshly turned mounds of earth ringed the edge of camp. Black gravediggers, their faces grimed with clay and choking dust, leaned against shovels and picks, contemplating their grisly work. Overhead, scraggly flocks of vultures wheeled lazily against the darkening sky.

The whole complex was a bewildering maze of tents, men and wagons, horses and equipment, seemingly strewn about at random. But the thing that struck Wiley most was the silence. He suspected it was simply because the men were too tired, too beaten, to talk. Down-trodden officers and ragged foot soldiers, many of them barefooted and swaddled in bandages, wandered around the dusty camp like zombies, their limbs dragging and lifeless, their eyes fixed and glassy, their lips reluctant to move.

WILEY FOUND TALMADGE hunkered down outside his tent cleaning his musket.

"Well, look what the cat's done drug in," Talmadge said, rising slowly and embracing him.

Wiley was amazed at how much his old friend had aged since he last saw him. There was an overall grayness about him—in his hair, his eyes, even the color of his skin—that was both shocking and terrifying.

"Welcome back, hero," the big man said. Even his voice seemed somehow different—softer, mellower. "Come on over here by the fire and let's set a spell. We got us a powerful lot of catching up to do."

Wiley followed him over to the tent and dropped his gear. He sat down. Talmadge poured them a cup of coffee, then eased himself down next to Wiley. He slapped his thigh and said, "You're a sight for sore eyes, boy, you know that?"

Wiley laughed. "You too, Tal."

"I want to hear all about it, son, everything, right from the beginning." He fixed his eyes on Wiley and said, "Especially how you handled those bushwhacking Yankees."

Wiley shrugged. "I'm afraid there ain't much to tell."

Talmadge threw back his head and gave a hearty laugh. "Don't be shy, boy. It's all over camp. The way you took on those murdering marauders and saved that young lieutenant's life."

"I didn't exactly save his life, Tal…"

"Let me see the medal," Talmadge cut in.

The medal…

Because of all the things that had happened in the past few weeks, Wiley had forgotten all about the medal given to him back at Chimborazo. "Ah, it's nothing," he shrugged. "Besides, all I did was shoot a blue coat."

"That ain't the way I heard it," Talmadge retorted. He leaned closer. "I heard you put a whole passle of 'em on the run. Got yourself a little nick there, too, I see," he said, taping Wiley's bandaged shoulder. "How do you feel?"

Wiley grimaced. "A little sore, but I reckon I'll make it." He finished the coffee. "What about you fellows? I heard about the big fight up at Gettysburg."

Talmadge leaned back and slowly shook his head. "You heard right, boy. Lost a lot of good boys up there in Yankee country. For no good reason, neither." He looked away for a moment. "Old Longstreet should have known better than to send us across that field the way he did. It was murder, pure and simple. Dang near killed the whole bunch of us."

"What about Buster and Smalley?"

Talmadge grimaced. "Both of 'em were cut down in the first wave. I found 'em laying next to each other in the grass. They…They were holding hands." He looked straight at Wiley. "Can you imagine that? They were holding hands…"

CHAPTER 33

THAT MORNING, as the wagon creaked and rumbled toward town, Wiley was very much on Martha Ann's mind. It had been more than a month since she'd last heard from him, the longest period of time since he'd been away. She tried not to worry, tried to convince herself that nothing was wrong, that he was fine.

But it was so hard. Ever since the death of Charles, she had been terrified that something dreadful was going to happen to her husband. The thought of Wiley getting hurt—or worse—was a torment that stayed with her constantly.

She sat up front next to Monroe, who was driving. Sarah sat in the back holding Joanna against her massive bosom and humming a beautiful old spiritual. Indigo sprawled in the back, long legs dangling off the side.

It was a spectacular summer day, not a cloud in the sky. Butterflies flitted across the dusty road, dipped and wheeled over the fields and meadows. A warm breeze sighed through the pines. It was a lonesome sound, a sad, soul-crushing sound that made Martha Ann miss Wiley even more.

Monroe sensed her mood. "Thinking about Mr. Wiley?" he asked.

Martha Ann tried to smile, but tears formed in the corners of her eyes. She looked away, not wanting Monroe to see her crying.

The wagon rolled on a few more yards before Monroe said, "Now, don't you worry none, Miz Martha Ann. Mister Wiley knows how to take care of himself. He's gonna be just fine."

High overhead a pair of crows squawked furiously at an approaching hawk. The hawk circled the field twice before vanishing over the woods, the crows hot on its tail.

"See those old crows?" Monroe asked, pointing skyward. "What they're doing is protecting their territory. Soon as that old hawk gets the message, he'll leave 'em alone and go back home."

Monroe fixed his eyes on Martha Ann, hoping she'd get the point. "Pretty soon, old Abraham Lincoln's gonna git the same message. Then Mr. Wiley and all the others are gonna git to come back home."

———

MARTHA ANN'S SPIRITS SLUMPED even more when they pulled into town and saw a large crowd of people gathered around a big green wagon parked across from McDaniel's Feed & Seed Supply Store.

The green wagon meant only one thing—"Cap'n Dex" was in town.

Rudolph Dexter—or "Cap'n Dex," as he styled himself—was the biggest slave trader in the region. In recent years the practice of buying and selling slaves on the open market had all but disappeared in Georgia. But once in a while, Cap'n Dexter would roll into town with a wagonload of "choice African stock" and auction them off to the highest bidder. The whole county usually turned out, more to see the legendary Cap'n Dex with his stovetop hat and cracking whip than anything else.

Martha Ann gave a faint gasp when she saw Cap'n Dex. He was strutting around the wagon, whip in one hand, bill of sale in the other.

"Step right up, folks, and set your eyes upon the finest choice black African stock this side of the Congo River," Cap'n Dex trumpeted. "What we've got here folks is an entire family—firm, fresh and full of nature-blessed health and strength, ready for your inspection, my friends."

The auctioneer paused for dramatic effect. "These handsome darkies won't last long, let me assure you." His eyes roamed the crowd. "Come one, come all, let me hear your wallets talk."

Chained to the wagon were four Negroes—a tall, ruggedly built male, an attractive woman and two small children. The man and woman were stripped to the waist. Both children—a boy and a girl—stood stark naked before the gaping crowd.

The children were frail, puny little things, their skin black as

Kentucky coal. They clung to their father's legs, afraid to turn loose, even when the auctioneer prodded them with the whip. The little girl was crying.

Cap'n Dex tapped the side of the wagon with his whip and ordered the mother to make the girl hush up. "Or so help me, I'll whip her to the bone," he growled.

But the little girl wouldn't stop crying. If anything, the pitiful wails grew louder as she tried to hide her head between her father's legs.

Someone in the audience yelled, "Hey, Cap'n Dex, if you can't control that little darkie, what makes you think any of us can get her to mind?"

"I don't think they even understand English," someone else cracked, then the whole crowd burst out laughing.

Cap'n Dex glowered at the little girl. He didn't take kindly to darkies who didn't do exactly what they were told. He didn't much care for ribbing either, especially from country clods who didn't know spit from the back end of a mule. But if he couldn't get the girl to hush, he might lose this sale. His reputation was on the line here.

He yanked out his whip and shook it in the little girl's face. "Now, are you gonna stop that infernal bawling, or am I gonna have to whip you?"

The girl's eyes widened with fear. It was obvious she didn't understand a word the man was saying.

"There," he said, convinced that she had finally gotten the message. "That's better." He turned around and faced the crowd. "See, a little firmness is all you need with these people."

He climbed onto the wagon and held his arms high. "Time's a-wasting, folks. This might be your last opportunity to invest in a whole family before…"

Across the way, Martha Ann said to Monroe, "Let's go, Monroe. We don't need to stay and see any more of this."

Monroe started to flick the reins when, suddenly, the little girl began crying again. Her mournful wails drowned out the trader's voice. Fuming, he pulled out his whip and jumped down off the wagon. "I warned you," he snarled, drawing back his whip. He let the whip go, and it cracked like gunfire across the little girl's naked back.

When Martha Ann saw the whip lash out, she pulled Joanna

against her so she couldn't see. "Why can't somebody stop him?" she lamented to Monroe.

Monroe flinched—then felt Sarah's strong hand on his arm. "No, Monroe," she said firmly. "You can't do anything."

Sarah was right and Monroe knew it.

Dexter raised the whip again, but before he let go, the girl's father lunged toward him. A couple more inches and he would have had him by the throat. But the chains held, cutting deep into the man's ankles and wrists.

The crowd exploded in laughter.

"Hey, Cap'n," another man laughed. "Better watch that one. You got yourself a real tiger there."

Dexter was beside himself with rage. For one thing, these ignorant bumpkins were laughing at him as if he were some kind of backwater clown. For another, this black brute had tried to attack him—and that was something that, under no circumstances, could be tolerated, especially in front of potential customers.

This time he raised the bloodstained whip and let it fly across the black man's chest. The big Negro flinched but did not cry out. He merely glared at the slave trader. Twice more Dexter's whip rang out, cutting into the man's chest and shoulders. When he raised his whip a fourth time, one of the Negro's hands broke free and seized Dexter by the throat.

Dexter screamed. He kicked, he flailed, he lashed out at the black man with his whip. But it was no use. The big Negro was too strong, and his grip quickly tightened around the auctioneer's throat until his tongue leapt out from between his teeth and his eyes bulged from their sockets like overripe grapes.

With a defiant roar, the big Negro flung Dexter to the ground. He landed with a thud in a tangled heap at the feet of the startled onlookers.

For several long moments the enraged father just stood there, frothing, fists clenched, eyes on fire, chest heaving in and out, daring anyone else to challenge him.

Suddenly, a single shot rang out. The big Negro's eyes went wide. He grabbed his chest, then toppled forward, crashing like a fallen tree in the dust at the feet of his daughter.

Automatically, every eye turned and saw Zeke Taylor, the smoking revolver still clutched in his hand.

This time there was no cheer from the crowd, no foot-stomping applause. There was only stunned silence as the onlookers watched the little girl, a bewildered look on her small face, crawl slowly over to her dead father and throw her arms across his naked chest. The girl was quickly joined by her brother and mother, who commenced wailing and tearing at their hair.

Dexter picked himself up, dusted off his hat and looked at the dead Negro. Then he turned slowly toward Zeke. "You fool," he barked. "You stupid, stupid fool!"

"But, Cap'n," Zeke said, calmly holstering the pistol. "That buck was gonna kill you."

"Like hell he was," the auctioneer thundered. He scratched his head, still staring at the dead Negro. "You just cost me a thousand dollars."

The Reverend Thurmond pushed his way through the benumbed crowd toward the dead Negro. He leaned down, saw that he was dead, then rose slowly and faced the sea of silent faces pressing around him.

"Is this what you want?" he thundered. "Is this why our sons and fathers and husbands are off fighting and dying on the battlefield? So that they can protect the likes of you?" He shook his fist angrily. "And to think you call yourselves *men*."

The minister stormed off, thrusting his way past the mumbling men and women who seemed rooted where they stood. Behind him, he could still hear the eerie wailing of the children and their mother.

When he saw Martha Ann in the wagon, he turned and walked over. "Sorry you had to see such a spectacle, Martha Ann," he said, shaking his head in disgust.

Martha Ann pulled out a handkerchief and dabbed at the corners of her eyes. "It's this awful war, isn't it? It's turning us all into... savage beasts."

"That's part of it," the white-haired preacher replied. "But I'm afraid the devil has a lot to do with it, too."

He reached up and tapped Monroe's hand. "Sorry you and your family had to see it, too, Monroe."

"Ain't nothing new to us, Reverend," Monroe replied. "We've seen it all before."

The reverend started to go, then stopped. "Oh...I was sorry to hear about Albert."

Martha Ann blinked curiously. "Albert?"

A surprised look flashed across the preacher's face. "You mean you haven't heard?"

Martha Ann swallowed apprehensively. "Heard what?"

"Why, he's dead." He waited a moment before adding, "He was killed a few weeks ago over in Alabama. The telegraph came just this morning." He reached up and touched Martha Ann's hand. "I'm so sorry, my dear. I thought sure you already knew. Why, I'm on my way out to Nancy's right now to help with the plans."

Albert...dead? Dear God, no, Martha Ann was thinking, please don't let it be true. First William, then Charles. Now Albert.

Would Wiley be next?

CHAPTER 34

GARRETT NESMITH INCHED HIS WAY along the edge of the creek, cane pole in one hand, full can of earthworms in the other. He was barefooted. The dark, wet mud oozing up between his toes felt cool and mushy in the simmering September heat. He kept a close lookout for moccasins as he tromped along, mindful of the bushy overhangs and thick clusters of palmettos and cypress knots lining the bank.

It was late afternoon. In a couple of hours, twilight would descend, and the swamp would be bathed in blackest shadows. If he hurried, Garrett could make it to Nora's Pond and back before it got too dark. The last thing he wanted was to be caught in the swamp after dark.

Nora's Pond wasn't really a pond. It was a slough, part of the creek's original bed before the channel shifted course centuries ago and left it cut off from the main stream. It was named after Nora Peterson, an old blind woman who, legend had it, fell into the black waters and drowned long before Garrett was born.

It was a spooky old place, but it was the best fishing hole in the county. Those brave enough to go there around sundown usually went away rewarded with a delicious mess of redbreast.

Garrett wasn't far from Nora's Pond when he heard a rustling sound in the bushes straight ahead. He stopped, craned his head to hear better. Somebody—or something—was headed his way. He froze. Whoever or whatever it was, they were coming in an awful hurry. His heart raced wildly as he looked around, half expecting to see a bear or bobcat come lumbering out of the woods toward him any second. What would he do? He had nothing to defend himself with, except his fishing pole and pocketknife.

Then it was quiet again. No more rustling sound. No more strange stirrings in the bushes. Only the preternatural dead weight of silence.

Garrett looked left and right, straining to hear. Had he imagined the whole thing? That was certainly possible. Swamps could play strange tricks on a person's mind, especially in the late-afternoon gloom. He took a deep breath and held it. Maybe all he had heard was the wind. Yeah, that was it. Just the wind.

He took a few more steps, then stopped when he heard the noise again. Crunching. Rustling. Only this time it was accompanied by what sounded like voices. Human voices. Low and garbled, wafting on the breeze. At one point he thought he heard the whimper of a child. That was odd. Garrett wondered who would be foolish enough to wander around the swamp this time of day with a small child.

Moments later a group of blacks emerged from the woods. There were perhaps a dozen in all, men, women and children, carrying bags and satchels and a few ragged old suitcases. They moved quietly, furtively, crouched and hugging the shadows.

Garrett started to call out—then stopped. Something inside him suggested that might not be a good idea. Instead, he ducked into some bushes and waited.

The group continued its slow, silent journey up the wooded path until they came to an old foot-log spanning the creek. A couple of adults went first, saw that it was safe, then waved for the others to follow. The remaining adults scooped up the children and started across the log.

Garrett was intrigued. What would a group of blacks be doing out here slipping around in the middle of the swamp at night? Certainly not fishing, since none had a pole, And what were they doing with all those suitcases?

The answer came to him almost as quickly as it had formed in his mind. They were running away. That was it. They were fugitives fleeing some plantation.

He watched until the last person crossed the log and faded into the dark woods on the opposite side. He was about to rise when a twig snapped behind him. He froze. A moment later he felt cold steel against the back of his neck.

"On your feet, boy," a deep, menacing voice said.

Garrett turned slowly around and found himself looking straight into both barrels of an old shotgun. His eyes followed the length of the barrels until they rested on the face of a big, bearded black man. The man wore a patch over his left eye. He also wore a broad-brimmed hat, which was pulled down low over his head, and a long black coat. Inside the coat, tucked inside his trousers, Garrett could see a pair of pearl-handled revolvers.

"I said, git up," the black man growled, waving the shotgun. "Now!"

Garrett jumped up and flung his hands into the air. The big man eyed him curiously a moment, then inquired, "You out here by yourself, boy?"

Garrett gave a nervous nod.

The big man glanced uncertainly around. "You sure?" he demanded, eyes narrowed and fixed on Garrett.

Garrett nodded again. Faster.

"What are you doing out here all by yourself, huh?"

Garrett swallowed hard. "Fishing," he replied, pointing toward his pole.

An exasperated sigh escaped the black man's lips. He looked Garrett over, a troubled look in his one good eye, as if trying to make up his mind what to do. "Fishing, huh," he grumped. "You sure you weren't spying on us or something?"

"Spying?" Garrett asked innocently. "I don't even know who you are."

"That's a likely story."

The big man still seemed uncertain about what to do. His eyes scanned the woods, searching the shadows. It would be dark soon, completely dark, and there would be no way out of the swamp then. He had to get this thing over with in a hurry.

"Git down on your knees, boy," he commanded.

Garrett didn't like this idea. "My knees?"

"Yeah, your knees. Now, do it!"

"But, why?" Garrett replied, fear creeping into his voice.

"Don't ask so many questions, boy! Just do it!" the big man thundered, raising the shotgun and pointing it straight at his midsection.

Garrett dropped to the ground. The big man walked slowly behind him, pressed the barrel against the back of his head. Garrett flinched when he heard the shotgun being cocked.

"Hate to do this, boy," the black man said, almost apologetically, "but I ain't got no choice…"

Garrett wanted to say something but nothing came out. All he could do was make a faint, gurgling sound in his throat.

"Just close your eyes, won't feel a thing…"

Before the big man could pull the trigger, a strangely familiar voice rang out: "*No! Don't shoot!*"

Garrett's eyelids fluttered open. He looked around and saw Indigo Collins, suitcase in hand, sprinting through the woods toward them.

The big man with the shotgun did not take kindly to having his work interrupted. "What did you say, boy?"

"I s-said…don't s-shoot him," Indigo pleaded. "I know him."

The big man laughed. "You mean to tell me you know this little white boy?"

Indigo nodded. "He's a f-friend."

"Well, you know the rules. We have to kill him. Can't take no chance at this stage."

Indigo pushed his way between the shotgun and Garrett. "If you shoot him, then you'll have to s-shoot me, too."

That struck the big man as funny. "Are you crazy, nigger, or are you just plain dumb?"

"Look," Indigo blurted, "he ain't g-gonna turn us in." He looked at Garrett and asked, "Are you, Garrett?"

Garrett was thoroughly confused. "Turn you in for what?"

"You have to promise not to t-tell anybody what you s-saw out here. Nobody. Not a soul." Indigo paused, pleading with his eyes. "Say you'll promise, Garrett!"

Garrett nodded uncertainly. He still didn't have a clue what any of this was about.

Indigo heaved a sigh of relief. Eyes twinkling, he smiled and said, "This is it, Garrett. Don't you understand? I'm leaving for Glory Land."

"Glory Land?" Garrett replied, dumbfounded. What was Indigo going on about?

"Remember what I told you before? About the Underg-ground Railroad? Well, this is it. I'm on it now, and it's g-gonna take me to f-freedom, all of us."

So that was it. The Underground Railroad. Indigo had often told him about the Underground Railroad, a secret organization that supposedly helped slaves escape to freedom up North. According to what Indigo had told him, it was a network of paths through woods and fields, river crossings, boats and ships, trains and wagons, that eventually led to Philadelphia or Baltimore or New York City or some other city where they would be free. Some went all the way to Canada.

So Indigo was finally leaving.

Indigo continued: "Mr. Still—Mr. William Still—he...he's in c-charge of this trip. Says all we g-gotta do is follow the Drinking Gourd—" he paused, pointed toward the heavens—"and the North Star. He's taking us up to Philadelphia where everybody's g-gonna be free. Then I'm g-going back down to see Mister Lincoln about joining the c-cavalry."

"Okay, boy, that's enough," the big man said, moving between them. To Indigo he said, "You run on ahead, and tell the others I'm coming. I have to stay here and take care of this."

"But, he said he wouldn't t-tell anybody. You c-can't kill him."

"I have to, boy. That's my job. Now, git!"

"*No!*" Indigo said defiantly and refused to move.

The big man sighed. "Look, boy, do you want to jeopardize the whole operation? We turn this white boy loose and he's gonna go running back and tell the other white folks. They'll have the dogs on us by morning." He shook his head. "This is the only way."

"But he's my friend. He ain't gonna t-turn us in..."

This time the big man pointed the shotgun at Indigo. "I ain't got time to stand here and argue anymore with you, boy. Now, either you git out of my way, or so help me God I'll kill you, too."

Just then a tall, slender black man wearing a green silk vest and high black boots stepped from the shadows. In a voice that rumbled with authority, he said, "Put that gun away, Jesse."

The big man lowered the shotgun reluctantly. "But...Mr. Still...I...I thought, I mean..."

"There'll be no killing here tonight," the stranger retorted in that same deep, authoritative tone. He looked at Garrett, then fastened his steely eyes on Indigo. "That was a brave thing you just did, boy. Putting your life on the line for a white boy."

"He's my friend," Indigo sobbed.

The stranger turned toward Garrett and said, "We should all have friends like that."

The big black man said, "Mr. Still, if we don't kill that boy, he's gonna go running back and tell the sheriff. You know what that would mean."

The stranger seemed unconcerned. "Then we'll just have to move a little faster," he concluded.

"But, Mr. Still..."

"*Enough!*" William Still ordered, silencing the big man with a wave of his hand. He smiled at Garrett and said, "He isn't going to turn anybody in. Are you, son?"

Garrett shook his head. "No, sir," came his reply.

William Still smiled. "Good. Then it's all settled, Jesse. You run along and join the others. Tell them to go on. Indigo and I will catch up with you shortly."

"Mr. Still, I think you're making a big mistake."

"Then it's a mistake I'll have to answer to."

The big man glared at Garrett a moment longer, then turned around and lumbered off into the woods.

"Time to go," Mr. Still said to Indigo.

Indigo turned toward Garrett again and said, "Take c-care of yourself, Garrett."

"You, too."

"Look in on my ma and p-pa for me?"

"Sure."

Indigo grinned. "Maybe we'll see each other again s-sometime s-soon."

"Maybe."

Then the two Negroes were gone, crossing the foot-log and fading like phantoms in the dark shadows on the opposite side of the creek.

CHAPTER 35

ACORN HALL WAS EASILY THE GRANDEST HOUSE in all of Wilkinson County. Built back in the late 1840s as the summer home of a prosperous Savannah banker and cotton merchant, the handsome, plantation-style mansion had passed through a series of hands until 1854 when it was acquired by Franklin Futch, the wealthy new mayor of Irwinton. It was just the place for a young, up-and-coming lawyer like Futch, who had seen his triumph in small-town politics as the only first logical step toward higher office—perhaps the governor's chair some day, or even the Confederate senate.

After moving in, Futch worked hard to see to it that his rambling mansion became the social center of the county. Prominent businessmen and politicians from all across the South dropped in occasionally to close deals and plot strategy. It wasn't uncommon to find celebrated artists and men and women of letters hobnobbing at Acorn Hall, attending teas, lawn parties, chamber recitals and the occasional pro-states' rights rally. Governor Brown was a frequent guest, as were Robert Toombs and Howell Cobb, the brainy, young "fire-eater" from Macon who was fast making a name for himself in the secessionist movement. Rumor had it that Jefferson Davis, the strikingly handsome senator from Mississippi, had spent the night there at least once before he became president of the Confederacy.

That evening, as he stood in the doorway of his home welcoming a seemingly endless flow of guests, Mayor Futch couldn't help reflecting on his good fortune. The sawmill business he had founded in Irwinton had prospered beyond his wildest dreams. So had other investments, from cotton and corn to banking and railroads.

Not only did he sit on the boards of three major Georgia banks and a railroad company, he owned several small businesses around the state, including livery stables, commodity stores and a variety of farming operations. No miser, he gave freely to charities and the arts and helped fund a number of select political organizations.

Not bad for a poor boy from the Virginia backcountry, he reminded himself as he shook hands and made small talk with each arriving guest. Especially one whose parents had been scalped by wild Indians, leaving him behind to grow up in a Quaker orphanage near Savannah. But little Franklin Futch had worked hard at the orphanage, persevering in a variety of subjects from Latin to geography to literature and astronomy. He showed a special aptitude in business and mathematics. By the time he was thirteen, he was keeping books for the orphanage and helping with the budget. Two years later he won a scholarship to a small, prestigious Pennsylvania college. It was there, the following year, he met his future bride, Cora Hampton Belmont, the sweet but rather dull and unattractive daughter of Jules Ferguson Belmont, a wealthy rice and cotton planter from Georgetown.

It was love at first sight for both of them. How ironic, Futch had often mused, that the daughter of one of the most powerful families in all of Dixie should show interest in a poor, overweight orphan boy from the Virginia frontier. The courtship lasted until graduation, after which they were married at St. Michael's Episcopal Church in Charleston, a lavish affair attended by the low country elite and gentrified "cottoncrats" from Vicksburg to Richmond. Upon return from a month-long honeymoon in Europe, Belmont gave the young couple a near-bankrupt plantation he owned near Beaufort. The gift came with an ultimatum: "Make it profitable within two years, boy, or as God is my witness, I'll take it back and kick your fat hide out into the streets."

Anxious to impress his new in-laws—and at the same time keep a roof over his head—Futch went to work right away. He thinned the slave stock by selling off unproductive hands and replacing them with young, healthy ones. He sliced the payroll wherever possible, including many overseers and paid farmhands, preferring to utilize the services of slave trustees in most field operations. He also sold off several unprofitable tracts of timber and used the capital to re-invest in the expansion of his cotton holdings. All the while, he plowed money into the rapidly expanding railroad business. When the Charleston to Hamburg line was formed, he put up investment capital, then successfully lobbied to have the track cross near his property-—an effort that paid off handsomely down the road.

Six months later, the plantation—Pelican's Point—was showing a healthy profit. Old Belmont was so delighted by his new son-in-law's enterprising spirit and flair for business he gave him another planta-tion to overhaul, this one near St. Marys near the old Florida border. Within months, the second plantation was up and running, too.

During those early years it seemed as if everything Franklin Futch touched turned to gold—plantations, railroads, banks, what-ever. The newspapers in Savannah and Milledgeville were calling him Georgia's "Golden Boy." *The Augusta Chronicle* hailed him as "the next great leader of our great and sovereign state."

It was only a matter of time before Futch was seduced by the siren call of politics. When he decided to run for mayor, there was never any doubt that he would win. Thanks to the Belmont name and the friends he made in office, he kept on winning, year after year. But that wasn't enough. Deep down, Franklin Futch wanted more, lots more. After secession, the secret came out that what he really wanted now was a seat in the Confederate senate, or, at worst, the next vice-presidential nomination.

Unfortunately, his world had fallen apart when Cora came down with yellow fever and died. Overnight, his dreams of higher officer vanished. So did the support of his former father-in-law, who bitter-ly blamed Futch for his daughter's death. Even before his daughter was cold in the ground, Belmont had taken back the plantations, the cash and stock that he had once so freely dished out to his young son-in-law. Futch was left alone with the boys and Acorn Hall, which he had bought with his own money.

PREDICTABLY, CATHERINE POTTER was the last guest to arrive. Predictably, every head turned when she entered the room, hanging on the arm of young Fred Sherwood, the banker's son. She looked radiant in a blue satin dress with leg-of-mutton sleeves and white gloves. Her flaming red curls spilled around her shoulders in tight, jeweled ringlets that seemed to catch fire in the glow of the twinkling chandeliers.

Mayor Futch shook Sherwood's hand, then bowed graciously toward Catherine. "My dear, Catherine," he beamed, "I'm so glad you could come. You look positively gorgeous this evening."

"Why, thank you, Mayor," Catherine gushed, long eyelids fluttering. "These days, what with the war and all, it's positively impossible for a woman to keep herself up proper-like."

The mayor laughed. "Yet, you always seem to manage to exceed beyond one's expectations."

"Oh, Mayor Futch!" Catherine gushed. "You certainly know how to charm a girl."

The mayor leaned forward and pretended to whisper. "Where's Joseph? Is he not with you this evening?"

Catherine sighed. "Oh, you know Joseph. He…He had other business to take care of." She tapped Sherwood's arm and said, "Freddy here was kind enough to be my escort tonight."

"Such chivalry," Futch said flatly. He glowered at the boy, then: "Would you mind excusing us for a moment, Freddy?"

Without waiting for a reply, Futch took Catherine by the arm and led her toward the center of the room. "I want to introduce you to a couple of people," he said, steering her past the crowd of some fifty guests, most of them eating and chatting noisily around a long table covered with food, flowers and drinks.

"Evening, Mayor," a tall, bushy-haired man called out. "Great party tonight."

Futch smiled when he saw Henry Scully, one of the county's leading planters, and said, "Thank you, Henry. Glad you could come."

"We wouldn't miss it for the world," replied Scully's wife, a big, bosomy woman who stood at the table stuffing herself with cake.

The mayor steered Catherine across the great room in the direction of the fireplace where two dignified strangers were engaged in heated conversation with a group of guests. One of the men was tall and singularly handsome and wore a priest's collar; the other was slight in physique, stoop-shouldered and ghastly pale.

"Excuse me, Mister Vice-President," the mayor said to the slight, stoop-shouldered man with pasty-white complexion, "I'd like to introduce you to Mrs. Catherine Potter, one of our town's leading citizens and true defenders of the cause."

Only then did Catherine recognize "Little Alex"—Alexander H. Stephens—the vice-president of the Confederate States of America.

"It's a pleasure to make your acquaintance, Mrs. Potter," the vice-president said with a warm bow.

"Why, thank you, Mister Vice-President, the honor's all mine."

Next, Futch turned to the tall, white-haired gentleman standing next to the vice-president and said, "Bishop Elliott, Mrs. Catherine Potter. Catherine, allow me to introduce you to Bishop Stephen Elliott of Savannah."

"So good to meet you, Catherine," the bishop said in a voice rich with culture and fine breeding. Catherine couldn't help noticing that the bishop's eyes were as clear and blue as a summer sky. "Are you by any chance Episcopalian?"

Catherine smiled and said, "No, but I've always felt I should be."

The bishop gave a hearty chuckle. "Well, we'll just have to see what we can do about that," he joked.

Futch leaned forward and said, "The bishop and Vice-President Stephens were just discussing Lincoln's Emancipation Proclamation and the shameful impact it is already having on our Southern way of life."

"Oh?"

"Well," the vice-president began in a weak, surprisingly high-pitched voice, "the cornerstone of the Confederacy—indeed, our whole way of life—rests upon the simple, great truth that the Negro is not equal to the white man, and that slavery—subordination to the superior race—is his natural and normal condition."

The vice-president was paraphrasing his famous "cornerstone speech," the one he had first given in Savannah back in 1861, but Catherine did not know that. Nor did Mayor Futch or anyone else in the room, for that matter, with the possible exception of Bishop Elliott.

"Little Alex," as the vice-president was known, paused long enough to taste the punch, then continued: "I'm afraid that all Mister

Lincoln has done is to awaken in the slaves an unnatural desire for freedom—a freedom they can neither understand nor truly appreciate."

"Here, here," Futch interjected. "I say that, from the beginning, Mister Lincoln's only intention was to unleash the hellish passions of the unfortunate Africans, to tempt them with false promises and offers he knows full well shall never come to pass."

Catherine could not tear her eyes away from the handsome bishop. "And you, Bishop Elliott?" she asked, intoxicated by his watery-blue eyes. "What do you think about Mister Lincoln's proclamation?"

The bishop smiled and said, "I agree in principle with the vice-president and mayor. My feeling is that Mister Lincoln has miscalculated the will of his own people and the determination of Southerners to preserve the status quo." He took a sip of champagne and continued: "I find it ironic that where Mister Lincoln could have freed the slaves—such as in Maryland and the other border states—he chose not to. But where he couldn't—that is, down here in the Deep South—he chose to try. That might turn out to be a serious blunder for the whole Republican Party."

NO ONE NOTICED Joseph Potter slip through the doorway and stagger across the room. He stopped at the punch table, found a crystal glass and filled it to the brim with champagne. He smiled to himself as he gazed about, weaving unsteadily on his feet.

Joseph downed the drink, then helped himself to another. He finished that one, too, then cleared his throat and said in a loud voice: "Everybody...May I have your attention, please?"

The room fell deathly silent. Startled guests shrank in terror when Joseph pulled back his long, black coat and withdrew a long-barreled Colt Revolver. "I said...May I have your attention?" he shouted. He raised the revolver and waved it around. "This will only take a moment, I assure you."

Catherine recognized the sound of her husband's voice. Her heart sank when she glanced across the room and saw him standing by the punch table, weaving back and forth with the gun in his hand.

Oh, God, she said under her breath.

She made her way toward him, pushing past the terrified guests, some of them already bolting for the door.

When she got to him, she said, "Joseph…What on earth do you think you're doing?"

Joseph smiled at his wife. "Oh, hello," he said. "Having a good time?" He looked around the room, pretending to be impressed. "Great place our illustrious mayor's got here. Regular showplace."

"You're drunk," Catherine hissed.

Joseph made a mock gagging sound. "Drunk?" He laughed. "I've had what you might call a little nip. Plan to have another one, too."

"Why are you embarrassing me like this, Joseph? What do you want?"

Joseph turned on her. "What do I want?" He found the question amusing. "I'll tell you what I want," he said, pouring himself another drink. "I want this war to end. I want food for hungry children. I want freedom for the slaves. I want justice for everybody, including the Indians who used to own all this land we're fighting over." He gulped down the champagne, then hurled the glass to the floor. "But, most of all," he added, "I want my wife. That's what I want."

Catherine pressed closer. "How dare you come here and disgrace me like this, Joseph Potter. How dare you!"

Mayor Futch walked over, saw the glass, then the gun. In a calm, careful voice, he said, "Evening, Joseph. I was asking about you earlier."

Joseph laughed. "Why, thank you, Mayor," he said, wiping his mouth with the back of his coat sleeve. "That's downright sporting of you. I mean, a rich, powerful man like yourself, asking about a little old storekeeper like me. I find that touching."

"Joseph…" Catherine warned.

The mayor looked at the gun again. He said, "Why don't you come on over here and eat something, Joseph? There's plenty of good food."

"Thanks, but no thanks. I'm not hungry."

Futch hesitated. "Then just what *do* you want, Joseph?"

"I came to get my wife."

Futch looked at Catherine. Before he said anything else, a man standing near the door shouted, "Why doesn't somebody go get the sheriff? Can't you see this man is clearly insane?"

Joseph heard the remark and spun around. "And drunk to boot," he roared, laughing and waving the Colt around again.

Several women screamed.

"Joseph, please," Catherine pleaded.

Futch took a deep breath, then said, "Joseph…if you don't put away that gun I'm going to have to ask you to leave."

Joseph completely ignored the mayor. He looked around the room, noting the elegant architectural features, the oil paintings, the glittering chandelier, the cowering mob of wealthy guests in fancy gowns and formal black attire. He saw the mounds of food and drink piled up on the fancy tables.

His eyes came back to Futch and narrowed sharply. "So your fancy guests think I'm insane, huh?" A dry chuckle issued from his mouth. "Well, when's the last time any of you looked in a mirror? I mean, just look at you now. All of you, strutting around here like high-and-mighty gods and goddesses." He paused, toyed with the revolver a moment, then continued: "Stuffing your fat faces and drinking champagne while children are starving and soldiers on the front lines are eating rats and bark."

"Joseph, please, you're making a fool of yourself. Go home," Catherine implored.

Joseph turned on her. "And you, my fair wife. Look at you. A regular Southern belle, aren't you? Pretending to be a high-and-mighty patriot. Waving the flag all the time. Begging me to be one of the boys and join up for the cause."

"This is a disgrace!" snarled a plump, white-haired woman. She was clad in a shimmering, floor-length gown studded with jewels and sequins. "Can't someone do anything about this lunatic?"

When two men tried to rush him, Joseph waved the revolver at them. "Uh-uh-uh," he warned teasingly. "I wouldn't do that if I were you. This old gun here can make a hole in a man's chest big enough to poke a fist through."

"Joseph!" Catherine screeched. "Put that gun away! You're scaring everybody half to death."

Mayor Futch found the strength to say, "I must ask you to leave,

Joseph. I'm afraid I must ask you to leave now."

Joseph pondered the mayor's ultimatum for a moment, then slowly lowered the gun and relaxed. "I'm going, Mayor, I'm going." He paused, looked straight at Catherine and said, "I just dropped by to tell you I've decided to join up after all. I'll be leaving first thing in the morning."

Without another word, he stuck the gun back in his pants, turned around and walked away.

The moment he left the room, Henry Scully wiped his forehead and blurted, "Somebody should notify the sheriff so he can lock that man up. He's dangerous."

Vice-President Stephens sauntered forward. He stuck his hands in his pockets and said, "I beg to differ with you, sir, but from what I saw, I'd say that he was one of the bravest young men I've ever seen in my life."

The comment caught everyone by surprise. "I beg your pardon, Mister Vice-President," Mayor Futch said, thoroughly bewildered by it all.

"It took courage to stand up to all of us like that," the vice-president replied. "Real courage. That man is a true warrior."

CHAPTER 36

HIS NAME WAS EDWARD, but they called him Eddie. Eddie was only two years old when he came down with the fever, the same brain-devouring fever that swept down from the Carolina high country in the early 1840s, smiting young and old alike.

There was nothing anyone could do for the boy but put him to bed and pray—pray that a merciful God would somehow see fit to make him better.

Eddie never got better. Instead, he slipped into a coma one frosty Saturday morning in late December. He died on Christmas Day. It was so cold they had to wait almost a month before they could put him in the ground.

"It is not ours to reason why this had to happen," the boy's stern-faced father, Jeremiah Walker, said somberly after tossing the first spade full of ice-flecked dirt onto the crude pine box that served as the boy's casket.

Later, after shoveling in the last pile of earth, Jeremiah Walker walked away from his son's grave and never once looked back.

When they returned to the cabin, he gathered his family around the table and told them they were never to speak of the dead boy again. His memory would live on in their hearts forever, he said, like a burning candle in the night.

But he was with the angels now, and they were to put the boy's painful death behind them and move on. There were too many other things to think about, he explained, too many things that pertained to the living and not the dead.

No one ever mentioned Eddie's death again. It was as if it had never happened, as if the boy had never been born.

Martha Ann Nesmith had been a mere baby herself then, only four years old. But she never forgot about her little brother or his great suffering before a kindly angel came and took away his pain.

Even now, as she sat before a crackling hearth gently rocking her own sick baby, Martha Ann could still recall the pain in her father's voice that day at the funeral. She could see her mother, all bundled in black, her red, swollen eyes and trembling fingers. She could hear the wails of those who had come to pay their last respects, the wind howling mournfully through the lonely snow-covered forest where they laid the boy to rest.

"Our Father...who art in Heaven," Jeremiah Walker intoned, his deep, rich voice cracking in the twisting wind. He loomed over the dark grave, a towering giant of a man, all gray and weathered, bowed, hat in hand, surrounded by the cloaked and veiled mourners. "Hallowed be thy name, thy kingdom come, thy will be done, on earth, as it is in Heaven..."

Her brother's final screams still rang in her ears, the screams that for so long had penetrated those long, dark nights and nearly driven her father mad with grief. The end had come suddenly and mercifully with Eddie drifting off to sleep. Martha Ann could still remember every painful detail—the smell of the ointment applied to her brother's frail little body, the lonely crackle of embers in the fireplace, the bitter wind that clawed and scratched unceasingly at the window late that night while little Eddie's corpse lay clean and white and stiff on the kitchen table awaiting burial...

THE SOUND OF JOANNA COUGHING brought Martha Ann back to the present. She pulled back the blanket and gazed down at her child—so soft and delicate, almost doll-like in her innocent slumber. As always, she was struck by Joanna's uncanny resemblance to her father—the same dark eyes, upturned mouth and rosy complexion.

Wiley. The very thought of her husband brought her back to the brink of tears. It had been so long now, so long. How she missed him! She desperately longed to sink into his strong arms once more, to feel him against her, all around her, to have him shield her from this awful night. She wondered where he was at that moment, what distant and nameless battlefield he might be sleeping on.

Her gaze drifted toward the mantel where his father's old musket used to hang. She remembered the day Wiley had taken it down and cleaned it up to take with him off to war. That was the day she had made him promise to return safely home.

"Don't you worry, Punkin," he had told her, that boyish grin on his otherwise manly face. "I'll be back soon. I promise…"

That was more than two years ago—and still he had not returned. The letters continued to pile up, and she was grateful for each and every one that came. She kept them in the bottom drawer of a table beside her bed. Every night she pulled them out and read them over and over again, sometimes going back to the first few he had written from North Carolina on his way to Richmond. They were magical, those letters; they kept her sane in an otherwise insane world; they were her spiritual link not only to her husband but also to a far more innocent time on earth.

Another cough. This one louder, scratchier than the others. Trembling, she reached down and touched Joanna's forehead.

She gasped.

The child was burning up!

Sweet Jesus! She heard herself whispering among the flickering shadows. Please don't let my baby die. Please don't take her away from me like you took Eddie so long ago. Not now. Not on a night like this…

There came a loud knocking at the door, and Martha Ann's head reared up. At first she thought it was the wind. But when she heard the pounding a second time, she got up, lay Joanna on a small cot by the fire and moved slowly toward the door.

She pressed her head against the door and called out, "Who is it?"

"It's me," a woman's voice came back over the wind. "Sarah!"

Sarah! Martha Ann almost cried out with joy when she heard Sarah's voice. Brushing back tears, she unlocked the door and flung it open wide.

Sarah stood in the doorway, bundled in an old black coat and blanket. "I saw the light on and thought something might be wrong," she explained. Her big, dark eyes twinkled like fresh-cut diamonds in the inky darkness spilling in from the door.

"Oh, Sarah, thank God," Martha Ann said tearfully. She waved her inside and closed the door against the cold. "It...It's Joanna. The poor child's burning up."

Sarah threw off her coat and rushed straight for the bed. "Let me see," she said, bending low over the little girl.

Martha Ann whispered a silent prayer as she watched the black woman's hand glide smoothly across her child's forehead. After checking the inside of the girl's mouth and her ears, Sarah straightened and asked, "How long has she been like this?"

"All night," Martha Ann explained, trying not to cry. "Coughing. Wheezing. And the fever. Do you think she's going to be all right?"

Sarah reached down, picked up the sleeping child and held her to her bosom. "Get me some cold water and all the spare blankets and towels you can find," she said, stepping near the fireplace. "And bring me some fresh lemon squeezings, if you have any. Any kind of citrus will do."

"Of course," Martha Ann answered quickly, already running toward the kitchen.

It was only then that Martha Ann realized how much her arms ached from holding the baby so long.

―――――

THEY WORKED ALL NIGHT, the two of them, bathing Joanna in cold water and forcing cold liquids down her parched and swollen throat. Sarah used up all the lemons in the house, rubbing them against Joanna's temples, under her armpits and behind her tiny knees. Several times she applied drops of lemon inside her nostrils and on her tongue.

Sometime before dawn the fever broke.

"She's gonna be all right now," Sarah said wearily, dabbing at Joanna's forehead with a wet cloth.

Martha Ann almost collapsed with relief when she heard Sarah utter those words. She fell to her knees beside Joanna's bed and prayed. "Thank you, God," she whispered. "Thank you for letting me keep my baby..."

When Martha Ann felt Sarah's strong hands on her back, she rose and hugged her. "How can I ever repay you, Sarah…for what you've done?"

Sarah smiled. "Pay me? Pay me for what, child?" She took Martha Ann's hands in her own and squeezed them tightly. "The baby's gonna be just fine, now," she said. "That's payment enough for me." She waited a moment, then said, "Just keep giving her plenty of cool water. She'll be up and around, hollering her head off in no time."

For the first time that night, Martha Ann felt the weight of a million worlds lift off her shoulders. She even managed a smile. "You know, I honestly don't know what we'd do around here without you and Monroe."

Sarah patted her hand and said, "We're all in this together, honey. Don't you ever forget that."

At that moment Joanna opened her eyes. "Mommy," she called out from the bed. "It hurts."

Martha Ann bent over her daughter and kissed her forehead. "I know it does, sweetheart, but Sarah and I are going to make it all better. Aren't we, Sarah?"

"We sure are, baby. You'll be feeling good as new in a little while."

Martha Ann tucked Joanna back in bed. "Go back to sleep, sweetie. In the morning I'll fix you a big breakfast with fresh milk and honey. Won't that be nice?"

"Um-huh," Joanna replied, snuggling beneath the covers.

The women waited until the child was fast asleep, then walked into the parlor and sat down.

"Tea?" Martha Ann asked, heading straight for the teapot that hung over the fireplace.

"That would be nice," Sarah replied, rubbing her own tired arms.

———

WHILE MARTHA ANN POURED THE TEA, Sarah looked out the window and noticed the first faint, pinkish rays of dawn streaking across the dark landscape. Monroe would be waking soon and wanting his breakfast. Then she thought about her own child, Indigo. Tears welled up in her eyes as she recalled that afternoon long ago when he had stood on the back porch in the dusky twilight and told her and Monroe goodbye.

"I'll write you as s-soon as I get to Philadelphia," the boy had promised, clutching the battered brown suitcase close to his chest. "And when this war is over, I'm g-gonna send for you. I want you b-both to c-come to Philadelphia and live with me."

Monroe hadn't been particularly pleased with that suggestion, but he let it pass, seeing as how he probably wouldn't be seeing his son again for a very long time. Deep down, Monroe was actually proud of Indigo. The boy had guts. He was going far away to make a new life for himself, one which the boy believed would be a far sight better than the one he had known. In a curious kind of way, Monroe even envied the boy for having the courage to follow through with his dream. If he and Sarah were ten years younger, who knows? Maybe they'd be following him on this journey.

Monroe pulled his son close and hugged him tight. The only thing he could think of to say was: "You take care of yourself, boy. Always remember that people are people, no matter where you go. There's gonna be some good ones, and there's gonna be some bad ones. You just try to stay away from the bad ones."

Indigo shook his father's hand and said, "I will, Pa. I will."

Sarah pressed another sack into her son's hands. "Some more biscuits and cheese for the journey," she explained.

"But, Ma, I already got enough f-food to last a m-month," Indigo complained.

"It's gonna be a long trip," Sarah retorted. "You never know when you might need something to eat."

Indigo crammed the sack of food inside his coat. "Well," he said, staring, "I guess I should get g-going. The others are w-waiting for me down at Nora's Pond."

Indigo hugged them both again and moved slowly down the steps. Halfway across the yard, he turned slowly around one last time and waved. Then he was gone, blending with the shadows.

Sarah and Monroe had stood on the porch for the longest time, unable to tear themselves away. As they stood there, listening to the whippoorwills and the soft wind sighing through the pines, the moon rose high and bright over Wilkinson County.

"HERE YOU GO," Martha Ann said, handing Sarah the cup of tea. When she saw the sad, far-off look in her friend's eyes, she leaned close and asked, "Still no word from Indigo?"

Sarah shook her head slowly. "And it's been almost six months," she sniffed. "I just know something's wrong."

Now it was Martha Ann's turn to console Sarah. She wrapped an arm around the big woman's shoulder and said, "You know how the mail is these days, Sarah. Besides, I'm sure he's been real busy getting settled and all that. You'll hear from him soon enough."

Sarah forced a smile. "That's what I keep telling myself," she replied, choking back tears. "But, it's so hard...so hard when you don't know."

It tore at Martha Ann's heart to see her friend on the verge of tears. In fact, she couldn't recall ever having seen the big woman cry. Sarah had always been so strong, so controlled—so solid—that she seemed incapable of mortal grief or pain. What possible comfort could a weak, indecisive woman like Martha Ann offer a being of such noble strength and stature?

She put both of her arms around Sarah's neck and held her. "Sweet, sweet, Sarah," she sobbed. "I do know what you mean. God in high heaven, I know what you mean."

CHAPTER 37

COLONEL SAMUEL PLAYER stood in the shade of a giant bay tree, calmly surveying the perimeter. It was a hot morning in early June, and a dry haze hung low over the woods outside the crossroads town of Cold Harbor. The tall, lanky Georgian knew it was only a matter of minutes before the Union infantrymen massed across the way would come charging toward them. This time, when they came, he and the men of the 49th would be ready. No need standing around waiting for some pompous higher-up to come along and tell them what to do, not when they could already be doing it themselves.

All night long the colonel had moved among his men, urging them to dig deeper, work harder and faster in setting up the sophisticated defense system of parapets, trenches and earthen embankments that ringed their camp.

"Hurry, boys, hurry!" the young colonel pleaded, scurrying from one trench to the next. "Put your backs into it. We haven't much time!"

So they dug and they hacked and they sawed in the dark, furiously at times, almost like men possessed, dragging logs, widening trenches, piling up great heaps of earth to use as a shield against Yankee bullets and bombs. They worked until their backs ached and their fingers bled, and still they didn't stop.

At first, a few wiseacres from other units laughed at them for working so hard.

"Hey, if you Georgia boys want to kill yourselves so bad, why don't you just wait a little while and let Billy do it for you?" one South Carolinian from Kershaw's division teased. "It'll be a whole lot easier on your backs that way."

But the Georgians kept working through the night, mindless of the crushing heat and humidity, refusing to slow down except for an occasional drink of water.

When an officer from a nearby regiment wandered over and saw what Player's men were up to, he was so impressed he ordered his own men into action.

"Do as the Georgians, boys," he bellowed. "And most of you might live to see another day."

Before long, every rebel commander on the front line was urging his men to do the same. By three a.m. the echo of clattering shovels and banging pickaxes could be heard clear across Totopotomy Swamp as brigade after brigade of Confederates rolled up their sleeves and went to work.

Long before the first rays of sunlight began to filter through the gloomy pines of Cold Harbor, an incredibly sophisticated network of overlapping trenches, fire zones and protective embankments had emerged.

Although they couldn't know it at the time, what they were building was a deathtrap for the twenty thousand or so boys in blue hunkered down half a mile away.

"Excellent work," Colonel Player said proudly upon completion of the defense system. "It'll be a cold day in hell before the Yanks can penetrate this line."

"What now?" a young aide asked.

The colonel slowly removed his garrison cap and wiped the sweat from his forehead. "Now we rest," he said wearily, "and wait."

———

WILEY LAY FLAT ON HIS BACK, staring straight up at the stars, the first he'd seen since the rains had begun back at Spotsylvania. There was the Big Dipper and the Hunter, the Seven Sisters and a couple of other constellations he vaguely remembered from boyhood. So beautiful. So cold. So far away. They made him think of home and the little family he'd left behind. The baby daughter he'd never seen.

Joanna.

Almost without thinking, he reached into his haversack and pulled out a stack of crumpled letters. He rummaged through them until he found the one he was looking for. He opened it up and pulled out the latest picture of Joanna that Martha Ann had sent him several months earlier. In the flickering firelight the two-year-old looked almost angelic. She was barefooted and standing on the steps in front of the house, attired in a white cotton dress covered in ribbons. She was smiling.

Tears formed in the corners of Wiley's eyes as he rubbed his fingers gently across the image of his daughter's face. So beautiful. So like her mother's, Wiley thought, captivated by his daughter's bewitching smile and big, round eyes.

He put the picture back inside the envelope and carefully tucked the stack of letters back inside his knapsack. He wiped his eyes and lay back down, curling up inside his blanket. As he lay there gazing up at the stars again and listening to the lonely sounds of the swamp all around him, a barrage of tormenting questions flashed through his mind: Will I ever get to see my own daughter? Will I ever get to touch her? Hold her in my lap? Kiss her sweet cheeks?

How many nights over the past two years had he lain awake in his sweat-soaked blanket wondering those same thoughts? He closed his eyes. Visions of Martha Ann and Joanna continued to cloud his mind. They were so real he could almost smell them, hear their gentle voices floating on the night wind.

When sleep finally came, gently embracing him in its sweet blackness, a final prayer was forming in his mind: *Please get me through this one more time, Lord, just one more time, that's all I ask…*

⸺

MUSKETFIRE rattling in the distance brought Wiley to his feet.

He peered over the trench wall and saw sporadic tongues of flame darting between the trees several hundred yards to the east.

Skirmishers, Wiley thought, reaching for his musket.

Suddenly, the whole world seemed to explode in a deafening crescendo of cannonfire. The ground shook, and thick puffs of white smoke floated up like ghostly wings from the dark ground, drifting over the ragged tree line.

"Incoming!" someone yelled.

But Wiley wasn't worried about the shells whistling toward them. They were coming from batteries far behind enemy lines. As every Rebel veteran knew, Union gunners were notoriously lousy shots. And, at that range, the canisters and shot lobbed at Confederate positions were falling harmlessly in no-man's land between the two lines. Only occasionally did a stray round crash into the trees, smashing limbs and showering the Rebel defenders with debris.

What concerned Wiley was the long line of Yankee infantry forming in the shadowy mists a few hundred yards away. He could already see them, the sea of flags fluttering high over the blue columns. He could hear them, too, their canteens clanging and boots thudding, a frightful sound that betrayed the awesome size of their force. Clearly visible were the mounted officers galloping to and fro, swords drawn and gleaming in the pre-dawn light, barking orders.

All at once the shrill cry of Yankee bugles filled the air, followed by a long roll of drums that seemed to go on forever. Then, at 4:30 a.m. exactly, the first long line of infantry began to move forward.

The final, bloody assault at Cold Harbor was underway. The whole thing would be over in less than half an hour, but the incomprehensible carnage wrought in that brief span of time would shock survivors on both sides.

Talmadge, looking lean and haggard in the early morning gloom, was at Wiley's side in a flash.

"Hope your trigger finger don't get the cramps today," the big man said. He checked his own gun to make sure it was ready. "I got a feeling you're gonna be needing all ten of 'em this morning."

In the fading darkness, the Federal army came, two lines of them, one well in advance of the other, stepping smartly to the beat of the drums, pausing occasionally to fire, then dropping to their knees to reload. On they marched, stepping faster, a single blue wall of smoke and musketfire cracking and popping in the sticky morning heat.

Officers scurried among the ring of Rebel defenders, swords flashing, ordering the men to stay low and hold their fire.

"Steady, boys, steady," Colonel Player cautioned, watching the Union approach through a pair of field glasses.

Wiley leaned flat against the embankment, the cold wood of his musket pressed hard against his cheek. He sighted down the long barrel, felt the steel curve of the trigger with his index finger. Any second now the order would be given to open fire. While he waited, Wiley scanned the long line of advancing blue coats until he finally settled on the man he would shoot first.

Seconds ticked by. Minutes. Still the long, roaring lines of enemy infantrymen came, and still there was no order to open fire.

"What do you suppose they're waiting for?" Wiley whispered to Talmadge.

"Beats me to Sunday and back," Talmadge retorted. "But if they wait much longer, those ol' Yanks are gonna be right on top of us."

Up and down the line, long, gleaming rows of muskets faced the charging blue wall like stiff metal serpents pointed and ready to strike. Any moment the pre-dawn stillness would be shattered by the roar of five thousand muskets spitting solid sheets of flame and death against the doomed soldiers now double-timing toward them.

Colonel Player raised his sword. Sweat poured down his face, staining the gilded braid on his collar.

"Be patient, boys," he shouted, waiting to give the signal. "Just a little longer now."

More tense moments passed as the Confederates waited. Men fidgeted in the ranks. They coughed, cleared their throats, wiped sweat from trigger fingers and furrowed brows. Some held their breath. Here and there whimpers could be heard, as well as the soft, choking sounds of men in prayer.

Soon the Yankees had drawn to within three hundred yards. Two hundred. A hundred. How much longer could they wait? anxious men wondered. How much longer...?

The boys in blue were so close now Wiley could hear them clearly, grunting, groaning, swearing and praying among themselves as they charged. He could even see the face of the man he would kill first. He was a tall, broad-shouldered man, a sergeant, probably in his mid-twenties, sporting a red mustache and thick matching sideburns. In that instant Wiley wondered what the man's name was, where he came from. Did he have a family back home? A child, perhaps? A little daughter he'd never seen?

"*Fire!*"

The order echoed down the line, jolting the men into action. Five thousand fingers yanked triggers; five thousand muskets barked at once; and five thousand Yankee infantrymen fell to the ground in a single convulsive heap, grasping chests and heads and bellies. The men immediately behind them stumbled over the dead and wounded, some crashing to the ground before regaining their balance and charging on.

A second volley of Confederate musketfire ripped into the re-formed line of blue coats, knocking hundreds more off their feet. Some of the wounded men tried to rise, only to be felled by sniper fire.

The Yankee charge finally stalled less than fifty yards away. The dazed blue coats staggered about, as if wondering what to do next, forming easy targets for Rebel marksmen who took advantage of the confusion to mow them down. They continued to fall by the dozens, whole companies of them, ripped and shredded banners fluttering to the ground beside them.

The charge ended when there were no more Yankees left on the field of battle to charge. Seven thousand blue coats lay dead less than fifty yards in front of the Confederate lines.

FOR THE FIRST TIME IN DAYS, Wiley felt relaxed. The big battle was over. Except for one private who caught a ball in the shoulder and had to be evacuated to the rear, nobody in his outfit was hurt. It was almost as if a band of angels had been there hovering over them the past two weeks, shielding them from the shot and shell of the hard-charging Yankees.

Still, it was sad to see so many of those brave blue coats cut down like that. He could still hear the agonizing screams of the wounded as they lay writhing and dying on the battlefield, roasting in the hot morning sun. It was terrible the way the generals just let them lay there hour after hour. Why didn't somebody call a truce so they could go collect the wounded and bury the dead?

As he listened to their cries, Wiley couldn't help wondering where the Yankees' angels had been that long, bloody morning at Cold Harbor.

Talmadge found Wiley sitting on a log beside a little brook, pen and pad in hand, his bare feet dangling in the cool water. The big man plopped down next to him, pulled out a plug of tobacco and stuffed it inside his cheeks.

He unlaced his boots and stuck his own dirty feet in the water. "Guess you've heard the latest," he said, splashing his feet around.

Wiley stopped writing and looked up.

Talmadge stuck a finger inside his mouth and adjusted the wad of tobacco. "We're moving out. First thing in the morning, from what I hear."

Somehow that didn't surprise Wiley. "Where to, this time?" he asked, rubbing his bare feet.

"Across the river somewhere. Petersburg, I think."

"Petersburg?" He rubbed his chin thoughtfully. "But that's clear around south of Richmond. What about Grant?"

Talmadge drew in a deep sigh. "They say that's where Grant's heading. Word is, he's trying to sneak back across the James so's he can come up into Richmond from the south."

Wiley sighed deeply. "That old boy never gives up, does he? I mean, you'd think that after what happened here, he'd finally get the message." Wiley paused, put away the pad and pencil. "I wonder how many more Yankees we've got to kill before he realizes he can't beat Uncle Robert."

Talmadge cut loose a thick wad of greenish-brown juice. It landed with a splat against the trunk of a small pine sapling. "Reckon that's why they call him 'the butcher.'"

CHAPTER 38

JOANNA WAS IN THE YARD playing with Freckles, her favorite rag doll, when she saw the lone rider coming. "Mommy," she called out excitedly, "somebody's coming!"

Martha Ann jumped up from the spinning wheel where she had spent the morning working on Wiley's new uniform and hurried toward the open doorway. She looked out, saw the horseman coming hard, great clouds of dust billowing up behind him. At that distance it was impossible to tell who it was.

"Come inside with Mommy, sweetheart," she called out to her daughter.

"But, Mommy…"

"Joanna, do as Mommy says," Martha Ann said firmly. "You know what you're supposed to do."

"Yes, ma'am," the little girl replied dejectedly. She toddled up the steps and went inside the house. When she reached the ladder that led to the loft, she turned toward her mother and asked, "Can I take Freckles with me?"

"Of course, sweetheart. Just hurry."

Joanna let out a little squeal of delight. "Did you hear that, Freckles? You get to come up and play hide with me."

"Remember to be real quiet. Don't say a word until Mommy says it's okay. Will you and Freckles do that for me?"

"Um-huh."

"Good. Now off you go," Martha Ann said, shooing her up the ladder.

When the little girl got to the top, Martha Ann put a finger against her lips and whispered: "Remember: not a word."

"Yes, ma'am," Joanna whispered back. Once upstairs, she knew exactly what to do. Months of practice had taught her to crawl under the bed and pull the quilt down over the side. There she and Freckles would be safe.

Martha Ann waited until Joanna was safely under the bed, then hurried back over to the front door and pushed it shut. She bolted it, then hastened to the backdoor and locked it, too. That done, she bustled around the house, latching shutters as she went. Her last stop was in the kitchen, where she opened a drawer and pulled out a long carving knife. She ran a finger down the length of the blade to make sure it was sufficiently sharp. Satisfied, she went back into the parlor and waited by the window.

When the lone rider galloped into view and she saw that it was Garrett, she almost cried out with joy. "Thank God," she said, pressing her eyes shut with relief. She threw back the latch and swung open the door.

Garrett hopped down from the horse, hitched it up and headed up the steps. He stopped suddenly when he saw Martha Ann standing in the doorway clutching the long knife.

His eyes fixed on the knife. "Whoa," he said, backing up.

Only then did Martha Ann realize she was still holding the knife. She gave a nervous laugh, then lowered the knife. "Sorry," she said sheepishly. "Guess I overreacted."

Garrett nodded as though he understood perfectly.

Martha Ann said, "I mean, there are so many army stragglers roaming the countryside these days. You just never know who might come riding up."

Garrett pushed back his hat. "Ain't it the truth," he said, relieved to know that his sister-in-law hadn't intended to carve him up with the long kitchen knife. "I heard a group of 'em tried to break into old Bart Clanton's place just last week."

"My goodness. Was anybody hurt?"

"Aw, you know old man Clanton. He chased 'em off with his shotgun. Nicked one of 'em, too, from what I hear. Some old bummer who should have known better than to go messing around with old Bart Clanton."

Garrett wiped the sweat from his brow and looked around.

"Where's my favorite little pumpkin eater?"

Martha Ann nodded toward the house. "Inside."

"Inside? How'd you get that little tumbleweed to go inside on a day like this?"

Martha Ann drew a deep sigh. She suspected Garrett already knew why—why she was so afraid, why she locked the doors and sent her daughter scurrying up the loft every time she heard hoof-beats galloping up the lane. Ever since that episode with Zeke more than a year ago she had been terrified that he'd return someday when Monroe wasn't around. And today Monroe had gone into town to pick up supplies.

Garrett narrowed his eyes and asked, "Has Zeke Taylor been bothering you again?"

"No. Not lately, anyway. But I don't see the need in taking any chances."

Garrett smiled. "I know what you mean. That old Zeke Taylor is one bad seed, all right. I wouldn't put nothing past him." Garrett snapped his finger. "Almost forgot," he said, trotting back to his horse and reaching inside his saddlebag. "You've got a letter from Wiley."

Wiley! Martha Ann's heart leapt with joy. It had been more than a month since the last letter. That was back in late May, right after the big fight at Spotsylvania. It was only a short note, really, but enough to inform her that his unit was on the move, trying to block General Grant from making a sweep around Richmond. She didn't exactly know what that meant, but it was common knowledge that the primary goal of the Union's new commanding general was to capture the Confederate capital. Farther down in the letter Wiley had mentioned they were headed to a little place along the Chickahominy River called Cold Harbor. As she read the letter she couldn't help thinking what an odd name that was for a town.

"Hope it's good news," Garrett said, handing her the letter.

Martha Ann looked at the postmark: Richmond, Virginia, CSA. "Thank you, Garrett," she muttered. She started to open the letter, then stopped. "Would you like to come inside and have a glass of tea? I've got some fresh-squeezed lemonade, if you'd prefer."

"Boy, would I," the boy exclaimed. "I've never seen it so dry before. And so much dust. If it don't rain pretty soon, I reckon we're all just gonna dry up and blow away."

They went into the parlor. "Joanna," Martha Ann called out, "you can come down now, sweetie. Somebody's here to see you."

Joanna poked her head out from beneath the bed and asked, "Who is it?"

"Come see for yourself," her mother replied. To Garrett, she said, "The lemonade's in the kitchen. Go help yourself. There are some tea cakes on the table, too."

At that moment Joanna appeared at the top of the ladder. When she saw Garrett, her eyes sparkled with delight. "Uncle Garrett! Uncle Garrett!" she squealed.

She flew down the ladder, straight into her uncle's waiting arms.

"How's my little pumpkin eater?" Garrett inquired playfully. He teased her a moment, then said, "Come on, let's go get some lemonade and cookies."

"Will you carry me?"

"Sure," Garrett replied. He bent down and turned his back toward her. "Hop up there," he told her.

Joanna hopped onto his back. With both arms locked securely around his neck, he hauled her into the kitchen piggyback-style, put her down and poured them each a tall glass of lemonade.

Back in the parlor, Martha Ann sat down in the rocker by the window and opened the letter. It was dated June 11, 1864:

My darling wife:

I apologize for not having written in such a while, but we've been on the move for weeks, with hardly enough time for a meal, let alone to write a letter. I miss you and the baby so much. Not a moment goes by that I don't think about you, wondering if you're both well and safe. I was sorry to hear that Indigo left. I hope he'll be happy wherever he winds up.

We have just come away from the biggest fight yet with the Yanks. It was in a little swamp near Cold Harbor, not far from Richmond. The bloodshed around The Wilderness and Spotsylvania Court House was awful, but this business at Cold Harbor was enough to turn one stone cold to the idea that anything noble could ever come out of war.

I am proud to say that we gave the Yanks a good licking, and old

General Grant finally got wise and backed away. The victory was sweet, but there was a dark side to the fighting that left me and most of the boys chilled to the core. In all my years of fighting this unholy war, I have never seen so many men killed so fast in one place.

They came at us early on the morning of June 3, charging straight toward our lines. They came in waves, screaming, yelling, artillery shells lofted by their batteries exploding all around us. Col. Player had us hold our fire until they had drawn so close we could see the sweat running down their necks. Then we let them have it with everything we had. It was a fierce volley that flattened the first line. They kept coming, and we gave them another dose of lead and shot that took care of the second line, too.

Although it seemed like hours, the major fight was over in less than half an hour. The colonel (who fought so bravely that day it made me proud to be a Wilkinson County Invincible) said the Yankees lost close to seven thousand men killed and shot. Our side lost about a thousand.

The wounded lay piled up on top of each other and surrounded by the dead for almost three days. The air was laden with insufferable smells. We breathed it in every breath, tasted it in the food we ate and water we drank. For some reason, Grant and Lee refused to agree to a truce so that stretcher-bearers could go collect the wounded and bury the dead. In all that time, in all that boiling heat, we could hear those poor boys screaming and crying out for water.

By the time the generals got around to allowing details to go in and fetch the wounded, it was too late. Every one of them had died...

I overheard one of the officers say that this isn't war, it's murder...

We're on the move again. I'm not quite sure where we're headed this time, but rumor has it we're on our way down to Petersburg, just south of Richmond, where we hear Grant is supposed to be planning another assault on the capital. We have been told that it is our job to defend Richmond to the last man.

I'll write you again when we get there. With any luck, Grant and Lee will soon come to their senses and end this unholy war.

Your loving husband,
Wiley

Tears were streaming down Martha Ann's cheeks by the time she finished the last page. She put down the letter and turned slowly toward the window. In the fields beyond, she could see green rows of cornstalks rippling in the warm June breeze. A layer of reddish dust seemed to cover everything—trees, yard, porch and fence.

Oh, Wiley, she sobbed quietly. You promised you'd come home. You promised…

When she heard the kids, she quickly wiped her eyes. She didn't want them to see her crying.

"Well," Garrett asked, "what'd he say?"

He was standing in the doorway, glass of lemonade in one hand, fresh-baked tea cake in the other. Joanna, her mouth smeared with cookie crumbs, clung to her uncle's leg.

"He's been in another big battle," she replied.

"Where?" Garrett asked eagerly.

Martha Ann shook her head. "Some little place outside Richmond called Cold Harbor."

"Cold Harbor?" Garrett scrunched up his face. "That's a funny-sounding place."

When Joanna saw the redness in her mother's eyes, she scrunched up her face and asked, "Mommy, why are you so sad? Is it because of something my daddy said in the letter?"

Martha Ann scooped the girl up into her arms and said, "No, sweetheart, it's nothing like that at all."

"Then why are you crying?"

Garrett grabbed his niece and started steering her toward the door. "Come on, pumpkin," he said. "Let's leave your mommy alone a few minutes and go outside and see if we can catch a dragonfly."

"A dragonfly? I don't want to catch a dragonfly."

"Okay, what about a butterfly?"

The little girl brightened. "Oh, goody. I love butterflies."

They scampered out the door, leaving Martha Ann alone to plumb the depths of her own dark and endless sorrow.

CHAPTER 39

"Ain't nothing gonna make me go back there, nothing." Private Lester Murphy squatted at the edge of a shallow stream, dabbing at his wounded arm with a wet bandanna. He was a wiry little man, and the dull glint in his pale gray eyes hinted at a weariness only veterans of many months on the front lines can ever truly know. His uniform was ragged and gray, and the cracked brown boots on his feet were caked in mud and blood and were missing part of their soles.

After cleaning and dressing the wound, Murphy looked over at his companion, a lean, muscular private who lay face down in the grass, his breath coming in short, choppy gasps. "I say let's high-tail it outta here now while we still got our legs and half a chance. What do you say, boy?"

John Nesmith rolled over and looked up at the sky. His round, bearded face was smeared with mud and stained by gunpowder. He pulled himself to his knees. "That's crazy talk, Lester. We can't just run away like that."

Murphy unscrewed his canteen and dipped it in the clear water. "Crazy?" he retorted. "I'll tell you what's crazy, boy. Going back. Going back there to die. That's what's crazy."

John knew that Murphy had a point. They had just fought their biggest battle of the war, an awful scrape, during which superior Yankee forces had washed over their thin lines like water flowing over a cracked dam. He remembered the smoke and the screaming, the sound of cannon and musketry, the awful pain in his left arm as a Yankee ball passed clean through, leaving a hole the size of a silver dollar. Then he remembered falling, getting up sometime later, crawling over bodies, some of them mangled and dead, others twitching and moaning, then he was on his feet, running, running, clambering over more bodies and horses, finally stumbling into a shallow trench somewhere near the rear of the battlefield.

That's where he'd found Murphy crouching in the trench, face smeared with mud and blood, a wild, disoriented look in his gray eyes. Murphy had pulled him down and held him, neither of them moving or hardly daring to breath, while the battle continued to rage all around them.

Some time later, the two of them had crawled out of the trench and run into the woods. They didn't stop running until they came to the stream.

"Drink up, boy," Murphy rasped. "Then we gotta get our tails out of here."

John sighed heavily. "Lester, you're just not making sense. We can't desert our outfit like this."

Murphy rolled his eyes. "What outfit are you talking about, boy? You mean those corpses back there?" He gave a faint laugh. "Hell, boy, we ain't got no outfit no more. They're all dead, every last one of 'em, dead as rusty doornails."

John ripped part of his sleeve away and examined the hole in his left arm. Incredibly, the bleeding had stopped. But it still hurt pretty bad. Wincing, he said, "I know, but it wouldn't be right for us to leave. We have to go back."

Murphy shook his head. "Back where? Didn't you hear me, Nesmith? Ain't nobody left to go back to. Nobody. The whole outfit, wiped out. Grissom's dead. Morgan's dead. Hank. Callahan. The whole blamed bunch of 'em. I saw 'em all, back there in the grass..." He paused, rubbed his eyes. "Even the cap'n."

John's heart sank. "Captain Jacobs, too?"

"Him and his horse. Cannon got 'em both. Blowed slap to pieces."

"Are you sure?"

Murphy sighed. "Of course I'm sure. Saw it with my own eyes. Blowed apart. Just blowed apart. One minute they were there, the next they were gone. Boom! Just blowed apart."

Murphy scratched his scraggly beard and looked around. "Now, unless you want to hang around here and wait for the Yankees, I suggest we git while we still can."

This time, when John tried to rise, the pain in his arm made him double over. Murphy leaned over, looked at the wound. "I've seen worse, but that there flesh wound's pretty bad," he said. "We got to git you some help. Come on, there's bound to be a doctor around here somewhere."

Murphy helped John to his feet, then said, "We'll find a place to hide out till dark. Then we'll move out, head west, keep going till we can't hear no more shooting. Maybe all the way to California."

"That's a long way off, Lester. We'll never make it."

"Sure we will, boy. Sure we will."

———

IT WAS ALMOST DARK when they came to a narrow dirt road flanked on both sides by thick woods. They stopped, looked both ways, then headed left, keeping near the edge of the woods where the shadows were deepest.

A little later Murphy slowed down and said, "You know, Nesmith, we've been fighting them Yankees now going on three years, right? And you wanna know something? I ain't never yet figured out why."

"I don't reckon it really matters anymore, Lester."

"No, don't reckon it does. Maybe it never did." He laughed. "Maybe we been fighting this whole dang war for nothing."

———

THEY HAD JUST PASSED an old abandoned farmhouse when they saw a group of soldiers headed their way.

Both men froze in their tracks.

"You see what I see?" Murphy whispered.

"Looks like a patrol."

"Yeah, a damn Yankee patrol," Murphy concluded. "Git down, quick!"

They jumped into a clump of bushes beside the road and lay there for several minutes. "Think they saw us?" John finally whispered.

"Naw," Murphy wheezed. "We'd be dead by now if'n they did."

Murphy raised his head slightly and peered through the bushes.

He ducked back down quickly and said, "They're headed this way, all right. Just lay low till they pass."

Through the bushes, John was able to count eight Yankees, all of them clad in dusty blue jackets, forage caps and armed with what looked like Spencer repeating rifles. The young officer leading them carried a sword in one hand, a Colt Revolver in the other.

The two Confederates waited until the squad was well out of range before peeking over the bushes. "That sure was close," Murphy said.

Suddenly, a voice behind them said, "Okay, Rebs, on your feet!"

Murphy spun around and saw two Yankees pointing rifles at them. One of them, a sergeant, cocked his rifle and growled, "I said on your feet!"

The Rebels scrambled to their feet.

The sergeant was a clean-shaven, barrel-shaped man with a flat, piggish nose and big, bulging eyes. "Well, well, well," he chuckled, "what do you know, a couple of Reb deserters."

His companion, a scrawny, baby-faced private, snickered and said, "I think they're spies, Sarge."

"I think you're right, Briggs," the sergeant replied. Still grinning, he said, "The captain's sure gonna want to meet you two boys." He shoved them both with the barrel of his rifle. "Move!"

THEY STAGGERED DOWN THE ROAD for a half-mile, then veered across a cornfield until they came to a small camp. Half a dozen Sibley tents were set up in a small clearing behind a ruined tobacco barn. Some fifty Union soldiers lounged about the camp, most of them passing jugs of whiskey back and forth.

John gasped when he saw the bodies of four Confederates dangling from ropes strung from a tree.

"Say hello to a couple of your compadres," the big sergeant chuckled. He poked John in the back with his Spencer and said, "Keep moving."

"What you got there, Sarge?" a young private called out. The soldier staggered, clearly drunk from the jug of whiskey he held with both hands.

"More buzzard bait," another soldier laughed.

They stopped in front of a tent, and the sergeant went inside. A moment later he reemerged, followed by a short, stocky Federal captain clutching a half-empty whiskey bottle.

The captain straightened as he looked them over. "So," he said, wiping his mouth, "more deserters, huh?"

He took a seat behind a plank table outside his tent. "Bring the prisoners over here, Sergeant," he said. He poured himself a drink from the bottle and looked up at the two Confederates. "I'd offer you boys a drink, but under the circumstances, I'd say it'd be a waste of good liquor."

The sergeant chuckled again, never once taking his eyes off the two prisoners.

The captain knocked back his drink, then folded his hands on the table and said, "So, you're a couple of spies, huh?"

"No, sir," John said quickly. "We aren't spies, sir."

The big sergeant laughed. "We caught these Johnnys hiding in the woods, sir. Just like the others."

"I see," the captain replied, eyeballing first John, then Murphy. "And you're sure they're spies?"

"That's what it looks like, Cap'n Clark. Just a couple of mangy, no-account Rebel spies."

The captain leaned across the table and stared hard at Murphy. He had a weary look on his face, as if he'd been through this too many times. Once upon a time he might have been a handsome man. But in the gathering gloom of a bombed-out cornfield, dirty, tired and very drunk, the weary Federal captain resembled an over-stuffed scarecrow that was starting to come unraveled.

"Is that right, boys?" he asked. "Were you aiming to spy on us?"

"No, sir," John said quickly. "We don't know the first thing about spying."

"I figure they were counting the troops, Cap'n," the sergeant interjected with a sneer. "Just like the others."

"You've got it all wrong," John protested. "We were just...We were just...you know..." He faltered, suddenly ashamed of the truth. Whatever he said, however he tried to explain their situation, they'd be disgraced, maybe even hanged like those others.

The captain lifted an eyebrow and said, "You were saying, son?" John steadied himself. "Well, sir, our outfit came under heavy fire back there. But I reckon you know about that. Most all of our boys were killed. Back there in the cornfield. You must have heard the fighting. We…We were the only ones left that we know of…"

"That's a likely story," the sergeant groused.

The captain poured another drink. He took a sip, leaned back. "So, if you aren't spies, then what were you two boys doing back there, huh? Running away? Skulking? Were you deserting your ranks?"

"I…" John stopped, unable to answer. "Yes, sir," he finally said, suddenly wracked by shame and humiliation. It was bad enough for your own side to know you were a coward; it was even worse when the enemy knew. He said softly, "We were running away because there wasn't any use staying back there. All the others are dead."

The captain's bloodshot eyes narrowed. He stood up and banged his fist on the table. "Damn it to hell, a couple of skulkers, and here in my court, to boot!" he roared. "If there's anything I hate worse than spies, it's skulkers." He leaned over the desk and glared straight into John's eyes. "I'm a good mind to shoot you Rebs right here myself."

He sat back down and poured himself another drink. Then, after adjusting his cap and belt, he said, "Sergeant, assemble the men. Looks like we're going to have another court martial. The charge is desertion."

"Yes, sir, Cap'n, sir," the sergeant replied gleefully.

"But you can't do that!" John screeched. "I mean, it ain't right. All we were trying to do was get back to one of our units. Everybody was dead back there. Dead, I tell you! Don't you understand?"

"Save your breath, Reb," the sergeant drawled.

Murphy nudged John and spoke for the first time. "Relax, boy. They ain't gonna hang us. They're just puttin' us on, havin' a little fun." He grinned, pushed back his cap. "Shoot, they can't try us for somethin' we didn't do. Don't you see that?"

John wasn't so sure. He turned around and glanced toward the row of dead Confederates swinging from the tree behind them. "What about them?" he asked Murphy.

"Aw, they probably were spies or something," he said. "Poor bastards just got caught, that's all."

"What do you think they're going to do with us?"

Murphy chuckled. "Probably try to scare us some more, then send our behinds back to some prison camp."

"Prison?"

"Sure," Murphy said confidently. "But think about it. It won't be so bad, see. At least we'll get fed regular, and we'll be off the front lines." He smiled at the captain. "Ain't that right, Cap'n, sir?"

The captain poured himself yet another drink and knocked it back. "Sergeant," he barked, "bring me another bottle of whiskey. Then I want a full court assembled in five minutes. Might as well get this thing over with."

Murphy winked at John. "Relax," he whispered. "Just play along with 'em. They ain't gonna do nothing. Trust me."

The big sergeant with the big, bulging eyes turned toward a couple of privates and said, "Boys, take this couple of Rebel pukes over to the tree to get ready for the trial."

"Sure 'nuff, Sarge," one of the soldiers said. He poked John with his rifle and said, "Okay, Rebs, you heard him. Let's go!"

John and Murphy had no choice but to follow the guards across camp until they came to the hanging tree. John looked up and saw the gray, swollen faces of the Confederate corpses. They had obviously been dead for several hours. Their tongues, black and thick, protruded from their lips, and their eyes bulged unnaturally from dark, hollow sockets. Fat, green blowflies buzzed around their heads.

The guards hustled them over to another table and told them to stand at attention. While they waited, John was conscious of two sounds: the buzzing of the blowflies and the steady creaking of the ropes around the dead Rebels' necks.

The captain, now attired in tall black boots and a formal coat, walked over and took his place behind the table. Opening a book, he said, "Court is now in session." He shuffled through some papers, then looked up and said: "Men, we are gathered here again to determine the guilt or innocence of these two Rebel soldiers, captured fair and square this afternoon and duly bound over for trial in this here court."

The captain paused long enough to open the new bottle of

whiskey the sergeant had brought him and fill his cup. After downing the contents, he hiccuped, then said, "Traitor soldiers of the so-called Confederate States of America, you have been charged with spying and the lesser charge of desertion. How do you...*hic*...plead?"

John glanced nervously at Murphy. "Not guilty, sir," he said. "We were just..."

The captain cut him off with a brisk wave of his hand. "Just a yes or no answer will suffice, soldier."

John took a deep breath. "Not guilty, sir."

The captain looked at Murphy and asked, "And you? How do you plead, Reb?"

"We ain't no spies, if that's what you mean," Murphy said contemptuously.

"You were both caught red-handed by legal Union forces, whose sworn testimony before this court suggests one of two things and perhaps both: You were spies, for which I condemn you to be hanged by the neck until dead, and you were deserters, for which I also condemn you to be hanged by the neck until dead."

The captain swatted at a blowfly and continued: "Gentlemen, since this court can't make a determination which count to try you on, I reckon it'll have to find you guilty on both charges. It is my duty to order your immediate execution—by hanging." He banged his hand on the desk. "Court adjourned!" Then: "Sergeant, carry out the sentence of this court!"

"No!" John shouted. "Wait...You can't...I mean, we're not guilty of anything. We're not, honest..."

"Move it," the sergeant commanded, poking John with his rifle.

———

"ANY LAST WORDS?" the captain asked.

John and Murphy sat astride a pair of horses, hands tied behind their backs, thick ropes knotted around their necks.

"Yeah," Murphy growled. "See you in hell, Yank." To John, Murphy said, "Sorry I got you into this mess, Nesmith."

John looked around. Darkness was closing in fast. In another few minutes the moon would be up, riding high over the trees, and the stars would be shining bright. But he and Murphy would not live to see either.

"It wasn't your fault," John replied softly.

Murphy closed his eyes. "See you on the other side, boy."

John had stopped worrying about death long ago. Too much blood and too many corpses had made him utterly numb to his own mortality. When his turn came, he wouldn't be afraid. Dying would be as natural as getting up in the morning. He'd seen too many of his friends killed over the past couple of years to come to any other conclusion. The amazing thing was that he had lasted this long. He thought about his brothers—Charles, William, Albert, James Madison and Wiley. He would soon be joining Charles and Albert and William, but he now prayed that the others would somehow make it out of this war alive.

Captain Clark, sword drawn, staggered over to the mounts. "Gentlemen, prepare to meet thy maker…"

From out of nowhere there came a series of loud, popping sounds. In that instant the captain dropped his sword and fell to his knees, clutching his chest. A thin stream of blood pooled around his hand, trickled through his fingers to the ground.

A wave of gray-clad soldiers burst into the clearing, shouting and shooting. Three more Yankees toppled to the ground. A fourth raised his rifle to return fire but was cut down in a hail of bullets. Several other Yankees managed to reach the far edge of the woods before another wave of Rebels rushed into them, shooting them point-blank.

Out of the corner of his eye, John saw the wounded Union sergeant lumbering toward Murphy's horse, hand raised. He screamed when the sergeant's hand smacked the horse, causing it to lunge forward and leaving Murphy dangling and kicking at the end of the rope.

Grinning, the sergeant turned toward John. He raised his hand to strike the horse, but in that same instant, a Confederate officer ran over to him and shot him in the back of the head with a revolver. The big sergeant staggered, and the officer shot him again, this time directly in the forehead. The sergeant crashed to the ground like a sack of potatoes.

A young Rebel private reached John's horse and held it before it could bolt.

"Cut 'em down, boys, hurry!" the Confederate officer yelled. He looked up at John and said, "God Almighty, this ain't no way to treat a son of the South!"

A couple of soldiers helped John off the horse and untied his hands. John yanked off the noose, rubbing his neck and gasping for air.

"Are you all right, son?" the officer, a major, asked.

"I...think so," John replied. Then he remembered Murphy. He spun around and saw his friend still swinging from the rope. "Somebody help me cut him down, quick!"

The officer grabbed John by the arm and shook his head. "Too late," he said. "Neck's broke. Poor devil's done turned blue as a goose."

John dropped to the ground and heaved his insides out.

The major reached down and helped John to his feet. "What outfit are you with, soldier?"

Gradually recovering, John said, "They're all dead. Except for Murphy and me." He corrected himself. "Except for me."

"That them back there in the cornfield?"

John nodded. "What's left of them."

The officer resheathed his sword and draped a gloved hand over John's shoulder. "Looks like you boys went through hell out there today. How come you and your friend here got away so clean?"

John wiped his eyes, then cleared his throat. He could still taste the warm vomit in his mouth. Weakly, he said, "We were out foraging when the Yanks hit, sir. We could hear them, screaming all over the woods. By the time we got back to the lines, there was nothing left. Nobody. It was all over."

The officer rubbed his bearded chin and grunted. "That so?"

"Yes, sir. And my friend there..." He shuddered at the sight of Murphy's body sprawled beneath a blanket. "We were on the road trying to find a friendly regiment when a Yankee patrol caught up with us. They said we were spies..."

"Well, you're one lucky trooper," the major replied. "That's all I can say. He glanced down at Murphy. "Wish I could say the same about your friend there. Oh, well, he died for the cause. We'll see that he gets a proper burial."

CHAPTER 40

"GRAMMY, were you ever a little girl?" Jane Nesmith looked at her granddaughter and laughed. It was the first time she had laughed in months.

"Of course," she said. "But it's been such a long time, child, sometimes I can't remember."

Joanna was sitting on her grandmother's lap, playing with a pretty silver necklace dangling around the old woman's neck. At the end of the necklace was a small, heart-shaped locket containing miniatures of Jane Nesmith's own parents, now long dead.

Joanna fiddled with the locket, then unsnapped it and stared at the tiny portrait of her great-grandparents. "Grammy, why did your mommy and daddy have to die?"

"Goodness, child, now what kind of question is that?"

"Were they sick?"

"No, sweetheart, they weren't sick."

Joanna scrunched up her nose and contemplated her next question. "Well...did somebody kill them?"

"Joanna!"

"Did they have an accident?"

Jane Nesmith sat upright, genuinely shocked by her granddaughter's line of questioning. She stared at her in baffled silence.

But before she could think of a reply, Joanna asked, "Then what happened, Grammy? Did they just go away like my daddy and never come back?"

The question cut deep, causing the old woman to feel faint. She sank back down, fanning herself. "Who told you your daddy isn't coming back?"

Joanna looked at her grandmother with child-like curiosity. "Nobody. I just know he isn't coming back. He's never coming back because he's dead."

———

"MOMMY!" JOANNA SQUEALED when Martha Ann opened the door and entered the house.

Joanna jumped up from her grandmother's lap and ran toward her mother, arms outstretched. Martha Ann put down the packages she was carrying, bent down and scooped up her daughter in her arms. "I missed you, sweetheart," she said, hugging her tightly. "Did you and Grammy have a good time while Mommy was gone?"

"Uh-huh," Joanna replied indifferently. Then: "Did you bring me a present?"

Martha Ann kissed her daughter on the cheek and said, "Let me see now," she said in mock contemplation. She put her down and reached for one of the brightly wrapped packages. "Here, why don't you open this and see?" she teased, handing her a long, flat box with a pink bow on top.

"Oh, goody," Joanna replied, tearing open the package. "Oh, goody, oh goody oh goody..." When she'd finished ripping off the paper, she opened the box and pulled out a new silk dress. It was white and covered with little blue bows and ribbons. "It's beautiful," she squealed, holding it up against her.

"I had a feeling you'd like it," Martha Ann said.

"Can I wear it to church in the morning?"

Martha Ann nodded. "Of course you can."

Still pressing the dress against herself, Joanna raced toward the mirror in the back bedroom. When she was gone, Martha Ann looked at her mother-in-law and smiled. "Sorry it took so long in town. How did it go here?"

Mother Nesmith stiffened. "I think you need to have a little talk with Joanna."

"Oh? What about?"

"She was asking a lot of questions."

"Questions? What kind of questions?"

"Crazy questions," Mother Nesmith replied, a concerned tone in her voice.

Martha Ann sat down on the sofa next to Mother Nesmith. "I'm afraid I don't understand."

The old woman grabbed both of Martha Ann's hands and held them against her bosom. Martha Ann could see tears forming in the corners of her mother-in-law's eyes. "She doesn't think her daddy's coming back home."

Martha Ann blinked in amazement. "What…?"

"She thinks he's dead."

"But that's…that's crazy."

"That's why you need to talk to her." She paused, listening to her granddaughter laughing and playing in the next room. "Although you'd never know it at the moment."

"I'll talk to her. Thanks for letting me know."

Mother Nesmith sighed. "I suppose we shouldn't be so surprised," she said softly. "After all, she's never even seen her father, has she? To her he's nothing more than a word, a fairy tale she keeps hearing us talk about."

When Martha Ann heard the wagon pull up out front, she rose and said, "That must be Monroe now. Are you sure you can't stay the night with us? Joanna would love it."

Mother Nesmith got up and put on her shawl and bonnet. "Not this time, I'm afraid," she said, tying the bonnet under her chin. "The only place these old bones can rest anymore is in my own bed."

Joanna bounded into the parlor, still clutching the dress. She swirled around the room and said, "It's the most beautiful dress in the whole world. I'm going to keep it forever and forever."

Martha Ann said, "Grammy's leaving, sweetheart. Let's give her a big hug."

Joanna stopped dancing long enough to say, "I thought you were going to sleep with me tonight, Grammy," she said disappointedly.

"Another time, child."

Martha Ann said, "Give her a big hug, sweetheart."

Joanna reached up and hugged Mother Nesmith around the waist. Then she reached up on her tiptoes and kissed her on the cheek. "I love you, Grammy."

"And I love you, precious," Mother Nesmith replied. She tapped her on the nose and said, "See you at Homecoming in the morning."

Joanna's expression brightened. "Oh, yes, ma'am. And I'll be wearing my new dress."

———

THE REVEREND THURMOND'S Homecoming message was remarkably brief that morning. He talked about the history of the church, some of its early founders and the great contributions they had made to God and country. He deliberately avoided any mention of the war, except during the closing prayer.

When the service was over, everybody adjourned to the picnic grounds next to the cemetery. The men set up tables and chairs in the shade of the old sycamore tree while women brought out the food. Children dressed in their Sunday best scampered about, hopping over tombstones, climbing trees and spitting watermelon seeds at each other. Noticeably absent were a large number of the menfolk who were off fighting the war.

When the time came to eat, Reverend Thurmond rose at the head table and bowed his head. "Lord, bless this food we are about to receive, and we beg you, Merciful Father, to make us mindful of the many great blessings you have bestowed on us." He lifted his haggard face toward the heavens, spread his arms and added, "We pray that you will see fit to end this war soon...and that you will bring our boys safely back home to us..."

"Amen," several men shouted, and everybody dug in.

"Any news from Joseph?" Martha Ann asked Catherine, who had just sat down beside her with a plateful of food. It was the first time she had seen her sister since Joseph had gone away. And that was months ago.

Catherine shook her head. "Not a word."

Martha Ann waited a moment, then dared say, "I'm sorry. I know how much you must miss him..."

Catherine laughed softly. "Sometimes, I suppose." She looked at Martha Ann. "I know you might find that hard to believe now, but it's true."

"I believe you, Catherine."

"Poor, sweet Joseph. I suppose he had his good points, you know."

"My goodness, Catherine, you're speaking of him as if he were dead."

"He might as well be. No man leaves his wife for six months without telling her why."

"But you know why he's gone, Catherine. He enlisted…for you. That's what you wanted, isn't it?"

Catherine's lower lip trembled. For a moment, Martha Ann thought she was going to cry. "I suppose so."

NOBODY NOTICED the gray-clad rider approaching until he had galloped into the churchyard and halted.

"Why, it's Freddy Sherwood," Catherine said. Her eyes widened in disbelief when she noticed the crisp, new uniform the young banker's son was wearing.

Lieutenant Sherwood dismounted and strode briskly toward Reverend Thurmond who was seated in the shade next to Mother Nesmith.

"Good afternoon, Freddy," the preacher called out, "We're glad you could join us."

"I'm afraid this isn't a social call, Reverend," Sherwood said, turning to face the crowd. He straightened and said: "Ladies and Gentlemen…May I have your attention, please? Everybody?"

When the crowd had quieted down, he put his hands on his hips and said, "I'm afraid I've got some bad news, folks." He paused to catch his breath, then continued: "We've just got word that Atlanta has fallen. General Hood has retreated into Alabama, and the city is in flames…"

"Oh, no," someone gasped, then the whole congregation was in an uproar.

"Please…Please," Lieutenant Sherwood shouted, waving for silence. "That isn't the worst, I'm afraid." As soon as the crowd had settled down again, he said, "The Yankees are on the march, and they're headed this way."

Once again, the crowd erupted in a series of gasps.

"Now, the good news is that General Phillips' division is in Griswoldville to block any advance in this direction."

Bart Clanton rose slowly to his feet and said, "Phillips? Why, that old fool ain't no commander."

"I'm afraid he's the best we've got," Sherwood said.

"Then we're in a heap of trouble, folks. All that old fool's got is a bunch of gol-dang schoolboys. What can they do against the likes of Sherman?"

Sherwood sighed. "I guess we'll have to just wait and see," he said.

He started to go, then stopped when he saw Catherine. He walked over to her and said, "Hello, Catherine...Martha Ann." He hesitated a moment, then said, "Catherine, I saw Joseph a few weeks ago..."

"Joseph! Where?"

"Outside Jonesboro. He was with Hood's forces. He...He asked about you."

Catherine brightened. "He did?"

Lieutenant Sherwood nodded. "He sure did. Let me tell you, that husband of yours is one fighting fool. I've never seen a man charge into battle so hard. Why, he was an inspiration to the rest of us boys."

Catherine drew a sharp breath. "You said...was. Do you mean...?" She let the question hang.

Lieutenant Sherwood lowered his gaze. "I don't know," he said softly. Then: "The fighting was some of the heaviest I've ever seen. Boys were falling all around me. Artillery shells raining down on us and bursting everywhere. Smoke so thick nobody could see more than a few yards in any direction." He took a deep breath. "The last time I saw him he was leading a charge straight toward a Union gun emplacement."

"My God," Catherine whimpered, then threw her head against her arms and wept.

Martha Ann placed a comforting arm around her sister's shoulders. It was the first time she had seen Catherine cry in years.

CHAPTER 41

IN THE EARLY HOURS OF THE MORNING, Martha Ann Nesmith lay sleepless in her bed. She was trying to pray. She got up without making a light and knelt down in her white cotton nightgown. She pressed her forehead to the Bible, which was open to one of her favorite passages in Psalms.

"Blessed be the Lord, my rock, who trains my hands for war, and my fingers for battle, my lovingkindness and my fortress, my stronghold and my deliverer, my shield and He in whom I take refuge..."

The only sounds in the room were the faint hiss of the oil lamp, the tick of the mantel clock and her low, muttering voice.

She rolled her tear-soaked eyes toward the dark ceiling. "How much longer must the suffering go on, Father?" she called out in the dark. "How much more must we endure?"

She continued to stare at the empty ceiling, as if expecting an answer to her question any second. When no answer came, she threw her head upon the bed and wept.

"GONNA BE A COLD WINTER," Monroe said.

He was standing in the middle of the hog pen, rake in hand, staring up at the gray October sky. Sarah sat on a wooden stool by the gate, watching over little Joanna while Martha Ann slopped the dozen or so hogs and pigs that crowded around the hand-hewn trough.

"See those clouds?" Monroe asked, pointing to a band of wispy white streamers directly overhead. "They're coming down from the north. Wouldn't surprise me none if we had us a real snowfall this Christmas."

Sarah laughed. "Snow? Monroe Collins, you old fool, when was the last time you saw any snow way down here in the south of Georgia?"

Leaning against the rake handle, Monroe gazed across at his wife and said, "Read the signs, woman. They're everywhere, plain as day. All you gotta do is watch the birds and the squirrels and the bugs. Ain't never seen so many critters piling up for winter this early."

He cranked his head upward again and rasped, "Mark my word, we're gonna have us some snow this year. Some real snow."

Martha Ann finished with the hogs and wiped the sweat from her brow. "Well, in that case, we better get busy chopping so we can bring in an extra lay of wood."

"Oh, don't you worry none about that, Miz Martha Ann," Monroe said reassuringly. "I'll see to it that you and the little one get plenty of good seasoned hardwood laid aside and all the fat lighter you'll need to last you from now to Easter."

"Then I reckon you better get busy before we find ourselves snowed in," Sarah teased.

Martha Ann got up and stretched. She trudged through the mud over to the fence and gazed across the brown, flat fields that spanned off in the distance. She had never seen the place look so dreary and desolate. Maybe Monroe was right. Maybe it was going to be a cold winter.

Another long, cold winter without Wiley.

Tears welled up in her eyes as she thought about her husband and the hard time he was having at the front. From the tone of recent letters, things hadn't been going well for the Army of Northern Virginia lately. Everyone was blaming Grant, but Wiley said the new Union general was only doing his job, even though his job was killing Rebel soldiers. "You can blame a man for a lot of things," Wiley had written, "but you can't blame him for doing his job."

The letters made it clear that the biggest problem was food. The boys were down to one-third rations, which meant a biscuit and bite of meat no more than once a day. Some were going without meat for days at a time. "There are more boys foraging the woods for grub than are actually doing the fighting," the last letter had informed her. "Nobody knows how much longer we can go on like this. If Grant doesn't get us soon, hunger will take us all."

It pained her to think of Wiley having to go without food way up there so far from home. She sighed, thinking that perhaps Elizabeth was right after all about this whole mess. Although Martha Ann could never take such a radical attitude toward the war and the Confederate government, such views were spreading like wildfire. All this bickering and fighting among the folks back home while the menfolk were off fighting and dying seemed wrong.

Sarah glanced over and saw the change that had come over Martha Ann. "Something wrong, child?" she called out.

Martha Ann wanted to smile and pretend that she was fine, but the tears streaking down her cheeks betrayed her true feelings. She wiped her face with the back of her hand and sobbed. "No, nothing, it's okay."

Sarah put Joanna down and said, "Why don't you run along, child. Your mama and me need to talk."

"Okay," the little girl replied, hopping down and dashing off across the yard.

The girl was almost three years old now. She was tall for her age, but skinny and full of freckles and bruises that she got from playing so hard around the lot. Her favorite pastime was hunting frogs and rocks. The frogs couldn't stay, but there were so many rocks in the loft where she slept that Martha Ann feared the rafters were going to cave in.

Sarah walked slowly over to Martha Ann and stopped. "Well," she sighed, "you sure don't look okay. What's troubling you this morning, girl?"

Martha Ann watched Joanna scamper across the yard, pigtails flying and bare feet skidding across the grass. She sighed and said, "I don't know how to say this, Sarah..." She hesitated, searching for the right words.

Sarah waited. "But what?" she asked, intrigued.

Telling Sarah and Monroe she couldn't afford them anymore was going to be the hardest thing she had ever done in her life. But the truth was, she was broke, flat broke. It had been months since

Wiley had sent any money home. The way things looked, it might be a long time before another dime arrived.

"It's just that..." she said falteringly. "Well, you and Monroe have done so much for us. My heart breaks that we've not been able to do more for you."

Sarah's bright eyes twinkled with understanding. She let Martha Ann go on.

"You see...It...it's the money, Sarah. It's the money." Her voice trailed off and she fought back tears.

"What money you talking about?"

"That's just it, Sarah. I don't have any more. It's gone. Every last cent that Wiley left me." Martha Ann dabbed at the corner of her eyes with her apron. "What little we get from Wiley's mother barely puts food on the table."

She wiped her eyes. "And until Wiley comes back..." She was tempted to say, *if* he comes back, but refused to phrase it that way. "Until Wiley comes back, I just don't have enough to pay you anymore."

Sarah draped her massive arms around Martha Ann's shoulders. "Lordy, lordy, child, is that all you been frettin' about? You ain't got no money?"

Martha Ann nodded. "I...I guess I'll just have to let you and Monroe go. You can still live in the house, of course. You can always live there, as long as you want to. But I guess you'll have to find some other work. I can't pay you anymore."

Once again a smile lit up Sarah's broad, black face. She took Martha Ann's face in her hands and stared deep into her eyes. "Now, you listen up to me, Miz Martha Ann, and you listen real good. How long have we known each other, huh? Ever since you were a little baby, that's how long. Now, that's a long time in my book, and if you think for one minute that me and my Monroe are gonna up and go high-tailing it out of here just because you done come across some hard times—just because you can't pay us right now—then you're badly fooled, child. Badly fooled."

"Besides," she added, drawing Martha Ann against her heaving breasts, "we ain't stayed on here all these years just for the money. Goodness, no, child! We're here because you're like family to us, you and Mister Wiley. And now this little one. Ever since the slavers sold us away from our parents, you see, we ain't had no family, no real family. Don't get me wrong—your daddy took real good care of us. But you and Mister Wiley—why, you're our family now. You've been good to us, real good. And we love you, child, just like you were our own flesh and blood."

CHAPTER 42

MAYOR FUTCH WAS WORRIED SICK. He crouched behind his polished mahogany desk, a fearful, agitated look on his face, listening to the angry roar of the townsfolk outside his office window. All morning long they had been gathering on the courthouse lawn, women and children mostly, chanting, shouting, demanding food and an end to the Confederate War Tax. They carried placards and banners denouncing the war, the Richmond government and President Davis. Some were even calling for a separate treaty with Lincoln's government, with or without the permission of Governor Brown or President Davis.

Now they were shouting for the mayor to come outside and listen to their demands—as if he, the simple mayor of a small, one-horse town on the backside of nowhere—could do anything about their complaints.

But what could he do? What could one man possibly do or say that would change the way any of them felt? The war wasn't his fault. Nor should he be blamed for the food shortages, the skyrocketing inflation, the bumbling, embarrassingly inept governments in Milledgeville and Richmond.

Futch stared at the gilded portrait of his beloved wife hanging over the mantel. Thank God she was not around to witness this madness. Then he looked at the twin oval portraits of his sons and thought the same thing. He was glad now that he had had the foresight to send them abroad more than a year earlier to stay with friends until the crisis passed. The very thought of his boys having to endure another year of this chaos would have been maddening in itself.

Then he caught a glimpse of his own reflection in the glass bookcase and almost gasped. He hardly recognized the face that stared back at him. Three years ago his hair had been thick and brown and wavy on the sides; but the image in the mirror was that of an incredibly old man, white-haired and bald and wrinkled, a haunted, hollow look in his watery eyes. He had this infernal war to thank for that, too.

The mayor slammed his fist against the glass, shattering it. "Goddamnit!" he shouted at his own broken reflection. "What more can I do?"

It wasn't his fault that the people were suffering. It wasn't his fault that the government came and stole their food, their livestock, then had the nerve to send agents down here to force them to pay taxes. Why was everybody blaming him?

He got up slowly from the squeaking chair, walked over to the tall window and looked out across the lawn. What he saw chilled him to the bone. Women and children barefooted and in rags. Toothless old men hobbling around on crutches. Gangs of ragged, grizzled veterans, some of them limping and missing a limb here and there, all of them marching back and forth across the lawn, screaming and snarling at one another like so many rabid animals.

It terrified the mayor to think that these were his own people, the same simple, God-fearing folks he had gone to church with, the same ones who had kept him in office these past dozen years. Now they were nothing more than a mob—a lousy, low-class mob bent on destroying his reputation. And maybe the whole town in the process.

SHERIFF POINDEXTER, tall and gaunt and clad in a long black coat, dusty white hat and black boots with jangling spurs, stood on the courthouse steps trying to restore order. His thick white mustache drooped past the corners of his mouth, trailing down past his square chin like a pair of gleaming walrus tusks.

"People...please!" he bellowed, arms outstretched, eyes red and swollen from worry and lack of sleep. "If you all will just calm down and hear me out..."

"We're tired of hearing what you have to say, Sheriff," a plump, rosy-cheeked woman hissed. She hitched up her hefty belly and roared, "We want to talk to the mayor!"

"Bring out the mayor!" another woman shouted. "We want to talk to the mayor!"

Soon the whole crowd was chanting, "We want Futch! We want Futch! We want Futch!"

Elizabeth Nesmith had heard enough. She waited until the chanting died down, then sprang up the courthouse steps, turned around and confronted the crowd. "Sisters!" she shouted, waving for silence. "Sisters and children and fellow citizens…Let me have your attention, please!"

The crowd fell silent almost at once. Every eye seemed to focus on the tall, handsome woman shrouded in a dark blue shawl. She wore no bonnet. Her hair, gleaming like fine, white river sand in the noonday sun, had worked loose from the bun on top of her head, curling down around her shoulders and giving her an angry, slightly mad look.

"It is clear," she said, icy blue eyes flashing, "that the mayor and the rest of our leaders are afraid to face us out in the open. It is equally clear that they are as much a part of this corrupt political system as are Jefferson Davis and Alex Stephens. That being the case, I say we have no choice but to take matters into our own hands."

Sheriff Poindexter took two jangling steps toward the fiery speaker. "Now, Elizabeth," he said wearily, "I know how upset you are about James Madison and the rest of the boys off fighting. I know how upset all of you are about the inconveniences and suffering brought on by this terrible war. But what you're talking about here is wrong, plain wrong…"

Elizabeth whirled around to confront the sheriff. "Is it, Sheriff? Is it wrong for the people to want to eat? Is it wrong for the people to stand up to a system that robs them blind, takes food out of the mouths of babies? Is it wrong for the people to be outraged with the so-called leaders of our great cause who live in fine houses and ride around in carriages and eat and grow fat while the rest of us have to try to make do on bread and water?"

The crowd exploded in agreement with Elizabeth. "You tell 'em," an enraged woman rasped.

A cross-eyed woman with two disheveled boys clinging to her skirts stepped forward and asked, "Why does the mayor still get to live in his fancy house with silver and servants when the rest of us have to scratch and claw just to feed our children?"

"It isn't fair!" another young mother cracked. "He and his family get to eat meat and potatoes three times a day while we go hungry!"

Sheriff Poindexter knew the situation was getting dangerously out of control. One wrong word, one careless move and there'd be a regular rampage in the streets of his town. He'd seen more than a few such demonstrations in his time, enough to know they always turned out ugly. The trick, of course, was to get a handle on the ringleader. That meant Elizabeth Nesmith.

"Elizabeth," he implored, "I want all of you to know that I fully sympathize with your feelings. But, by God in high Heaven, I'm still the law here, and it's my job to uphold my sworn duties!"

Elizabeth snapped, "If the duty of the law is to stand idly by while our children go hungry, then I say we no longer need the law."

Once again, Elizabeth's outburst was greeted with wild cheering.

Elizabeth turned furiously toward the crowd, then reached inside her cloak and pulled out a long revolver. "I say *this* is our new law!" she shouted, raising the gun high in the air.

The sight of the gun electrified the crowd. Several women rushed forward in a single mass, cheering, laughing wildly. Some of them clutched nursing babies to their breasts.

When Sheriff Poindexter saw the gun, he knew he had lost. Still, he was the sheriff, and his first instinct was to try to take it away from Elizabeth. But when the woman swung the long gun around and pointed it at his chest, he thought better.

"Just stand back, Sheriff," Elizabeth warned, "I know how to use this."

The sheriff raised his hands, took a tentative step backward. "Elizabeth…please, for the love of God…"

"For the love of our children!" she screamed, cutting him off. "We are doing this for the love of our children!" She lowered her voice and warned, "Don't try to stop us, Sheriff. I don't want to hurt you…but I will." Waving the gun, she charged down the steps. "Are you with me, sisters?" she yelled.

"*We're with you!*" they roared back.

"Then follow," Elizabeth told them, turning and striding across the lawn toward the row of stores across the street.

———

MAYOR FUTCH'S worst fear had now become reality.

From his second-floor office window inside the courthouse, he watched the women go from store to store, watched them exit moments later, arms filled to overflowing with food. Bags of potatoes and rice were dumped onto waiting buckboards they had commandeered, as were loaves of bread, vegetables and canned goods.

The amazing thing was how serene it all seemed, how natural, almost expected. It was as if someone had thrown open the gates to Paradise, and the sinners were all rushing in to claim their rightful salvation. Some of the merchants actually appeared eager to help the looters clear out their stores. A few joined ranks with them, singing, laughing, moving on to the next store, and the next...

Wherever they found a door locked, they kicked it down or smashed windows. Storekeepers who stood in the way or otherwise resisted were taken outside and summarily bound to hitching posts.

"Food! Food for the children!" the jostling crowd shouted everywhere they went. "*Food! Food for the children!*"

The chanting echoed up and down the street and across the town square, a continuous, undulating roar that pierced deeply the soul of Franklin Futch. At last, he thought, still gazing out the window, the end of civilization. The barbarians were finally loose and storming the gate. Rome was burning. How sad. How utterly sad that it must all end this way.

Anarchy in his own hometown was something he could not—would not—bear.

He turned away from the window, strolled over to his desk and opened the middle drawer. He reached inside, pulled out a small derringer. The sight of the gun repelled him, yet he caressed it lovingly, almost as if it were a delicate flower, as he walked over to the mantel and stared into the long-dead eyes of his wife.

"Forgive me," he said, then put the gun in his mouth and pulled the trigger.

CHAPTER 43

EARLY ON THE MORNING of September 15, Garrett Nesmith rose and dressed quietly. While his mother slept in the next room, he crept into the kitchen, sat down at the table and scribbled a note.

The note read:

Dear Ma:

By the time you read this, I'll be gone to join the cavalry. Please don't be mad at me. I'm doing this because the Confederacy needs me. Plus, I want to avenge the deaths of my brothers. I would have woke you up to say good-by, but I knew you'd cry and try to talk me out of going. Please don't worry. I just want to make you proud of me.

Your loving son,

Garrett

PS I took the sorrel with me, since you need your own horse to join the cavalry.

Then he tacked the note to the mantel shelf, went outside in the pouring rain and saddled up. He took one last, long look at his home, then mounted up and galloped off in the wet darkness.

He had intended to go straight to Macon where he had heard General William Walker was rounding up volunteers to serve in General Joseph Wheeler's cavalry command. But on the outskirts of Clinton he ran into a column of ragged gray troops who informed him that Wheeler was no longer in Georgia. Nobody knew Walker's whereabouts.

"Where's everybody going?" Garrett asked a grizzled veteran

who limped along, using his rifle as a crutch. Garrett was puzzled because the gray coats appeared to be heading in the opposite direction of Atlanta, where all the fighting was raging.

"Where do you think, boy?" the old soldier wheezed. Then a defeated look came into his eye. "Home. We're going home. Everybody's going home."

Garrett was confused. "But what about Atlanta?" he asked. "What about General Johnston and the Army of Tennessee?"

The old soldier made a grunting sound that was somewhere between a laugh and a groan. "You better ask John Bell Hood about that, boy. Best I recollect, there ain't no more Army of Tennessee. Least ways since that fool Hood took over."

Hood? Who was Hood? Johnston was supposed to be in charge of the forces defending Atlanta against Sherman.

Bewildered, Garrett trotted over to a young private who sat slumped against a tree. Garrett saw the bandages and the blood and he knew the private—who couldn't have been a day over eighteen—was wounded pretty badly. The boy lifted his head slowly when Garrett came over. Garrett could see he was crying.

"Are you retreating?" Garrett asked.

In a choking voice, the boy soldier said, "The Yankees whipped us good. We…We tried to stop 'em. But there were too many. Just… too many." His voice trailed off for a moment, and he seemed to be reliving some awful moment in battle. A new urgency suddenly came over him. "If I was you, I'd run, run as fast as I could, 'cause the Yankees are coming. Can't be more'n ten miles up the road."

Yankees! Were they really so close?

The prospect of the enemy being so near both thrilled and terrified Garrett. He had to find General Walker's outfit, had to find it in a hurry so he could join in the effort to drive the blue-bellies back.

"Thanks," he told the wounded boy soldier, then spurred his horse and galloped away.

———

THE ROAD TO CLINTON was littered with dazed and wounded men, broken-down wagons and stragglers, old men and young boys mostly, clomping and sloshing through ankle-deep mud, their eyes fixed and frozen, as if the light had gone out of them and there was nothing left to see as they scraped and shuffled along.

The lucky ones rode wagons or clung to the backs of artillery limbers. Most, however, trudged wearily along on foot, slipping and sliding in the muck, occasionally falling. Along the way Garrett passed shell-blasted farmhouses and barns, some of them still smoking and hissing in the rain. Every now and then he caught sight of a civilian darting among the ruins. Sometimes they would race toward the retreating soldiers, holding out hands in a silent appeal for food.

Then Garrett saw his first Yankee, a young, blond-haired boy about his own age. The boy, bundled beneath a billowing blue poncho, was one of some twenty Federal prisoners being herded down the road by a Reb guard detail.

There was a look of stark terror etched on the Yankee boy's powder-blackened face. As they passed, Garrett caught the young soldier looking at him apprehensively. Garrett dipped his head and smiled. The Yankee smiled back nervously.

Garrett wondered if the young Federal prisoner had left his mother a note before he had run off to join the Union army.

Some time later he came to a lonely stretch of road and slowed down. Where was the main camp, he wondered? Surely he hadn't missed it. In the pouring rain it was difficult to see more than a few yards in any direction. Shielding his eyes with the back of his hand, he scanned the woods on both sides of the road, searching for some sign of the camp.

Suddenly, a rain-soaked Rebel jumped out of the bushes, musket raised high. "Halt, there!" the soldier croaked.

"Don't shoot!" Garrett blurted, reeling the horse around. "I'm a Southerner!"

The Rebel guard's bearded face peered out at him from beneath the folded hood of a billowing poncho. "That's a good way to git yoreself kilt, boy," the guard snarled, then slowly lowered his musket.

Steadying himself, Garrett said, "I'm looking for General Walker's outfit."

The guard rubbed his chin. "Ain't no general by that name in these here parts."

Garrett started. "But he's *got* to be. They told me his camp was around here somewhere. I'm looking to join up with his cavalry unit."

"*The cavalry!*" the soldier hissed, as if the word had a bad taste to it. "What you looking to hook up with that mangy bunch for, boy? Those cavalry boys ain't no good. Can't fight. Can't shoot. All they do is ride around and eat up all the forages and make trouble for the rest of us." He spat onto the ground, wiped his mouth. "And when they git into trouble, they call on us infantry boys to come save their hides."

Growing desperate, Garrett pleaded with the soldier just to tell him where headquarters was. He'd find the cavalry command on his own. The sentry rubbed his grizzled chin warily, then groaned. "Well, I don't reckon that can hurt none, seeing's how you done got yore mind made up and all." Pointing straight down the road, he said, "Just keep going. About half a mile up the road you'll see the main camp. Can't miss it 'cause of the smell. Maybe somebody in there can tell you something."

Before turning away, the guard coughed and said, "But you best keep yore head down, boy. These here woods are crawlin' with blue-belly sharpshooters."

Garrett thanked the sentry and galloped away.

———

HALF A MILE UP THE ROAD Garrett came to the edge of a sea of tents—gray and sagging in the downpour. In his young life, Garrett had never seen a more miserable sight. It wasn't just the clumps of maimed and wounded men who lay everywhere, some huddled beneath lean-tos and tents, others face up and shivering in the pouring rain. Nor was it the sad, defeated look on the faces of the officers and men he saw. No, it was the overall bleakness, the melancholy hopelessness that stabbed at his soul like a dull, rusty knife.

He dismounted and waded through the mud over to a group of soldiers hunched beneath a canvas tarpaulin.

"Can somebody tell me where I can find General Walker?" he called out.

One of the men, an emaciated old graybeard with a bandage wrapped around his forehead, found the question amusing. "General Walker, aye?" he cracked, stroking thin wisps of white beard. "Let's see, now, sonny...Last time I saw him he was laying belly-up in a cornfield outside Atlanta. Had a hole in his head big enough to poke yore fist clean through."

Garrett felt his knees start to buckle. General Walker, dead? No, it wasn't possible! General William H.T. Walker of Augusta was a hero, one of the most valiant officers in the Confederate army. His actions at Chattanooga had been written up in all the newspapers.

Garrett suddenly felt sick.

He caught himself, then asked, "Can you tell me who's in charge?"

One of the soldiers, a bearded, bowlegged private who looked and smelled as if he hadn't had a bath since the fall of Fort Sumter, nudged one of his comrades and chortled. "I'm in charge, boy. Whatcha' think about that?"

The other Rebs cracked up. They hooted and wheezed and slapped their legs as if they had just heard the funniest joke in the world.

Only Garrett wasn't laughing. He swallowed hard. He knew the men were putting him on, and he knew he had to be careful what he said. "I...I was looking to join up," he mumbled. "Can you tell me who I need to see?"

The men exchanged astonished glances, then burst out laughing again. The bowlegged private spat a huge chaw of tobacco juice in Garrett's direction. It landed at his feet. "Join up?" he asked. "Join up with what? This ain't no kiddie outfit, last I checked, sonny-boy."

Garrett's cheeks reddened with rage. He glared at the men contemptuously. "I was told they needed riders for the cavalry."

The bowlegged private let go another wad of tobacco. This one landed closer to Garrett's foot. "The cavalry!" he sneered. "I told you, sonny-boy, this ain't no kiddie outfit!"

Just then a short, clean-shaven man wearing a captain's uniform walked over and said, "What seems to be the trouble here, boys?"

The bowlegged soldier spat again and said, "Ain't no trouble, Cap'n. We wuz just havin' a little fun with the boy here."

The captain looked at Garrett. "Can I help you, son?" The captain had sad, lifeless eyes, and a thin stream of blood trickled from his lower lip.

Garrett was so relieved by the officer's intervention he wanted to shake his hand. Instead, he snapped to attention, puffed out his chest and said, "I was looking for General Walker, sir. But they…they told me he was dead."

The captain sighed. "That's right, son. He fell almost two months ago outside Atlanta. Are you a relative?"

"No, sir. I just heard he was looking for volunteers. For the cavalry."

The trio of soldiers burst out laughing again.

The captain fixed his gaze on the soldiers and said, "At ease, men." In a firm tone, he said, "Why don't you boys just go on back to your posts. I'll take care of this."

The men wandered away in the rain, still slapping themselves and guffawing.

After they had gone, the dark-eyed captain turned to Garrett and offered a weak, apologetic smile. "Don't let them get to you, son. They don't mean any harm. You see, those men have been through a lot these past few days." The captain paused, rubbed his bleeding lip with the tip of his fingers. "Now, then, was there something else you needed?"

Garrett still stood at attention. "Well, yes, sir, there was, sir. I mean, I reckon there *is* something. You see, I heard the cavalry needed some volunteers. I'm here to offer my services."

The captain smiled, impressed by the boy's naive enthusiasm. He looked him over and said, "How old are you, son?"

"Almost seventeen," Garrett said proudly, a measure of authority in his voice.

"Almost seventeen," the captain replied softly, as if conjuring up some painful memory. He rubbed his lip again, tasted the blood on the tip of his finger and winced.

"That makes you sixteen now, doesn't it?"

"Yes, sir. But I'll be seventeen in two months."

Another long, dispirited sigh escaped the officer's mouth. "Are you sure about this, son? Riding in the cavalry is a hard job."

"Oh, yes, sir, I'm sure. I've been waiting to ride with the cavalry ever since the war started."

The look on the captain's face seemed to say: You and how many others? All young and wet behind the ears, just like you, bellies on fire, ready to charge off and conquer the world with a sword and a dream of glory. He didn't want to even think of what had become of most of those boys.

"Well," the captain concluded, "I sure admire your spunk. Tell you what. See that big tent over there?" He pointed to a wedge-shaped canvas tent on the far side of camp. "That's General Alfred Iverson's divisional headquarters. You go on over there and ask for General Anderson. He's General Iverson's brigade commander. Tell him I sent you. Captain Vason of the 10th Confederate. General Anderson's the man you need to see about the cavalry."

Garrett could scarcely contain himself now. It was happening. At last it really was happening. "Thank you, Captain," he blathered, saluting the dark-eyed officer again. "Thank you very much."

He reached out to shake the captain's hand, then thought better of it and yanked his hand back. He couldn't remember if soldiers were supposed to shake hands with officers. He spun around and started to back away, then stumbled and almost fell. Regaining his composure, he saluted again and hurried away.

"Good luck, son," the captain said softly behind the boy's back, a melancholy smile on his face.

———

GARRETT HITCHED THE SORREL outside the big canvas tent. He strode toward the open entrance, which was flanked by two trim, sour-faced guards wearing short jackets and tall black boots. Long, curving sabers dangled from each man's belt, as did a pair of gleaming revolvers. A drooping rubber overhang protected them from the rain.

"I'm here to see General Anderson," Garrett explained.

One of the guards, a handsome, curly-haired fellow with bushy sideburns and a walrus mustache, pushed back his garrison cap and said, "Is that so? And just what might be the nature of your business, sonny?"

"I'm here to join the cavalry."

The guards looked at one another but said nothing. The first one—the handsome one—wore red sergeant's stripes on his sleeves. "You want to join the cavalry, huh. Can you ride a horse, boy?"

"Sure can," Garrett replied.

The guard looked him over appraisingly. "Wait right here." He disappeared inside the tent.

When Garrett saw the second guard staring at him, he grinned and said, "Hello."

The guard, a beefy, round-faced corporal with thick lips and a pug nose, ignored him.

"Been in the cavalry long?" Garrett asked, trying to break the ice.

"Long enough," the trooper replied flatly. His gaze wandered past Garrett toward some distant point beyond the hills to the west.

Garrett followed his gaze. For the first time, he became aware of a dull, thumping sound off in the distance. It sounded a lot like thunder. "Are those cannons?" he asked.

"Yep," came the guard's glum reply. "Union batteries. Napoleon twelve-pounders."

Cannons! Garrett had never heard cannons before.

The guard shifted his gaze back to Garret and said, "And they're getting closer."

The slender sergeant emerged from the tent and said, "The general will see you now, boy."

"Thanks," Garrett said, ducking as he pushed back the flap and stepped inside the dry, spacious tent.

Garrett couldn't believe he was actually standing inside an officer's tent. His eyes wandered the room, gradually adjusting to the musty gloom. It was dark and smoky and smelled of stale tobacco and mildew. Above his head, the rain pounded mercilessly on the roof.

Brigadier General Robert H. Anderson stood in the center of the room next to a big desk. He was a small, thin man no more than thirty years of age. He had narrow shoulders and a thick brown mustache that all but concealed his narrow chin. Two officers clad in full battle dress stood on either side of the general. One was a tall, skinny lieutenant with shoulder-length blond hair. The other, a broad-shouldered colonel, leaned against a walking stick. All three officers were puffing on long-stemmed clay pipes.

Without looking up, the general waved Garrett closer.

Garrett stepped hesitantly toward the desk and snapped to attention.

"The sergeant tells me you want to join the cavalry," the general mumbled.

The general's voice was low and monotone. Garrett had to lean forward to hear. "Yes, sir," he replied.

"Can you ride a horse?"

"Yes, sir."

The general pulled out a leather pouch and stuffed fresh tobacco into the bowl of his pipe and lit up. He drew deeply, watched smoke rings coil and swirl toward the drooping roof. "Well, seems to me that a fine boy like you might be wasting his talent in the infantry."

Garrett shifted nervously while the general looked him over.

"Do you own your own horse?" the general asked.

"Yes, sir. Right outside the tent, sir."

The general smiled. "Good, good," he said, puffing on the pipe. "Then it's settled. You're a horse soldier now." The general walked around the table and scribbled something onto a piece of paper. "The pay's ten dollars a month. But I wouldn't go spending it all in advance. My men haven't seen a dollar in over four months."

Only then did Garrett notice how the general favored his right arm. When the general saw the look on the boy's face, he smiled and said, "A little wound I picked up three months ago, compliments of a Yankee general named Garrard. You get used to little things such as this."

The elegant general's words and mannerisms were dignified and graceful, almost to the point of being showy. "What's your name, son?" he asked.

"Nesmith, sir. Garrett Nesmith."

"Well, Mister Nesmith, you're Private Nesmith now. A trooper in the Confederate Cavalry. What do you think of that?"

Garrett's chest swelled proudly. "It's a real honor, sir."

"Ever fired a revolver, Private Nesmith?"

"Yes, sir."

"Ever used a sword?"

"No, sir. But I'm a fast learner."

"That's good to hear, because with General Sherman's sixty-thousand Yankees breathing down our necks there sure ain't no time to teach you."

The general turned toward the lieutenant and said, "Lieutenant, take Private Nesmith over to supply and see that he gets a pair of pants and a jacket. Try to find him some decent boots that fit and a sword and revolver—if we have any left."

"Right away, sir," the lieutenant replied, reaching for his cap as he headed for the door.

"Oh...one more thing, Lieutenant. Be sure to write down the boy's name and address of next of kin." The general looked at Garrett and winked. "Don't worry, son. It's just a formality. We do that with all our boys."

"Let's go, trooper," the lieutenant said to Garrett.

Trooper...

The lieutenant had actually called him *"Trooper."*

At last.

CHAPTER 44

THE FIRST GROUP OF YANKEES rode into town shortly after sunrise. There were a dozen of them in all, ten enlisted men armed with Spencer carbines and two young officers with swords clanging at their sides. One of the riders, a Negro servant, carried the Stars & Stripes.

They stopped at the edge of town and looked around. Seeing that it was safe, one of the officers, a tall, longhaired captain wearing a black patch over his left eye, motioned for them to advance.

Sheriff Hiram Poindexter, looking tired and wane in a dusty black coat and wide-brimmed hat, stood in front of a crowd of about thirty men and women watching silently as the blue-coated invaders trotted up Main Street toward them.

It was a strange sight—Yankees trotting up Main Street. But the sheriff wasn't surprised. He had been expecting them for days, ever since the fall of Atlanta and the sack of Milledgeville. With no Confederate army standing in their way, the Yankees had marched straight across the state in two long columns, one snaking northeastward toward Augusta, the other angling southeastward from Macon and Milledgeville in the direction of Sandersville and Millen.

The best that General Joe Wheeler's outmanned, outgunned band of cavalry could do was nip at the heels of the invaders in a gallant but doomed effort to slow them down.

Then, two days ago, Georgia's last hope had collapsed in the freezing snow and rain at Griswoldville. On a gray, sloping hillside not far from the smoking ruins of the little town, Sherman's well-entrenched veterans, armed with repeating rifles and Parrott ten-pounders, had quietly and methodically slaughtered more than six hundred brave young Georgia militiamen and cadets who had tried in vain to turn the Federals back. Word of the massacre, along with rumors that Sherman's men were plundering and burning everything in their path, sent shock waves rippling across Wilkinson and other neighboring counties. Terrified citizens fled south, taking their livestock and slaves with them, or toward Savannah, thinking they'd be safe along the coast. Those who couldn't or wouldn't leave boarded up their homes and buried their valuables in the woods and swamps for what they hoped would be safekeeping.

Now they were here, the same marauding conquerors who had chased the gallant John Bell Hood out of Atlanta, leaving the city behind in flames.

As he watched the advance party draw near, Sheriff Poindexter grimly wondered what would happen next.

He didn't have to wonder long.

The Federals had drawn to within twenty yards of the courthouse when, suddenly, a single shot rang out. Clutching his head, the longhaired Federal captain wearing the eye patch slumped in his saddle, then toppled to the ground, dead.

Thinking they were under attack, the Yankee troopers quickly dismounted and formed a defensive circle in the middle of the street. The Negro servant with the flag stood in the middle, one hand on the flag, the other waving a long-barreled revolver.

A few seconds later old Bart Clanton darted out of the shadows. He ran hard for a seventy-year-old man, and fast, and he was headed straight for the Union troopers, aiming an old musket.

When Poindexter saw Clanton, he yelled, "Bart...you crazy old fool. What have you done?"

"Get out of my way, Sheriff!" the old man bellowed. "I'm gonna kill me some more Yankees."

He raised his musket to fire again, but it jammed. Before he could fix it, the Yankees rushed over and seized him. They tied his hands behind his back and dragged him, kicking and screaming, over to the courthouse steps.

The surviving officer pointed his finger at Sheriff Poindexter. "You Rebs will pay for this," he snarled.

Bart Clanton lay thrashing on the ground between his captor's legs, a wild, disoriented expression on his face. "They killed my boy!" he shrieked. Tears were spilling down his craggy face. "They killed my little Petie…"

Then he went quiet, curling up and burying his face in his hands.

"Take him away!" the Yankee officer ordered his men.

Sheriff Poindexter faced the officer. "Wait," he pleaded. "He's just an old man, crazy with grief because his boy was killed in action."

The lieutenant looked at the sheriff contemptuously. "I'm sorry, mister, but he killed my captain. We're gonna have to hang him."

"Hang him?"

The lieutenant turned to face the crowd. "That's right…hang him," he yelled. He swung his sword around dramatically. "And we'll hang anybody else who tries to interfere with our mission here."

"But, officer, he's just an old man. Look at him. What possible harm can he do to you now?"

"I'm afraid that's the law, Sheriff," the lieutenant said. "Now, if you'll kindly order your people out of the way, maybe we can avoid any more unnecessary bloodshed."

Greta Underwood, plumper than ever and wearing a long white shawl and hat, rushed forward and grabbed the officer's arm. "You can't do that!" she screamed in his face.

The lieutenant drew back, then pointed his sword straight at the woman. "My name is Lieutenant Patrick H. Flannigan of the United States Army. You people are traitors to my country. I will advise you that I can do whatever I want to down here in Rebel territory—even draw and quarter an ugly old she-Rebel like you."

The officer's harsh outburst silenced the crowd. He lowered his sword and forced a mock smile. To his men he said, "Now take that murdering old traitor away and string him up. *That's an order.*"

"Yes, sir," the ranking Union enlisted man replied.

While the other soldiers stood guard, two privates dragged Clanton up the courthouse steps. One threw a rope over a rafter, then tied the other end around the old man's neck. When the rope was secure, the soldier pointed toward the banister. "Get up there, old man," he ordered.

Without saying a word, Clanton got to his feet and climbed the banister. It was as if he had given up all hope, his spirit drained.

Greta Underwood clapped both hands over her mouth. "Can't somebody do something?" she sobbed.

"What about it, Sheriff?" another man yelled. "You're not gonna just stand there and let these murdering blue-bellies get away with this, are you?"

Poindexter closed his eyes, sighed. They were right. He was the sheriff in this town, and he had to at least try to save Bart Clanton's life. But how? What could he do? The old fool had just killed a Yankee officer. Shot him dead right in the middle of the street. There was no way these soldiers were going to listen to him or anybody else. In fact, they'd be lucky if the Yankees didn't burn the whole town down in retaliation. They'd done it before.

Throwing up his hands in a futile gesture, the sheriff lumbered over to the lieutenant, who was busy cleaning out the dead captain's pockets, and said, "I beg you, Lieutenant...in the name of humanity... in the name of God...let the old man live."

The lieutenant pushed himself to his feet. He dusted off his jacket with his gloves and tugged at his belt. There was fire in his eyes and ice in his voice as he said, "This has been a long war, Sheriff. I'm tired. My men are tired. We're tired of all the killing and all the blood. We're tired of the stinking heat down here and the bugs and marching and all the months we've been away from our families." He drew a breath before continuing. "So, I hope you can understand, Sheriff, when I tell you that I'm not feeling particularly humane today. Especially not with my captain lying over there dead with this Rebel's bullet in his brain."

The lieutenant buttoned up his jacket and straightened his garrison cap. Then, assuming a dignified pose, he turned to his men holding the prisoner and said, "Carry out the sentence at once."

"No! Please, God, no," Greta Underwood whimpered.

Poindexter put his arms around the woman's shoulders and drew her close. "I'm sorry, Greta," he said sadly. "There's nothing we can do."

Bart Clanton gazed out over the crowd, a glazed look on his face. His eyes were puffy and red, but he was no longer crying. Instead, his expression seemed to be one of utter resignation. He was thinking: The sooner this is over, the sooner I can get to heaven—and the sooner I can be with my little Petie again.

All at once he noticed a boy standing near the back of the crowd. The boy looked oddly familiar and seemed to be smiling right at him. He was dressed completely in white, and there seemed to be a strange light shining all around him.

Clanton blinked in disbelief. Could it be? No, no, he thought, it wasn't possible, had to be a trick of the light. Then the boy smiled at him again, and the light around him seemed to grow even brighter. Suddenly, the old man knew. His dry lips moved slowly, mouthing a single word: "Petie…"

Then one of the soldiers pushed him off the railing and he was left dangling in midair. He didn't kick, didn't struggle, didn't even cry out as the darkness closed over him. There was a popping sound as the old man's neck elongated and his head twisted unnaturally to one side. Then he was dead, long before the creaking rope stopped swinging his body around in wide circles.

CHAPTER 45

MARTHA ANN HAD JUST DOUSED THE FIRE in the hearth and crawled into bed next to Joanna when she heard footsteps on the front porch, followed by a loud banging on the door.

She got up, put on her robe and walked down the hallway. In the warm afterglow of the firelight, she could see the clock on the mantel. Eleven-thirty. She wondered who on earth would be calling this time of night. That thought was followed by a sudden cold certainty that Zeke Taylor was back.

But that was impossible, she reassured herself. Zeke wouldn't dare come back, not after the way Monroe had handled him last time.

"I'm coming," she called out, lighting the kerosene lamp. She pressed her ear against the door. "Who is it?" she asked.

"It's me, Miz Martha Ann, Monroe. Open up, hurry!"

There was a rare urgency in Monroe's voice that frightened her. She flung back the latch and opened the door.

Monroe stood wet and shaking in the cold. He was breathing hard, as if he had been running a great distance in a hurry.

"Monroe…What are you doing out this time of night?"

"Ain't no time to explain, Miz Martha Ann," Monroe said quickly. "I've got to get you and the baby away from here, fast!"

Martha Ann held the lantern higher so she could get a better look at Monroe's face. She could see that he was shivering, and his eyes flashed wide with fear. "What's wrong, Monroe? What are you talking about?"

"Please, Miz Martha Ann, there ain't much time. You've got to come with me now."

"Go where? What's gotten into you, Monroe Collins?" She stared at him in utter bewilderment. "Come on inside out of that rain," she said, motioning him inside the house. "You look like you've been running clear across the county."

"I have, Miz Martha Ann," Monroe said flatly, then stepped into the dark hallway. He removed his hat and wiped the rain from his face.

"Now…Would you like a hot cup of tea while you tell me what this is all about?"

Monroe shook his head. "No time." He heaved a heavy sigh. "I don't mean to worry you none, Miz Martha Ann, but it's the Yankees."

Martha Ann's mouth fell open in shock. "Yankees?"

Monroe nodded. "Yes, ma'am. They couldn't be no more than five, six miles up the road. And they're coming fast, burning and shooting everything and everybody that gets in their way."

Martha Ann drew her robe tightly around her neck. "Are you sure?"

"Yes, ma'am. That's why you and the baby have got to come with me now. Before they get here."

Martha Ann braced herself against the wall. Could it be true? She had heard all the rumors about General Sherman's men and their ruthless march from Atlanta. Only three days ago a group of them had ridden into town and killed old Bart Clanton.

Monroe said, "It's just awful what they are doing to the poor white folks, Miz Martha Ann. Just awful." He swallowed hard. "Why, they burnt down the Burkhalter place slap down to the ground."

Sally and Henry Burkhalter and their five children lived only six miles across the creek. They were Martha Ann's nearest neighbors.

"Good heavens!" she gasped, flinging her hands to her face. "Poor Sally."

"I hate to tell you this, Miz Martha Ann, but they're all dead."

Martha Ann let out a sharp breath. "Dead?"

"The Yankees shot every one 'em. Then they stole everything they could take off and burned their house down. Just burned it down to the ground."

"But…why?"

"On account of Mr. Burkhalter being off fighting in a Rebel offi-cer's uniform, is why." Monroe shifted uneasily. "Miz Martha Ann, we can talk about all this later. Right now I've got to get you out of here."

"But, where will we go?" Martha Ann asked shakily.

"You and the baby are gonna come stay with me and Sarah. You'll be safe there. We'll hide you till the Yankees are gone."

Martha Ann quickly weighed her options. "You're right," she said. "We must leave. I...I'll just go get Joanna and a few things."

Monroe smiled with relief. "Good. I'll go around back and hitch up the wagon and bring it around."

Monroe opened the door and stepped out onto the porch. "Everything's gonna be just fine," he said, turning around and smiling. "You'll see. Don't you worry one bit."

After Monroe had gone, Martha Ann hurried into the bedroom and woke Joanna.

"Wake up, sweetheart," she said gently.

Joanna sat up and rubbed her eyes. "Was I having another bad dream, Mommy?" the little girl asked.

"No, sweetheart. I want you to help me get you dressed as fast as we can."

"But why? Are we going somewhere?"

"Yes, sweetie, that's why we have to hurry."

"Are we going to see Grammy?"

"No, sweetheart, we're not going to see Grammy."

"But why can't we go see Grammy? We never get to see Grammy."

"We'll go some other time, sweetheart."

She worked fast, pulling off the girl's nightgown and helping her into a warm dress and shawl. Then she tied a woolen scarf around her neck to protect her from the wet night air.

"Can I take Freckles?" Joanna asked.

"Of course, sweetie. I wouldn't think of leaving her behind."

Martha Ann packed a few of her daughter's things in a canvas bag. In addition to Freckles, she let her pick out two of her favorite toys—a teddy bear and another little doll—and they went into the parlor.

"Wait here," Martha Ann told Joanna. "I've got to pack a few things, too."

She hurried into the bedroom and threw a few clothes into a big brown traveling case. Finished, she hurried back into the parlor and found Joanna rocking back and forth in front of the fireplace.

Suddenly, there was a loud knocking at the front door. That would be Monroe, Martha Ann told herself, snapping the case shut and rushing toward the door.

When she opened the door, she saw a tall, broad-shouldered soldier standing in the doorway. He was wearing a blue uniform.

She almost screamed when she saw the revolver in the soldier's hand.

"Evening, ma'am," the big soldier said, tipping his hat politely.

Martha Ann backed away from the door. "Who are you? What do you want?"

The soldier just grinned. "Oh, I was just passing by. Mind if I come in?"

Martha Ann's heart catapulted into her throat. A Yankee! Right here in her own house. What should she do? "No," she stammered. "I mean...yes...I do mind. You can't come in. Please go away!"

She started to slam the door in the soldier's face, but he was too quick, too strong. Laughing, he blocked the door with his hand, then pushed his way inside the hallway. He glanced around the room, tapping the revolver against his leg.

"Reckon you're all alone," he said, pleased with his observation. He smiled when he saw the little girl sitting by the fireplace. He smiled at her and said, "Hi, there, little darling."

"Hello," Joanna replied.

The soldier's grin widened. "Nice place you got here, ma'am. Real nice and dry," he said.

Martha Ann retreated toward the fireplace. "Please...I must ask you to leave." She shuddered. "Or else, I'll...I'll..."

The big soldier took a step toward her. "Or you'll what?" he said mockingly. Now he was standing so close she could smell his foul breath washing over her. "Now, you just relax, little lady. Ain't nothing to fret about, long's you act real nice and friendly."

"Please...I have a little child," she sputtered.

"So do I, ma'am," the soldier snapped back. "Back home in

Pennsylvania. About that same age, too."

He noticed the suitcases and bags beside the door. "Going somewhere?" he asked coyly.

Martha Ann bit her lip to keep from screaming. "Yes…My daughter is sick. I was going to take her to the doctor," she stammered.

The soldier threw his head back and roared with laughter. Martha Ann thought she had never heard such a horrible, repulsive sound come from a human mouth. It reminded her of pigs being led to slaughter.

The soldier rammed the barrel of the pistol against her neck. Leaving it there, he began to slowly peel away the shawl, exposing bare flesh.

"No, please, don't," she whimpered.

The soldier leaned forward and whispered in her ear. "You just relax, darling. I said I ain't gonna hurt you, didn't I?"

Until that moment, Joanna had kept quiet. But when she saw the gun and the big man touch her mommy she burst into tears. "Mommy…"

Martha Ann managed to twist out of the soldier's embrace. She stumbled across the room and scooped Joanna up in her arms. "It's okay," she said, trying desperately to disguise the fear in her voice.

Still sniffling, Joanna asked, "Is that man going to hurt us, Mommy?"

Martha Ann hugged her close. "Of course not, sweetie. Of course not."

The soldier lumbered over, placed the revolver against Joanna's head.

"No!" Martha screamed. "Don't you dare touch her!"

"Then get rid of her," the soldier bellowed. "Git rid of her now, or so help me God I'll blow her head clean off!"

Martha Ann looked at Joanna and said, "Go upstairs, sweetheart. Go up there and play until Mommy calls you."

"But, Mommy…I want to stay here with you."

"No, sweetie, you can't, not right now. Do this for Mommy, okay?"

"But I don't want to. I'm scared."

"There's nothing to be…"

The soldier cocked the pistol and snarled, "I said get rid of her, lady, or so help me…"

"Mommy! Mommy!" Joanna screamed, throwing her arms around her mother's neck and burying her face against her bosom.

The soldier made a groaning noise, then pulled the girl away from her mother and threw her to the floor. He then grabbed Martha Ann and pulled her against him. With Joanna crying her heart out in the background, he ripped at Martha Ann's shawl and blouse.

"Run, Joanna, run!" Martha Ann shrieked.

At first Joanna didn't know what to do. Then, instead of running away, she rushed over and started pounding the soldier with her tiny fists. "Don't you hurt my mommy, don't you dare!" she yelled.

The soldier brushed the girl aside, raised his gun and pointed it at her head. "I told you," he growled. "Either she goes—right now—or you'll be scraping her brains off the floor. You got five seconds."

Almost hysterical, Martha Ann tried to spin loose. But the soldier held her fast. "No, please, don't hurt my baby," she wailed.

"I warned you…"

"No, please!"

At that moment a shadowy figure burst through the open front door. Before the Union soldier could react, Monroe had crossed the parlor and buried a pitchfork deep in his chest. The soldier staggered backward, knocking over a table.

"You…You stinking, rotten nigger," the big soldier bellowed, clutching at the pitchfork protruding from his chest. "I'm gonna…blow…your black head off…too…"

He tried to raise the revolver but couldn't. In the dim light of the lantern, Martha Ann saw the Yankee's eyes turn glassy smooth. He tottered for another couple of seconds, then, groaning and wheezing, collapsed to his knees. Gurgling sounds issued from the dying man's throat as he struggled with the pitchfork.

He dropped the revolver. For several more seconds he swung his beefy arms in a grotesque dance of death, then tumbled face forward onto the floor and died.

As soon as she was sure the man was dead, Martha Ann rushed over to Joanna and picked her up. "It's okay, baby," she said, trying to shield her from the sight of the dead man. "It's all right now, it's over."

"We best hurry," Monroe advised. "Other Yankees will be here any minute."

Monroe carried the bags out to the wagon and tossed them in the back. Then he helped Martha Ann and Joanna up onto the seat. "I'll be back soon as I take care of that soldier," he said. "Won't take but a minute."

Martha Ann and Joanna waited while Monroe disappeared inside the house. Martha Ann tried not to imagine what he was doing with the soldier's body. When he returned a few minutes later, he climbed up beside them and said, "It's done. Ain't nobody ever gonna find that Yankee now."

In the distance, the sound of gunfire shattered the dark stillness. Off toward Irwinton, a curious pink glow lit up the night skies.

Monroe clicked the reins, and the wagon lumbered away.

Martha Ann didn't once look back at her house.

CHAPTER 46

C ATHERINE STOOD IN FRONT of the mirror at the back of the shop quietly admiring herself. Not bad, she reminded herself. Not bad at all. Almost twenty-three years old and there wasn't the first sign of a wrinkle or blemish. No thanks to Joseph, of course.

As she moved toward the front counter, patting her hair and smoothing out the wrinkles in her dress, she wondered where she'd be today if she had married somebody important—Freddy Sherwood, for example, the banker's son and now a fine officer in the army—instead of that do-nothing Joseph Potter.

Instead, here she was, stuck in this two-horse town in the back of beyond running a dumpy dry goods store with no friends of any real value. Fate could be so unkind, she fumed.

Catherine looked up at the clock. It was almost noon and still not the first customer.

"Damn this war," she heard herself say.

Business had been slow enough since the start of the war. Now, with Joseph gone, it had all but disappeared. Unless things picked up soon, she might have to face the grim prospect of closing the store. In her heart, she continued to blame Joseph.

The front door opened, and two middle-aged women she knew from church sauntered in. They were Greta Underwood, the church organist and leading town gossip, and Agnes Blanchard. Both women were trembling and appeared to be almost out of breath.

"Why, ladies," Catherine said, a concerned tone in her voice. "You sure seem to be in an awful hurry this morning."

"My lord in heaven," Greta huffed, fanning herself with a silk handkerchief. "Haven't you heard the latest? The Yankees are headed into town. Thousands of them."

Catherine's hand flew to her throat. Yankees? A tingling sensation swept over her as she pondered the possibility. She had never seen a real, live Yankee before. The group that had galloped into town earlier had been only a small advance party. The main force was scheduled to follow in a few days.

"Are you sure?" Catherine asked.

"Of course, we're sure," Greta replied indignantly, as if anyone would dare challenge the veracity of her words. "And from what we hear, they're coming in an awful hurry, too. You best do what everybody else is doing, and that's hide everything you can, then close up and go home."

"Greta's right, Catherine," Agnes chimed in. "You sure don't want to be around town when they get here." Touching Catherine's arm, she leaned forward and whispered, "There's no telling what those animals might try to do."

The doorbell tinkled again, and the two women jumped. They were relieved to see Sheriff Poindexter step through the door.

"Morning, ladies," the sheriff said, tipping his hat.

"I suppose you're here to tell me about the Yankees, too," Catherine said.

The sheriff looked taken aback. "Yes, ma'am," he said, eyeballing the two women. "As a matter of fact, I am. Some of Sherman's raiders have drawn to within a mile of town already. Some of our boys tried to stop 'em out at Polecat Bridge, but there were too many. Just too many. From what I hear, it was a massacre."

"Good heavens!" Greta gasped. "Those poor boys. What do you think we should do, Sheriff?"

Sheriff Poindexter removed his hat and ran his fingers through his silvery-gray hair. "If I was you ladies, I'd grab all the valuables I could get my hands on and just high-tail it into the swamp. Or, better yet, try to get as far south of here as possible."

Agnes was utterly aghast. "You mean…just leave town? Leave our homes? Why can't our army do anything about it? Where's General Wheeler? Isn't he supposed to be looking out for us?"

"Ma'am, General Wheeler's already got his hands full. Besides, I reckon he ain't got more than a handful of boys with him. Sherman has well over sixty-five thousand, last report I heard."

"Mercy!" Greta exclaimed. She grabbed Agnes by the arm, and together they started toward the door. "Come on, Agnes," Greta chirped, "we've got work to do out at the church before the Yankees get there."

After the women had left, Sheriff Poindexter turned to Catherine and said, "You ought to think about leaving, too, Catherine."

Catherine stared at the sheriff for a moment. "I thank you for your concern, Sheriff, but let me assure you that it will be one cold day in purgatory before I run away from a few Yankees."

The sheriff shrugged wearily. "Suit yourself, ma'am."

He tipped his hat again and left the store.

Yankees!

And an uncommon thrill swept over Catherine.

THE YANKEES MARCHED INTO TOWN late that afternoon. The first thing they did was cut down the Confederate flag and run up the Stars & Stripes over the courthouse. Then they proceeded to set up camp. Within an hour the entire courthouse square and much of Main Street was awash in white canvas tents and wagons. Hundreds of soldiers milled about, building breastworks and shoring up batteries.

Later, amid a flurry of drumbeats and bugles, a detachment of officers led by Brigadier General Charles R. Woods arrived. They went straight to the courthouse and were met by Sheriff Poindexter and a small delegation of citizens, including Reverend Thurmond, Hamilton Dewberry and Judge N.A. Carswell. After a brief, informal ceremony, the town was turned over to General Woods.

"I can assure you and your people that no harm will come to them as long as they abide by the rules I have set forth," the general announced. "But should one of your citizens step out of line, I shall enact swift and terrible punishment. Do I make myself clear, gentlemen?"

Sheriff Poindexter nodded. "We understand martial law," he said softly. "There will be no trouble from the citizens of Irwinton."

"Good," the general said. "Now, our first order of business here is to acquire suitable quarters for me and my staff officers. Major General Osterhaus, our corps commander, will be arriving first thing in the morning."

"Accommodations will be arranged," Reverend Thurmond said.

Sheriff Poindexter sighed. "General," he announced, "as the sheriff of this county, I am concerned not only about protecting the lives of our people but their property as well."

The general smiled. "Of course, of course. My men are professional soldiers, not common criminals or renegade guerrillas like some of your Rebel bands. Our intention is to pay for our stay and all services required of your town. And, in the unlikely event there are certain—shall we say—transgressions, we will reimburse you fully for any and all damages. And I will deal with my men accordingly. You have my word on that."

CATHERINE WAS SO EXCITED she could hardly contain herself. Several times in the course of the afternoon she had ventured outside the shop to observe the commotion and was rewarded with more than a few winks and propositions from soldiers. The fact that it was against the law for civilians to fraternize with the troops made it all the more appealing.

One blue coat in particular had caught her eye—a handsome young officer sporting a thick red beard that matched the flame-colored sash around his narrow waist. Earlier that afternoon, he had dashed to her rescue when a trio of privates had surrounded her on the walk outside her shop. The officer—a major—had dispatched the grubby privates with a sharp command and wave of his sword.

Catherine was struck not only by the major's good looks but his gallantry as well.

"Thank you," she had told the young major.

The officer dismounted and bowed courteously. "I must apologize for the actions of my men, ma'am," he said, sweeping his hat forward. "They've been on the march a mighty long time, and unfortunately, some of them have forgotten their manners."

Catherine's eyelids fluttered. "There's no need to apologize, sir," she gushed. "But I do appreciate your gallant gesture on my behalf, nevertheless."

The major clamped his hat back. "Is there anything else I can do for you, ma'am?" he asked.

"Well," she started, "there is one tiny little thing…"

"Anything," the major cut in. "You just name it, ma'am."

"If it wouldn't be too much trouble, I would appreciate an escort back to my shop. It's that one…" She pointed to her shop across the street. "Just over there."

The major smiled and said, "I would consider it an honor…the least I could do for a lady so beautiful and charming as you." As he gave Catherine his arm, he leaned over and said, "Allow me to introduce myself. I am Major Sam Ferguson." Then: "May I be so bold as to ask your name?"

"Catherine Potter." She hesitated. "*Mrs.* Catherine Potter."

"Oh," Major Ferguson said disappointedly. "What a pity."

He marched her across the street to the store. When they reached the door, Catherine lowered her umbrella and said, "Thank you again, Major. I hope it wasn't out of your way."

"Not at all, Mrs. Potter," he replied. "The pleasure was all mine."

There followed an awkward moment of silence, with neither knowing what to say. Finally, the young officer tipped his hat. "Till we meet again," he said, bowing dramatically. He saluted and walked away.

Catherine watched him walk away, thinking, *It might be sooner than you think, my dear young Major Ferguson.*

CHAPTER 47

"**W**ORRIED, BOY?" Garrett turned to his left and saw Pete Lacy leaning across his horse toward him. "A little," he admitted to the older trooper.

Lacy shifted in his saddle and said, "You should be. There's better'n a thousand Yankee dragoons on the other side of that creek. I figure we got no more'n six hundred. Most of 'em green runts like you."

"That don't bother me none."

Lacy chuckled. His tall, lanky frame seemed to swallow the small gray horse beneath him. "We'll see about that soon's the shootin' starts."

They were in the front ranks of a long line of horse-mounted troopers facing a shallow creek. On the other side, hidden by a wall of rhododendron and a dense cropping of trees, waited the enemy. Judson Kilpatrick's devils, Garrett glumly thought, as he stared across the sluggish little creek toward the dark woods.

For weeks Confederate cavalry forces under Wheeler had been sparring with Sherman's wily little Union cavalry commander as he raced about the countryside, burning, raiding, trying to screen the Federal advance through Georgia. Now, acting on a tip that Kilpatrick was planning a strike against Augusta, the outnumbered Rebel cavalry had hurried to cut them off at Buckhead Creek thirty miles away.

Unconsciously, Garrett's right hand reached for the sword clamped to his belt. The handle felt cool and comforting in his grip.

The Rebel cavalry unit had been in position for the better part of an hour. The riders were tense, irritable, as they waited for the order to move out. Even veterans like Lacy were growing impatient as they sat, eyes narrowed, shoulders hunched forward, glaring across the water toward the unseen enemy.

Garrett shifted in his saddle. His bottom was sore, chapped from days of riding. His shoulders ached. His eyes burned from straining so hard in the early morning mists. Like Lacy and all the others, he wanted the waiting to be over. He was ready to charge, get it over with. No more delays.

At one point the thought occurred to him that maybe the Yanks weren't really there. Maybe they had high-tailed it sometime during the night. Skedaddled. Cut and run. Maybe the officers knew it, too, and were keeping it a secret. Maybe this was nothing more than another training exercise.

But the occasional rattle of Yankee sabers gave them away, as did the monotonous snorting of their restless mounts. Every now and then Garrett could even hear the unseen riders talking nervously among themselves.

Finally, around eight o'clock, a brown-bearded general came bounding down the line, waving his sword and barking at the Confederates to get ready. The general halted a few yards down-line from Garrett. He was an enormous, slab-shouldered man whose big brown eyes and round face gave him a curious bovine appearance.

"That's General Robertson," Lacy whispered. "General Wheeler's chief of staff. You keep your eye on him, son. That boy's a born fighter."

The general was soon joined by several other officers, including Captain Vason. The officers met at midstream and parleyed for a few moments before splashing off in several different directions.

Garrett tensed. This is it, he told himself. This is how it is going to be. Any moment now the signal would be given and they would go plunging forward into battle. His first battle. Banners flying. Sabers clashing. Bullets splitting the early morning air. Men would charge and scream. Some would die.

For the first time in his young life, Garrett would come face to face with death.

This was the moment he had been waiting for. The supreme moment of battle. All that training. Drilling. Riding. Shooting. Marching. Charging. Waiting. It meant everything. It meant nothing.

Garrett sat ramrod straight in the saddle, one hand on the saddle horn, the other clutched tightly to the helm of his saber. Beneath him, the sorrel pawed and trampled the soft sod at the edge of the creek. He listened to the sounds of impending battle all around him. Men breathing deeply. Chests heaving in and out. Horses snorting. Uniforms stained black with sweat and dirt. Eyes glazed with fear…

Oh, Ma, I should have at least kissed you goodbye…

Lacy, the veteran, saw the kid shifting uneasily next to him. "Relax, boy," he said. "Cavalry charges don't take long. We move in, hit 'em hard and fast, then the whole thing is over, just like that."

Just like that, Garrett thought. Somehow he didn't think going into mortal combat would be quite so simple.

"Just remember to stay low and keep your sword high," Lacy reminded the boy. "You'll come out of this thing just fine."

Garrett started to say something, but faltered. Why couldn't he be more relaxed like Lacy? He studied the veteran out of the corner of his eye. How could he be so calm? Lacy was a real trooper, an experienced horseman who had ridden with Nathan Bedford Forrest before coming back to Georgia and being assigned to Brigadier General Robert H. Anderson's brigade under the division command of Brigadier General Alfred H. Iverson. Garrett was grateful to be riding next to him, the wily old veteran who knew everything about the cavalry. For reasons unknown, Lacy had taken the boy under his wing right from the start and showed him the ropes. Now, Garrett was hoping he'd be able to make the old man proud.

Captain Vason trotted toward the middle of the creek and halted. He studied his men for a moment, allowing a mournful gaze to sweep up and down the ranks. Then, with a forlorn flick of the wrist, he swung his horse around to face the opposite bank. Slowly he withdrew his saber and pointed it skyward. A ray of sunlight caught the tip of the blade and seemed to set it on fire.

"Standards at the ready," the captain barked. His voice seemed oddly muffled in the still morning air.

"Standards ready!" came the spirited reply of several troopers whose mission was to take the regimental banners into battle and defend them with their own lives.

"Sabers…drawn!" Again, the captain's voice sounded soft and hollow, unreal.

Immediately, six hundred steel sabers were unsheathed and raised toward heaven. The sound of so many sabers being drawn at once sent a cold shiver down Garrett's spine. It was a sound unlike anything he'd ever heard in his life.

From across the creek came the muffled echo of similar commands being given up and down the hidden line of Union warriors.

Captain Vason removed his cap and casually attached it to his saddle horn. He bowed his head, offered up a small, silent prayer, then faced the dark woods once more. A mad fury seemed to come over him then. He swung his saber around in a circle several times, tilted his hatless head forward, opened his mouth and yelled, "Ready on the right?"

"Ready on the right, sir!" a lieutenant in that direction replied.

"Ready on the left?"

"Ready on the left, sir!" another officer roared back.

The captain closed his eyes and sucked in a deep breath. "*Charge!!!*"

The word seemed to explode from his mouth, reverberating through the ranks. All at once, the long line of mounted Confederates sprang forward. Screaming and shouting at the top of their lungs, they hit the creek with a resounding splash, six hundred horses strong, crashing and careening into the swirling water almost at the same instant.

As Garrett's horse plunged into the creek, he felt himself being carried forward by a power he had never known, some unknown force that laid claim to his mind and body. Everything around him seemed to blend into a watery blur as he charged on, not really seeing or hearing, just drawn steadily forward by that same invisible energy.

When he saw the waves of blue-clad troopers rushing toward him, screaming and swinging swords, a voice deep within his soul cried out: *At last...the moment of truth!*

The two lines of cavalry met in midstream. They twisted and knotted, a wild confusion of clashing sabers and shrieks and revolvers spitting smoke and fire. Men yelled and screamed, toppling from horses and vanishing amid pounding hooves and churning water.

In the heat of battle, some riders threw away their sabers and pulled out carbine rifles that clacked and popped.

"Keep going, Georgians!" the Confederate captain yelled. "Remember who you are! *Remember who you are!*"

The sight of the captain's sword flashing in the early morning light gave Garrett renewed energy. He surged straight ahead, oblivious to the bullets whizzing past his head and flashing sabers singing all around him. Like a being possessed, he continued his ferocious charge, swinging his bloodied sword left...right, left...right, slicing and slashing until his arm ached.

The first Union trooper he encountered was a heavyset corporal who made a groaning sound as he swung his saber at Garrett. Garrett hitched out of the way, and the Union trooper's blade whooshed past his head, cleaving air. Without the slightest hesitation, Garrett brought his sword straight down on top of the Yankee's shoulder. The soldier screamed and tumbled from the saddle.

Garrett wheeled around and saw another rider bearing down on him. Garrett drew back on the reins, swinging the sorrel around, and the Yankee horseman galloped past. At that precise moment, Garrett thrust his saber forward, penetrating the Yankee's side and killing him instantly.

Garrett continued to lash out with his sword, striking first one Yankee, then another. He seemed to be out of control now, slicing, jabbing, poking, penetrating, a madman on horseback. His fierce actions had not gone unnoticed by his comrades, who cheered him on, waving their hats each time the hard-charging rookie found another mark.

The battle ended with the piercing blast of a Yankee bugle signaling retreat. Almost at once, the surviving blue coats whirled their steeds around and galloped back into the woods, gradually disappearing in the drifting smoke and fog. A few brave troopers remained behind to pick up their wounded and to snatch up standards and flags that had fallen into the blood-soaked waters.

And then it was over. The Federal thrust had been turned back. Augusta had been saved.

For a long time the victorious Rebels cheered and threw their hats into the air, taunting the defeated Yankees and daring them to come back for more. But the Yankees did not come back. They had had enough of the hard-charging Rebels for one day.

Garrett felt a strong hand reach out and touch his shoulder. He turned around and saw Lacy, a big grin on his smoke-blackened face. "You did just fine, boy," Lacy said, "You did just fine."

"HEY, TROOPER, is your name Nesmith?"

Garrett was sitting on a log outside his tent polishing his sword. It was the day after his first battle, and he was feeling more than a little sore.

When he looked up and saw the lieutenant looming over him, he jumped to his feet and saluted. "Yes, sir, I am, sir."

"Come with me. The general wants to see you right away."

"The general?"

"That's right," the lieutenant replied. "He wants to see you in his tent. Now."

GARRETT FOLLOWED THE LIEUTENANT across the camp to General Iverson's tent. Once inside, the lieutenant saluted and said, "This is Private Nesmith, sir."

General Iverson, a tall, clean-shaven man clad in a red flannel shirt and gray trousers, rose slowly from his desk and walked over. "Thank you, Lieutenant," he said, staring straight at Garrett.

A fragmentary dread oppressed Garrett as he stood facing the general. Had he done something wrong? Had he broken some kind of rule? He groaned inwardly. Were they going to kick him out of the cavalry for doing something he wasn't supposed to?

"General Anderson tells me you did rather well yesterday at Buckhead Creek," the general said.

The general was now smiling. Garrett felt himself relax.

"In fact," the general continued, walking around Garrett as if sizing him up, "I've been hearing a lot of good things about you lately, Private Nesmith. That fight yesterday morning was one of many promising reports I've heard about you."

"It was nothing, sir," Garrett said shakily. "I was just doing my duty."

"Yes, well, I suppose you were. But if we had a few more boys like you just doing their job, this war would have been over a long time ago." He leaned back, folded his arms across his chest. "Your action at Buckhead Creek helped saved Augusta, son. I think General Kilpatrick will think twice before he tries to run past us again."

The general reached inside a box on his desk and pulled out a pair of shiny gold bars. "Do you know what these are, son?" he asked, holding up the bars.

Garrett stared at the bars. He cleared his throat and said, "They look like officer's bars, sir. Captain's, I think."

The general smiled. "You are correct, son. They are captain's bars. And, as of this moment, they belong to you."

Something deep inside Garrett seemed to turn over. For several long moments he couldn't move, couldn't breathe. Couldn't talk. It was as if a pair of giant hands had wrapped around his throat and were slowly starting to squeeze.

Garrett honestly didn't know how long he had stood there gaping at the shiny golden bars—it could have been five seconds, it could have been five minutes—before the general said: "As your commanding officer, and on behalf of Corps commander Major General Joseph Wheeler, I want to thank you for what you did out there on the field of battle yesterday. Thanks to your bravery and unselfish devotion to duty, our Confederate forces were able to carry the field. That's why I am now promoting you to the rank of captain. The promotion won't be official until the orders are cut, but I want you to understand that, as of this moment, you are now a captain in the cavalry of the Confederate States Army."

The general pinned the bars onto Garrett's shoulders, then stepped back and saluted him. "Lieutenant, see to it that Captain Nesmith here gets a proper uniform."

CHAPTER 48

MARTHA ANN SAT BY THE WINDOW in a handmade rhododendron rocker watching the rain come down in great, gushing sheets. It was a cold, wild rain that blew in from the east, transforming the bleak November landscape into a patchwork of quivering bogs and oozing brown mud puddles.

Behind her, snuggled beneath a pile of blankets, lay Joanna. The child made soft snoring sounds while she slept.

Martha Ann was thinking: *I've never felt so lonely in my entire life.*

The sounds around her seemed to be united in a cruel conspiracy against her: the hissing rain, the crackling fire, the ticking of the mantel clock, the steady creaking of the rocker, even Joanna's gentle slobbering noises made her feel totally alone, stranded on some distant and lonely shore.

Without thinking, she slipped a hand into her bag and fingered the stack of letters from Wiley. Even her hand felt detached, as if it belonged to someone else.

"Oh, Wiley," she whispered, staring out the window. "I miss you so much."

Her eyes turned slowly away from the window and wandered around the small, cozy bedroom. Other than the bed and home-made rocking chair, the only other piece of furniture in the room was a battered old pine dresser that Sarah's grandfather, a slave, had made for her back in Sparta. Sarah had done her best to make the room as comfortable as possible. Monroe had even gone back over and brought back a wagonload of valuables and stored them in a closet—the silverware, glassware, photo albums and what few pieces of jewelry she owned.

"Those Yankees are so busy looting and raiding the big houses they won't think about looking here," Monroe had assured her.

So far, two weeks after she had moved in with them, the strategy had worked. From her window she had watched several groups of Yankees come and go, but none had bothered to search the house.

One afternoon a group of Federals had knocked on the door to check for Confederate sympathizers. Monroe and Sarah had met them at the door and offered them fried chicken and cornbread. All during the meal, Monroe and Sarah praised the soldiers for liberating them from their cruel masters. They especially were grateful to Abraham Lincoln and "Massa Sherman," whom they called the "Angel of the Lord."

"He's the man that rules the world," Sarah shouted in slave dialect, then brought out berry cobblers and fed them to the appreciative soldiers.

From the backroom where she and Joanna hid, Martha Ann heard the Federal officer say, "You niggers are free now. Why don't ya'll just pack up your things and leave this cursed land of the Confederates? By the time General Sherman gets through with it, there won't be nothing left but graveyards and buzzards."

Monroe had smiled and told him they had planned to leave but were staying back to welcome General Sherman to Georgia. "We wants to see the Angel of the Lord," Monroe explained. "Soon's we gaze upon his mighty face, we can go on to Glory Land."

———

AS SHE WATCHED THE RAIN slosh down outside her window, Martha Ann couldn't help thinking about Wiley, wondering where he might be at that very moment. How many hours had she spent looking out her own window back home, hoping, praying to see him coming riding up the lane any second?

She was so deeply engrossed in thoughts about Wiley she almost didn't hear the soft knock at the door. A second later the door cracked open, and Sarah peeked her head inside the bedroom.

"There's someone here to see you," the black woman said softly. There was an edginess to her voice that made Martha Ann shudder.

"Who is it?" Martha Ann asked.

Sarah rolled her eyes in mock disgust. "You better come see for yourself. I'll watch the baby."

Intrigued, Martha Ann got up slowly and left the room. She passed through the small living room, opened the front door and walked out onto the porch. It was dark now, and the rain was coming down in great, gushing sheets that hammered and hissed against the shingled roof.

"Martha Ann," a woman's voice called softly from the far end of the porch.

Martha Ann turned around. Catherine, clad in an overcoat and bonnet, stepped out of the shadows, a tall red-bearded soldier dressed in a blue Yankee uniform at her side. They were both dripping wet.

Catherine pushed back her bonnet, allowing her red hair to spring free. She smiled and said, "Monroe told me you were here. How have you and Joanna been?"

While her sister spoke, Martha Ann couldn't take her eyes off the handsome young Union officer at her side. "We're doing the best we can," she said coolly.

Catherine pursed her lips nervously and said, "Martha Ann, I've come to say goodbye."

"Goodbye?"

Catherine sighed. "I'm going away." There was both sadness and excitement in her voice. "Sam here is taking me back to Boston with him."

"Boston?" Martha Ann glanced at the soldier again, then back to her sister. "What are you talking about?"

Catherine drew the tall soldier against her. "We're going to get married, Martha Ann. Isn't it wonderful?"

Martha Ann felt as if she had fallen off a mountain. She looked at the soldier again—a tall, strapping fellow in his late twenties or early thirties. He had a well-groomed beard and twinkling blue eyes. Even in the dim light of the porch she could tell he was exceedingly handsome.

"Married?" Martha Ann heard herself ask. She was more angry than shocked, and the tone of her voice revealed that. "But Catherine…you're already married!"

Catherine gave a little laugh. "Oh, Martha Ann, you know

Joseph isn't ever coming back. He's dead. How many times do I have to tell you that?"

"Dead? Dead? Catherine, how do you know that? How can you say such a thing?"

Catherine sighed. "I just know it," she said with a casual wave of her hand. "I haven't heard a word from him in over a year."

"But that doesn't mean he's dead!"

Major Ferguson stepped forward, removed his cap. In a gentle, almost hypnotic voice he declared, "I love your sister, ma'am. I want to take her away from here and make her my wife. I promise I'll take good care of her."

Catherine leaned forward and hugged her sister. "See? Isn't he a prince?" She hesitated, then added, "and he's a major. A major in General Sherman's artillery corps."

Martha Ann felt her senses slipping away. She staggered, caught herself, then leaned against a post. For the first time in her life she felt something close to hatred for her sister.

Then, as an icy gust of rain blasted across the porch, she found the strength to say, "Catherine...How could you?"

Catherine looked at the officer for support, then back at Martha Ann. "My dear sister, don't you realize there's nothing left for me here? Irwinton is a dead town. Everything here is dead or dying, just waiting to be buried." Her eyes suddenly flashed. "Why don't you come with us?" she asked quickly. "You and little Joanna. We'll go to Boston and build a brand-new life."

She waited, assessing her sister's reaction. "Before you say no, dear sister, just think about it. No more cornfields. No more hog pens. No more...Well, Boston is a lovely city, and it'll be just wonderful! Now, won't you come with us, please?"

Martha Ann backed away in disgust. She couldn't believe this woman standing before her was actually her sister, her own flesh and blood.

"Just look around you, Martha Ann," Catherine continued, sweeping one arm around in circles. "Here you are, shut up inside a slave house. Too scared to go back to your own house. Is that any way to live?"

Martha Ann felt nothing but contempt for her sister. Backing slowly away from Catharine, she whimpered, "I have to go inside now. The baby needs me. Please, just go. Just go away and leave me alone."

"But Martha Ann," Catherine persisted. "Please think it over. We're leaving in the morning when Sam's regiment pulls out. He's taking a furlough so we can go up to Boston and get married."

Furlough. How easily that one word rolled off Catherine's tongue. Martha Ann closed her eyes, bit her lip to keep from crying. How many times had Wiley written to her in the past three years announcing that he was coming home on furlough? Only to have his hopes—and hers—dashed at the last moment. Of all the many reasons to hate this Yankee officer standing on the porch in front of her, *that*, Martha Ann surmised, was the most important.

Anger blacker and deeper than she had ever known suddenly welled up inside her toward this man, this Yankee, this enemy soldier who dared come to her and talk about furlough when her own husband hadn't been home in almost three years.

Out of nowhere, Catherine said, "I know what you're thinking, Martha Ann. But it's been years since you've seen Wiley, right? Years! Do you honestly think he's ever coming back home?" She made a cackling sound. "No, dear sister, this war is going to claim him, just like it did Joseph and William and Charles and all the others."

Major Ferguson stepped forward, still gracious as ever. "Ma'am, I don't want to sound out of line," he said in a calm, gentle voice, "but I have a brother back home who I know would be tickled pink to meet a beautiful Southern lady like yourself, maybe even make you his wife. He's a good worker and a God-fearing Christian provider and will take real good care of you and the little girl your sister has told me about."

"He's right, Martha Ann," Catherine interjected. "You've got to think of little Joanna as well as yourself."

That was all it took to push Martha Ann over the edge. "*Get out!*" she screamed, so loud, Monroe and Sarah both opened the front door and peeked out. "Both of you, get out of here right now!"

Catherine said, "Martha Ann, don't be foolish. Think about it. Think about what you're passing up!" Martha Ann shrieked. "Just...Just get away from me. I don't want to ever see you again, ever!"

Catherine grabbed the major's arm and led him down the steps through the pouring rain toward the buggy. Before climbing up, Catherine turned and shouted, "Don't be a fool, Martha Ann. This might be your last chance!"

Major Ferguson helped her into the buggy, then hurried around to the other side and climbed up. A jagged line of lightning sliced down from the dark sky, briefly illuminating Catherine's moon-shaped face.

At that instant, Martha Ann knew she would never see her sister again. She sank to her knees and cried out as the wagon sloshed away into the night.

CHAPTER 49

THE RAIN-SOAKED HILLS OF VIRGINIA can be a cold place at three o'clock in the morning, especially if you think you might have only a few more hours to live. Clad in a tattered regulation poncho and garrison cap pulled down over his ears, Wiley paced the dark perimeter, nervously eyeing the long rows of campfires flickering across the valley. Those campfires belonged to the enemy. Come dawn, the valley would be flooded with Sheridan's Yankees charging straight up the ridge toward them.

This time, Wiley feared, the Rebels wouldn't be able to hold. They would break and snap like twigs, and the war would be over.

But there would be a price.

As Wiley surveyed his own men's miserable camp, he wondered how many more of his friends, now sleeping comfortably in their ragged tents, would live to see another twilight? Taste the morning dew once more upon their parched tongues?

Ever since the fall of Petersburg, the pathetic remnants of the once-proud Army of Northern Virginia had been on a steady retreat westward. Rumor had it that Lee was hoping to link up with Johnston near Danville or Lynchburg, then swing down into North Carolina and challenge Sherman before he could join Grant in Virginia. Some said Lee was taking what was left of his army into the mountains where they could hide out and continue to wage a guerrilla campaign against the Union forces until Great Britain or France joined the struggle against Lincoln's government.

So far, neither plan was working. Twice, at Five Forks and two days later at Sayler's Creek, Union forces had caught up with them and given them a good licking. Against all odds, the ragged, dispirited Confederates had managed to escape the combined clutches of Sheridan and Meade. Now, beaten and hungry, they were running for their lives.

Wiley switched his musket to the other shoulder and continued pacing. He wasn't afraid of death. He had walked through the Dark Shadow so many times over the past three years that death had now become meaningless, much like an old friend, the kind of friend who invites himself over to your house, eats all your food, then leaves without so much as a thank-you note.

No, it wasn't death that caused Wiley to dread the coming light of day. It was Martha Ann and the baby. What would happen to them if he fell in battle? What would they do? They couldn't continue to rely on Monroe and Sarah, not without money coming in.

A rustling in the bushes behind him. Wiley spun around, unflinging his musket in the same motion. "Halt!" he shouted, straining to make out a trio of shadows moving slowly toward him. "Who goes there?"

"Don't shoot," a thin, bearded private called out. "We're friendly."

Wiley lowered his musket when he saw three Rebs step out of the bushes. "You boys going somewhere?" Wiley asked accusingly.

One of the soldiers, a big, lumbering hulk in gray rags who long ago had outgrown his uniform, shifted his haversack. "And what if we are?" he growled.

Almost apologetically, the first soldier said, "We're going home. I hope you ain't figuring on trying to stop us."

Wiley stiffened. "You mean running away."

"It ain't running away, boy," the big soldier groused. "If you had half a brain, you'd put down that pea-shooter and come with us."

Wiley sighed. "Come on, you boys can't be serious."

The big private hitched back his shoulders and said, "Serious? Let me tell you about serious, boy. See those campfires over there? Must be fifty thousand Yankee riders and infantrymen. That's serious."

"Yeah," the third soldier agreed. "In the morning these woods are gonna be full of Yankee soldiers and Confederate corpses. I ain't figuring to be one of them corpses. No, sirree."

Now it was the small, bearded private's turn to speak up again. "I know what you're thinking, friend. But these boys are right. We ain't deserting. There ain't a coward's bone in a one our bodies." The soldier paused, fidgeted. "What's your regiment, soldier?"

Wiley hesitated. "The 49th," he replied. "Wilkinson County, Georgia."

The wiry private smiled. "We know you boys," he said happily. "We fought with you at Malvern Hill and were with you at Sharpsburg and Gettysburg. Why, you saw how we charged across that field. And Fredericksburg? We were there with you all the way. Do you remember Chancellorsville? How we run those old Yanks like rip? Same thing at Cold Harbor. We were all there together—you, me and these old boys here, plus a lot of other boys who weren't so lucky. Hell, friend, the truth is, we done fought our hearts out. There ain't nothing left in us to fight no more. We just want to live now. Go back home. Be with our families again. That's all."

"Goddamn war's over," the big soldier glowered. "If you stay back, those Yankees are gonna skin you boys alive tomorrow."

The second soldier shifted nervously beneath the weight of his bedroll. "Come go with us," he urged. "Ain't no use staying back here and getting yourself killed tomorrow for nothing."

Wiley shook his head. "For nothing? Are you saying that all those boys that fell with us at The Wilderness and Manassas and in the Crater fell for nothing? Is that what you're saying, soldier?"

The soldier shifted again, suddenly embarrassed. "No, of course not, that ain't what I'm saying at all…"

"Well, that's sure what it sounds like," Wiley interjected. Steeling himself, he said, "Don't you see? If you boys run off now, then all of that dying will have been for nothing. The whole war…everything…for nothing. Is that what you want?"

The big soldier spat a wad of tobacco. "Save the fancy words, hero. We're leaving." He pointed a thick finger straight at Wiley. "And don't you try to stop us!"

"You boys are making a big mistake," Wiley said.

The big man walked over to Wiley, jabbed a finger against his chest. "Tell it to us at your funeral, hero."

"Leave him be," the skinny private said. To Wiley, he smiled and said, "Sure you won't come? I'll wait for you to get your gear."

Wiley shook his head in disgust. "No. You go on with your

friends there. And good luck if you get caught. You know what they do to deserters."

The big soldier snarled, "Ain't nobody gonna catch us, hero. Want to know why? Because nobody gives a damn no more. Nobody. Not even the almighty Robert E. Lee hisself." He readjusted his gear, then added, "Come on, boys. The scent of death here makes me want to puke."

The first soldier stuck out his hand and held it there for several seconds. When Wiley declined to take it, he said, "You're a good soldier, friend. I wish I was half as good as you."

Only for a moment did Wiley think about lowering his musket and detaining the three deserters. He should have, he knew, but no power on earth could have made him try to hold those boys back. Not after what he had seen in their eyes—the desperate yearning to get home, to feed their bloated bellies, to sleep under peaceful stars once more.

———

"WAKE UP, BOY, time to rise and shine."

Wiley groaned. He rolled over, yanked the dew-stained blanket over his head. He'd been asleep less than an hour, having been on picket duty most of the night. Every bone in his body ached from the damp night air, every muscle and tendon screamed out in pain.

All he wanted to do was crawl back under the blanket and go back to sleep. Forget about the pain. Forget about the war.

Dream.

Dream...of pleasant valleys and sunlit meadows far away; of pine-scented forest lands and ripe, rustling cornstalks in the July sun and red-breasted perch jumping in cool, black waters; of a woman named Martha Ann, his wife, and a little girl named Joanna, a little freckle-faced girl with red pigtails and big, round eyes the color of noonday skies in springtime—all waiting for him, waiting, waiting...

Suddenly, Wiley became conscious of a long-forgotten smell. Groggily, he sniffed the chill morning air, still laden with dew and mist. If he didn't know any better, he could have sworn that what he was smelling was bacon sizzling over an open fire. But that was impossible. The last time he'd tasted bacon was back in

Richmond, and that was months ago.

He slowly opened his eyes, saw Talmadge's big face looming over him. Talmadge's beefy jaws were moving up and down, trying to wolf down what looked like a moldy biscuit and a greasy slice of ham. *Food!*

Surely he was dreaming. It had been so long since he had seen bacon—let alone smelled or tasted it—he had a hard time convincing himself he wasn't hallucinating. Sometimes that happened to hungry men on the front lines. Back in the trenches of Petersburg, a young private from B Company had gone over the top one day when he mistook a squad of enemy pickets for a herd of grazing cattle. The poor boy had gone plumb loco with hunger—but that didn't stop the Yankees from shooting him dead on the spot.

Oh, well, Wiley had thought, The Good Lord has different ways of dealing with hungry men.

Ever since Five Forks and the retreat from Petersburg, the food situation had gone from bad to worse. The officers had told them to keep going, to step smartly, that plenty of rations awaited them at Amelia Court House some thirty miles to the east. There they could fill up their bellies, eat until they burst!

Spirits renewed, the men raced forward, sometimes whistling, singing and swapping jokes as they thought about the mountain of food waiting for them just a few more miles down the road. Even sporadic clashes with pursuing blue coats failed to dampen spirits as they hurried along, stomachs on fire with hunger pangs, mouths watering at the prospect of food being so nearby.

But when the famished troops reached the little railroad village on the morning of April 3, 1865, the supply train was gone. By a tragic mistake, the train had been diverted to Richmond and had been captured by Yankees! Not only that, the heartbroken, starving Confederates also learned that the citizens of Amelia County had already been cleaned out by Confederate impressment crews. There was nothing to eat. No food of any kind.

Ever since, the men had been reduced to foraging the forests and fields for cone nuts and palmetto roots, mulberry and pine bark and juniper twigs. In short, anything they could get their hands on, from the leather on their boots to butchering the occasional dog or cat that made the mistake of wandering into their ranks. Some men were detailed to follow along behind the horses and mules and snatch up kernels of corn dropped by the animals. Afterward, they'd wash and boil the corn, and not one soldier lucky enough to receive a portion complained.

So they had continued their grim march westward, toward the smoke-ringed mountains in the distance, toward the sleepy little village of Lynchburg. They stumbled along, more dead than alive, tearing branches off trees and gnawing buds, while artillery mules collapsed, unnoticed, in roads turned to mire by rain. Some men wandered off on their own into the woods to search for food. Some never came back. Other men, driven mad from hunger, muttered to themselves, fired their muskets at shadows, sometimes hitting and killing fellow soldiers.

The cruel march continued, with Federal units nipping at the Confederate army's heels each step of the way. Every now and then the Rebels would collide with a stray Yankee patrol, and a fierce firefight would break out. Most of the Confederates, however, weakened by hunger, merely went through the motions of returning fire before fading into the trees themselves or the Yankees pulled back. A large number simply surrendered, throwing themselves on the mercy of their captors and begging for food.

That aroma again…mouthwatering, teasing, intoxicating…

Talmadge licked his fingers and grinned. "Gonna be one helluva day."

Wiley watched while the Alabamian devoured the food. He couldn't tear his eyes away from the biscuit and chunk of meat, the globules of fat trickling down into Talmadge's thick beard and running down through his sausage-like fingers.

"Where did you get that?" Wiley finally asked, still stunned by the sight of food.

Talmadge smiled. "Some of the boys on forage detail got lucky this morning," he explained. "Came across a couple of fresh-kilt Yanks on the other side of the creek with enough grub in their haversacks to feed a whole company of Johnny Rebs."

Talmadge watched his friend's eyes grow wide with disbelief—and hunger. "Oh," he teased, reaching inside his own haversack and pulling out another biscuit and chunk of ham. "Almost forgot; this is for you." He tossed the food to Wiley. "I'd make it last if I were you. No telling when we'll see our next mouthful."

Wiley tore into the bread and meat as if it were going to be his last meal. No morsel of food had ever tasted better. Miracles really do happen, he thought, chomping and munching until it was all gone.

Then, licking his fingers, he realized it was morning.

"Did I miss reveille?" he asked, savoring the sticky grease on his fingertips.

"Wasn't no reveille this morning," Talmadge drawled.

Only then did Wiley become conscious of a dull, muffled roar off in the distance. The roar grew steadily louder, low and ominous, rolling across the surrounding countryside in one continuous, mighty wave. Wiley thought of mountains crashing and icebergs breaking up and sliding into churning seas. Beyond the tree line several miles behind them, small puffs of smoke wafted skyward.

"Grant," Talmadge said out of the corner of his mouth, completely without emotion.

Wiley uncorked his canteen, guzzled down several huge gulps of tepid water. He wiped his lips and growled, "Damn, don't those boys ever give up?"

HALF AN HOUR LATER the army was on the move again. A light rain was falling, but few men noticed as they trudged silently forward, each grim and silent in his own thoughts, the muffled roar of cannon-fire echoing behind them as Grant's forces drew closer and closer. Unknown to the Confederates at that moment, units of Sheridan's cavalry were already circling them to the south, hurrying to cut off any hopes they might have of retreating into North Carolina.

They came to a narrow, winding creek and halted. There a young officer informed the men that the city of Richmond, so long the symbol of Confederate resistance and strength against a host of enemy campaigns, had fallen and at that very moment was being consumed by tall, crimson flames set by rampaging blue coats.

A great sadness swept through the ranks. Some men cursed the Yankees and vowed revenge. Others dropped to their knees and wept bitterly. A few took the news calmly, while dozens of ragged, barefooted veterans, already disheartened by hunger and fatigue, simply melted away into the woods.

But those who remained were told to take heart. Couriers had been sent on ahead to Lynchburg and Farmville with requisitions for food.

"Each of you shall feast like kings when we reach Lynchburg," the same young officer, a major, informed the Rebels. "And when that is done, we will turn around and deal with the enemy. And, God willing, he shall be repaid a thousand times over for the misery he has brought upon our fair country."

"Why don't we stand and fight them now?" one old grayback yelled.

"Yeah," grunted another soldier. "Give us another crack at 'em. We'll show 'em what the Army of Northern Virginia is made of."

"We'll fight till hell freezes over for General Lee," another shouted.

Soon men were shouting up and down the line their desire to stand and fight. They whistled and cheered, stomped and hooted, strangely energized by the opportunity to avenge the fall of their beloved capital city. Their many voices had been transformed into one tumultuous roar, a tidal wave of emotions and anguish that threatened to break out of control.

The young officer, at first thrilled by the men's mood, suddenly became apprehensive. He stepped back, fearful of losing control. He almost expected the yelling, giddy Confederates to go charging off toward the enemy any second. He honestly didn't know what to do.

Then, from out of the misty forest there galloped into view a tall, white-bearded rider. At the sight of the horseman, the men grew strangely quiet.

"Well, blow me off my horse," Talmadge whispered to Wiley. "It's the old King of Spades hisself."

General Robert E. Lee, looking tired and worn, but resplendent in full dress uniform and golden spurs, drew up directly opposite Wiley's column and halted. He removed his hat, even though it was still raining, and waved it high in the air.

"Men," the famous general said in a voice so soft, so possessed of wisdom as to seem almost supernatural, "I know how each one of you feels regarding the enemy and the shame he has brought to our beloved capital. But, I assure you, to stand and confront him now would be a mistake, a terrible mistake."

The general gazed up and down the ragged line of Confederates. His clear blue eyes seemed to settle on Wiley, and for the briefest of moments, Wiley had the eerie feeling that the great general was speaking directly to him.

"We must keep moving for now," Lee continued, his fine silvery hair and whiskers now dampened by the rain. "We must reach Lynchburg and re-form our units. And then you must eat. We must all eat and refresh ourselves. Then, when the time is right and God is willing, we shall move upon the enemy with swift and all due diligence. And make no mistake about it, we shall prevail."

A multitude of cheers was lofted into the air, along with hats, blanket rolls and haversacks.

"Three cheers for General Lee!" someone shouted, and immediately three cheers went up.

The great general stood and watched his men for another long moment, then whirled his horse around and galloped back into the rain-soaked woods.

CHAPTER 50

THE REVEREND GEORGE F. PIERCE knelt in the musty darkness of his tent, silently staring at the huge wooden cross nailed to the center pole. He had already said his prayers. Now he was waiting for God to tell him what to do.

Outside he could hear the men starting to stir. They would be breaking camp at first light, anxious to put more miles between them and Sheridan's rapidly pursuing legions. Pierce was no military man, but he knew it was only a matter of time now before the Yankees caught up with them again. This time, he feared, it would take a miracle to save Lee's Army of Northern Virginia.

But Reverend Pierce had stopped believing in miracles a long time ago.

He lifted his eyes and gazed mournfully at the cross. "My God, my God…why has thou forsaken us?" he cried, then buried his head in his hands and wept.

Ten months earlier the preacher had left his small congregation in the North Georgia foothills to embark on a great crusade for Christ on the front lines in Virginia. The purpose of that crusade was to save souls, but it was also aimed at helping revive the sagging morale of the men on the front lines.

Like many men of the cloth, the diminutive preacher had gladly answered President Davis' call to come to the spiritual aid of the South's beleaguered army. No one needed to remind him that his homeland was under attack from all sides—not only by Northern aggressors clad in blue uniforms but also by legions of demons unleashed by unholy agents of Satan.

"It is imperative that you assail these demons and drive them forth from the field of spiritual battle," the president's aide had instructed the revivalists before sending them off on their dangerous missions.

But almost a year of tending to souls from the snowy valleys of the Shenandoah to the blood-soaked trenches of Petersburg had left the young minister feeling bitter and betrayed. He blamed everybody—but most of all he blamed God.

Why had the God of Abraham turned his back on his children and unleashed such unholy carnage? How much more must they endure? How many more gallant soldiers must die? How many more lives shattered? How many more children must be left fatherless before their cries were answered?

"Why don't you answer me?" Pierce shouted at the cross? "I've done everything you've asked of me, *everything*. What more must I do? *What more?*"

Just then a shadow fell across the threshold. "Preacher?" a young man's voice called out.

Pierce turned slowly and saw a young private, probably no more than seventeen, standing just outside the tent. He wiped his eyes quickly. "Yes?" he faltered.

"Could I...have a word with you, preacher?" the boy said nervously.

The minister pushed to his feet, straightened. "Of course, son. Please come in."

The young private ducked as he entered the tent. He leaned his musket against the tent post, just beneath the cross, then removed his hat. Bareheaded, he looked even younger: curly brown hair, blue eyes, pink, dimpled skin.

The boy fidgeted for a moment, as if uncertain how or where to begin. Finally, in a voice tense and cracking, he blurted, "I'm scared, preacher. I'm real scared."

Pierce felt a tugging at his heart for the frightened young soldier standing before him. He wanted to reach out and hug him, to tell him that it was okay to be scared, that God would look after him, would always be there to take care of him.

Instead, he asked, "What are you afraid of, son?"

Shuddering, the boy said, "I don't know if I can go through

another battle." He sounded afraid, like a terror-stricken child. "I'm so sick of all the killing, all the dying." He paused, wiped his eyes. "I...I just don't know if I can watch another man die..."

For several seconds neither spoke. The only sounds were the quiet drumming of rain on the roof of the tent, the wind sighing through the pines outside the door. Suddenly, Pierce felt a tingling sensation in his breast, then an old familiar warmth started to stir deep within his soul. The feeling spread quickly to all parts of his body, touching, comforting. Soon he was feasting in his new-found strength.

Pierce turned slowly to the cross and opened his heart to the quiet rapture. "Fear not, my son," he said softly. "God has a purpose for our being here, and he will see us safely through..."

———

LATER THAT MORNING, the Reverend Pierce stood on the back of a wagon, surrounded by five thousand ragged troops. The men were swaying and weeping, arms outstretched and eyes locked on the rain-swept heavens.

"You must fight and die, fight and die...like Joshua," the preacher roared in a voice laced with lightning and thunder. "There must be more baptisms of blood, but you must fight, my friends, fight till the streets and hills run red with the blood of your enemies. You must bare your breast as well as your spirit in this great struggle, so that our great land will be cleansed of those corrupt Northern meddlers who would seek to contaminate our world with their evil ways."

As he spoke, Pierce's eyes blazed with an ancient fury. His whole body shook and quivered, and he seemed to be transformed from a weak backwoods preacher into a true Holy Warrior on fire with the love of Jesus and his Father's Miraculous Grace.

One after the other and in droves, the soldiers fell to their knees, into the mud, lips trembling, tears flowing down dirty cheeks into scraggly beards caked with blood and bits of mud. Some rose to their feet and rocked back and forth, crying out, eyes brimming with tears of pure joy. Others caught up in the Holy Spirit crawled around on their hands and knees, barking like dogs and braying like donkeys.

Pierce raised both arms again and shouted: "I call upon our great God Almighty to let loose the electricity of insulted Heaven, so that it may fall with destructive violence upon the serried host of the enemy..."

A chorus of "Hallelujahs" echoed among the teary-eyed crowd. "Praise be to God!" they shouted back.

"And remember," Pierce intoned, "while we kill the bodies of our enemies, may the Lord have mercy on their sinful souls as General Lee, our own God of Battle, leads us forward to victory in the name of Jesus Christ, our Lord and Savior..."

CHAPTER 51

A PALE MOON WAS RISING HIGH over Big Sandy Swamp as Sheriff Poindexter pulled up in front of the dimly lit tavern. He got off his horse and stood for a moment, listening to the crickets and sniffing the sweet night air. It was amazing how calm and peaceful the swamp could be at midnight.

He hitched his horse to the rail, then pulled out his revolver and checked the chamber to make sure it was loaded. Satisfied, he stuck the gun back inside his coat and reached for the single-barreled shotgun hanging from his saddle.

Cradling the shotgun, he made his way across the yard toward the tavern. Off to the side he saw several mounds of earth with crude signs reading: *Death to Yankees*—grim reminders that a small Union patrol had wandered too far into the swamp when Sherman's army had passed through Wilkinson County the previous November.

Pearl's Place was the rowdiest tavern in Wilkinson County. Before the war it had been a somewhat respectable watering hole for local farmers and other honest citizens who liked an innocent nip now and then. In the years since, it had become a notorious hangout for army deserters and drifters and desperados.

The tavern was actually a dilapidated, three-room shack that sat at the edge of the swamp five miles from town. The front room was the bar where roughnecks liked to drink and gamble and occasionally cut each other up. The two backrooms were reserved for the painted ladies and their low-life clients.

Sheriff Poindexter had never liked going out to Pearl's alone, even in the best of times. But as sheriff he sometimes had no choice. Tonight was one of those times. That's why he had brought along the shotgun.

He trudged up the creaking steps and hesitated at the door, listening to the laughter and rambunctious beer-hall music coming from within. He sighed. Might as well get this over with, he told himself, then pushed open the door and went inside.

The room was dark and smoky from stale tobacco and kerosene lamps and smelled like warm beer and cheap perfume. He looked around, slowly sizing up the place. He recognized a few hard cases lounging by the bar and a couple of the women hanging onto them. One of the men was wearing a military coat and garrison cap.

Pearl Maddox, the owner, was leaning over the bar, puffing on a thick cigar and chitchatting with a couple of customers the sheriff had never seen before. He was a big, sweaty man with dark circles under his eyes and heavy eyelids that gave the impression he was about to fall asleep any second.

"Evening, Sheriff," Pearl called out when he saw the sheriff enter the bar.

Poindexter ambled over to the bar and leaned across the counter. "Hello, Pearl," he said, gazing up at the long, decorative mirror behind the bar.

Several customers got up when they saw the sheriff and bolted out the door.

Pearl poured the sheriff a glass of whiskey and shoved it across the bar toward him. "You're bad for business, Sheriff," he said in a thick drawl. "What brings you out to these parts, anyway?"

Poindexter downed the whiskey. "Work," he said. His voice was flat, utterly lacking emotion.

Just then the door to one of the back rooms flew open and a half-naked woman scampered out, screaming. A second later a wild-eyed roughneck holding his pants up with one hand and a bottle of whiskey in the other charged out after her. When they saw the sheriff, they turned around and darted back into the room and slammed the door.

The sheriff shook his head. "Some place you got here, Pearl," he said, reaching for the bottle.

Pearl's fat cheeks rolled back in a wide grin. "It's an honest living," he chuckled. Leaning forward, he said, "Say, you wouldn't be looking for a little action, would you, Sheriff? I got a new little hussy from Savannah that'll turn your socks inside out, if you know what I mean. Cost me two thousand dollars to bring her here, but I figure she's worth it." He winked. "Tell you what, since you're the high sheriff, I'll let you have her for two hours—on the house."

Poindexter made a grunting sound as he downed his second drink. "You know I'm a married man, Pearl."

"Yeah, yeah," Pearl acknowledged. "I was just trying to be nice. But I'll bet you ten to one that below that toy badge you've got a pecker just like the rest of us."

"Maybe," Poindexter replied glumly. He wiped his mouth and again glanced up at the gaudy mirror behind the bar. "You've got bad taste, Pearl."

Pearl's eyes flicked toward the mirror, then back at the sheriff. "What's wrong with my mirror?" he asked, feigning surprise.

"It's...I don't know...somehow out of character."

"Well, ain't nobody else ever complained about it before," the big bartender snarled.

Poindexter grunted in amusement. "No, I don't reckon they'd dare."

Pearl grabbed a cloth and started wiping dirty glasses. "So, if you ain't looking for action, then what are you doing here, Sheriff?"

Poindexter sighed. "Actually, I was looking for somebody. Zeke Taylor. Thought he might have been out here tonight."

Pearl pretended to think hard for a moment. "No, can't say he has. In fact, I haven't seen old Zeke in some time now."

Poindexter narrowed his eyes accusingly. "Don't lie to me, Pearl. I'll shut you down and tear this place apart if you lie to me."

"I...I wouldn't lie to you, Sheriff," Pearl recoiled. "You know me better than that."

Poindexter reached slowly across the counter and picked up the whiskey bottle. He rolled it around in the palm of his hand for a couple of seconds, then hurled it with all his might against the long mirror behind the bar. Pearl dove behind the bar just as the mirror exploded in a cascade of broken glass.

Pearl got to his knees and peeked out from behind the counter.

"Are you crazy?" he screamed at the sheriff.

The sheriff grabbed another bottle and heaved it at another unbroken part of the mirror. The impact was equally devastating.

He grabbed a third bottle and started to throw it.

"Okay, okay," Pearl blurted, waving his hands in surrender. "I'll tell you what you want to know if you'll just stop wrecking my place."

Poindexter smiled and slowly lowered the bottle. "I'm waiting," he said impatiently.

Pearl wiped his bald head with the same dirty rag he'd been using to clean the glasses. He swallowed hard, then nodded toward the second back room. "If you tell him I told you, I'm a dead man."

"Thanks, Pearl," the sheriff said. He dropped a ten-dollar bill on the counter and said, "Buy yourself a new mirror."

Then he picked up his shotgun, slung it across his shoulder and headed slowly toward the back room.

He was halfway across the room when the backroom door opened and Zeke Taylor stepped out. He was holding a long revolver in one hand, a half-naked girl in the other. When he saw the sheriff, he yanked the girl in front of him.

"I hear you've been looking for me, Sheriff," he sneered.

Poindexter straightened when he saw the gun. "I reckon you know what I'm here for, Zeke."

Zeke grinned. "I figured you'd be coming sooner or later, Sheriff. What took you so long?"

"I've been kinda busy."

Zeke laughed. "Yeah, I know what you mean." He leaned down and gave the squirming girl a kiss. "I've been kinda busy myself."

"Put down the gun, Zeke, and let the girl go."

"And what if I don't?"

"Then I'll have to kill you."

Zeke gave a nervous laugh. "Who do you think you're fooling, Sheriff? You ain't gonna shoot me, not with all these here witnesses. Why, it'd be cold-blooded murder."

Poindexter sighed. "It's your choice, Zeke. Either you come with me peacefully to stand trial for the attempted murder of Hamilton Dewberry or I'll kill you where you stand."

Zeke rolled his eyes, unimpressed. "Aw, that old Yankee-loving

DEEP IN THE HEART 357

abolitionist had it coming, Sheriff, and you and everybody else in town knew it. Besides, that was a long time ago. Hell, I don't even hardly remember it."

"Well, Mr. Dewberry ain't never forgot it. Maybe Judge Carswell can help refresh your memory."

"Carswell? Sheriff, there ain't no way I'm gonna let you take me in to that old hanging judge."

The sheriff fixed Zeke with a granite-hard stare. "Like I said, it's your call, Zeke. I'm going to count to three, and if you ain't turned that girl loose and dropped that gun by then I'm gonna kill you."

Zeke's eyes scanned the room, frantic for help. He waved his gun at a couple of low-lifes cowering in the corner. "You boys ain't gonna just sit there and let him take me in, are you?"

When nobody moved to help him, Zeke knew he was on his own. He cocked his gun and pulled the girl tighter against him.

"*One…*"

Zeke glared across the room at Pearl. "Pearl, you fat-headed, loud-mouthed sonofabitch, I hope you burn in hell…"

"*Two…*"

Zeke, now crazed with fear, pushed the girl out of the way and pointed the revolver straight at the sheriff.

"*Three.*"

Zeke fired his revolver but the bullet sailed wide, crashing into a kerosene lamp behind Poindexter. Before he could cock the gun to fire again, the sheriff swung the shotgun down off his shoulders, aimed and fired.

The single blast slammed into Zeke's chest and face, knocking him backward against the wall. He seemed to hang there in death, as if impaled, before slowly sliding down and leaving a long trail of blood on the wall.

Sheriff Poindexter lowered the smoking shotgun and walked slowly over to examine the body.

"Murderer!" a girl screamed. It was the same half-naked girl Zeke had been holding as a shield only moments ago. She rushed toward him, throwing herself against him and beating his chest with her fists. "*You killed him! You killed him!*"

Poindexter grabbed the girl's wrists and pushed her away. "Calm down, little lady, or I'll have to throw you in jail."

"You wouldn't dare," the girl hissed, then reached inside the sheriff's coat and pulled out his revolver.

Before Poindexter realized what was happening, the girl cocked the gun and pointed it straight at him. "I loved him," she sputtered. "He...He was going to marry me. Now he's dead and...and I'm gonna kill you!"

Another blast...another scream...and the girl lay dead at the sheriff's feet, a pool of blood forming beneath the gaping hole in the back of her head.

Poindexter looked across the room and saw the smoking rifle in Pearl's hands. The big man was not smiling. "You just cost me two thousand dollars, Sheriff," he said.

CHAPTER 52

GENERAL ROBERT E. LEE was not in a particularly good mood. He had slept in the rain the night before, an unnaturally cold spring rain that had drenched his bedroll and uniform and left him shivering and feeling feverish. On top of that, the arthritis in his shoulder hurt so bad he could hardly move his arm.

But the worst pain came when he rode forward that morning and saw his battered, barefooted army in full retreat.

"My God!" he wailed to several equally soggy aides at his side, "Has the army been dissolved?"

General Billy Mahone came up in a flash. "No, General," Mahone replied. "Here are our troops, ready to do their duty!"

But when Lee gazed about and saw the despair in the eyes of those troops, his spirit sagged. How could men such as these—wet, cold, shriveled by hunger and disease—how could they possibly be asked to obey another command? How could they march another mile? Fight another battle?

Tears came to the general's own haunted eyes as he watched the ragged remnants of his once-proud army fade into the early morning mist.

Indeed, Lee's army was in its final stages of disintegration. The road to Lynchburg, where he had hoped to find fresh provisions and respite for his men, was littered with dead and dying Rebels. Wagons and broken-down artillery caissons blazed in the pouring rain. Unopened boxes of ammunition exploded. Shells burst, throwing up dense columns of smoke that spiraled skyward. Exhausted soldiers and worn-out mules and horses lay beside the road where they fell, indifferent to Lee or orders by other officers to form up.

An officer caught the look on Lee's face and asked, "Do you think it's time we talked to General Grant, sir?"

Lee bristled at the suggestion. "I trust it has not come to that!" he fired back. "We certainly have too many brave men to think of laying down our arms. They still fight with great spirit, whereas the enemy does not."

"But, sir…"

Lee waved his hand for silence. "If I were to intimate to General Grant that I would listen to terms, he would at once regard it as such evidence of weakness that he would demand unconditional surrender—and sooner than that I am resolved to die. Indeed, we must all determine to die at out posts!"

Lee righted himself in the saddle. Leaning, he reached out and snatched a Confederate battle flag from a skulker running rearward. He wheeled his charger around and headed straight for the ranks.

"I will strike that man a blow in the morning," Lee shouted, holding the flagstaff high so that every man could see it. The wind caught the flag and snapped it around his silver crown, brushing his shoulders and face and wrapping his body in red.

"Uncle Robert's" gallant display of courage shamed many of the fleeing men and brought others to tears. But it failed to halt the hemorrhage of dispirited Confederates retreating from the field.

Nor did it slow the steady streams of advancing blue coats.

———

THE NEXT DAY Sheridan's cavalry caught up the Confederates near Appomattox Court House, and a fierce battle ensued. It was to be the Army of Northern Virginia's final skirmish.

"Looks like this is it, Georgia boy," Talmadge said to Wiley. The big Alabamian squatted against a soggy embankment, his bloodied and bearded face tilted toward the rain. His eyes were gray and hollow, the eyes of a corpse. His voice was the voice of the dead. "Don't reckon it'll be much longer now."

Wiley was struck by how much his old friend had aged in recent weeks. All that marching and fighting had done it, plus the endless days without food and drinking water so rancid it kept the boys running into the woods every few minutes. Talmadge was only forty-five but he looked more like seventy-five. His thinning hair was white and speckled with dried blood. His grizzled, ashen-gray face was streaked with mud and more flecks of dried blood. He reminded Wiley of a sick old dog that had finally run its last trot.

Between bouts of coughing and wheezing, Talmadge clutched at his bleeding side. A Yankee ball had caught up with him back at Sayler's Creek, but a sharp knife and jug of whiskey had kept him alive.

"Let me see that," Wiley said, checking the bandage.

Talmadge waved him away. "Ah, it ain't nothing," he rasped, then coughed again. "We got more important things to worry about right now."

He was right. Wiley knew the Federals would be making a final charge any minute now, the third that morning. This time, when they came, it would probably be the final curtain call. But as he gazed up and down the jagged line of gray coats huddled in the rain, he knew those old Yanks would pay dearly for their victory. It might be the Confederates' last battle, but by God they'd at least go down swinging.

Wiley flipped open his cartridge pouch and felt around inside for a new packet.

The pouch was empty.

Empty.

His fingers clawed around inside the leather pouch, desperately probing for one last nonexistent round. He turned it inside out. Nothing.

It was no use.

He had run out of ammunition.

With a shrug, Wiley leaned back next to Talmadge, their shoulders touching. He closed his eyes and waited.

Nothing to do now but wait.

———

A SHARP PAIN IN HIS SIDE brought him around. It was Talmadge, poking him with his elbow.

Wiley opened his eyes, saw the big man leaning over him. For one horrifying moment, he thought he was looking at a dead man, gray, swollen and stinking, rising from the grave.

"What now?" Wiley asked.

Talmadge sucked in a deep breath of air that rattled around inside his throat and pushed himself to his knees. He wiped the mud from his eyes. Still clutching his wounded side, he cut loose a wad of tobacco juice—his last plug.

"I told you a long time ago I wasn't gonna let nothing happen to you," he rasped.

Wiley wanted to laugh and say, "Well, you're sure doing one lousy job of it," but didn't have the strength.

"Just want you to know I'm a man of my word." Talmadge peered over the trench wall and looked around. "Come on, this might be my last chance to save your hide."

Wiley managed to ask, "What are you talking about?"

"We're getting outta here."

Wiley's eyeballs rolled around behind his eyelids. "Where?"

"Just follow me," Talmadge barked back. "This old boy ain't about to roll over dead. Leastaways, not yet."

Before he knew what he was doing, Wiley was on his knees following the big man along the trench wall. They kept low, hugging the mud, low-crawling at times, bumping and sliding silently along the narrow trench. They moved surprisingly quickly, dragging themselves across bodies, some of them so badly mangled they no longer looked real. Old men. Young boys. Eyes bulging skyward. Mouths open wide, full of rain and frozen in death's final agony. Fingers twisted around the grips of rifles or simply coiled upward at grotesque angles.

At one point Wiley's hand slipped, and he found himself staring into the fixed, frozen eyes of a dead major. Where the major's mouth should have been there was a large, gaping hole filled with mud. Bugs slithered in and out of the hole.

"No," he heard himself say, only it was more like a scratchy exhalation of air.

He felt his insides heave. Groaning, he pushed himself away from the dead major quickly, vomit spewing on his chest, feet, hands, everywhere. He shook uncontrollably, gasping for breath.

He finally caught up with Talmadge, watched the big man

scramble over the side of the trench wall. Two dead Confederates, one of them wearing captain's bars, lay face down in the mud. The back of the captain's head was missing.

"Poor bastards," Talmadge grunted.

He clambered over the side, reached down and tried to pull Wiley up behind him. "Come on, boy," he rasped. "Gotta keep moving."

The mud gave way twice, each time causing Wiley to slide back down into the death-filled muck. On the third try Talmadge caught his arm and yanked him over the top.

"We should have done this a long time ago," Talmadge wheezed. "Hell, this ain't no war. This is murder. Plain and simple."

They kept crawling until they reached a small patch of woods and stopped long enough for Wiley to catch his breath. Then they were off again, scudding and sliding through the mud, fingers clawing up huge chunks of clay and dirt as they worked their way deeper into the woods.

When they came to a clearing, Wiley rose to his feet and looked behind them. Through the smoke and driving rain, he saw nothing but dead Confederate soldiers as far as the eye could see. Scattered here and there were the rotting, mangled carcasses of horses and shattered wagons. Trees uprooted and splintered like toothpicks. Craters deep enough to drive a team of mules through. A nightmare come to life.

Vague forms stirred in the shadowy mists swirling about the battlefield. Occasionally, Wiley caught glimpses of a face, nothing more, as wounded men wandered, dazed and bleeding, through the carnage.

Not far behind them came more voices, interspersed by the steady *ker-thump! ker-thump!* of artillery blasts, soon followed by the sickening, metallic whine of projectiles hurtling through the air.

They straggled forward, the two of them, grasping at each other for support. They kept low, avoiding contact with other soldiers either lost or running away in confusion. Wiley wondered what would happen if they ran into an officer.

Up ahead, barely visible in the rain and drifting fog, loomed some kind of building. A house. Or what used to be a house. A very large house.

"There!" Talmadge pointed, pushing Wiley in the direction of the house.

An eternity seemed to pass before the pair of Confederates crossed the field and reached the house. It was an old plantation-style place, grand and handsome even in ruins. Part of the porch was missing, as was a section of the front wall. Only three of the house's six massive white columns remained to support what was left of the roof.

They walked up the wide steps and looked around. Most of the triple-hung windows were shattered and the paneled shutters splintered and hanging at odd angles. Straight ahead the massive paneled door was opened part way to reveal a dark hallway. If the inside of the house was anything like the outside, it must have been a grand place indeed before the arrival of the two armies.

Wiley hesitated at the door. "We can't do this, Tal," he said.

"Can't do what?"

"Run away. We can't run away like this. If we do, we're no better than those skulkers who skedaddled last night."

Talmadge draped both hands across Wiley's shoulders and sighed. "Wiley, Wiley," he said wearily. "I want you to listen to me, boy, I want you to listen to me good." He drew another deep sigh. "You want to see that sweet little woman of yours again, don't you? And that little gal?" He paused, letting Wiley think it over. "She's gonna need her pappy."

Wiley knew the old warrior was right. But he still didn't like the idea.

Talmadge turned loose and backed away. "You ain't got no choice, boy. So, come on. We still have a chance to save our hides if we hurry. If those Yanks break through back there, we're done for. You ain't never going back home. They'll put you in a prison way up there in New York or somewhere so far away that little gal of yours will be a grown woman before you get to see her. Is that what you want?"

It didn't make sense, yet Wiley knew Talmadge was right. It was wrong to run, sure, to abandon one's comrades on the field of battle. But the way Wiley now saw it, they didn't have any comrades left to abandon. They were all dead or dying. Those who remained would soon be dead, too, or taken prisoners.

But he and Talmadge were alive and free, and suddenly that seemed awfully important.

CHAPTER 53

WILEY HAD BEEN RIGHT about the house. It was as
magnificent on the inside as it was on the outside.
Although he had never been inside such a grand house
himself, he had often imagined what it would be like. Back home in
Wilkinson County, there were a couple of places that could right-
fully be called mansions. There was Mayor Futch's big house at the
edge of town. Another was owned by the Sutter brothers who
farmed a couple thousand acres of cotton along Big Sandy Creek.
The Sutters worked their spread with a couple of hundred slaves,
and rumor had it that some of those slaves lived better than a lot of
whites.

But this place—it was like a palace!

"Let's split up," Talmadge said. "You go that way and look; I'll go
this way."

As they went their separate ways, Wiley didn't have the foggiest
clue what they were supposed to be looking for.

Wiley wandered through a pair of double-arched doorways into
another spacious hallway, past a winding staircase and carved interi-
or columns rising to the lofty ceiling. Priceless treasures were
strewn about everywhere. Glittering chandeliers. Oil paintings
encased in gilded frames. Lamps. Tall-case clocks. Fancy, hand-
carved pieces of furniture still arranged as if the owners had just
stepped out for a Sunday afternoon stroll. Even the wallpaper, a
rich, rosy damask pattern, looked almost kingly.

But the war had left its dirty fingerprints on just about everything. Sofas, chairs, tables, books—all smoked and covered with
thick layers of mildew and dust. Bits of plaster sprinkled down from

the ceiling, littering furniture and Oriental rugs and finely polished floors. Patches of green mold grew on walls and floors. Stringy cobwebs looped down from cornices, snagging everything that moved.

Such a shame, Wiley thought, brushing back a sticky strand of cobweb as he moved deeper into the house.

Gray fingers of mist curled through the lonely rooms, adding an eerie touch of melancholy to the gloomy ruins. This was the kind of place where people saw ghosts, Wiley figured. Old houses full of death and sorrow. Old houses where the spirits of the dead still mourn for the world they left behind.

He entered another room and stopped. Beneath a chipped and stained chandelier in what Wiley assumed was a library or music room was a very large piano. One of its gracefully curving legs was missing, leaving it tilted at an awkward angle. Wiley could only imagine the sweet music that must have once flowed across those cracked and peeling keys.

Wiley heard the floor creak behind him. He turned around, musket raised.

"Some place, huh?" Talmadge said, treading lightly into the room.

Wiley lowered his musket. "Yeah." He waited another second, then asked, "What now?"

Talmadge sighed. "Just let me think a spell," he replied, plopping down into a leather wing chair. Clouds of dust billowed up from the chair, making Wiley sneeze.

Wiley noticed Talmadge's wound. He was bleeding pretty badly. The bandages had soaked through, leaving tiny droplets of blood everywhere he went. He had to make the big man stop, if only for a few minutes, to give the wound time to heal. Otherwise he was going to bleed to death.

Yet the Yankees couldn't be far behind them now. The roar and clang of gunfire had dimmed considerably, an indication that the fight was probably winding down. By now, his regiment was probably in full flight. Those still alive, he grimly reminded himself.

As if reading Wiley's thoughts, Talmadge said, "At least we're still among the living."

"We're done for, Tal," Wiley fired back, an agitated tone in his voice. "We should have stayed and fought with the other boys."

Talmadge shook his big head slowly. "You want to give me one good reason why, boy?"

Wiley pressed his lips to say something, but Talmadge cut him off. "Let me tell you something about war, boy," the big man said in an uncommonly serious tone. "There ain't no glory in war, no matter what the politicians and the generals tell us. Boys who fool themselves into thinking such wind up getting themselves killed. And there ain't no glory in death, neither."

Talmadge pushed himself to his feet, using his musket as a crutch. "We ain't whipped yet," he said, suddenly brightening. "I told you I'd think of something." He winked. "Got you this far, didn't I?"

Wiley shrugged and said, "I still say we shouldn't have left the others."

"Hush. Let me think."

Wiley heard the telltale whine of an incoming mortar round. A split second later there was a deafening crash in the front yard. Windows rattled and shook, and more plaster cascaded down from the ceiling.

"You better think a little faster," Wiley said.

Talmadge sprang to his feet. "There's got to be some old hole around here to hide. You go upstairs and have a look-see. I'll check down here, try to find us a root cellar or something. Let's go!"

Wiley moved quickly, heading back into the hallway and up the winding staircase. He took two steps at a time, carefully at first, but when another shell landed closer to the house, he sprinted up the remaining steps.

He moved cautiously from room to room, no longer admiring the furnishings, no longer envious of the former occupants, but galloping instead through each passageway, kicking over furniture, banging open doors, desperate to find some place to hide.

He came to a bedroom and stopped. It was big and dark and filled with choking dust and debris. Against the far wall stood a handsome four-poster bed, surrounded by expensive-looking tables and chairs. In the center of the room stood an amazing object—a white marble statue of some ancient god clutching a gracefully curving harp.

Wiley's eyes went back to the bed again. For one tantalizing moment he was tempted to lie down, stretch out on the wonderful-looking bed and relax, go to sleep. He couldn't remember the last time he had slept on a real bed.

He slammed the bedroom door shut and moved on down the hall. The next room he came to was a small sewing room. He walked inside and looked around. Thick clouds of dust covered everything, but he was able to make out several pieces of beautifully embroidered works of art—pillows, dolls, scarves, dresses, pin cushions, samplers. Needles and pieces of material lay scattered about.

He gasped and reached for his empty musket when he saw a tall figure lurking in the far corner. He relaxed when he realized it was only a mannequin sporting a faded pink dress.

On a table next to a set of sewing pins lay what looked like an old photo album. Wiley ran his fingers over the embossed cover, slowly opening it to the first page. *The Denson Family*, the initial entry read. Below the name were two oval portraits of a handsome man and woman. The caption read: *Ansel Denson, aged 35, and Isabelle Mavis Denson, aged 30.*

The date was May 15, 1855.

Almost ten years ago.

Wiley put the album down and started out of the room. That's when he noticed a small crack of light coming from the ceiling. When he looked closer, he saw that it was an attic door of some kind. Energized by his discovery, he pulled over a chair, climbed up and pushed open the door.

It was a vast room—dark and empty except for a couple of old boxes and trunks and a few other items scattered about. A perfect place to hide! He yanked off his knapsack and tossed it inside. His letters to Martha Ann would be safe up there in the attic until he returned with Talmadge.

He was halfway down the stairs when he heard a gunshot.

"Talmadge," he said apprehensively.

He hurried down the stairs, not slowing until he found an open door leading down into what appeared to be some kind of basement. He took several steps down into the darkness, then stopped. "Talmadge?" he whispered cautiously. "Are you okay?"

Silence.

He descended a few more steps. "Tal? You down here?"

Movement in a darkened corner.

Wiley spun around and saw a young Union soldier cowering in the far corner. He was shrouded in shadows, but Wiley could tell that he was young, very young, probably no more than sixteen or seventeen.

Wiley raised his musket and aimed it at the boy.

The boy threw his arms straight up. "Don't shoot...please," he begged. His voice was that of a child. A terrified child who had just done something wrong.

A shapeless mass on the floor near the boy's feet caught Wiley's eye. He blinked, trying to adjust his eyes to the darkness. Then he saw it—Talmadge's body, sprawled at a twisted angle. A fresh stream of blood gushed from his forehead.

"Tal?" Wiley called out fearfully.

"I...I didn't mean to hurt him...honest," the boy sobbed. "My gun...just went off."

Wiley felt like his heart had been ripped out of his chest. He tottered, felt his knees buckling. "No...no...no," he sobbed, unable to tear his eyes away from his dead friend's body.

Still shaking, he raised his rifle and pointed it straight at the boy's chest. He tugged at the trigger, even though he knew the gun was empty, willing the gun to somehow fire anyway so that Talmadge's killer would die.

But the boy was crying, and he was so young, oh, so young, with big blue eyes and tousled blond locks and a round, pink face that belonged at his mother's breast. Oh, God, why did he have to be so young? Wiley wanted to know. Why? All he could think about was Petie and Delk and Coop and all the other boys with innocent blue eyes and round, pink faces whose lives had been snuffed out in the flowering of their boyhood.

Wiley slowly lowered his musket. He staggered over to Talmadge's body, bent down and touched his cheek with his fingers.

"Rest easy, old friend," he whispered, then pulled off his jacket and draped it across the big man's face.

Fighting back tears, Wiley rose slowly to his feet and glared at the boy. *Why*, he wanted to ask, but before he could get the word out the boy shuddered and said, "I didn't mean to kill him. He...He was going to shoot me. My...My gun went off. It just went off. I'm sorry."

A blinding wave of fury washed over Wiley. With all his heart he wanted to run over and club the boy Yank, smash him to a bloody pulp. Strangle him. Stab him cruelly with his bowie knife. Watch him bleed and slowly die. In that moment of madness, Wiley blamed the boy not only for Talmadge's death but also for the war, the endless suffering, the long years spent away from his wife and daughter. He felt himself shaking, quivering uncontrollably, every muscle in his body poised and yearning to spring forward, to kill the Yankee intruder with his bare hands.

Then the urge passed.

Wiley closed his eyes for a moment, the image of the frail, blond youth with the tangled blond curls ingrained forever in his memory. Suddenly, for no reason at all, anger gave way to pity. He dropped his musket. The sound of the gun clanging on the cold stone floor echoed eerily through the muffled gloom of the basement.

"Where are you from, boy?" Wiley heard himself ask. It was a simple question, but oddly out of place under the circumstances. When the boy faltered, Wiley said, "I'm not going to hurt you, son. I just want to know where you're from."

The young Yankee swallowed hard. "Pennsylvania," he replied.

Several seconds passed. Out in the yard, Wiley could hear the sound of musketry and shells falling. Maybe the Yanks hadn't licked the Rebs after all. Maybe there was hope in old Lee's army yet.

"What are you doing down here, anyway?" Wiley asked the boy. "Why aren't you out there with the rest of your outfit."

The boy dragged his sleeve across his face, wiping away the tears. "I just couldn't take it anymore," he sobbed. "Out there...Just couldn't take it anymore."

Wiley nodded as if he understood, as if he understood everything now. In a strange sort of way, he felt himself drawn to the boy Yank. Perhaps that was because they had shared something in common. Both had reached the point where the thought of living seemed to outweigh that of dying for no good cause. Isn't that what homesick soldiers had done since the beginning of time? Whenever a war or cause became unbearable, they simply threw down their weapons and went home.

Wiley smiled at the boy. "Go on home," he said. "Get out of here. Go back to Pennsylvania and never think of this day again."

The boy gasped in rabid disbelief. He waited another moment, just to be sure he had heard right, then rushed past Wiley and up the steep flight of stairs, the sound of his footsteps echoing hollowly through the lonely house.

Wiley walked over to a basement window and peered out in time to see the young Union soldier scampering across the deserted front yard. He smiled. The rain had stopped finally, and it looked for all the world like the sun was trying to break through the clouds. Wiley even thought he heard the sound of birds twittering way off in the trees.

Only it wasn't birds he heard.

From out of nowhere there came another howling roar of airborne lead, then the deafening crunch of metal exploding against earth.

Wiley dropped to the floor and held his breath until the house stopped shaking. He rose slowly and peered out the window. The smoke gradually lifted. Where the boy Yank had stood only a moment before there now wafted a puffy white cloud of smoke.

"*No!!!*" Wiley screamed, pounding his fists against the windowsill. "*No! No! No!*"

He sank to the floor again and wept uncontrollably.

Some time later he dragged himself over to Talmadge's stiff body. He reached down, touched his friend's cold head.

"You were right, old friend," he whispered. "There ain't no glory. There never was."

CHAPTER 54

"**B**Y THE POWERS VESTED IN ME by our Almighty Father and the sovereign state of Georgia, I now pronounce you man and wife."

The Reverend Isaac Thurmond, looking worn and frail in his black suit and purple vestment, turned to the handsome young Confederate officer standing before him and said, "Son, you may now kiss the bride."

Major Garrett Nesmith looked at Amy and smiled. With trembling fingers he slowly lifted the veil and kissed her softly on the lips.

"Hallelujah, praise the Lord!" Sarah Collins shouted from the back of the church.

She caught herself, smiling and squeezing Monroe's hand just as Greta's heavy foot found the organ pedals. Within seconds the old church was rumbling and rocking to the heavy strains of "The Wedding March."

Sergeant Indigo Collins—mustachioed, trim and handsome in a dress blue uniform with bright red dragoon chevrons on the sleeves and gleaming sword curving away from his side—was the first to shake the groom's hand.

"Congratulations," Indigo said. His voice was rich and smooth and showed not the slightest trace of a stutter.

Garrett embraced Indigo and whispered in his ear, "Thanks for coming, old friend. It means a lot to Amy and me."

Smiling, Indigo asked, "What are best men for?"

It was an odd sight—the groom in Confederate gray, the black best man wearing Yankee blue. A few days earlier they would have been mortal enemies on the battlefield. Today, with the war all but officially over, Garrett and Indigo were friends and countrymen once again.

Sarah Collins, sitting next to her husband on the back row, dabbed the corners of her eyes with a handkerchief. How handsome and grown up her two boys looked in their fancy soldiers' uniforms! So proud and strong, each having bravely gone off to serve a different cause. When Georgia had been threatened by invaders, young Garrett rushed off to defend her honor. Indigo had answered the call in a different way—a way which, quite frankly, Sarah felt was closer to God's chosen plan.

But none of that mattered now. The war was over, and both of her boys were back home, praise the Lord! Thanks to Mister Lincoln—God rest his troubled soul—the Union had been saved. It was a new day, a brand-new day. Of course, there was still a lot of healing to be done, but Sarah figured there would be plenty of time for that. *Plenty of time.*

Arm in arm, Garrett and Amy turned and started down the aisle. Behind them toddled the three-year-old bridesmaid—little Joanna, her bangs and long, flaming pigtails garlanded with bows and ribbons. She wore her favorite white dress and clutched a bouquet of fragrant spring flowers.

Mother Nesmith sat in the front pew between Martha Ann and Elizabeth. She was smiling. For the first time in years, there was finally something to smile about again. Still, Martha Ann could sense the old woman's pain as she watched her youngest son stroll slowly down the aisle, his beautiful, blushing bride draped on his arm. The others were gone—James Madison, Charles, Albert, John, William and Wiley—but at least there was Garrett to carry on the family name.

Martha Ann's eyes glistened as she quietly recalled the day four years earlier when she had walked down this very aisle arm-in-arm with Wiley. How handsome he had looked with his dark, flashing eyes and boyish grin and broad shoulders as he held her in his strong arms before the altar. She closed her eyes, reliving the moment he first kissed her, how her heart had fluttered when Reverend Thurmond pronounced them man and wife.

It was the happiest day of her life—until that arrogant young major with the golden hair and jangling spurs came riding up with the terrible news that would turn her world upside down and shatter her dreams forever...

Mayor Joseph Potter sat alone near the back of the church, silently cursing the war and all it had cost him. He unconsciously rubbed the stump below his right shoulder, the sleeve tucked under and folded flat against his side. An awful price to pay for other men's folly, he fumed. And for what? What had been the gain?

He closed his eyes and thought about Catherine—his dear, sweet Catherine. More beautiful than a summer sunset, more tempestuous than a winter wind. And now she was gone. A bitter-sweet smile crept across his face. How could he ever have deluded himself into thinking a woman such as Catherine would remain his forever? He should have turned her loose long ago, saved them both a lot of grief. He sighed wistfully. Trying to hold onto a woman like Catherine was like trying to hold onto the wind.

Still, he missed her terribly. Not a day went by, not a single hour, that he didn't think about her. Her bewitching smile and dancing eyes followed him everywhere, guiding him through the daylight hours and lighting up his tortured dreams at night.

Compared to the loss of his beloved Catherine, Joseph's missing arm seemed a trivial thing.

Inside his jacket pocket was the crumpled note she had left behind the day she ran off with her Yankee boyfriend. He had found it tucked inside the cash register in the store:

Dear Joseph:

In the unlikely event you survive this war and return to Wilkinson County, I am writing this to tell you that I have gone away to make a better life for myself. I hope you aren't too angry with me and can somehow find it in your heart to forgive me for all the heartache and pain I have caused you all these years. I wish you well, and pray to God that he will see you safely through this war. You deserve better, dear Joseph. You have always deserved better.

As always,
Catherine

In spite of it all, Joseph still held out hope that she would some-day return. It was, admittedly, a slim hope, but one that had given him the strength to reopen the store and get on with his life. A few weeks after his return from North Carolina, where he had battled Sherman's forces with Johnston at Bentonville—and also where he had lost his arm in the final, fierce engagement of the war—a group of townsfolk had approached him and talked him into running for mayor.

"This town needs you," Colonel Samuel Player had urged him. Player, the former commander of the Wilkinson County Invincibles—and one of its few survivors—pledged his support in the race. "As the local representative in the state legislature, I will personally see to it that Irwinton gets all the help possible to rebuild what Sherman destroyed."

Joseph won easily.

Catherine would have liked that.

———

THE PROCESSION was halfway down the aisle when the church doors suddenly creaked open. A lone figure stood in the doorway.

Garrett and Amy halted when they saw the gaunt, bandaged fig-ure clad in a tattered gray uniform. They stepped aside as he limped into the church and made his way soundlessly down the aisle.

The music stopped. Every eye stared blankly at the intruder, whose dirty, tear-filled face seemed to glow in the soft light filtering through the stained glass above the altar behind Reverend Thurmond.

Martha Ann rose slowly, gasping in disbelief. Was it a dream? A cruel trick of the light? She steadied herself against the back of a pew. Oh, God, she heard herself moaning, oh God…

She almost cried out when she recognized the face of the man she hadn't seen in more than three years.

Wiley came to her like a shadow out of a dream. Time stood still as their eyes locked, neither daring to touch for fear the other might vanish. The years rolled quickly backward. *Wiley standing bare-chested at the woodpile, showing Martha Ann how to chop wood. The two of them standing on the back porch watching a fiery sunset. Now they were in*

Savannah on their honeymoon, the dark Southern sky lit with fireworks and the roar of martial music echoing through the rain-soaked night. Their last day together at the train station, their last kiss, Wiley leaning from the window, the train fading into the gray mists...

In her mind, Martha Ann relived the many long, lonely nights, the endless stream of letters, the years of fear and anger and frustration. *Don't worry, Punkin, I'll come back...I promise you I'll come back...*

Then they were gone, dimming like a bad dream the moment Wiley reached out and touched her.

Wiley. Gaunt and grim, *but alive!*

"Punkin," he whispered.

Then something seemed to break inside him. Choking back tears, he took her in his arms and kissed her. He kissed her cheeks and eyes, her forehead and temples, her ears, her neck. He pressed his face into her hair, unable to drink in enough of her fragrance.

Martha Ann clung wordlessly to her husband, whimpering, weeping, secretly praying this was not a dream.

Wiley felt a tug at his pants leg. Pulling away from Martha Ann, he looked down and saw a little girl, a little girl with red pigtails and bangs and pretty satin ribbons in her hair. She handed him a flower.

"This is for you," the little girl said.

Something inside Wiley came unraveled. His lips parted to speak, but no words came out, only a dry hissing sound. He stared at the little girl for several long moments, trying to sort through the kaleidoscope of emotions rushing, tumbling through his brain.

Then, trembling, he dropped to his knees and gazed deep into his daughter's eyes for the first time. *So blue and clear. Just like her mother's.* Just the way he'd always imagined.

Joanna crinkled up her nose. "Are you my daddy?" she asked with all the innocence of a summer rainbow.

Wiley smiled, blinking back tears. "Yes," he said softly, "I am your daddy."

Joanna clasped her hands. "Oh, goody," she giggled. "Does that mean you'll go home with us?"

"Yes," Wiley rasped. "I'm going home with you."

He reached inside his pocket and pulled out the tiny locket

Talmadge had given him. He opened Joanna's hand and placed the locket inside her palm.

"This is for you," he choked. He folded her tiny fingers over the locket. "It's very special."

Joanna's sparkling blue eyes opened wide in joyous disbelief. "Oh, thank you," she chortled. Looking up, she said, "Look, Mommy, look what my daddy gave me!"

Only then did Wiley reach out and hug his daughter. Only then did he press his hard lips against his little girl's soft cheek.

Reverend Thurmond waited for the right moment, then raised his hands and nodded toward Greta Underwood. Beaming with joy, she crashed her foot down on the organ pedals, and her thick fingers collided with the keyboard. Once again, the little church seemed to explode in music and song.

Wiley gathered up Joanna in his arms and turned to Martha Ann.

"Let's go home," he said, and they started for the door.

AFTERWORD

When I was a small boy, I dreamed of becoming an artist. In those days, real drawing paper was hard to come by, so I drew pictures on cardboard boxes, the backs of school papers, calendars, envelopes, paper bags, meat wrappers from the butcher shop of my Uncle Bill's grocery store—in short, anything I could get my little hands on.

There were the usual jet planes and rocket ships, but mostly I drew Civil War pictures. Pencil portraits of Lee and Jackson and Grant hung on the walls of my room alongside pictures of great battles like Gettysburg, Shiloh, Manassas, Petersburg and Vicksburg. My favorite, however, was a giant mural depicting the Battle of Atlanta, which I copied from memory after a trip to the Cyclorama. That single picture, done in chalk and colored pencils, measured more than 24 feet long.

My teachers were so impressed they had me stand up in class and talk about it. It was a torturous, terrifying moment, but at least I got to talk about my favorite subject, the Civil War.

Long before my twelfth birthday, I knew I would grow up to be a great artist. But not just any artist. I wanted to be a Civil War artist. I wanted to paint pictures of men charging into battle. I wanted to capture the smoke and roar of cannon and muskets. I wanted to go back in time and come face to face with those hollow-cheeked boys in gray and blue who fought and died for causes few of them truly understood.

Then I grew up. All those boyhood dreams of becoming a Civil War artist gradually faded. My old paint brushes crumbled and fell apart. Old canvases cracked and dried up. After the dark ages of Vietnam and college, I found myself struggling to survive as a journalist. There would be no art career. My paintings would never hang in museums and grace the pages of *Civil War Times Illustrated*.

In the mid-1980s, while teaching journalism at Georgia Southern University, Wally and Ann Wildenradt approached me about doing a book on Ann's great-grandfather, a private who served with General Robert E. Lee in Virginia. At the time I was simply too busy grading papers and running down freelance writing assignments to take time off to write a book. But the Wildenradts, God bless them, kept pressing. They wouldn't give up. They wanted me to write a screenplay. They wanted me to write newspaper and magazine articles, a book. Before long the idea for *Deep In The Heart* had begun to materialize. What sold me were the dozens of old letters that Ann's grandfather had written to her grandmother during the war. When she showed me the letters—and explained how they had come into her possession—I was hooked.

Many of the letters had been written—but never mailed—by Private Wiley Nesmith while serving with the 49th Georgia Infantry Regiment—the "Wilkinson County Invincibles." When he surrendered with Lee's Army of Northern Virginia at Appomattox, he hid them in an old farmhouse—apparently thinking he'd come back and get them some day. He never did. There they remained, crammed behind some old wallboards, for more than 120 years, rotting and gathering dust, until the early 1980s when the new homeowner came across them during renovation. Intrigued, he contacted a Civil War buff who was able to track down Ann Wildenradt, who was living in Statesboro, Georgia.

The letters themselves are far from literary masterpieces. Written in the simple phonetic style common to uneducated Confederate foot soldiers, they are painfully plain. But what they lack in sophistication they more than make up for in passion. Here we see a homesick Georgia farm boy eager to stand tall and do his duty proudly, ready to "run the Yanks like rip" if necessary to end "this unholy war;" a husband and father haunted by an unquenchable desire to survive the war so that he can return home to his beloved wife and baby. The letters also reveal the hardships, touching reminders of the courage and fears that plagued ordinary foot soldiers on the front lines.

Five years ago, after reading transcribed copies of those letters many times over, I set out to write the book. My research took me to the killing fields of Beaver Dam Creek and Malvern Hill, Fredericksburg and Chancellorsville, Spotsylvania and Cold Harbor. I couldn't get Wiley out of my mind. His ghost was with me every step of the way, from the shell-blasted crater at Petersburg to the gloomy hills of Sayler's Creek and beyond to Appomattox. At every stop, I couldn't shake the image of Wiley and all the other boys from Georgia huddled around campfires, ragged, bellies on fire with hunger, dreaming about life back home, dreading the next morning when bugles would blare and they'd go charging across smoking fields of battle. At Fredericksburg, I walked along the solemn Sunken Road where his unit stood facing Burnside's charge. At the Wilderness, I found the spot where he was wounded. I saw the Bloody Angle at Spotsylvania, followed the line of retreat from Petersburg to Appomattox. In Richmond, I wandered among the long, lonely rows of moss-draped tombstones inside Hollywood Cemetery searching for the unmarked grave of one of his brothers who had died during the siege of Richmond.

Wiley survived the Civil War, unlike most of his brothers. In 1876, he and Martha Ann moved from his ancestral home in Wilkinson County to Bulloch County, Georgia, where he operated a small country store. During an influenza epidemic in 1917, his beloved wife went home to be with the angels. Alone now, white-bearded, frail, forever cursing the Yankees for leaving him with a "bum" leg, Wiley continued to putter about the little store. One cold November afternoon, after nodding off in front of the fireplace, a spark ignited the quilt on his lap. The burns proved fatal. A few days later, on November 27, 1924, the proud old warrior was laid to rest beside his beloved Martha Ann.

E. Randall Floyd
Augusta, Georgia, 1998

ABOUT THE AUTHOR

E. RANDALL FLOYD is a nationally syndicated newspaper columnist, motion picture screenwriter and best-selling author of several books including *Great Southern Mysteries.*

A former European correspondent for United Press International, he worked for the *Florida Times-Union* and the *Atlanta Journal-Constitution.* His lectures on Civil War history at Augusta State University helped inspire *Deep In The Heart.* He lives in Augusta, Georgia, with his wife, Anne, and their son Rand, 6, where he writes full time.

LECTURES & BOOKS

E. RANDALL FLOYD offers lectures on a number of topics, ranging from strange and unusual aspects of Civil War history to the paranormal. If you want to contact Mr. Floyd to arrange lectures, guest appearances or autograph signings, please call the Augusta office at (phone & fax) 706-738-0354 or write: Harbor House, 3010 Stratford Drive, Augusta, Georgia 30909, for further information. Or, you may e-mail him at rfloyd2@aol.com.

To order additional copies of *Deep In the Heart*, send $24.95 plus $4.95 postage & handling to: HARBOR HOUSE, 3010 Stratford Drive, Augusta, Georgia 30909.

OTHER TITLES
BY
E. RANDALL FLOYD

Great Southern Mysteries	$8.95 Softback	$16.95 Hardback
More Great Southern Mysteries	$9.95 Softback	$16.95 Hardback
Great American Mysteries	$9.95 Softback	$18.95 Hardback
Ghost Lights and Other Encounters with the Unknown	$9.95 Softback	$18.95 Hardback
America's Great Unsolved Mysteries		$19.95 Hardback

Please add $4.95 shipping and handling for the first book, $3.00 for each book thereafter.

To order, send your request to:

HARBOR HOUSE
3010 STRATFORD DRIVE
AUGUSTA, GEORGIA 30909
706-738-0354

I understand that I may return any books for a full refund, for any reason, no questions asked.

Please allow four weeks for delivery. Mr. Floyd would be happy to autograph all ordered books. Please indicate how you would like each book to read.

ATTN: COLLEGES, UNIVERSITIES, QUANTITY BUYERS
Discounts on these books are available for bulk purchases.
Write or call for information on our discount programs.